A PROMISE KEPT

JAK ANGELESCU

DEDICATION

I'd like to dedicate this book to my best friend Holly, who never stopped believing in me and for listening to me reread this book to her a million times and for her endless insights, support, opinions, and for being my muse for the female protagonist. I love you more than you'll ever know.

To Kye Feher for asking me about my book a year after I stopped working on it and lit a candle under my ass and for always believing in me.

To Rowan, my fire lily and fellow author, for reminding me that "nothing is too unbelievable" and keeping my imagination wild.

To my mom and dad who never got to know the end but loved my work regardless. I love you both and miss you dearly.

To my editor Jason, for the two year-long bout of being understanding and supportive through my father's death, my unbalanced life, and helping me to be the author I never thought I could be.

To anyone who ever felt they weren't good enough for felt like they were a defect in society and unwanted. You are seen, loved, and valued.

To Brian Haner Jr. for being a role model and supporting this heartfelt endeavor.

And last but definitely not least, to the two men I kept dreaming about who inspired this whole series.

1

_____

"Captain Radal!"

The young voice in the darkness echoed throughout the small village. Rain pelted the dark soil while torches along broken pathways and on modest homes attempted to stay aglow. Such cozy little dwellings they were, made of rustic wood and small enough to hold but a single family. But their humble appearances were littered by rain barrels thrown about and broken wagons. The flowers alongside had been trampled by the outbreak of livestock and horses that had been set free.

And in all of this there was the warm glow of those torches and lanterns. One moment the spark of life would flicker in hope to all who could see it only to be quickly extinguished the next.

Chaos had erupted in Nakhan, a small northern village that was wildly unprepared for such a night. Prior to that evening, it had been a beautifully warm spring day. The wild grasses of the pastures had already felt the refreshing rain of a gentle storm earlier. This storm was not the same.

The villagers, their voices ringing of fright and terror, ran every which way in a frantic attempt to hide. An invisible colossus was the sole perpetrator causing the innocent to scramble for safety, though they knew not in which direction to find it.

The voice of a young man called again, "Captain! Where are you?"

He looked left and saw a mob of villagers running by him, all bundled in loose, plain clothing, and covered in soot and rain. His lips firmly pressed together, and he hurried through against the nightmarish scene on pathways filled with more pushing people, screaming children, and houses crumbling from being engulfed in flames. Each straw of the thatched roofs wilted up in embers, crawling with smoke and flames.

But he slid in the mud and came to an abrupt stop, crouching and covering his head. A window of one of the farmer homes blew out. All he could see were the flames coming out and swallowing the side of the house.

There was no choice but to ignore it.

His black hair gleamed with fiery hues from the torches he ran past. His breath was heavy, and his blue eyes portrayed a hint of fear to anyone who could see them. Escaping seemed impossible.

"No!" the young man shouted to himself as he squeezed his eyes together for a moment as he ran. His breath left his chest as he wiped his face. "I will not break. Not now. Not at this moment!" At least the rain would hide his tears.

In the blinding commotion, a middle-aged woman with soaked and ratted blonde hair suddenly collided with him and, falling to the ground, began hurrying to gather the things she had dropped. She was a peasant woman with barely anything, and so what she had dropped was all she had left. With her voice shaking and unstable, the young man lifted her from the mud.

His voice fought against the raging winds and sounds of roofs ablaze. "These things do not matter!"

Her eyes watered as she desperately thrashed in defiance. It was clear that whatever it was she dropped was of utmost importance to her. "I protest! These belong to my—"

He lifted her with ease and pushed her off. "Leave them be! They hold no value if your life ends tonight. You must go find shelter—"

Screams followed. And they were not the screams of the people.

Above and inside the skies, creatures appeared in the flashes of the storm. Everyone was racing around to protect their lives down below.

There they were, no longer the unseen. The horrors of the night descended without reason and without warning. The young man clutched the woman to his side to hold her near, both of them in awe at the presence of what was crawling high above them. The winged black beasts ripped apart the dark sky with their flaming breath. At once a putrid stench of decay and rot filled the hot wind.

The woman drew a frightful breath. "Oh stars above," she stammered slowly, "what are those creatures?" Her hands locked toward her flowing nightgown that would have been a beautiful linen color earlier, but now it was filthy with mud, sweat, and horse manure.

He would always see those monsters in his memory the way they were in the reflection of his eyes that night. Taunting him. Taking away his home and his people.

"Miss!" He pushed on. "Go hide underground in your meat cellars! We are not safe on the paths!"

She looked to him, and the unknown of what time would bring to her was creeping like a plague in her blood. The village bell began to chime, and together they suddenly looked up at it. He was utterly confused, as those who pulled the rope to signal the bell had fled the tower. Once more the beasts let out their howls. His throat clenched and his stomach rolled from the smell of their opened mouths. Although he turned and winced, he quickly glanced back to witness their actions. One seemed to become still, gently moving its wings to maintain its altitude, at least so it sounded like.

In unison, they all opened their gaping mouths to engulf the entire roof of the tower in a searing inferno. They began to attack the tower, pulling it apart piece by piece. Their flaming breaths displayed it all for him to see. There was no bell ringer in that tower. It was simply being destroyed.

All of that beauty that took far too many years to create was destroyed in seconds. The once-white stone had now become singed into soot and blackness as the belfry rang harder and the shaft began to fracture. The sound was deafening.

Quickly, he looked back to the woman and pushed her onward. "Should this tower fall, you and I will surely be in the path of death. LEAVE!"

When he brandished his sword, she finally ran away.

He looked about. Where was his captain? He had little time to think of the possible places to search. In the middle of his racing thoughts, he had remembered enough of Radal to assume that the captain, being a family man, must have still been at home. Despite yearning for a time of rest to think, the young man felt the flush of heat when a house caught fire nearby. He was running out of time. He slipped in the drenched soil and rushed toward the outer boundaries of the village and the captain's home.

The sound of an escaping cattle herd alerted him to the stampede, and so he mounted a nearby feeding crate, waiting for them to pass. He could finally rest, but his chest hurt, for the armor he wore was becoming far too heavy for a boy merely fifteen years old. Heaving and sweating, he began unbuckling the shoulder latches for his breast plate.

"Come now, calm yourself," he spoke with a breathless whisper. "You will find him. Stay calm."

The latches released, and he pushed off the breast plate. Immediately jumping off the crate, he continued toward the outer circle. Despite all the commotion, his well-trained ears heard more hooves and a whinny coming to his left.

He turned to see a young stallion with a coat as black as his own hair suddenly appear and muscle his way alongside him.

"Ah, come closer, my friend!"

The young man reached out as if his body would be swept away in a current and his stallion's mane was his only way out. Readily obeying his rider's command, the young horse raced closer, and with one easy reach of the waving mane the man pulled himself up to straddle.

"Faster, Rikaana! We have to get to the outer fields." He kicked hard into the horse's belly and held on for the fast race against the seconds that were quickly slipping away.

They sailed over the broken pathways and viscous soil, hearing cries for help that couldn't be answered now. To his right, a little home's thatched roof was breaking under the pressure of the beast creeping atop it. The young man could see in the fleeting moment he passed that it was only a matter of time before the beast would destroy it with its burning winds. His heart ached to think there could be a family inside, and with his current mission consuming his energy he was powerless to help.

The talons crushed the brittle rooftop. The young man heard the house breaking into ruins behind him. He wiped his tears and the rain from his face and quickly turned away. A few moments later, he finally reached the surrounding farmlands that had not yet endured what the village had.

The captain's home was in sight. It was a slightly larger home with numerous thatched ridges, a maze of fences that kept livestock contained, and a quaint porch made with burkold wood that sat underneath an awning. The livestock had been set free, and the house was still intact, bringing a fleeting sense of relief to the head-strong man.

"Radal!" he called out. Gritting his teeth, the young man clutched the horse's mane. "Rikaana, you must move faster!"

Closing in on his destination, he quickly shifted his legs to one side and jumped off to rush up the wooden stairs and break the front door down, but he was not of size nor strength to do such a thing. *Oh, of all the times to be so youthful in stature and so useless in strength,* he thought. The rain and his sweat mixed and dripped down his ashen cheek, and with one loud scream of frustration the young man banged harder on the door. He was determined. Even though he had removed his breastplate, he still wore his spaulders and taking a step back, slammed his shoulder hard into the door. It would not budge.

"Captain, you must be here! I see your horse outside!" He drew in a deep breath and moved closer to press his ear to the door. The captain *was* inside, as his voice made plain. .

"I must go! This is my duty! Agrona, take our son to the meat cellar and do not come out until you hear the three chimes of the bell!"

The young man tried the door once more, but it would not move. It was clearly locked, and for good reason.

The captain's wife responded, "Radal, please! Let these villagers fend for themselves! Please! Have you not done enough?" A child wailed, and the woman shouted in earnest, "Think of our family for once! We need you here!"

"No, take your hands away from me. I have thought of my family every day. Agrona, they came for our strongest guardians, our guaradas, last time. If they come once more, they come for men of strength. I must protect my men and our village."

Outside, the young man turned and winced at all he heard. Pressing his forehead to the door, he steadied his breath to allow his aching heart to steady. He heard the captain's wife once more.

"What if you leave and I hear the four long tolls of death? I'd die an angry woman if that were to be you!"

Suddenly like a clap of thunder, the young man almost fell forward when the door opened. He regained his posture and saluted, "Captain Radal, I am—"

But the young man was pushed away. Captain Radal was a sizable man, more so than any of the other Guardians yet smaller in frame than the enormous guaradas. With broad shoulders and a chest as proud as the northern mountains, even in utter chaos he held a stalwart appearance of assurance and dignity. Radal was not only the young man's captain but also his mentor and a father figure since the death of his parents. In that moment, he was earnest to do anything the captain asked of him.

"Come, Staghen. Let's make haste." Radal cleared his throat from the smoke that was coming from the village, and he lifted his head to look onward. The rain bathed the specks of his blond facial hair, and he wiped it quickly. "We must remember our protocols. You were too young to recall when this happened the first time." He adjusted his spaulder. The brown leather gauntlet of his left hand shifted as his large arm flexed. "But I am aware and have trained you well. All that's left is to do it," he finished with a husky, deep voice.

Radal fixed his hair, glorious long blond braids that hung tightly behind his ears in many different thicknesses and lengths, showing he had been preparing for some sort of ceremony that evening. Even in the dark and endless night of horror, the jewels in his hair seemed to sparkle like the stars that should have been seen by all, glittering like brilliant children at play in the sky.

"Yes," Staghen began, "I believe we could formulate a plan. They are attacking men of strength like you said. The guaradas have formed their circular unit around the school, where I have sent the children to hide."

His captain was now at his side, and he truly felt all would be cared for.

Radal's voice rose heroically, "Excellent work. I knew I chose you as my malakae for good reason, however my greatest concern is—"

How intimidating a second can be.

A moment.

The captain heard a coming sound and immediately pulled his successor, also known in Nakhan as his malakae, into his chest and away from the house, turning his back to whatever destruction that came to shield the younger one. Several howling, blackened fiends landed on the captain's home, and within seconds flames spread across the roof. The heat of the flames being enough to catch fire with dampened wood was a clear indication of the real danger at hand.

Radal pivoted and looked to his home. With wild eyes, he struggled to maintain his composure. To the hellish beasts and all who could hear, his voice roared, "No, no, no, no! My family is inside!"

They heard his wife's shrill voice drowning in the catastrophe. Before anything else could happen, Radal skillfully drew his sword. He would never stand for this. Not again.

The three creatures stood on their hind legs, which left them at a height that would double that of the tallest man. "If it is *I* you seek, then come here to find me!" He analyzed their movements, how they crawled on the burning roof. "COME FOR ME, YOU COWARDS! LEAVE MY PEOPLE ALONE!"

It appeared they heard his challenge. Their wings snapped furiously as they began to advance toward him. He turned to that young man who would one day take his place, his malakae. "Staghen, please! Get my family out of there!"

Choices. Protect the captain or save his family. It seemed all things went quiet in Staghen's eyes as he saw his captain's strong face calling to him, the blues of his eyes narrowing. Radal's rain-soaked hair was plastered to his jawline as his eyes narrowed, scrunching his brow. He could hear the flames burning, his heart pounding, the creatures descending from the roof. But as a malakae, he had to do what was asked of him regardless of the outcome. His heart split asunder. Of course the outcome mattered, but it truly depended on who was affected most. It was as if at that very moment he felt within his young heart that he knew the captain's plans, and he was not formidable enough to stop it. His lips tightened. His heart went numb.

The malakae reached to grab the captain's shoulder. "Please, Radal," he spoke nervously. "Be careful."

The captain forced him forward. "Go! I'll get them away!" Radal whistled for his horse and mounted it, quickly proven right. The beasts left the burning home and took up the chase.

Staghen watched his captain's image fade further and further beyond the burning fields, so tragic were their ember glows. All of the farmers' work had been obliterated. But he would remain valiant in his work and firm in his promise. Looking over his shoulder, he saw that there was little time to get the family out.

Inside, the woman held her son, and her eyes widened with the sense of the impending doom. "Gish lana, Derjaun," she whispered, attempting to hush the boy.

The back of the home was burning, and there was no way to get to the cellar. The burning roof was collapsing. She closed her eyes and heard the crackling of the wood. The noxious smoke infiltrated her precious lungs. Coughing, she pulled her wool shawl over her son's mouth and leaned her head against the wall again. Her eyes witnessed the dancing flames flowing up the back wall of the kitchen, and the window shattered.

The lines on the sides of her lips formed, and her mouth quivered. She squeezed her son. Once more she coughed and began to sob. If she fled the house, where would she go? She could not see now, and it was getting harder to breathe. The house was in flames almost everywhere, and her heart's clock ticked quicker. Time was running out.

"Sheylee!" the child suddenly cried, looking about. "Paposa left us here!"

"No, my child, he did not. He left to go fight to protect our people. He is the captain. It is his role." She brushed her hand to his face as they hid in the corner.

Their eyes met. "Sheylee, are we going to die?"

She stroked his warm face to soothe him. The embers fell around her. Her eyes were tightly closed as her trembling lips kissed her son's forehead. With the child's eyes awakened to all things around him, he heard his mother humming to him.

Outside, Staghen held his hands above his head when the front awning started to fall. The burning sensation became almost suffocating as he hurried left and right. The wood of the house cracked under the force, and the flames shot out the side glass windows blowing out everywhere. Inside, he heard the young boy scream in fear.

"I have to get inside!" Staghen shouted.

To let the captain's family die and be burned alive was simply not an option. Once more he kicked the door, thinking that surely with the fire it would be weakened enough. But instead of this the wall began to crumble in a wretched blaze. Sparks flew as he shielded his eyes but saw the opened front window. It too was quickly being devoured by the heat, but it was his only option, even if it meant his face enduring permanent disfigurement.

The malakae kicked the old porch chairs away and came to the window and looked inside. Attempting to calm himself, he felt with his hands that the glass was far too hot to touch. The heat may have become too much for the family inside to bear. He had no choice but to act.

With the soot and sweat stinging his eyes, he reached for his sword and used the hilt to break the glass as fast and efficiently as possible. The moment the window broke, he gasped through the choking heat that was rushing to escape to the cooler air outside. They wouldn't last much longer. It was as if he felt the anger of abandoning his father figure being exerted into this one life-saving task. Honor the captain, that was all he had to do.

Agrona heard the sudden sound busting through the window of the front, sending broken glass shards flying. The woman squeezed her son, believing those beasts were coming through. "Leave us alone!"

Agrona felt all she could do was scream in terror and cry. She did not want her or her son to die.

The figure stood easily on two legs and hurried over. She looked and saw it was the malakae!

"Malakae Staghen!" she cried with wilting eyes. "How did you get in here?"

"Agrona, come!" He extended his arms. "Let me carry him."

"My malakae, how are we to escape? These fiends are everywhere!"

"Come with me." He pulled the boy to his shoulder and using his free hand helped the woman to her feet. "Hold your head low and cover your mouth with your scarf. We will leave out the bedroom window!" The little blond boy fit under the man's left arm, and the mother took his hand. The young man turned with a soiled face and spoke to her, keeping her as low as possible, "I did not see damage to your bedroom window! I presume this means the fire has not claimed your room just yet!"

"Let's hope so!" Agrona shouted back as she ducked. The common rafter above suddenly collapsed, and Agrona let out a shrill scream, covering her head immediately.

"It's alright. Keep moving. Let me be your eyes!"

Continuing into the next room, the man shifted the young boy to hold him in both arms, and he glanced urgently about. "We have little time. This room will be next to go. Here, hold him. I'll break the window."

She grabbed her son as the man lifted the sole chair in the room and hurled it through the glass. "Both of you first!"

The mother obeyed his orders in the most desperate hustle of her life. Even though the young orphaned malakae was smaller and younger than Radal's wife, his muscles were exceedingly developed to handle such stress. He lifted her out the window first and then coaxed the child enough to be able to lift him through afterward to his mother. Above his head, he heard the wall plate beginning to give. He heaved himself out and picked up the child. He would normally carry the child over his shoulder, but never in such a dangerous situation. He held the mother's hand, and with Derjaun under his right arm they fled to safety.

Outside there was absolute chaos. The beasts were inside the Inner Circle of Nakhan. With the child under his left arm and pulling Agrona with his right hand, the malakae braved the fleeing stampede of horses, oxgog, pigs, and kaku birds set free from the neighboring farmhouse. It was almost impossible not to trample over any slow-moving bird, but he had no other choice. He was desperate for rest but continued to pull the mother harder.

"Come, Agrona," he shouted into the night. "I know your breath is gone, but they are still here. I have to get you to the barn."

The child in his arms looked about as the prairie blaze reflected in his blue, fear-stricken eyes. The malakae pulled the mother closer to shield her head under his arm. "The ashes are still falling, and I can't have you burned. Keep your eyes closed. I will lead you!"

Agrona was crying hard. She stumbled, and her chest felt overwhelmingly tight from panic and smoke. Everything in her body hurt. However, no one could understand the pain inside the malakae's soul. He no longer knew if Radal was alive, but Radal would never have thought of anything else except the task at hand. He must do the same.

They made it to the barn safely. The young man, Staghen, that brave malakae, held his cloak over both of them. "Here, cover yourself in the hay. I will stay with you."

Inside his mind was nothing but the sensations of urgency, panic, and fright, yet he was surprised by how easily he was able to mask his true emotions with the blanket of bravery.

This was the first time in his entire young life that he had been in a predicament like this. He flopped against the wall to sit and closed his eyes, but his face tightened. Looking to the locked double doors of the barn, he thought of going after Radal, but doing so would leave his family vulnerable. He calmed his nerves and glanced to the right and saw Agrona rocking Derjaun in her arms, calming the child's cries.

A memory then came to his mind.

At one point in his life, he had been in that same position, not with his own mother or father but with Radal. His parents had died during an infectious season and succumbed to the illness before he could ever really remember them. His first real memory was looking up into his captain's eyes while being held, a sweet sentiment coming along with the words the captain always spoke to him.

He whispered fondly into the night, "I will always be here for you."

The young child rolled out of his mother's arms to climb nearer to Staghen. He looked up to the man and with a soft voice as to not attract any further attention from the beasts outside, he said, "You saved my sheylee and I, Malakae Staghen. Thank you." The young boy curled up alongside him.

All the young man could do was soothe their nerves with a smile. "You are welcome, dear one. One day you will be as strong and mighty as your father. You will carry his sword as well and do the same as I have done." He paused in thought. The child had the most wholesome eyes. The malakae then helped the boy lie down. "Here, Derjaun. You and your sheylee will sleep here for the night. I'll stand watch."

"But what about you?" Derjaun suddenly whimpered.

"What about me?"

The young boy was curious about Staghen's demeanor. All of what had happened did not even appear to fracture his bravery. "Aren't you scared?"

Strangely, that little question gave Staghen time to steady his fears, which truly were rioting within. But calmly, he answered with a lie, "Guardians don't get scared."

He made certain that the woman and child were both hidden from sight. After rising to his feet, he turned toward the front of the barn. His expressive eyes focused with every sudden sound, and his ears felt the blood of his heart racing. He was afraid but very thankful that the barn was built with stone walls and wooden rafters.

A heavy sigh left his young chest, and he moved stealthily toward the window and found himself turning a water pail upside-down to sit on top of it. He gathered his shoulder-length black hair on top of his head to allow his neck to cool. He looked toward the woman, who was combing her fingers through her son's blond strands.

How could anyone sleep during such a night? Agrona sat in a pile of comforting hay while her child lay across her lap, his head resting in her arms.

The captain's wife stayed awake until her son's eyes began to grow heavy in need of rest. When the child found himself tired enough for slumber, Agrona sat forward. Her dark eyes found the malakae now pressing his ears to the wall of the barn.

"My brave malakae, what of my husband?"

"I know nothing of your husband right now, Agrona." He sighed heavily and lifted his chin to peek above the barn's windowsill. "Rest your eyes."

The woman lifted her tattered sun-kissed golden hair to be able to comfortably lie next to her child. The howls echoed all around outside. With every harsh force of the wind to the wood of the walls, Agrona's skin jerked, and her throat tightened. No one could truly know if the next gust of wind would be the deathly blaze from those creatures.

Time was both a gift and a curse that evening. What a blissful thing it was for the Vin Gruinelle family to rest, and yet how unkind it felt to Staghen that he was to remain sentinel, torn between going after Radal and staying as he was told to. The young man glanced outside once more, peeking to see the engulfing flames of the town in the distance. He leaned his head down in thought and felt his stomach knotting. The urge to vomit was strong. Tears came, but his dutiful mind and consciousness fought them. Moments passed as he clenched his fists, his heart rapped against his ribs, and his lungs filled loudly in frustration.

He could no longer stand for it.

To protect the family meant to bring Radal safely home as well, for they would be without a father and a husband if death occurred. Staghen's mind was set, and he hurried to ensure that the family was well hidden in the hay and horse blankets. He grabbed his sword on the ground, sheathed it, and hurled himself out the window into the formidable night.

Agrona woke in the early dawn after what seemed like a brief second of sleep, yet it was not the light of the morning that woke her. Rather, to her relief, it was the sound of the bell. Yet this sound was odd to her. For it didn't seem to be ringing by the usual rocking of the pull but rather struck with something repeatedly. One looming ring called out with its song throughout the village.

Though surely damaged, the bell tower never actually fell. All of its stone had fallen to rubble, but the wooden rafters it hung to had fallen across the ruins, allowing it to be struck but sadly not rang. The creatures had spared their most precious landmark. And not only this, but the battle had obviously come to an end.

Her dark-brown eyes flitted in every direction to make sure it was safe to rise from the hay-covered stone floor, "Oh!" she exclaimed.

Agrona got to her feet. She was quite lithe as a younger maiden, but now with her hard work she was sturdy in frame, and it made her movements easy. The tolls continued for the second time throughout the village. "Derjaun, awake, my boy! It is over." Happiness washed over her exhausted face of sun-kissed skin and age lines. "Hurry, my dearest child!"

Derjaun rolled over and rubbed his eyes. Gleaming joy was the face he wore. "Sheylee, Paposa saved us all! Right?"

She could not withhold her excitement. She hoisted her son high into the air. As the third toll sounded the victory, she tossed him higher, swirling around the barn and dancing with him.

"Yes, your paposa has done it once more! Our village is spared, and we are all safe!" She kissed his cheek with the aggression of a mother's love.

Some women know the burden of the heart when loving a man in the position of a warrior and a protector. And for Agrona it was no different. She loved Radal truly and completely, but when Derjaun was born the idea of losing her husband to his work had given her a never-ending conflict.

The double barn doors opened, letting in the dusty brilliance of the day, and still Agrona wore a smile as she turned to see who entered. Soft sediments of nature gracefully hovered in the beaming light that illuminated the barn. She repositioned her son to her chest, holding him close while he nuzzled her. Her dress was as filthy and exhausted as her face, but her expression still beamed like an ornament of happiness. The sun outside was warm and comforting in that brilliant spring day.

"Why, my dear malakae. Welcome. Please take us inside, will you?"

His clothes were burnt, his body wet with sweat. He stumbled in and did not respond. Soot covered his face, and her eyes wandered to the blood on his gloves.

Agrona noticed he was beyond fatigued to answer. "Oh, you should rest. I'll go inside. I suppose we do not need an escort. But the blood on your hands, where is this from? Are you hurt? If you follow me inside, I will mend your wounds and…"

Silence. Agrona edged toward him while her son put his knuckles to his mouth in confusion. She searched his eyes for an answer. "Malakae? Why do you move without an answer to me?"

The fourth toll followed. And with this toll, the pause that could last a thousand years ceased all breath and life from her.

"Malakae?" Her quaking voice asked. Derjaun turned his head upward to his mother and saw the look she gave to Staghen. "Why am I hearing four tolls?" Her eyes hardened, desperate for an answer.

He moved forward and lifted his head. "I think we all know why." He was beyond his threshold for holding strong for others, and as brash as it may have seemed to utter those horrible words in such a way, he no longer cared.

"No!" the woman cried loudly. She placed her son on the floor and rushed to Staghen, who looked as broken as she felt. "No, it can't be." In all of her heartache, she shook him hard. "Tell me my love still stands and breathes the air I breathe! Tell me Radal is still alive!"

The young boy crawled over to the hay and sat with his knees pulled into his chest and watched his mother being held up by the young malakae, who hardly had the strength to stand on his own. Her screams were as strong as the silence that cast its ugly spell just moments before. Agrona bellowed in misery, and he struggled to hold her and attempted to console the new widow, but no consolation could be done. Her husband, Captain Radal Vin Gruinelle, had died.

Agrona pushed her face into the young man's shoulder, clutching his tattered crimson cloak. He himself could hardly hold her up, but in his predecessor's honor he tried with all of his might. However, she still fell to the floor, dragging her nails down his leather pants. And all of this Derjaun saw. He was a young boy, but he was not naive to what had happened.

Staghen saw Derjaun alone on the hay and settled Agrona to weep alone on her knees so that the young child could have some hope of comfort as well.

He knelt down and touched the soft, young skin with his glove. Minor smears of his father's blood graced the pale skin. Their eyes met. "Derjaun, I'm certain you understand."

"Yes," he said with emotions so thick he nearly choked on them, "my paposa is dead and won't come back." Derjaun's sky-blue eyes filled with water and despair. He cried into his knees.

The sound had made Staghen quite angered, but not for the reason one would think. He was told to stay to protect the family, and now he was told to stay to console the family. If he had gone after Radal sooner, would the outcome have been different? He drew in a deep breath and shuddered. He had to hide his own tears.

"Yes," the malakae concluded, "your father was found several miles away from the village. His wounds were many. I and several of his men carried him back home." A long sound of scraping metal being pulled from the scabbard on his back followed. "This sword is yours now."

"A sword?" Derjaun cried. He immediately slapped the blade away from Staghen's hand. "I'm a child, not a fool. I don't want a sword." He glanced up to the young man and screamed as loud as he could, "I want my paposa!"

With the utmost respect and honor, the malakae picked the sword up and laid it at the feet of the slain captain's son. He looked to the sword and to the boy, who gave the same reaction in return. Silence. It took every ounce of will for the young man to stay. He had not had his chance yet to mourn.

The sword was a longsword with the hilt embellished with the village's blue Yulan marble, silver in metal and boasting the dazzling filigree designs that were native to the Nakhanians. It was powerful and yet remarkably simple in its design. Nakhan was a very young village compared to others across the seas, and therefore their armory and weaponry still had some proficiency to achieve. Derjaun simply glanced to the brave young man and then back to the blade before him. He was quiet. Realizing his own anger, he picked it up and showed it to the malakae.

"Why is the end blackened?"

Staghen let out a breath and looked down. "From the heat of those creatures, the Annenji."

Derjaun simply touched it, and his mother stood above them. In the stillness of the tragedy, she witnessed the malakae's internal struggles. Although her bones were aching and her heart was torn from the loss of her beloved husband, she had to compose herself. Somehow.

"Staghen..." She held her hands together and lifted her disheveled blonde brows.

The young man rose to his feet and looked to her.

Her eyes watered, and she shook her head with an urging voice, "What are we to do? Do you really feel that you are ready to become captain? I know you are the malakae and would be next, but you are so young yourself. Although it is customary for the captain's son to reign in his place upon his death, Derjaun is barely a young boy."

Malakae Staghen combed his fingers through his jet-black hair, which was greasy and gritty. He had found her statements to be petty.

"Are we really at a point to be asking these kinds of questions? For stars above, woman, I have not even had a chance to mourn! You know, he was my father as much as he was Derjaun's. And here you are asking me these things. I don't even know my own name at this moment, I have not slept in nearly two days, and you come to me with these questions?"

He needed to step away from her and hide his face from the tears he could no longer fight. His face was usually handsome and youthful, with fair skin that was crowned with the blackness of luscious, thick brows, but now it was reddened with both heat and grief, and he felt he had aged a hundred years in a single night. His lips were burned and rough. Even speaking caused them to stretch in complete discomfort. At one point in his life his eyes were blue and clear. They were full of sparkling happiness and joy. Now they seemed gray. His life seemed gray as well. He looked outside to the burned pastures that were softened with the morning rain.

He had lost the only person in his life that he could turn to.

Quietly, the young man let out a constricted peep of sadness, but it was not audible enough for Derjaun or Agrona to hear. He wiped his hair from his face once more. His path was laid out for him, but it was not a path he was ready to walk. Yet against all of this and his fears, he was now a man and had no other choice but to be.

His lips parted breathlessly. "You asked me to stay, asked me to protect your family. But the last thing I heard from you was to stay. So even though I want to run, my father, I will honor your very last words." He centered himself with a long breath. "I will stay."

He swallowed hard. Removing his gloves, he felt the ability to answer Agrona's looming question about his readiness. "Agrona, if there is one thing I learned from your husband, it is that no one is ever really ready for anything. I'm hardly a man, and I fear I will never be half the man your husband was, but I must try my best."

Derjaun lifted the sword with both hands, and even still the sword was unwieldy for him. His eyes were enamored by his father's legacy. "Sheylee, this is really heavy. How will I ever hold this?"

"Have no fear, young boy," Staghen quickly replied, moving closer to him. "You'll grow into it one day."

He placed his hand on Agrona's shoulder, and she lowered her eyes to him. She was only a few inches taller than him. They had no choice but to find comfort in one another. The long pause allowed both widow and malakae to feel the cool breeze coming in through the barn doors. The subtlety of the quiet outside was both haunting and peaceful. While the little boy felt the smoothness of the blade, he looked to see his mother in a moment with the man responsible for saving them both.

"I am sorry for your loss, Agrona," the malakae consoled in his adolescent voice. "You know how much I loved Radal."

"Yes," she affirmed, gazing to the floor, her voice broken. "You were his other son by love but not blood. And yet after all of this time walking in his path, you somehow have his eyes." She whimpered and frantically rubbed her face from the coming thoughts. "I have no idea how I am to raise him on my own. My home and heart..." She paused in reflection, and her eyes glimmered while she confessed, "They will be forever empty now."

Abruptly the young man turned his head. He had no more strength or love to give. The realization of fate was becoming all too clear. "Your husband's ceremony will take place by midday."

Agrona watched the young man turn to leave, but what she did not see was him holding his own mouth. It was essentially Radal's love and teachings that kept him in line and alive. He found his sanctuary outside and watched the smoke of the buildings giving way to the wind. The storm of the night pressed on until early dawn, leaving the village entirely extinguished. There was so much work to be done. Nearly half the livestock had been either eaten or killed, homes and shops had crumbled, and the farmland was mostly dug up or charred.

He stood upright and began walking to the Inner Circle only to stop to dig up what was left of a vibrant orange root vegetable hiding in the turmoiled soil. He brushed the dirt and manure off of the skin to reveal the glorious color. It was the only kinip vegetable that could be spared. One would assume he would have consumed it due to the sickening emptiness of his stomach, but instead he placed it into his pocket to give it to someone who would need it more.

"Ha, I have trained to endure days without food. My people, however, did not." He kept walking through the sinking mud. It only then occurred to him that as he approached the village Outer Circle, with its families hurrying about, that he was truly an orphan now. Again.

All around he heard people trying to clean up after the disaster. Children were separated from their families, and many loved ones still needed to be found. It was immediately clear to him he was not ready to face what lay beyond the broken fence of the field boundaries. He drew in a deep breath, collapsed to the side of the fence's front gate, and cried. His tears dripped onto his black velvet Guardian coat. His tears dripped like the rain from the previous night against the black coat, tracing its way down the silver embroidery before finally landing on his leather pants. He mourned so hard with the idea that he had somehow failed.

Once more, he looked to the heavens above, hoping that Radal may answer. "I will miss you, my friend. I promise you I will stand in your guard and protect these people the way you have so many times. I assure you; your sacrifice will *not* be in vain." He pulled his shoulder-length black hair behind his ears, stood, and lifted his head. With his eyes focused and his lips firm, the young man walked into the despair that the chaos had left so unkindly behind.

Staghen walked with his shoulders back and his chest out. Even though this caused his upper back and shoulders to tear in pain, he had to appear composed to any who saw him. All of what he saw was a terrible sight to behold. Everywhere the clamor of his people rose above the rubble and destruction. He despised seeing fingers pointed, hearing shouts, yelling, and disruption. Malakae Staghen kept walking through it all, shaking his head. He looked to the left and witnessed a man having a verbal dispute with his lover, and to the right were many young adults fighting over who was going to clean the home. The remarkable new wrought-iron hanging signs that were gifts from the local blacksmith to the shopkeepers were melted to a point of being a blackened stream frozen in time.

Even the simplest things were destroyed. Window box planters that had just seen their first fragrantly bloomed herbs and flowers were withered down to charred remains and ash. It amazed him how ignorant, disgraceful, and ungrateful his people were. With all of the evidence of death around, every single villager should have been rejoicing to be alive. If Radal were to see such a sight, he would punish everyone for such unruly behavior.

He trudged through the broken facades and finally reached the Inner Circle, the place of Nakhan's wealth. The Market Center, the rich folk, the Guardians, the school, and the small infirmary were all in this circle. Although some shops existed in other circles and areas of the village, the Market Center was the heart of village commerce, especially for furs and hides. The lost captain and his family were supposed to reside in this part of the village, but Radal had built his home on the outfields so that his wife could continue the farm work she had so lovingly grown up with. The Inner Circle was also where the malakae himself resided. Oddly enough, the

Inner Circle had barely undertaken any damage. He wondered why.

A fellow young Guardian approached him and saluted by placing a hard fist to his heart, "Malakae, sir. Have you spoken to the Vin Gruinelle family?"

"I have," the malakae answered dryly as he continued to walk. The Guardian followed, and the malakae continued, "I must ask you to go gather Guardians to help the Vin Gruinelle family with their home. It is utterly destroyed. And once you are finished with this, summon all of the village to the center platform here in the Market Center for the ceremony. After all, our beloved captain gave his life to honor his vows to us, and he deserves to have such a ceremony in a place that's..." He paused to look around. "...not so desecrated. Now take your orders and move steadily with them."

"Yes, *Kapita!*" the man answered with a fist pounded to his chest.

The young malakae felt his nerves shake with the word. What a strange sensation he felt. *Kapita* was the word mostly used to address the captain in an honorary way. However, it was not uncommon for it to be used to salute someone of a high rank, and it made him feel quite uncomfortable, for he felt truly unworthy.

Pushing through the crowd near the center platform, he could *feel* the eyes upon him. To his left, the villagers held their loved ones who survived as if waiting for him to announce their return to the world of the living. To the right, he glanced to see the hope gleaming into the eyes of the lost and confused. Hard working farmer men were seen in their working clothes, all shielding and holding their wives and children. It was such a sad thing to see how their sienna woolen vests were frayed and wet. The aprons of the wives were both stained with blood of some unknown sort and soot. There he saw one of the farmers holding his wife in one arm and draping his other around his two boys.

The eyes of the two men met. In the eyes of the father he could see that he too was scared. Such glistening eyes they were, curtained by furrowing gray, bushy brows.

Staghen was all they had. And yet who was it that he could turn to? What star did he now have to follow? Who would he rise every morning for? It was just last night he knew that he would rise and follow the needs and desires of his people.

He gently pushed his way through the crowd to the small, wooden staircase and ascended to the platform. He surveyed the bright sky and the homes of the Inner Circle, taking a moment to be grateful that their strong burkold walls still stood. Although their rich mahogany hues were dusted and filthy, he observed the beauty of the flowers still in bloom in every clay planter pot. That was when his eyes fell upon his father's body.

Everyone experienced the young orphan's whirlwind of discomfort, for those flowers no longer seemed beautiful. The rain of sadness flooded the pooling of his heart. Radal Vin Gruinelle was brawny but beautiful, even in death. His majestic form lied upon a mat that was delicately graced with flowers from the pabi fields, and many gifts of his adoring people were placed beside him on the platform. His flowing blond braids were respectfully cleaned of the blood and soot and even brushed to be rebraided once more. His breastplate had been polished and cleansed. But no amount of work could hide those marks that were dug into the metal, left behind by the talons of the fiends. It seemed that even against the talons the metal had melted.

Amongst all of this was the crowning glory of Radal's lovely thick hair that framed his softly tanned face. As a young man, he kept it long, and it had only grown longer by the time he reached his thirtieth year of age.

How would an orphaned man ever grow to such prominence?

All grew quiet as he climbed to the top of the center platform. The serenade of silence touched everyone and everything. The malakae stood next to his father and gazed upon the brilliant human being. All of the adornments he wore were a true testament to the life Radal had lived. Staghen breathed deeply and turned to see the anticipating villagers.

His voice creaked and broke from either the shift of his coming and age or from the nervousness. The good thing was that no one would ever know the difference.

"My people of Nakhan, to my family, to all of you, who are now my family," he began, "I am a young man, but I was chosen by the brave Radal Vin Gruinelle to protect and lead you. In this time our hearts shall unite, may our tears begin as sorrow, but grace will allow it to become pride, and may that pride enrich this soil on which our heroes have lost their lives, and for this may they always have comfort in our strength."

He paused. In this moment he took a deep breath to survey those looking up to him. Was he saying the right things? Every speech Radal had given was eloquent, but Staghen was barely half his age, and he knew he had to speak well, hold a bold demeanor in delivery, and pause for breath. Yes, they still looked up to him, but now they would look *to* him. Several wild birds gathered on the deconstructed bell tower that was holding on for its last stance. Clouds gently blocked the blinding sun.

He cleared his throat. "We all know the wise words that Radal left us with, in that during the strength of the storms do trees root deeper. We as Guardians are not just your protectors; we live as we all should live. Valiant, strong, noble, loving, and wise. With every passing storm, we grow stronger. I have given his sword to its rightful heir; however I still raise my voice high, with utmost perseverance for the law of this land and the protection of my people. You all will rest well tonight," he called louder, lifting his head. "Forevermore, it is my duty to ensure that what happened to all of us last night will never happen again."

He spoke above all ears to be heard, "I, now Captain Staghen Viktraana, assure you that I will stand where you cannot, to fight what you cannot, and to see what you cannot see. This will be the last day that Nakhan, the village that Radal built for us with his own hands, will *ever* know misery!"

Then it came, like a swarming storm of bravery and calmness that once battered the weakened shorelines only to see that its merciless touch gave way to brilliant pearls. If only he could hear the applause of joy in such a time. When he was to be the new captain, he had envisioned a beautiful ceremony full of laughter, clapping, and joy.

After he discussed how the village would be and accepted his new life, the young captain of Nakhan descended the stairs to begin walking in the boots so woefully given to him. And yet with this, a new sense of pride soared into his spirit, and once more he lifted his face to feel the warmth of the afternoon star against it.

"I assure you, my friend, your people will all sleep well tonight and every night after. I promise you this."

2

The village touched the northern part of Aer Gala—a Nakhanian name meaning both *world* and *what all living things called home*. It was nestled to the south of a mighty snowcapped mountain range known as the Castonuje Mountains. Kneeling before the mighty range were scraping berry pine trees blooming their fragrant green hues and occasional flecks of vibrant orange berries. Many dark and rugged rocks bejeweled the skirts of the mountains. Between the mountain foothills and the Outer Fields of Nakhan was a dense and seemingly impenetrable forest of deciduous trees. Due to the fear of the beasts lurking somewhere deep within, no man or woman dared to venture so far. No one knew what rested on the other side. It was a wondrous mystery.

A four-day journey to the southeast was Persu, a grand kingdom that Radal gave praise and criticism to in one breath. No one could ever be quite sure as to why. It was as if Radal had known so much about Persu that he himself had been there before or perhaps even *lived* there at one point. Yet he never spoke of this to anyone in the village, except for a few stories to his son.

Staghen Viktraana could recall the day he learned about forging bones into his sword from Radal. It was an unusual and disgusting thing for him to think of, but Radal declared effortlessly that doing so made the swords stronger. It was never clear to anyone in the Guardians how or why Radal knew this, but the truth of it was self-evident. For even after a decade of training, not one man had a sword that fractured, bent, or broke.

Many years before Radal left their world, he playfully joked to a young and impressionable Staghen, "The usual way you have seen swords made is prone to overgrowth and makes it impure and soft."

Those thoughts were now bittersweet memories.

He wished on this day that he could think of Radal resting peacefully in his comfortable chair as an old and gray man, beside his old and gray wife whose golden skin would show her fine lines of hard work, and Derjaun would wield that sword with a long mane of the morning star, nearly as tall and muscular as his father was. But all of this would never come to be. Derjaun would have taken his father's place as captain. Maybe one day he would. Maybe one day the little Vin Gruinelle boy would grow into something miraculous. That was all Staghen wanted now.

Time had to pass. As Staghen Viktraana grew into a man of honor by his twenty-second year, Agrona had become a calloused mother.

Growing older as a single woman who still worked dawn to dusk in the fields had taken its toll on her heart and patience. With her son at side, now nearly twelve years old, she looked to his beautiful face. Derjaun had faithfully accompanied her for all these passing lonely years. One might ask, what else would a child do other than remain with his surviving parent?

Derjaun never took any interest in building relationships with other children at school. He took on the housework that had been the responsibility of his father. Before the morning star even yawned to wake, Derjaun's morning routine consisted of tying his boots up, grabbing his ax, and traversing to the large enclosure for their kaku meat birds. And oh how noisy those birds could be.

A terrible windstorm had once torn half of the fence apart, tossing it recklessly about the yard, and it was Derjaun alone who fixed it. Agrona had fallen ill during these times and was fortunate enough to survive, unlike the terrible fate that Staghen's parents endured. Derjaun was a willing boy who was grateful to care for his home, so she kept him from school so that he could cut down new wood and fix the property. It was his property, which he grew to love tremendously. He had learned from his father that he should feel privileged to call it "his" property, when elsewhere in the prefecture of Persu no citizen owned anything.

He only knew a trivial bit about the differences of Persu and Nakhan from his father. Whatever the *true* differences were, it did not matter to him one bit. His father taught him that it was important to delve into one's own efficacy before meddling in the lives of others. This lesson proved to be a good thing. As he aged, he knew how to build fences, raise livestock, fix the front stoop steps, and assemble doors all before he was twelve years old. Season after season he learned to mend and repair the damage the vicious, flying Annenji had caused to his home, as he was tired of watching his mother live in a house of disrepair.

Just like any morning, Derjaun found himself stretching out across his bed, which was a well-sewn mat stuffed with animal furs and feathers. A simple thing upon a simple floor. His narrow chest breathed in deeply to admire the warm and fresh summer air.

Derjaun stretched so deeply, twisting his back so that he rolled off and flopped about on the dirty wooden floor of his room. His hair had lost its dark-blond tone and was filled with more vibrant golds, yet it was not long enough to him. The people of Nakhan valued their hair. To them, longer, thicker, and more luxurious hair showed strength and health. If it bore white streaks, as if it were snow blessing their locks, it meant they were also adorned with the wisdom of many years.

After dressing in his dull-brown tunic and his beige stockings, he stretched his feet out and noticed how lifeless his outfit was. His stockings had holes in the toe area. How he longed for some sort of color in his garments. A sweet thought came to him as he lifted up and began searching inside his dresser for anything. There he found his royal-blue sash. Frantically, he tied it about his waist. Putting on his boots and grabbing his ax, the young boy hurried outside to the animals' water basin to rinse his face. For that moment, all time stood still. No boy so young cared much for time. He saw in the waters a reflection. Suddenly, he stopped. His ax no longer on his mind, he dropped it to grab a small lock of his hair to pull it, seeing the entire length. It went past his chin.

"Sheylee!"

The kaku birds scattered everywhere in clucks and cockles while the jubilant boy bounded back toward the house, calling his mother louder and louder. Although she was asleep, he could not contain his excitement one bit. It was true! His hair would grow to be like his father's. In through the back entrance of his home he ran, calling his mother even louder until she, half asleep, came from her room in her night garments.

She was dressed in fabric that had not been washed in moons, her blonde hair ratted from an unpleasant night's sleep, and she yawned heavily.

"Sheylee, come on!" he bellowed once more, grabbing his mother's hands.

"Derjaun," she sighed, "what in the stars are you hollering over?"

The boy quickly yanked her hands again, and his blue eyes gazed up toward her in wonderment. "My hair is longer than it has ever been!"

With little else to relish, they marveled at his hair, and through the chunks of blond his big eyes glistened. All Agrona saw was his sweet face, so innocent. Perhaps it was that his mother appreciated the sacrifice of his social life. He was innocent still, unlike other children who were already disobeying the rules to have fun. Or at least trying to.

Her eyes widened. "My son, you are becoming more like your paposa every sunrise." Overjoyed, she squeezed him to her chest, planting motherly kisses all about his soft face.

"Oh," he interrupted suddenly, "I want to get the fattest kaku this morning, Sheylee. You'll see how strong I am!"

With a pat on his shoulder, Agrona smiled. Her voice flowed as the nectar of a pabi fruit, glowing with its radiant orange hues in the forest trees, sweet and reassuring with every note. "You do that, my prince. And I will prepare the rest of our breakfast."

Pleased, Derjaun turned back toward the field. Around the house and over the fence of the yard, he raced with his heart pounding as freely as if he were running with the wild stallions of the mountains.

He thought of the exciting time when within a few years he would be of age to begin training for the Guardians, and how his heart soared at the idea of training under the man his father loved so.

The pigs grumbled in the mud on his left as he ran by shouting, "You all should feel blessed it's not you I'm after today!" He passed the pigpen and hurried by the wooden frame of the poultry house he was building. The dirt was soft underneath his feet, and his breath was free to breathe the pure air. The birds were roaming not too far from the house, and when he was near the wooden fence he skillfully vaulted it.

However, sitting upon the bird lot fence, he stopped. A sound came from across the lot. He surveyed, and his eyes widened. Creeping around in its substantial size was a pabi cat, lurking and studying the old wooden fence near the outfields. It was the fence that Derjaun had repaired when he was old enough to do so after the burning of the fields from the Annenji and once more after the wild storm of the season.

The cat had snow-white fur, sniffing at each post and trying to see if its head would fit through. Being such a massive animal, it would not. The kaku and lok birds mindlessly pecked at the ground with Derjaun and the cat on either side of them, and at the moment they were lucky that the cat was still being blocked by the fence. It began to reach an enormous paw through the wood.

He breathed softly while he whispered, "That's my livestock fence, you mongrel. You don't dare destroy it. I just finished it."

He thought to himself, *I didn't think pabi cats would come close to these fences. Why are they here? I didn't think they would run short of prey. I thought the gilda and oxgog herds were plentiful around this time.*

He put his hands on his hips and squeaked, "And I thought you liked fish, not birds."

The pabi cat, although a sacred beast to the Nakhanians, could be a gentle creature unless threatened. The animal possessed a fluffy long tail and piercing green eyes. While he enjoyed the beauty of the animal, he questioned how he would handle the situation should a serious altercation occur.

Suddenly, the animal extended its body and placed its front paws on the top of the fence, stretching to its own impressive length to climb. An easy feat it would be for such a creature to get over. If only the half-witted birds would notice the threat and take shelter in the nearby woodshed on their own.

The woodshed. *Yes, the woodshed!* Derjaun thought. There by the woodshed was an ax lodged into a stump. Perhaps he could herd the flock into the shed and have the ax to protect himself. He needed to get to it without causing a scene and disturbing both the cat and his flock. He would shut the door, lock up the birds, and hopefully be able to scare the cat away by simply swinging the ax.

All noble feats were easier said than done.

With light from the sun now stronger, he lowered one foot to the ground with not so much as stray twig rustling under his foot. While watching the cat sniff the top of the fence, he kept his eyes locked on the animal as he got down onto his hands and knees to crawl underneath the first fence. He felt his body gently trembling, yet he was far from afraid. The cat paused for a bit to rub its furry muzzle on the fence post, and it allowed him a few more precious moments to make his move to the ax.

He had to get to his ax; the lives of his cherished birds depended on it. All he could think of was protecting his home, and even if it meant killing the sacred beast without due law he would do it. He had lost all patience for beasts destroying his home.

He needed time as well and stealth. Pabi cats had immaculate hearing, and one small jostle of the littlest stone could send the hungry beast raging toward him. As quietly as he could, the boy moved to the flock's water basin. He lifted his hands gracefully and tried to keep his breathing steady so that nothing would disturb the birds or the cat.

Then one bird turned toward Derjaun and squawked at him.

Chaos erupted. He leaped and scurried in between the batting of feathers and harsh sounds. Everywhere he moved he was trying to keep them off of him, and it was a significant challenge. Feathers flew, beaks pecked, and all the ruckus left the boy fighting to stay focused on the ax. One bird charged right through him in a dire state of pandemonium, and a sharp beak pierced his skin. Blood ran down his shirt.

"Ahhhh!" he wailed in pain. "Get off, you idiots! I have to get my ax!"

All he could do was flail his arms as if he himself were a bird in fright, but it did no good. He was caught in a corner of the woodshed.

It was the sudden growl of the beast that finally told him he needed to try harder. The chime of death was beating faster by each passing breath.

The cat had climbed the fence and was descending toward a meal that had been almost too easily laid out. Derjaun looked to his right in panic, eyes wide and desperate for that ax. He crawled while the birds jumped and scratched all over him.

He could not call for his sheylee, not now. Not after he told her he was going to prove how strong he had become and most importantly how he could protect his home and her. This was the chance of a lifetime. If he got hold of that ax and fought off a pabi cat, surely he'd have Staghen himself pleading for the boy to join the Guardians, even without being the proper age.

With one fast glance to the right, he saw the cat appearing in his field of vision. Majestic, strong front paws slammed down to the ground heavily. It came fast for him, hungry for victory.

Suddenly he felt the ax's handle.

Derjaun rolled away from the birds and got to his feet, roaring a war cry to scare the animal off.

It didn't work. Instead, he received a response more horrific in tone and volume that was more aggressive than a thousand of his own war cries.

The large feline roared back, ducking on its front legs and waving a long, bushy tail rapidly back and forth.

He stepped to the left, slowly. "Oh no," he mumbled in shock. The cat was getting ready to attack.

He clutched the ax so that he wouldn't drop it. If he swung, he was going to have to swing *hard*. "You want to eat me?" he bellowed angrily. The animal closed in with movements ready to kill and let out another beastly call.

"Derjaun!"

Both the animal and the boy looked toward the sound. Agrona had been disturbed inside. She had heard the animal's primal sounds and came for her son at once. On the other side of the livestock fence, she lifted her dress to climb.

"Derjaun, hurry to me!" Panicked, she waived her arms and beckoned with arms stretched out. "I will help you over!"

"No, leave! He can climb fences. I have to fight him."

But no mother in her right mind would leave her son to fight off such a dangerous adversary.

"Derjaun, *listen to me!*" Agrona hopelessly shouted as she attempted to climb over the fence. Yet her long dress got caught under her slipper, and she slipped and fell on the dirt on the other side. She clutched her right wrist and elbow.

With aches in her aging hips, Agrona groaned and attempted to get up. The fall had hurt more than she had anticipated, and she rolled onto her hands and knees. Her hairpin had fallen out, leaving her hair falling all about her face. The linen gown she wore was even dirtier than it was earlier that morning.

The cat saw everything. Derjaun glanced back and forth in shock when the cat had noticed its chance at this new larger and injured prey. It lunged toward her. He was going to have to fight it.

His mother quickly shuffled back against the fence on her rear, and Derjaun heard her crying in terror. It was a horrible feeling to be so close to the most sacred and beautiful animal of all. Those sparkling emerald eyes should have been kind and sweet, but they were furrowed with white fur and accompanied by the baring of deadly teeth. Not wanting to watch her own death, she tucked and hid her eyes.

Yet instead she heard the wail of the animal. What a deafening and tragic sound. Derjaun had it by the tail! "Leave her alone!"

The cat turned abruptly, and it seemingly began to chase its own tail, for he would not let go of it. He let out yells, but they were far from calls of distress, more like the sounds of someone dancing with a partner that danced too fast.

Agrona panicked and urgently looked about the yard for something to throw. Derjaun slammed his heels into the dirt so hard that the cat let out a shrill of pain, its tail yanked unbearably hard. He quickly thought and climbed on top of the beast.

"Derjaun! Get off him!"

But the boy was stubborn, determined, and didn't have a choice. The cat began to frantically move backward, and its head thrashed left and right trying to toss the boy off, but he tightened his legs and grip and wielded the ax high. One of them was going to die.

"I will sell your coat to the king himself!"

His mother limped fast with her hand outstretched to stop the murder of Nakhan's most sacred animal. "Derjaun, no!"

The animal fought harder. Agrona cried in agony to prevent the ghastly event. She clutched her hands to her eyes, screaming louder until her face grew pale. "Derjaun, listen to me!"

The wild white beast had bucked hard enough to throw the boy to the ground. His adrenaline raced harder than his heart to get away, but as he tried he felt jousting claws swipe into his rib cage. It felt as if it broke every bone. The cat was atop Derjaun with a suffocating weight, but he still turned to fight. His teeth clenched to push the animal off, but the claws dug deeper into his left leg. He would never give up.

The battle was abruptly stopped by the sound of collapsing fences that came from everywhere, and the sound of horses broke the chance of such a victory. On his back, the boy felt the pounding of horse hooves in the ground. The pabi cat looked around, crouching to see it was surrounded by Guardians mounted on horses. It had to escape. The chanting and hollering of the strong men left the animal leaping over the fence to get away.

The boy rolled over and coughed from his back, and Agrona raced toward him with sobs of happiness. "Oh, my son! You have—"

"I failed," he whimpered with his head low. He pushed with every fiber of strength he had left to lift himself up. His youthful body was injured and bloodied. Scratches of the birds had left his clothes torn and parts of his body shredded and scraped with blood, but nothing in his physique could compare to the pain he felt in his heart. "I failed."

Agrona hurried to kneel by his side and kissed his face. "Look at me, my boy. How could you say such things? You saved both our flock *and* me."

Their eyes met. She brushed the dirty blond strands of hair from his glistening eyes and removed her shawl to press it to his side. How rough he looked, yet so sweet and kind. Her eyes reflected her pride for him, and with a stammering smile of emotions she spoke, "I have never been prouder of you than I am right now." She patted him a few times and compressed her shawl to the many wounds he had. "I did not lose you."

Derjaun, hearing the captain's voice, gently nudged his mother off of him to stand. Clutching the sides of his stomach, he attempted to hide his injury and bit his lower lip. His emotions were beyond reconciliation.

He needed to compose himself. He had to, because there before him came Staghen, mounted on his black stallion that now bore the significant weight of mature muscles.

"Aye-ya, Captain Staghen!" Agrona hurried to make her appearance more befitting of the captain's presence. She pointed her shaking finger toward her son. "Please, he needs medical care! Look at my white shawl about his waist. He's bleeding."

He waved a leather-gloved hand in her direction. "At ease, Agrona. Allow your heart's rhythm to slow steadily. You have been in distress and must rest." He turned to see the brave boy who showed pain and dolor. Staghen dismounted Rikaana, looking kindly at the boy.

Derjaun was not timid in front of Staghen. This was his time to show his worth. He was ready to truly wield his paposa's sword and anticipated the coming cheers.

But Staghen held his hand up at Derjaun's attempt to stand. "Stay down, young man. Lie on your back."

Derjaun hesitated briefly until Agrona nodded to him. He sat down on the dirt and lay down. The morning star's warmth coaxed his face to smile, and his body to breathe and relax.

Staghen removed his side bag, knelt by the boy, and called to his guaradas, "Search the outer fields and assure us that there are no more pabi cats."

Agrona heard the roaring voices of the large men. The horses were gone with a stamping of thunder and power.

The young Vin Gruinelle boy saw nothing but the blue sky and felt nothing but sadness. The captain looked at his eyes while he cleaned the wounds. It amazed him how Derjaun didn't even wince or grunt from the sting of the ulgg being poured across all the deep marks. Staghen smiled and began to work.

"Derjaun, I am exceedingly confused by you. I can almost see it," he chuckled heartily. "This dream of yours to be like your father. And I can see in your lost eyes that you feel you will never reach it. Your actions are misguided yet laced with honest intentions." He began piercing the torn flesh with the needle to sew, placing a gentle hand upon the boy's ribcage. "Your life is worth more than a few birds or a pig."

The young boy held his hands out to the sky in protest. "Captain, I was protecting my flock. The cat was going to eat them!"

Staghen grabbed his hands to place them back to the ground, less the stitching come undone. He tossed his long black locks that were adorned with partial ribbons and several braids that now hung far past his shoulders. He raised his right brow sharply.

"I...I understand this, Derjaun, but as I said your life is more important than that of your birds. Besides, I do not think it was necessary for you to attempt to cut the creature's head off. You above all else know how increasingly rare yet vital they are to our balance here. They keep the gilda deer from coming so close and eating our crops. These animals have not been truly spared from extinction yet. Do you risk sacrificing an age-old beast of our village for pride and strength, riches and valor?"

Agrona also came to sit beside her son. She stroked his hair to try to comfort him when she saw his head lean away from the captain, who firmly spoke again, "This animal is not to be destroyed and never will be. Is that understood? You could have briefly injured him and accomplished your goal. However, I believe you sought out the selfish glory of completely killing the animal for currency and pride, especially with what I heard you yell as I arrived."

Staghen focused on his work for a moment to allow Derjaun to think about what was said. He tightened the cross stitches more, and with the knot secure he kept Agrona's shawl pressed to the long wounds while he worked with one hand. He held the bottle of ulgg to Agrona. "Here. Clean what wounds from the birds you can."

She accepted the bottle and ripped a piece of her dress to clean her son's arm and neck.

With his innocence and bravery shattered, a tear rolled down Derjaun's filthy, blood-stained cheek. The son of Radal felt lowly, and his mother's face turned expressively to nurture him, rubbing away the tears.

"Captain, please forgive my son. I would be nothing but a bath of blood upon my own soil had it not been for his bravery. He desires so much to be like you, our brave leader, that at times he forgets his virtues."

The captain worked with care and diligence. "Well, if this be the truth, Derjaun," Staghen said with frigid hesitation, "may you be reminded that it is virtues that solely make a Guardian. You are more than admired for your daring bravery and risk of sacrifice to save your mother and your flock, but remember the cat only came to eat because it is hungry. You set to kill it because you were selfish. And this is not the heart of a Guardian. Do we have a mutual understanding, my boy?"

It took Derjaun no time to answer. "Yes, Captain."

Staghen pressed a little further to nurture the boy. "Your father told me something once that I think you may enjoy hearing, maybe not. Life, Derjaun, is always a stumbling climb up a mountain path that will *never* be familiar. I know you wish so much to be like your father, and what you do not know is that your heart is already just like his. But your pride is what needs mending. Sometimes we win, but sometimes we *must* lose. Your father told me this when I tried to fight the Guarada Theidran and lost badly. My shoulder was broken, and I suffered a concussion so great I was out of training for months. But it was not about winning. It was about climbing the mountain. I learned. I grew. So from this, I want you too to learn and grow."

Derjaun turned to look at the man who was ten years his senior and simply felt every word in his heart.

The captain turned to Agrona, raising his brows, "Let's get him to Dr. Crenon. His wounds are deep and need better care."

"Yes, Captain," she responded.

He slipped his strong arms underneath the boy's damaged body, allowing his head to rest against his chest.

The young boy sighed while being carried. For a moment, Derjaun looked up to Staghen's strong face. He felt the captain's breathing against his side, and he could feel how easy it was for the captain to carry him. It enabled Derjaun to melt in the embrace and relax. His father had carried him the same way numerous times when he had gotten hurt as a little boy. He looked to the ax on the ground and groaned aloud.

Agrona asked, "My son, what is it that troubles you now?"

He sighed once more and watched as they passed his ax. "I have to fix the fence again."

"Oh, come now, my boy," laughed Agrona. Her hand reached and brushed his shoulders. "This too can wait. After all, Staghen may command others to fix it for you, since it was his men who broke through it. But mind you, the captain is right. We must get you to the care of the doctor. These wounds are deep."

"Yes, they are," Staghen said firmly. He heaved Derjaun onto Rikaana, gave him the reins, and turned to the widow. "See to it that he gets there safely. I'm going to stay behind and pick up the broken pieces of wood."

Agrona thanked the young captain and was on her way to lead Rikaana to the doctor in the Inner Circle.

On their way, Derjaun had a curiosity that needed to be quenched. "Sheylee, you told me that paposa wore wounds much deeper and would push on throughout many battles. He didn't care about his injuries."

"He did this because he had no choice, Derjaun," Agrona warned. "You don't need to lose your common sense to be brave like him. He did it because there was no other choice. You have a choice."

He turned over his shoulder to see the mess that was left behind. The entire field and stockyard had grown quiet from the event.

"Sheylee, why is it that Staghen's horses broke through the fence instead of jumping it?"

She laughed again, rubbing the belly of the black stallion to guide him onward. "The Guardian drafts are horses that possess frames much too heavy for jumping and leaping well, my son. They are horses meant for charging into battle, meant to carry heavily armored men. They carry the big guaradas. You know that."

"Oh, *forgive* me for not paying attention to the horses that broke through the fence. I may or may not have been too busy with a pabi cat! I wonder if the mountaineer horses are as large as the guaradas' horses. I remember paposa telling me that their coats are as white as pabi cats and are strong, wild, and enchanting. I wish I could see one."

She chuckled. "Yes, the Guardian horses are quite large in size. But you know they must be in order to carry their riders, who are also very large. Maybe one day you'll see the mountaineer horses if they come down from the high elevations and get close enough to graze on the grasslands. They usually do so right before the snowfall of winter."

Within time, the two were edging closer toward the Inner Circle, where the doctor lived. People stared at the boy with blood in his hair and torn shirt, and the children ceased their playtime to gawk. Agrona noticed Derjaun holding his head high.

She snickered and looked forward. "Be careful of your pride, Derjaun."

He frowned at her. "I'm injured from a brave battle to protect my flock, and I protected my mother from getting her face mauled off. I'm riding on Rikaana. What do I *not* have to be proud of? Nakhan needs me to be proud and strong," he argued. Once again he looked at her in confusion and hope. "Does it not? It is supposed to be my legacy now. How can I do what I must do if no one allows me to think for myself?"

"One day, yes. But for now, allow Staghen to be your hero. You lost your father at an incredibly young age, and it's best for you to allow yourself a strong male figure still, someone to help make decisions for you."

He shook his head. "I'm sorry, Sheylee. It's…"

The boy let his thoughts trail off as he became enamored by the white, pillowy clouds in the sky. It hadn't occurred to him until then that he had no idea how to cope with losing his father. He had been caught between doing too much and not doing enough, being a man and still being a child. Perhaps his mother was right. It would be best to allow himself to follow Staghen's lead in all ways possible.

She smiled and lifted his dirty hand from his side to kiss it. "It's alright. I understand. Look, we're almost there. You protected me, so let me carry you the rest of the way. After all, I'm a farm mother. I'm used to carrying heavy things despite minor injuries."

Once they reached the doctor's house and tied Rikaana outside, Derjaun settled on a high wooden table that was covered in brightly colored blankets. They were freshly made quilts and white cloth, and

he rested his mind, admiring the embroidered floral patterns of
yellows and reds. Searching around the room, he noticed how many
windows there really were. The polished glass was framed with
white, lacy drapes. And on a nearby table, he saw cases of fine
medical instruments along with a desk that held a hefty book full of
herbal recipes, medicinal concoctions, and a water pitcher. Across the
room were several shelves, and the top one possessed several trinkets
that Derjaun couldn't name. A lone candle burned in the corner on a
stand. He gazed up to the ceiling. There were no cobwebs or signs of
dust or anything. He had been to Dr. Crenon's house once before
when he was younger, but he recalled that the room had been a bit
more unkempt.

The hustle of the village folk outside compelled him to look out
one of the many windows.

"Derjaun," his mother called from the chair next to the table,
"your wounds, do they not hurt?"

They hurt so mercilessly he had fought back every tear of pain on
the way here. The cat had truly clawed his ribcage. Dried blood ran
in deep, dark streaks along his side, and with every breath he felt his
rib bones expand into it, exacerbating the pain. His leg had been
bitten into, which he could not even recall happening.

He wanted to lie to keep his pride, but he concluded that it was
wiser to remember the conversation and speak the truth. "Yes," he
responded quietly and went back to looking outside.

Agrona began fanning herself.

He didn't go to the Inner Circle often, but he loved it when he did.
He staved off boredom by watching the business of the rich folk in
the streets.

He lifted his head. Far across the pathways, he saw a young girl
pulling her ragged brown cloak above her head. He leaned closer.
Her hair was dark brown, and her skin was white like Staghen's. It
was a very odd feature in comparison to other girls her age, who
often bore skin of richer hues and pigments, especially since she was
apparently a farmer girl. It appeared she was trying to sell bread from
a basket in her hand. She reached out to everyone who passed her by,

and yet no one offered to pay the two pences for the freshly made delicacy.

She looked around, calling politely for people to buy her bread. Still after moments passed, no one took any. She would disappear in the crowd of horse-drawn carts, Guardians, and children, only to appear again with the same amount of bread in her little woven basket.

"Sheylee," Derjaun whispered with his eyes still looking at the filthy girl.

"Yes?"

"Do you have two pences?"

She sighed and glanced impatiently around the room. "No, Derjaun, you are not buying bread from the farmer's daughter."

"But why not? Look at her." He pointed out the window. "Anyone can clearly see she is simply trying to earn money for her hard labor, and no one cares. I find that sad. After all, I have not eaten breakfast and am *starving*."

"Derjaun," she said firmly as she rose from her seat, "she is the age to begin her training as a woman of trades. If you fall for her clumsy act as a damsel in distress, then you teach her nothing. Now sit still. I hear the doctor coming."

Derjaun stared at her, but she quickly turned away. His heart was stung by what she said. He whispered, "I felt that you, as a farmer's daughter and now a farmer, would not see this as an act, nor would you see my kindness as being gullible."

Her eyes widened, and her mouth tightened.

The morning had not gone the way he had hoped. It seemed to him that everywhere he tried to reach people on a wonderful note they would slap him in the face and immediately condemn his acts of honesty.

But obeying his mother, Derjaun sat down in a severe case of aggravation, folding his arms. He groaned bitterly while still watching the young girl. As her face turned in his direction, he watched her brows raise sweetly to a woman passing by. He gave out a smile with happiness for her consistent kindness despite people being snide to her. He leaned closer to the window again and noticed something strange about her.

Her eyes were green.

It was completely impossible and abnormal for anyone in Nakhan. For as much as the young boy tried, he could not recall *one* person in Nakhan having such a trait. Green eyes were for the pabi cats.

Down the hall, they both heard Dr. Crenon walk with heavy stomps that even made the guaradas look like elegant dancers, and he walked fast with a huffy breath of masculine gruffing.

"Ahhhh, Derjaun, meh boy!" Crenon cheered happily as he entered. His round belly jiggled when the doctor laughed, and his face, although masked by his wiry black beard, was raised in a smile that no facial hair could hide.

"Oh!" He jumped at once, and for a fleeting moment his dark eyes twinkled. "Derjaun, what in de stars 'apenned to yeh? Yer bloody from yer hair to yer toos!"

When the doctor approached to begin cleaning the cuts, scrapes, and gashes, Agrona spoke on Derjaun's behalf, which did not make her son happy in the least. Derjaun knew very well that she would tell the story as if to make him appear a fool.

"He tried to fight a pabi cat," she stated.

"Ohhhhh," Crenon grumbled and shook his head, "dat is not sumtin fer a boy like yer age to be doin', Derjaun. Yer blessed to even be alive! Now, listen to yer sheylee and go get Guardians if dis 'appens again, ye 'ear?"

Derjaun folded his arms. "Please spare me. I've had enough lectures for the day."

While his wounds were stitched and mended, there was not one ounce of appreciation for his heart's desires. In his mind he remembered his father having to always answer to her, always having to explain himself to her. When he was a young child, he never noticed it. But now he was older, and all of this was placed on him.

Derjaun had rested at home for what seemed like an entire season nearly. Staying inside, butchering kakus, visiting his mother, and heavy housework were already his childhood. Yet now he had multiple injuries, and the doctor ordered him to *stay* in bed until his wounds were completely healed. The entire idea tore the boy's mind into a knotting frenzy of frustration. And he had many reasons for this. What a pain it was for him to watch Staghen lead in his father's place while he himself was trampled under someone else's foot.

The beautiful night sky had closed in on the tiny village, and both Derjaun and Agrona were in their quiet home. "Sheylee," he whimpered that evening in his bed, "Dr. Crenon says I can't go outside until my wounds are healed, but he also said that it may take several seasons for them to be completely better."

"Yes, my son." Agrona lovingly pulled the covers over him.

He looked over the blankets. "I want to go back to school this year, and I have to help you outside. I can't stay so long." His eyelids nearly closed from looking down, his voice weakened from realization. "And the Summoning Ceremony is tomorrow. I want to see who becomes a Guardian this cycle. I have missed the last ones, and before that I can't remember."

"Come now," she interrupted. "Let's not discuss this. You will rest tonight. Your body has been very strained. I think it best if you..."

"Yes, Sheylee?" Derjaun asked with a light of hope in his heart.

"Well, never mind this. We will talk some other time." She simply left his room.

How it agitated Derjaun when his mother left in what seemed like the middle of a conversation. No, deeper than that. She left in the middle of a confession, but he would never know what the confession was.

The boy, as far back as he could remember, always thrived when the Summoning Ceremony came around. Young boys would become young men tomorrow, and they would be fitted for armor, have special swords and shields made for them, and even more they would receive their own horses.

"My own horse," Derjaun whispered as he shuffled his blankets about his chin.

Guardians passed around near his window on foot. Their speech was of codes that only Guardians knew. Except for Derjaun. The entire language of the Guardians was derived in honor of Derjaun's lineage known as Gruic, and so he understood every word. As they passed by his window, he peered outward.

Their impressive presence outside lulled Derjaun to sleep until the song from the kabanana bird came. With the light of the blessed sun came the jewels of the morning dew sprinkled on the lush grass. It was always to be a calm morning in the outer fields. Except for this day.

He awoke with a smile. It was the day of the ceremony! Out of bed, he rushed to dress himself, ignoring the tearing sensation of the near-fatal wounds. He was always thrilled to start his day, but no day was any comparison to this one. "Gika-ma'ha!" His mouth fumbled happily as he tied his cloth pants. It was a Gruic phrase that simply meant, *it's morning*. "Today is my day to show Staghen that I'm still as strong as ever, even with my pabi cat scratches!" He lifted his shirt with naive hopes that his wounds would have somehow magically been healed. He saw that they had only dried. At once, his head lifted in realization. He shrugged easily. "Ah, so they are more like gashes. Oh, complete and total *war wounds*."

He then lifted a wooden comb to attempt to style his ever-growing manly mane, and proudly stated, "And he will see that I'm ready on this day. It's my day. I'm twelve years old. Even though I am not quite of age, Staghen has allowed young boys my age to serve in the Guardians if they do a just act! And my act with the pabi cat surely should suffice!" He laughed with overbearing excitement and his hands shook with his jostled nerves.

"Derjaun!" called Agrona.

He turned quickly, and his eyes became sore. *Sheylee will not approve of this.* He had to hide his body to appear he was still in bed. But it was of no worry to his heart. On this day, he knew Agrona would be in the village for quite some time, as it was mandatory for wives of Guardians, even if widowed, to attend.

"Derjaun!" she bellowed once again.

With much acting, Derjaun struggled to "wake" upon his mother entering the room. "Sheylee, is it still early?" He rubbed his eyes.

"Yes," she said merrily as she knelt by his side. He became more attentive after noticing his mother holding a package in her hand and had a smile upon her face. Unusually, she was already dressed as if heading toward the Inner Circle. Her brilliant long tresses were sparkling and washed, braided with ribbons that shone with new resilience. He noted mentally, *new resilience.*

"Sheylee," he said cautiously as he sat up to rub his eyes, "did you go into the village this morning?"

"I did, and I purchased this for you." The only sound he heard was the rustling of her pale-blue dress as she sat on the hard floor and gave it to him.

He tried to smile, and yet again it was an act. Her face seemed as if it promised a thousand wishes to come true, with her light eyes sweeping with sincerity. But if it was not an open allowance to attend the ceremony, it was no gift at all. He thanked her in the simple Gruic phrase of showing gratitude, "Min'ra mes vi, Sheylee."

He untied and opened the brown cloth.

It was a gift that was far from ordinary, twinkling in his eyes as a reflection of promises. A gift that, as the boy burst into tears to hug his mother, showed him that she was allowing him to attend the ceremony. It was the finest animal hide sewn into pants for him, plus hair ribbons with a vial of blackened flower seed powder for his eyes. It was usual for the newcomers to decorate themselves in bright colors to show their innocence and youth.

This was the moment that Derjaun waited for all his life. With his face pressed intensely into her sternum, he whispered, "You really *do* believe in me, Sheylee. Thank you. Thank you so much!"

His time had finally come to follow in his father's trail.

She kissed his head with a satisfied sigh. "I have always believed in you. But let's not stall this moment any longer. We need to get you bathed and dressed!"

He went through bathing, scrubbing, hair washing, nail cleansing, body oiling, and then came Derjaun's moment of pride, dressing his hair.

As he flopped on a creaking old chair in the kitchen, Agrona filed the prongs of the wooden comb so that his hair did not tangle or break in their splinters and chipped edges. "Your smile has not been so luminous in years, my son. Why, you can hardly sit still!"

The comb slipped through his wet hair while he sat next to the northern window to allow the cool breeze to dry it for him. He groaned affectionately with the stimulation of his scalp, all the tingles and delightful sensations adding even more reasoning to his happiness. The comb went easily down behind his ears, and for the moment Agrona removed it to see if any more filing was needed. Lifting it to her eyes, several thick cuts of hair were tangled inside of the comb's teeth, and she panicked. Stars forbid if he saw that.

"How is it, Sheylee?" he asked, lifting his chin in pride.

"Oh..." She quickly began yanking out the hair. "It's alright. I need to smooth the edges a bit more."

"Strange. I did not feel it even tugging my mane in the slightest. I combed my mane—"

He stopped immediately, knowing he'd said too much about what he'd done.

"You did what?" she asked in amazement.

"Sorry, Sheylee." He turned to her with regret. "I was up before you came into my room, and I brushed my hair that moment."

Agrona's light eyes seemed to bear the weight of confusion, "And your comb was filed properly?"

He nodded his head.

"Tell me," she said quietly, "did you find any hair in your comb's teeth?"

"No."

Stillness cast its blanket of waiting on the entire room, cloaking both son and mother with it. "Why? Is there a problem?"

Agrona jerked and shook her head. "No, my boy." She smiled. "Turn your head so I may finish."

And so he did. Sitting on the chair with anxiousness so great that he could not resist bouncing his knees and singing a song that his father sang often. Agrona, for the life of her heart and her son, could no longer match his happiness. Another lock of hair slipped out with her fingers.

She abruptly turned. "We need to dress you."

Derjaun climbed out of the chair and tripped onto the floor with an astoundingly loud sound. He lifted his leg where he bore the largest stitches. The wild beast had clawed and bit into his left leg nearly halfway down, and he shook it in discomfort. "My leg felt tingles, and it was awkward to stand on it."

Agrona laughed, "Come now, my son. It is your blood trying to heal your wounds. Don't be so silly! Your muscles are weak, for the sake of the stars above. You almost died recently."

She was confused and yet could not let it show. Her mind and heart had to clench dearly to the idea that it was her son's body healing and nothing more.

After they attended to their looks, Derjaun rushed out the door to take a flying leap off the steps. It was such a feeling of serenity that he enjoyed so many times before when he had done this leap of showmanship, yet this time he crashed hard into the ground. The pain was so vigorous he believed his knee bone had snapped. The freshly washed softness of his face slammed into the dirt.

"Derjaun, what am I to do with you?" Once more Agrona came to his side to pat off the dirt. "Do you want to look like a farm rat on this day? Stop flailing about so recklessly." Slightly agitated but even more amused, she brushed her hands down his shirt. "Are you hurt?"

"Sheylee," he whimpered, "I have done that so many times before. Why can't I now?" He could not hold his leg despite the agony it was set with. Why, if she saw he had been hurt she may turn him around and force him to get in bed again.

"How many times must I tell you? You are severely injured and need to be careful still. Your blood flow is uneasy these days because of the healing that's still happening."

The joyous boy pursed his lips and turned to hide a single tear.

"Ah, I'm sorry, my son. I care for you so much, and you need to learn you are not invincible."

"If you say so," he said to her with sparkles of a smile, attempting to lighten the emotions.

"Wonderful. Now let us go," she said cheerfully. They grabbed each other's hands and began hurrying toward the Inner Circle.

"Come on, Sheylee! Am I really faster than you?" Derjaun yelled behind to his mother, who was laughing as her hand was pulled far in front of her.

"I'm wearing heeled shoes! And I told you not to make such hasty movements!" she laughed.

Her son's spirit could not be tamed. Even with such injuries, he still somehow managed to run much faster than anyone else. Little did Derjaun know how much he truly was like his father right then. His leg hurt horribly, but he did not care in the least.

"And I'm injured! Come on, keep up with your new Guardian son!"

On the dirt paths they raced against the silver songs of the village bells. Everywhere people in their best garments hurried under clothing lines and out of shops for the momentous event. The two charged into the crowd once they reached the Inner Circle, and his heart was injected with a courageous lift so large that he hardly noticed how difficult it was for him to breathe. He coughed hoarsely.

His mother huffed when they arrived, "Now look what you've done. You've inhaled all this dust." She laughed at his expense.

"Oh, I don't care. Look, I see Staghen!"

Agrona patted his back firmly while looking toward the captain.

In the center of the Inner Circle, there was a wooden platform big enough to hold the captain, his malakae, four sorakhan Guardians (those who stood in rank below the malakae), and either the person being honored or the person being judged and tried for punishments. On this platform, Captain Staghen was offering his kindest smile to the Guardians next to him, conversing about the coming ceremony. In Staghen's young age of nearly twenty-three years, Derjaun could see how widely his back had developed. His hair was groomed as usual, glistening in deep-blue lowlights, but a maiden must have accented his waving hair with finger twirls and jinfish oil, for they seemed more lustrous than ever.

"Sheylee, look! There he is!"

"Yes, I see him. Wait here. I have to go inform him that I am allowing you to join if he wishes."

Surprisingly, Derjaun obeyed. When his mother left, he found himself looking about the crowd and wondering if that farmer girl was there.

Agrona scurried into the crowd and stopped at the stoop of the platform. Gently she called, "My Grace." With a polite bow, she couldn't contain the overwhelming joy she felt when she saw Staghen.

He turned to her. "Agrona." His arms opened for her, allowing his deep voice to come from his youthfully strong chest. When she came into his arms, they hugged one another lovingly. Although other women gossiped about Agrona pursuing Staghen, she always ignored them. Firstly, she was old enough to be a mother to him, and secondly she never wanted to marry another man. After all, Staghen himself vowed his heart was in his work, and he never seemed to take an interest in any lady. But it was clear many ladies took lustful interest in him.

"I come with great news, Captain," she said warmly as she held his leather-gloved hands.

He smirked. "Would it have to do with that boy jumping and waving his arms about in deranged madness?" He glanced in Derjaun's direction.

"Yes!" She looked back to the captain with excitement glowing in her eyes and a smile so wide it made her cheeks sore. She proceeded with a lift of happiness in her voice, "I have given him my blessings to join your men, but of course that is if he has yours." The gentleness in her eyes grew. The cutting hue of his blue eyes were always refreshing for anyone to gaze into.

He lifted his left hand in a gesture of uncertainty. "What of his virtues? Do you truly believe him to be morally ready?"

"If I may say, your Guardian Nikolag does not hold any more morality with the village women than my son does of his own innocence and attempts at good will. After all, Nikolag is a gollet, a seafarer of unbridled intentions and a nasty temper. I'm surprised you even allowed him on the Guardians."

They both shared warm laughter, and Staghen shook his head with his brows raised at the hilarity of the statement. "Yes," he said, "this is more than the truth. Ah, those gollets. Always out for something they shouldn't be getting into."

Agrona's heart raced like the rushing Gigannora. She waited. He sighed.

"He has my blessings."

Trembling in her hands, Agrona leaned to kiss his knuckles. "You have my warmest and most sincere gratitude, Captain. It has been his dream for so many years."

Staghen laughed and told her, "Yes, it has." He then gently gestured her off and with a scent of joy in his voice said, "Let us prepare for the ceremony."

Derjaun saw his mother pushing through a swarm of people, coming right for him with a stretch of pride upon her face. "Sheylee! Did he—" He was nearly unable to speak.

All his mother could do was pull him close. It felt as if she could not reach him fast enough to inform him of the captain's decision. When he was in her arms at last, her lips poured the final answer with tears down her glowing skin. "Yes! He said yes, my boy!"

But he didn't even get to thank his mother properly, for the young Vin Gruinelle boy was told to stand in a line toward the side of the platform with many other young boys who were one or two years within his age, and even some of the same age. He looked around with his chin held high as Staghen delivered a wonderful speech for the ceremony. He spoke of the honor he had in welcoming the youth of the next generation's strongest fighters and protectors and how pleased he would be to train these boys into becoming great men.

"So, with all my love being sent to their families, let the ceremony begin!" he concluded loudly. The gathering of people before him cheered happily in a unison song of glee.

The malakae, Vathra Saran, tossed his long hair behind his back before preparing the first training sword to be handed away. He possessed traits far different than Staghen, who was fair in complexion and had hair blacker than any jinfish oil could be. Vathra's hair was heavily straight, and it passed his biceps in length and carried the glorious color of blood in its tone. His skin was as rich of the color of blood, as it seemed so deep in warmth. It was just a part of his ancestry to be so rewarded in healthy tones. Suitably so, Vathra Saran possessed irises that matched his hair color. Vathra was the last of his lineage, known as the Sahinas, and he lost his only blood relative, his mother, in the fight of the Annenji. From all the loss of family, as Staghen himself had no one, the two men were self-announced brethren, loving and loyal to one another as family would.

"The first boy I summon is—" Staghen boomed loudly before pausing. "Astin Din Tannerg!"

Shouting echoed throughout the crowd while the first young boy stumbled up the stairs. Derjaun clapped and whistled for his new partner. Although he had never seen him before, he was proud to see the young boy so enthused.

Vathra hugged the boy, who now accepted a sword in his hand, a sword that was merely a dress sword for someone the size of Vathra. "My deepest love for you, boy," Malakae Vathra said.

But it was tenfold the honor to have Captain Staghen tie the cowhide lace around his waist. The dressing of the beads told a great story. Each bead that was red of color showed how many battles a Guardian had fought. The ivory beads were to show bravery or heroic acts of kindness. The more beads, the higher the ranking.

All of the boys were simply excited, bursting with the mental strain that their hearts longed to cease. Agrona began gazing about at the other boys when she saw her son rubbing his leg. He seemed to slouch. It felt like an eternity seemed to pass until it was finally his turn. She turned to him with her face as light as the star above and her hands clasped together with pride.

"And now," Staghen shouted, "the son of my predecessor, Captain Radal." He breathed. "Derjaun Vin Gruinelle!"

When his name was called, the young boy bounded up the steps like a deer in the fields. Only in the last few steps did his breath leave for just a moment. But he would be strong. Derjaun lifted his eyes to Vathra and calmed himself. It was his moment. His finest moment. If only his father could have been there to see his son take a sword that he could hold then, and in a handful of years he would truly be able to wield his late father's sword. He would be a man.

The malakae's eyes glistened. "Derjaun, you and I have shared the same dream. Congratulations to you and your mother." He kissed the boy's head. Derjaun breathed once more. The pressure where the kiss landed left his body feeling weak. Firing pain seemed to swim up his leg, and trying not to limp or let it show he utilized the energy of the crowd.

There he was, face to face with Staghen. "My boy," Staghen said in loving admiration for the boy's eagerness. "Congratulations, here is your—"

Suddenly a wave of blackness overwhelmed Derjaun's vision, and unconsciousness descended upon him. All the villagers called out in alarm, but Staghen caught the boy in his arms before he crashed into the wooden platform. Agrona's eyes busted in fright, and she immediately shoved people away without a care of hurting them. Her son had collapsed.

She pushed harder. "Leave my path! I must get to my son!"

"Derjaun!" the captain shouted to bring the boy back. All was in panic for the boy's life. The captain screamed mercilessly to all who could hear. "Get the doctor! He's fainted and losing color!" Staghen placed the boy on the wooden platform, opened up his mouth, and attempted to resuscitate him. He felt his heart beating, but with no breath felt he pressed his hands harder into the chest. "Derjaun!"

Staghen lifted the boy's head and tried to reposition his hand to hold the fragile neck. As Agrona came to her son's side, she saw that in Staghen's hand was a lock of hair so large that her son now had a bare spot.

Crying, she begged, "What has happened to my son?"

Staghen's eyes flooded as he shouted to his malakae. "Vathra! Rush for the doctor! Find him now!" His face was reddened, and his tone shaken.

The reason why the last boy of the Vin Gruinelle line collapsed was never known. Not even the doctor himself could understand what had happened. No one had ever been mauled by a pabi cat, so no one, not even a great doctor, could have been prepared for what had happened.

3

D erjaun's body could not heal properly from the attack, and he
was dying. The comforting warmth of summer came and left,
and the year was coming to an end. On a lowly, dark night at the end
of winter, the doctor spoke to the widow. The blanket of snow left the
entire fields mute save for the howling of the forest wolves.

In the warmth of his home, Dr. Crenon informed Agrona that she
must allow him free play and learning at school so that his last
season of living would be a wonderfully remembered one. It was
either that or bear the suffering and hurt knowing he would die
alone, without any friends, or even worse: without a legacy to live by.

The snow of winter eventually melted, and the young and sick
child barely made it through. It was now spring. Oh, but a chilly and
crisp spring it tended to be in that northernmost mountain village!
Although everyone and everything in this village was alive with flour-
ishing life and happiness, it was another day when Derjaun was
fighting with his mother to stay home from school. It was misery.
Absolute misery.

Agrona urged him sternly, "Derjaun, you dare again make a fool
of yourself this season? This is why the others taunt you. Ah, you are
just like your father. This was not one of his better characteristics."

Opening the curtains to let the warm light in, she raised a brow to her son, who was lying on his back with opened eyes. They had once been a warmed skin color around their lines, yet it had now faded into gray, and the lightest of his blues were forced out with all other signs of wellness, for they had become a sickly brown color with flecks of dying silver.

Derjaun, being too stressed with fatigue, found it difficult to smile. He listened before rolling over to face her. "Sheylee, it's not my fault. I tried to go to school over these last few seasons. I couldn't keep up because I had been tending to the farm for so long. I'm stupid compared to my peers, and that's that."

Agrona sighed, watching her child lie on the floor on his bed mat that should have been mended and stuffed with fresh feathers seasons ago. It had massive tears and became flat from all the time he had spent in it.

"I know you are sore and tired, but I want you to live and learn. You may learn something you've always wanted to learn. We cannot hold ourselves back out of fear."

Without being able to fight his mother any longer, Derjaun reluctantly agreed to go.

After dressing himself and eating what his belly could handle, Derjaun left the house and started his walk toward the Inner Circle. He walked like a lonesome soul. A soul without a sword, without a friend, and now without a purpose. The young blond boy felt the disease drain more than just his life. His absolute joyful disposition went as well. And one thing that began to boil in his mind more than ever was the feeling that his mother was one moment fending for him and the next scolding him. His heart ached more than his withered body.

In the middle of the uneven dirt paths toward the Inner Circle, Derjaun stumbled in one of the many deep grooves left behind from a farmer's cart. He coughed and regathered himself. "I'm not dead yet. I can do this," he confessed to the sky. It seemed as if the strength in his voice was medicinal for his tiring body. He looked at the sky, once more hearing something quite lovely.

The soft echo of some sort of forest bird called out to the sky from behind him. For a moment, he turned around to glance to the mountains.

Derjaun realized that out of all the stories he recalled of his father's tellings, not once did he recall his father telling him that he went to the mountains. No man was supposedly brave enough to go. With the unknown predators that lurked deep inside the forest, most men felt it unwise to leave the safety of the village. At one point in his youth, Derjaun had even recalled an old tale of a white wolf, monstrous in size and ill of temper, which was seen eating children near the forest. It was a silly idea, as everyone knew that no wolf would ever be white, nor would they eat children. But still the tales were either spread to keep the villagers safe or...perhaps something else.

"Oh, Paposa. Sometimes when I gaze into the great beyond their mighty horizon, I think of you." He turned his full attention toward the wonderful north. "Maybe you are there. Waiting for me. And what a pleasant thought it is."

It was as if Radal graced his son with an embrace, for Derjaun suddenly felt warm and happy enough to carry on to school. Once inside, he kept a low profile until he made his way to an unoccupied desk. Sitting down on the rickety wooden chair gave him a much-needed rest, and so he allowed his curiosity to roam about the room. He saw something new there that was not there last season. Above the teacher's desk was a long wooden plaque that read:

SHALL OUR BOOTS SLAM LIKE THUNDER, AND OUR SWORDS TEAR THE AIR LIKE LIGHTNING. OUR CHILDREN SHALL BE CARRIED AND OUR WOMEN PROTECTED, THE WEAK STRENGTHENED AND THE POOR SHALL BE THE WEALTHY.

Derjaun was incredibly happy, as this was the mission statement of the Guardians. It was the very phrase his father created to remind all of what the purpose of being a Guardian truly was. The timing of such a sight soothed him.

The voice of a girl suddenly caught his ear.

Derjaun lowered his head in fear of being bullied, his arms folded sorely on the wooden desk, eyes scarcely turning toward the sound.

"I said, bikva-vima!" she squeaked again brightly.

The thought of whether to be offended or amused at her ability to know his language sunk in his mind. "Noku tana medas bit vi-ha?"

The remark changed the once-excited female into a mere shadow of confusion. "Eh?" she asked and took the desk next to his.

With that, Derjaun finally conjured up the courage to face her.

There she was, smiling with skin as pale as the beautiful white clouds in the most royal of skies, and her cheeks that smiled so large were pelted with bits of redness as if burned by the sun. He blinked in awe. His memory shot through thousands of images in his mind, trying to remember where he'd seen her before. This smile was loving, caring, and friendly. His heart softened. He blinked while his cracked lips gently returned the friendly gesture.

This new girl possessed hair that was flaunting the colors of the ground's richest soils and laid straight across her shoulders that were a bit broad for a female. Perhaps it was due to her slight appearance of muscles that were impressive for someone of her gender and age. *She must be a field girl*, he thought. As Derjaun continued to stare, he wondered why she seemed so familiar.

Derjaun had not seen a girl with hair that dark or skin so white, and he was most entranced by the eye color he had never seen before. They sparkled with fields of lush green. Every other villager either had blue, gray, or brown eyes with the exception of Vathra. He was speechless and very, very nervous.

She giggled, "Are you always this quick with your mouth?"

He shook his head to regain his thoughts. "What do you want? I have no food."

She paused then said, "I didn't ask you for food."

"Well, you told me you were hungry." He brushed dirt off of his desk and swallowed hard as other children came to their seats. He sunk into his seat while his eyes loomed about. Class would be starting soon. His nerves shot out of his skin when her abrupt

laughter cackled. Derjaun turned toward her, completely embarrassed. "Why are you laughing?"

"I'm not laughing at you. I laugh at myself." As her clucking of
merriment continued, he allowed his mind to try and find a reason
why she laughed at herself.

Her laughter was a song for his broken heart. If only in that
moment this young girl knew what her voice mended for him.
Derjaun felt a deep, refreshing breath of air for the first time in half a
year. He asked, "Why do you laugh at yourself?"

"Ah, I have heard you say this many times around the village
square, so I thought it was your language to say hello." She leaned
back to rub her sore belly. "I'm such an idiot."

The timid boy turned back at his desk and grinned. He replied
quietly, "That phrase is osmehdit-das."

Her eyes yielded at the long phrase and she asked, "Who would
have such a long phrase for a simple meaning?"

Derjaun gathered the strength to sit upright and look to her. "It
was my father's language," he answered happily. "He created it. But
it's not so hard. Osmehdit means a simple hello. While osmehdit-das
means something more of a respectful version of hello. It literally
translates to 'greetings of kindness to you.' You know how everyone in
Nakhan tends to have their own language because of all the travelers
we get? Well, this is the one my father created."

"And who's your father?" she asked. The girl leaned her elbows to
her desk, rested her chin on her hands and turned her brightly infat-
uated eyes toward him.

Derjaun went quiet. Only after a moment he murmured, "Radal
Vin Gruinelle."

She gasped immediately and clutched her mouth. However
unnerved at her reaction, Derjaun was about to get a full joust of
more happiness and inquisitiveness from her. "You're Radal's son?
Derjaun?"

He was unable to understand if this girl would be abrasive or
genuinely nice. He had never known her before and therefore

believed he needed to act with some caution. After a pause, he looked back to her and nodded. "Yes, I am."

"Oh!" She reached to touch his shoulders, and he looked toward her hand when it did. She went on, "I've wanted to be a Guardian since I was a little girl! I've heard so much about you and your father. I remember him. You must be so honored!"

Never mind his honor. This girl had mentioned something so unthinkable and outlawed that he felt his stomach tighten. "You want to be a Guardian? But...you're a girl."

Her hand pulled from his shoulder. "It doesn't matter. I won't marry, and my passion for exploration, adventure, and more brings my heart the greatest pleasure. Why, I want to travel one day. Like a gollet. Far out to sea." She rubbed her heart through her worn and torn blouse. "I am a mere peasant girl, Derjaun, but I crave more from my life and blood than delivering eggs to the Inner Circle folk. This cincher I wear to help with field work, I'd give anything to trade it in for a breastplate." She looked out a large window. "I want to explore the mountains to the north along with their foothills unnamed and so much more."

He responded eagerly, "So you are a determined young girl who wishes to one day be a Guardian, sail the seas like a raunchy gollet, and explore the mountains?" He shook his head in disbelief with a kind laugh.

She looked happily back to him. "Yes! Or 'ehta,' to use your language."

Right as he was about to ask her why she carried so much adoration for the forbidden area, a smack of book leather against her desk made him jerk.

"Move your corpse, field rat! You're in my seat!" ordered a much taller boy with short, raven-black hair. It was Mozkin Ramath. He proceeded to throw the girl's writing scroll to the ground below. Derjaun lifted his eyes, and Mozkin screeched in laughter. "It's bad enough you are weakened with a beast's disease. Must you *smell* like one too?" He ruffled Derjaun's fragile hair with unsettling fingers.

The girl stood upright at once and hollered, "You compare him to the physical points of a beast, but it is you, Mozkin Ramath, who holds the unkind trait of what truly forms a devil, your soul. Ugh, I've grown sick of seeing your ugly face over these years. I can't wait to be rid of you one day!"

He barked into her face, "You'll have to deal with me until the day you die. So leave this seat, female! And stop using that language. You're not a Guardian and don't deserve to use it!"

The tension had rapidly escalated, and Derjaun wondered what his father would have done.

But she stood at once and slammed her calloused hands onto the desk and retaliated into his face, "Nagat!"

Mozkin chuckled with a head shake, "You are a little girl, Halo. Why do you attempt to talk in the Gruic language of the Guardians when you can never be one?" With this he pounded his heart in the ways of the Guardians. "I will be the next malakae, and soon I will be the captain. And you will attend to my every whim and command!"

Halo laughed as she shoved his hand away. "You are a disgrace to the Guardians. Why, you came to insult me, but if you were to be the captain one day you should know you actually saluted me with honor. To pound one's chest is an offering of loyalty."

Mozkin's face went pale. He looked about furiously to see if anyone else had caught the mistake while Halo continued to hold her stomach in taunting laughter. Derjaun held his head, hoping for the teacher to enter and yet contemplating if he had heard that name before, Halo.

His prayers were remarkably answered when the teacher, Lady Florn, entered the room and stopped the fight. With a distasteful gruff, the bully left them alone and ventured away to sit elsewhere.

"Well, *Halo*..." Derjaun smiled over to her. "...now that I know your name, thank you so much for defending me. But I have to tell you, most of your knowledge of the language is wrong."

"Oh, I know. It's such a difficult language to learn, but it is so beautiful to me. I try to listen to the Guardians in the fields while they train, but it's hard to hear when they speak so fast."

He extended a quivering, frail hand to rub her shoulder. A grin pushed past the obvious display of sickness and sadness. He consoled her with a voice that cracked in pitch, "It's fine. Would you..." He paused with exhaustion and winced. "Would you like to come over to my home after school? My sheylee can cook for us, and I can teach you my language."

The question appeared to make her halt the entirety of her very being. Then slowly, her hand came to her chest, she excitedly responded, "I would love that! Thank you very much!"

All throughout the day, he was comforted by her presence. Occasionally he would look at her during Lady Florn's many lectures, and the girl had no hesitation about helping him understand the material. She was patient. She was kind.

The hours of school came into the early afternoon, and Halo caught up with Derjaun before he was on his way home. It appeared to him that she truly liked him.

She asked, "May I walk you home?"

Derjaun shrugged and looked up toward the clouds in the sky with their gray and dismal appearance. The prelude of a spring storm was nearby. They were nowhere near matching the tone of his mood. He chuckled, "What? You have that backward! I'm the son of a Guardian. You know how much Guardians pride themselves on protecting the women of the village. It's our duty."

Halo playfully rolled her eyes. "You know, it's not very often I get such acts of kindness. You are definitely the son of a Guardian, and a good son at that," she responded.

His happiness allowed him to forget the pain that lodged into his feet and knees. "Then let's walk."

She hurried alongside him but stumbled suddenly. "Oh, I keep forgetting these paths can be a little uneven."

The blond boy stopped and looked at her. "Are you alright?"

Halo smirked back. "Of course I'm alright. I can be clumsy sometimes, I guess."

"I don't want you to fall. Believe me, it hurts when your body hits this dirt. Here, hold my hand. I may not be strong right now, but I hope I can be better than nothing." And then he held his frail hand to her.

The girl was mysteriously hesitant. She looked at his hand and peered at his eyes for a moment. Derjaun grew worried he had crossed a threshold of personal space.

But she finally responded, "Thank you. But you should know, not only are you much better than nothing, you are better than everything. You have been kinder to me in the few hours I've known you than most people in my entire life."

He firmly took her hand and responded, "Of course, you should know I could say the same for you."

Together, they walked toward the Outer Circle.

Derjaun, the sickly son of Radal, had befriended a girl who was fascinated with his family so much that his sickness did not deter her away from caring for him. He never thought that someone could find it in their hearts to dismiss his diseased ugliness, bony shoulders, and balding head. The two youths walked toward the Second Circle, where Derjaun realized he was far too enchanted by the moment Halo gave him that he nearly forgot about the excruciating truth in his blood.

All around she spoke to him about how despite the wealth of even the Second Circle she still preferred the lush fields where only the farmers and the poorer families lived. It was where the foliage was abundant in its uniqueness, and it seemed wildly tousled and therefore very favorable to her. She adored the planter boxes that snuggled underneath humble windows and the homely feeling of simple houses.

"I can hear the howls of the night sky much better in the outer fields," she suddenly said.

"Halo, I have to ask you something," Derjaun whispered as if frightened, but he could not resist. He had to know.

She stopped and turned to him, "Ask me anything, my friend."

Coughing, he asked, "You have no fear of my illness. Why?"

"Easy answer. I don't fear your illness. I can see your skin is sick, and your hair is dry and thin, but most importantly your spirit is sad. I was like you once. Maybe I'm still like you."

She smiled.

Derjaun almost interjected as he shook his head at the thought of her confession. "Wait, are you blind? How?"

He saw her lift her chest to sigh and look away. "I never said anything about that."

"Halo, I'm not that naïve. From the moment you stumbled, I paid more attention to your eyes. They look about in ways I've never seen. What happened?"

She was silent for what seemed like an eternity. Slowly, she folded her arms. With her head downturned, she spoke, "I'm not sure. I was born with this defect, and this is all I've ever known. Dr. Crenon has noticed my eyes slightly worsening as the years pass."

"Maybe this is why your heart is fiery with exploration?" he asked her honestly.

"Yes," she answered quickly. "This is exactly the reason. We never know what life may bring us tomorrow. Be it blindness, be it an illness, be it death from great bravery. I want to live first before I die, and I have yet to feel like I've lived."

Stillness came upon them. He could never imagine becoming blind. Of course he had his increasing illness, but he once knew a life of normalcy, and it pained him to know that this wonderful, kind soul may never know the same. He narrowed his eyes with sympathy and proposed, "Have you considered traveling to Persu? I'm sure their medical care is far superior to ours."

"I'm sure we both could go for the same reason, and yet we don't for the same reason as well. It is far too expensive to go." She pulled her coat about her, continuing, "I try not to let it affect me. I just don't want your sympathy. I don't want you to feel sorrow for me."

They finally made it to Derjaun's home and walked up the stoop. The door suddenly opened. Agrona, who was filthy from her hair to her slippers, wiped her hands on her apron and came out. "Derjaun, who is this young lady?" she asked merrily, her eyes squinting from the smile.

"Sheylee, this is Halo. But I uh, I don't know her surname."

Immediately Halo offered her hand to Agrona to introduce herself, "Halo Laankel, Miss Agrona. It's an honor to meet you."

"Why, yes, it is an honor to meet you as well, Halo. Come in," she said. "Supper is almost finished."

Derjaun reached for Halo's hand to lead her out back. "We'll be in later, Sheylee. Come on, Halo. I want to show you all the fences I've built and repaired a hundred times!" he exclaimed with bursting excitement.

She happily obliged, "Yes, show me everything. I want to see it all."

He turned and gestured down the stairs for her. "Be careful, my lady. There are a few steps here you should be cautious of."

Halo snickered at his behavior. "Derjaun, not only do your manners far exceed your age, but we walked up these stairs already. Surely you don't think my memory is as bad as my eyes."

"I'm sorry."

"Please don't be," she said with a smile. "I can also see them."

He still held her shoulders to ensure she got down safely. He was bewildered. "I don't understand. You can't see the deep holes of the paths, but you can see the soil-colored stairs?"

Halo finally felt her foot touch the dirt and tried to explain as best as she could, "I know it doesn't make much sense. But it is the contrast between the stairs I struggle with. I can't see how many steps there are, only that there are stairs there."

He paused. He was downright amazed but desperate to know more. By her side, he looked at the ground and rubbed his chin. Then he asked with a softened tone, "How do you know when you have reached the ground?"

Halo smiled and tapped the ground with her foot. "I can feel the texture change under my foot."

Derjaun gawked. "Even with slippers on?"

She quickly confirmed in laughter, "Even with boots on!"

"I'm stunned."

As they walked about the pasture and paddocks, Derjaun

explained all of how he fixed the fences, "You see Halo, when my father first built the fences, he had very little time to do so. So he did this old method to make what we first had called a split-rail fence. It was practical since there was so much wood to be cleared here, and they don't require a post or a posthole. And since their foundations are simple rocks, the wood doesn't rot either. Those were our first fences, but..." He paused to help Halo climb a fence to rest upon.

"But what?" she turned to ask.

Derjaun leaned over the fence top, resting his arms. He was quiet. His face seemed so sullen now.

A long time drew in at that moment, for it was emotionally hard for him to talk about it. "The Annenji destroyed it." He stared at the ground. "And my father could only teach me so much as I was so young. I found his building journal a few years after he passed and saw the type of fence he wanted to build eventually. But he never got to it." She was still watching him speak so emotionally from the heart. "So I built these fences in his, in his, well, um, his memory."

The farmer girl could see the pain in his heart. Her eyes almost began to water looking at how he was suffering so much. He attempted to pull himself onto the fence, but it was a horrible attempt. His leg and midsection were no longer strong enough to do so. He grunted and gave it a final heave, but she jumped off and assisted him in his true final push. She hoisted him onto the fence with the strength of a farmer. He sniffed his nose and turned to look down onto her face. The color of the gray skies washed through his hair.

"You helped me get down the stairs," she began as she heaved back up the fence herself, "and you assisted me up here." She pulled her hair to the side and looked at him. Her green eyes searched his face, and then she smiled. "So I wanted to help you."

There they were, simply finding solace in one another atop the sanctuary of the fence. They looked at one another for a long moment and smiled in unison.

She felt the northern winds come in refreshing and purifying breezes. The blankets of coolness brushed across her neck and gently lifted her hair from her shoulders. She closed her eyes softly to enjoy it.

She murmured, "You can almost smell the mountain air from here. But you should know, Derjaun..."

"What is it?"

She looked at him with a sincere smile. "Your father would love this fence."

Derjaun's body soared into the sky. He lifted his face to the beautiful passing clouds and found the restitution of his spirit he so desperately needed. He looked at her. "Thank you. I hope one day you know how much that means to me."

Agrona was washing the dishes after cooking supper, and she looked out the small and old kitchen window to see the pair far out into the northern pasture. While the wind cooled her hot and sweaty neck, she smiled and placed dishes to the left on a woven mat. She was out of fresh clean water, and even though she had a few more dishes to do she thought they could wait. She wiped her forehead with her apron and realized that this divine moment would probably not happen again. Her emotions had been woven like an unsightly mat, full of worn and used thread and had been trampled on far too much. No matter how hard she tried, she was going to lose her son. If only he had listened to her when she told him not to fight that awful pabi cat. If only Radal would have listened to her and stayed behind.

She began drying the dishes on the mat with a rag. "I will never love again. After my son sleeps, I will never love again. No one in these worlds can replace what I will lose nor will ever replace what I have lost."

She heaved her narrow chest in a deep breath. Her blonde hair was piled on top of her head with pins and twine. The pale light of the outside showed her stress lines while she looked at the two young ones starting to tease the pale blue kaku birds. She gathered herself and forced a faulty smile and called loudly through the window, "Come, you two, supper is ready!"

The strong girl quickly descended the fence and reached to help him down. He felt her arms around his sore belly, and she had practically supported his entire weight.

Derjaun released a breath of pleasantry. "Thank you." Immediately, he realized he could have taught her a Gruic phrase! And so he quickly finished, "Or was we say in Gruic..."

At once, both answered with glee, "*Min'ra mes vi!*"

So much laughter followed, and they began the walk back to the little home.

Once inside, they saw Agrona organizing all of the food onto the counter near the washing buckets. The buckets were large metal pails that were simply placed into two deep holes into the counter, and it was clear she had not finished all of the dishes. Halo took notice immediately and offered, "Agrona, may I finish your dishes for you? Or perhaps I could help set the table! I do these chores all the time at my home. And you look tired."

She placed her hands to Halo's back and pushed her to the table. "Nonsense. You are a guest. Here you will relax and simply enjoy supper. Besides, you can't see that well anyway. We don't need you to accidentally break something or hurt yourself."

The ending comment made Halo's body freeze, nearly petrify. For it reminded her of what her mother would say when she'd try to help in the kitchen. Yet Agrona went on, "After all, my son has never had a true friend before." She began placing the handmade plates onto the table, and the young girl sat down to study them.

When Agrona had turned to either gather more dishware or tend to the food, Halo lifted the plate in front of her and examined the lovely design of light-blue patterns. Derjaun watched her from across the table.

"Derjaun," she began curiously, "who made these plates? This design is amazing!"

He rubbed his hands together underneath the table. He had begun to feel exhausted and quite winded, and he was praying with all of his strength that neither his mother nor Halo would notice. "They were made and painted by my paposa. They were his wedding gift to my sheylee," he answered.

She asked in awe, "Was there anything your father *didn't* do?"

Agrona abruptly turned to put a stop to the conversation, and with a slight tinge of coldness in her heart she answered for Derjaun, "He didn't listen very well to his wife on numerous occasions."

"Sheylee!" he protested in disgust.

"Well," Agrona continued as she sat at the table with the prepared food, "it's true, Derjaun. You were only six years when he passed. I knew him far before these times."

Halo stared at Agrona and couldn't refrain from speaking, "Mrs. Vin Gruinelle, I am deeply sorry for your loss. I may not have lost a husband, but I too have lost in my own ways. And it hurts. But do you know what hurts the most out of all of this?"

Agrona sat down, straightened her back, lifted a glass to her mouth, tightened her expression, and looked at the little girl. "No."

Halo looked with urgency, leaning a little more forward to Agrona. "It is when we have lost so much and now have so little, but instead of celebrating the little we have we choose to abuse it and take it for granted."

Derjaun's eyes bulged, and his mouth opened. His heart pounded so hard in his chest as he looked to his mother to see her reaction. He *knew* Halo sensed something about the way Derjaun had been treated. Or maybe she didn't know at all and was simply fearful and imagining things.

Agrona sat the glass down and swallowed in thought. She swiftly spoke, "I agree."

Halo placed her hands under the table politely. "I'm glad. Thank you for this food, or as you would know it, *min'ra mes vi.*"

"Ha, Derjaun, you already taught her some of our language?" Agrona said aloud.

"No, not really. She already knew that expression."

"I see. Halo, Radal would have loved to know you."

It was then time for the three to enjoy one another's company over the little wooden table that was graced with food. Halo had learned that he not only fixed and built the fences out in the pasture but had also repaired the table and stools upon which they were sitting. Everything in that home was subtle and minimal, and it was a stark contrast to the inside of any Inner Circle home.

After supper, Agrona listened to them speaking in Gruic to one another out in the fireplace room. She was washing the dishes and heard almost every single word. The young and adventurous pair sat on the area rug by the fireside to enjoy the lessons together, and she listened to her son describe things to the girl who could not see. For once Agrona took in the deepest breath of her life. All of her tension left in that breath.

A few hours passed, and the sun began its descent behind the horizon. Agrona was sitting in her chair by the fireside and was reading when she noticed the fading light. "Oh, Derjaun. Perhaps I should get Halo home. It's getting quite late. We must have lost track of the time."

They all dressed in their shoes and began the long walk around the Outer Circle toward Halo's home, who lived on the entire opposite side of Nakhan. They could have crossed through the Second Circle and the Inner Circle, but it would have been busy with people closing shops down and heading home. Besides, the winds and the field grasses were too lovely to miss.

What a wonder it was to the boy, who at that moment felt like a true Guardian. Every now and then, he would watch his friend's steps to ensure her safety over the unstable terrain, and he would even go as far to describe what the fields among them looked like at night, and his description was full of tranquility to her. It was almost as if she could see the pale moon's glow upon every blade of flowing wild grass, every closed flower bud, and every rickety and old fence.

Agrona watched from behind and witnessed her son walking stronger than ever.

Upon arrival, Derjaun realized that it was completely true when Halo deemed herself a peasant girl, as she lived in the most rural part of the Outer Circle. As they stood on the outside of her home's fence, he watched the low-lit candles burn in the windows and looked at her. She seemed uneasy yet absolutely still, so he attempted to hug her to show her gratitude for all of what she had done for him. They both pulled into one another for a hug that his body had ached for.

There were so many things that he wanted to thank her for, and yet a simple embrace would never seem enough to do so. When her arms squeezed about his body, his eyes closed in adoration of the relief. No one could ever fathom what it felt like to have even some of that gruesome sensation removed, for even if some was removed the pain was so intense that any satisfaction brought tears of comfort to his eyes.

At one moment in his life, he feared he would have never known such warmth to exist. With the blooms of life did a mother love, but for someone not of blood to accept him was truly remarkable.

She whispered in her little voice, "I will see you at class tomorrow, Derjaun. And thank you, Agrona, for the wonderful dinner."

Abruptly, the young farmer girl turned to hurry inside.

The prelude of the storm never truly came.

The days became weeks of jubilant activities, and Halo and Derjaun grew completely inseparable. The pain of his disease faded from his memory. Although he still struggled to get out of his bed, the idea of going to school and seeing her made him want to get up. Yes, with her by his side, he truly felt invincible. To accompany these remarkable days, the nights of wonderful friendship came as well while their hearts bonded.

She knew many of his stories. She watched him one night tell the story of his father while they sat on the back pasture fence beneath a blanketing sky of stars. Derjaun, at the end of his father's tale, turned to see her smiling. The fields around them caught the wind, their longest blades of grass rustling, and the jewels in the sky sparkled brightly.

"You should know," Derjaun said timidly, "those stars remind me of your eyes."

She tried to ignore the compliment and looked to the grass below. "They are more like your eyes, light blue in color." She peered at him. "At least from what I can tell."

"But mine don't sparkle anymore," he said in an attempt for her to accept the compliment.

At once his friend felt her heart grow heavy in despair. "Oh, Derjaun, neither do mine."

He edged closer, attempting to see her eyes more clearly. "They do to me. I see courage. I see strength. I see so much in you. Why can't you see it for yourself?"

Silence. He coughed as they pulled away. He had to change the subject. Perhaps he had pressed the situation too far. He could see his dearly beloved friend was sulking in awful thoughts.

He asked, "Halo, do you ever bake bread or—"

They were again interrupted.

"Derjaun, it is time for Halo to return home!" Agrona called.

He sighed as she continued to wait for his question, but he never finished. All he could do was exhale with exhaustion and climb off the fence.

"I will walk with you."

"I'm sorry, Derjaun." She motioned with a gesture of her hand as she dismounted the fence. "You need your rest."

He suddenly worried that she was growing tired of his company or that he had crossed her threshold. His voice creaked in concern, "But why?"

"I, eh..." Her hand ran through her long, dark-brown hair. "I can make it home faster if I run. And I don't want you to wear yourself out. You were quite rough while playing today." She gave him a smile of reassurance.

"But, Halo, can you see sufficiently in this late light?" Derjaun quickly asked while he rubbed his nose that began to itch.

"It is no mind to you. I've done it many times before. I'll see you at school tomorrow. Also, please make sure you rest enough to come. My dear friend Jastin will be there, and I don't believe you have met her yet. She is often absent from school, and I know she will love you."

With nothing to say and no way to keep her, he watched her leave.

Halo occasionally had many strange aspects to her behavior. She threw rocks at boys, Mozkin included, she was excessively intelligent in all subjects, and more than anything she was *aggressive*. She had strength as sturdy as the untamed mountains and the cockiness of the Gigannora River. He could not argue with someone like her.

Derjaun, during the beginning of the new friendship, witnessed her shoving boys nearly twice her size to the ground. The knowledge to perform such acts was probably gained from watching the Guardians so many times.

His favorite trait of the outlandish and candid girl was her desire to follow the Guardians around the Inner Circle and attempt to walk as they did. How high she held her head, how straight and meticulously erect she kept her back, and even how she spoke to others in a naturally commanding tone. Now that she was more fluent in Gruic, it made her all the more believable.

All of these situations made him believe that she was outright attempting to overcome the village's societal ways that everyone had to abide by.

Yes, she seemed quite eccentric at times. Yet, not once, not *once*, had she ever acted so withdrawn as with what happened that evening.

Once Derjaun was preparing to sleep, a recollection of discussions filled his mind. She never talked about her past. Try as he might, the young boy could not even gather a clue to what the names of her parents were, if she had any siblings, how her poor vision ailed her, or anything.

He looked out the window. "Are you an orphan child? You can't be. I heard other people in your home when my sheylee and I first walked you back."

Derjaun was tired of mysteries. He already had the mystery of his disease and did not care to bring on another one of secrets from his friend. He swore to the stars he would ask her tomorrow what he yearned to know.

The following morning was a cool, breezy one, which made for the most enjoyable routine of combing his hair and getting dressed. His pale face was at one point sunken with the color of death, and the stench from the minor infections in his body would have easily taken over him. But this morning he felt different. Not only did he feel different, but he also *looked* different. After staring at himself in the old mirror, he lifted his arm to smell underneath. He sniffed a little harder.

"Oh, my stench is less today. I'll put a bit of pabi flower oil on here too."

He tipped the little amber jar of pabi flower oil on his palm, and after vigorously rubbing his hands together he patted the floral fragrance underneath his arms. His frame had become thin, wasting away every day. His shoulder bones were protruding through his oversized shirt, but he did not care. Death was trying to dress him more gloriously every morning in its own jealous way, but Derjaun would still smile through all of the visible signs of death's presence. His skin was dusted with the grayness of stormy skies, and his eyes were completely dull and lined with soft and sunken bruises of exhaustion. He could have been called almost skeletal to some.

The only true color of life his body seemed to possess were deep pink remains of his scars that covered his side and leg. He looked at his comb to observe if any improvement had been made to his scalp. He saw the teeth of the wooden comb tangled with more hair strands.

"What do I care?" he said out loud as his fingers struggled to loosen them. "I have a dear friend now who couldn't care less about my looks. I will look the best I can to—"

The pain came again. His kneecap shook violently. "Agh," he groaned at the coming torment. Quick breaths huffed from his drying lips, and yet once more the little joint of his leg stung in pain so great that he *had* to lie on his bed.

"Sheylee! Sheylee, please come!" he cried.

The doorway cloth slid open, and she came to his side. Lifting her long blonde tresses so that she could better tend to him, she fought to hold back tears while the sight of her son broke her heart.

"Derjaun, you have much pain?"

"My leg, Sheylee, I—" An immediate gasp for air interrupted his statement.

"Derjaun!" Agrona threw a blanket around his body, which began to jolt from the pain. "I'll take you to the doctor. You will be alright. Keep breathing."

His head fell into her chest, and with loud cries his eyes clenched. "Sheylee, my body is shaking!"

Agrona did not bother with dressing her feet properly to run to the Inner Circle. She lifted her son and fled out the door. As she launched onto the dirt-packed paths, all she could call for was the captain while she held her son in her arms. "Please! Someone find me the captain! I need a horse!"

People turned to the woman who held a sick boy and ignored her, moving about their own lives. "Ayook tana! Velvish-droyna!" Desperately, she tried all the languages she knew to beg for help, but she was left without any. Men and women of different ages turned their heads to move on in silence, and it was the unfortunate time when the Guardians were far into the fields during training, leaving only a few to manage the Inner Circle. She was left to do this all on her own. How in the stars would she manage to rush the boy in her arms alone? She had no idea, but it had to be done. For someone of her late husband's stature, it would have been like carrying the feather of a kaku bird, and she would feel delicate and fair with a similar sweetness as one. *If only he were here.*

The dirt path beat into Agrona's heels as her heart shattered trying to maintain the strength to carry him, all while running as fast as her spirit would take her. In this moment, her mind rushed further beyond what her body could endure. She was growing older, tired, and was losing the strength to be able to carry her boy in these frightening moments.

"Sheylee!" he called out suddenly. "I can't feel my legs! It hurts!"

As Agrona fought for her breath, she raced harder, trying to calm his nerves. She pulled him close. "I know, my love. You'll be alright. I promise!"

Her heart was torn asunder. She heard Derjaun cry for his father with every fiber of his being. He was scared to death that death itself was taking his life. He could not control his body, and the splitting pain in his side and leg was leaving him with no other option other than to cry in shrills for his beloved, heroic father.

He gasped in tears with loud and long cries that anyone in the town would have heard the pain he was going through.

Right as she approached the Inner Circle, the business of the location brought a more vigorous challenge. Her shoulder charged into people with loud pants of breath, shoving anyone and anything out of her way until they reached the stoop of the doctor's house. "Crenon!" she gasped.

As if that wonderful spirit that perhaps had protected him through the perilous winter had smiled upon her, Crenon opened his front door. "Agrona!" his large, furry face boomed.

The poor, helpless mother nearly tripped up the stairs and fought hastily for breath. "My son, he's shaking uncontrollably. Please, Crenon, help him!"

"'Tis alright, miss! Come in 'ere, quickly." Crenon guided her inside and quickly showed her to lay the shaking boy on the examining bed. All over the doctor saw the boy's muscles moving with obvious involuntary actions. For some mysterious reason, Derjaun's body would not stop quivering. Crenon checked his heart rate, and it seemed to be ironically stable considering what was happening.

Crenon sat back on his chair, his large belly in front of him. "Well, miss, der's nuttin dat seems to be a matter wit em. Dis shaking is hard to explain, but I can clearly see dat nuttin will 'appen to em. We jus need ta comfort em until it passes, yes? Per'aps hees body is trying ta sweat so dat it releases de sickness."

Agrona's eyes expressed her distaste of the diagnosis, but what else could she do? Heaving loud huffs of breath, the mother said calmly, "Yes, Doctor Crenon, I understand."

While Derjaun struggled to calm down, it was not until his sheylee lied next to him holding him close against her chest that he felt secure. "I wish I were stronger, Sheylee," he whimpered. He was afraid, and he was cold.

She sighed as her hand massaged his scalp lovingly. "You are. You're stronger than anyone I know. Let's let the doctor do his work."

Crenon stayed awake all night long studying the rare and unfortunate event. Throughout he managed to try to research his old text-
books from when he himself was a young scholar.

He questioned whether perhaps an infection had born the leg
needing to be amputated.

But no infection could be truly seen in the leg. The injury had
completely healed. The intense pink of the gashes were clearly now
scars. But then again, perhaps his studies were insufficient for such a
thing.

Dr. Crenon looked down at the naked body of the boy in an utter
state of loss. With a dry sigh and a fading wash of hope, he professed,
"I 'ate to say dis, but dis is the most rare and peculiar disease I 'ave
ever seen."

The doctor couldn't do anything more, and Agrona helped her
son home once the worst of his symptoms subsided.

They had returned home, and the carrying of her son on the
journey seemed to be extended due to the extra weight she bore.
"Here now, my precious heart," Agrona softly spoke as she covered
her son in his bed. She sat back, searching for a reason why the
doctor's orders had not worked yet. Why after so long, she pondered
regretfully, had the medicine and the rest proved worthless?

Her thoughts trailed off as she looked at the lone flickering flame
of the oil lamp near his mat. Far away in Persu, she had heard from
her husband that doctors toiled in research and medical glory, even
sewing fingers back on those who lost them during work or accidents,
and she was so certain that helping her son would be such a small
feat to them.

But...would he even live through at least three or four full morn-
ings and nights of traveling? Worst of all would be that Agrona
needed a way to get across the Gigannora, and although Persu offered
the passage by sturdy bridges, the picket to get across would have
taken her entire life savings, and for sure then she would not be able
to afford the care for her child.

Radal had spoken to her of what was called a *Red Lady* in Persu.
And those women could make her entire life's savings in one day. But

would she really subject herself to such work for her son? Would her late husband approve?

On and on the mother thought in her absolute grief of desperation. Yes, she could just move her family to Persu, but this was where she fell in love with Radal. It was the village she watched him build and where her son was born. It felt disloyal to leave her little village for a far greater prefecture. Even though the people of Nakhan never helped her with her son's illness, nor seemed to mourn for her loss of Radal, she had to stay for her son and for Halo.

And what would Derjaun do without his only friend? She always knew that being a mother was going to be a difficult experience, but she never recalled her own mother telling her it would be this hard.

All she could do was sigh in loss. She had no choice but to pray.

Her body rose to its tired feet, and with her voice low, she spoke to her son, "My son, I will be in the kitchen preparing our food, if you should need me again."

He thought. A moment of stillness passed in the room, and then another. But this moment was far more hurtful than its predecessor, as if every moment that passed meant his death was coming closer. "I'm going to school tomorrow."

Agrona answered immediately, infuriated that he would say such an asinine thing, "Derjaun, you must be out of your senses. You are not in any condition to go to school, not until you are well. And you will not leave your bed until I say so."

He scoffed, "Why? I feel like a pile of dung that's been stepped in too many times, and I feel that way too often. Halo makes me laugh, Sheylee."

"Derjaun," she scolded hotly, "I am sure she will come to you when her schooling is done. But you have been quite active lately, and surely you can see the results of your actions. It'll be alright. Halo can bring you your work and can visit you here."

The pressured mother left the room, but still he protested loudly after her, "I'm dying, Sheylee. Why can't I die happily? Just because you are a mother doesn't mean you're always right!"

"Derjaun!" she screamed from the halls, "it is the doctor's orders!

Now get some sleep!" She ignored his question. She did not have an answer and couldn't keep track of promises made in dire times.

The sick boy's cries came loudly with a sound so vile that it was unsettling to Agrona's heart. She knew she was bringing him suffering, but what could a mother do? Her heart told her to keep him bedridden, despite the loud shrieks of pain that she heard.

Later that evening, Derjaun ate supper with his mother. Together they sat in silent awkwardness around the little wooden table. He heard the rain sprinkling against the windows. Derjaun kept his head down, and since the candles in the kitchen were the only means of light it was difficult for Agrona to see his face, which made her emotions more agitated. The flickers of the glow of the fire had made his bruised eyes appear even more hollow, almost haunting and empty. She noticed his lips curled in a sour disdain toward what had happened earlier. He was angry with her and was attempting to hide it, but it was a losing battle. It was a pure signal that something was weighing on his mind. She stopped eating, unable to endure the frustrating moment any longer.

"My son, your sweet eyes have not looked into mine since dinner began," she softly said.

"I don't want you to see such eyes. They weep of sickness and long for companionship and health," he mumbled.

Agrona fought for her patience. This was becoming quite a routine discussion. Her worn hands set down the silverware and folded onto the table. "My love, your father taught you to be strong. Yes, you are ill, and you have a frail appearance, but do not forget your knowledge. Your father taught you courage and—"

"I have none! No one wants me to have any!" Derjaun interjected bitterly. "Sheylee, I can't find the strength nor wit to protect anything, and when I try, I am told to do otherwise! I am a coward! Halo had to protect *me* from Mozkin," he bellowed angrily, and Agrona's face glowed in concern. She allowed him to go on with an apparent choked-up outburst that needed to come out as much as his sickness did. "Why do you remind me how much I should be like Paposa with all he taught me? I can't be him. I will never be!"

Frightened by his own words, he shot out of his chair and went to his room. Agrona's motherly instincts tore her heart as she clearly realized that she was in denial about her son's fate, and it drove her to the need to comfort him, but a sudden clunk to the floor disturbed her. She rose immediately from her chair. "Derjaun!"

He had fallen in the hallway, his legs unable to carry him readily enough for the immediate reaction of fleeing for the room. She needed to act quick. His fragile body writhed in its own discomfort and wailing cries.

He hated himself.

No longer did he desire to bear burdens on his mother or the doctor or even Halo. He pulled violently at his own hair to become completely bald instead of letting the embarrassment of being half-maned show. Kicking against the wall and screaming until his face reddened, he cried until he could no longer see from the flooding tears. He was dying, and there was nothing he could do to stop it.

"Derjaun! My love, stop this. You are hurting yourself!" Agrona gave all of her struggling strength to contain him, but the death that prolonged itself into mere torture gave him the ironic gift of tolerance to anything, anything except his own emotions. She tried to hold his flailing body and hollered, "Stop it!"

When he heard the demanding and heartless tone, he did.

Agrona, tired from the incident and left with barely any strength of heart or body, put her son to rest again in his own bed. The situation had pushed him to the brink of exhaustion to where he fell asleep before she even lifted him. His eyes received a gentle kiss, and she left the room, pulling the cloth door closed behind her.

In the dining area, Agrona began cleaning the table on her own. Cleaning up the fallen hair was the worst, as it sealed the ghastly truth. Not only was he sick, but he was getting worse.

Agrona quickly prepared for her own time of slumber, and it was a miracle to do so quickly with how heavy her body felt. She combed her blonde hair free of all its dirt, slipped into her favorite night dress, and reluctantly climbed into bed. It then came to her that she was feeling as alone as Derjaun did.

Her widowed hands caressed the nearby unoccupied pillow that had not seen weight or witnessed the making of love for several painful years. She whispered to the night, "Oh, Radal, I have tried so hard for you, for us, to save our precious son." Her face burrowed deeper into the fabric of the pillow, longing for the brisk of his scent. "Perhaps I am destined to love men for currency. Would it really save our son?" The mother felt old as her face squeezed in sadness only to relax with the flow of lonesome tears. She could not resist weeping of her lost love.

Harder she wept to herself, holding the pillow that almost seemed to still carry his masculine scent in it. Or perhaps it was simply her imagination. She sighed, feeling the rich fragrance of his amber wood oils that kissed his strong skin. How much she missed him.

"I have failed you, my love. When our son finally rests, may he peacefully play with you and be held by you again. Then I shall live on, and it will be many years until I am in your arms again, and together we will embrace our healthy son."

4

Derjaun found sleep to be the least of his worries once the cold wind disrupted a somewhat peaceful rest. He dozed off and on throughout the stars little dancing, but he needed someone's comfort and felt an odd sensation that he may need to be there for that someone as well.

Halo's emotions had changed, and so he sensed she may not have been too happy either. Without his mother's knowing, he quickly dressed himself to slip out of the window in the dark night.

He needed Halo more than ever.

Getting out of the window was far from an easy task. The arms of the boy shook uncontrollably when he heaved himself up, and from lack of energy he fell without any grace to the hard dirt ground on the other side.

A discouraging groan escaped his lips, but he could not dawdle. The Guardians wandered through the village border right near his home, a very useful fact he learned from his father right before he died.

Perseverance was the proud medallion he wore around his neck, and it was nearly the only thing he could carry of any weight.

Life as Derjaun knew it was unfair. It lacked fairness in all aspects of itself. If he were to be found walking alone in the dark, he would have quickly been captured, scolded, and escorted home to bear another scolding from his mother.

Despite this knowledge of the possible coming of pain and humiliation, he held the beautiful thought of his father's bravery close to his heart. He eased on all fours with his bare feet touching flat and began to use his ears to observe the entire surroundings. Off to the mountain regions in the fields, a pabi cat attacked a pabi mouse, the size of the predator in proportion for the size of the prey. Horrible fat rodents, they were. Its shrieking died off as the rustling of the tall grasses faded with a final snarl. The cats were in the fields again.

The cool wind blew through the leaves of every tree, and although he caught the faint padding of footsteps, they were cloth slippers, not the boots of a Guardian. His father's skills of masterful stealth were something he excelled at, and it was a well-appreciated skill at this time of his life where not one soul allowed him any freedom.

A memory of his father's kind words entered the young boy's mind once again. He could see his father walking through the vast open field with him, holding his hand. He was a much younger boy.

"Derjaun, we all must remember. As the most graceful animal in our world, the noble pabi cat stalks in silence so that not even the grass is disturbed by its presence. May we learn this well, for we shall both exceed in strength and gentleness."

Derjaun shook the memory from his head before it became a heart-sinking distraction from the true mission at hand. But another thought could not escape his mind. Why were the pabi cats seeming to come so close to the village again? Was the pabi cat in the field that night the same one that attacked?

But the way was clear, the air was still, and he had to cut out another distraction.

Tiny homes came into sight, perfect to crawl behind and maneuver under the fences that restrained livestock, and he crept around the unoccupied pathways that nestled between the houses and eventually lead to an intersecting main road. Derjaun found himself knowing every crevice and path, building, and bridge that Nakhan had. He was completely swift in his movements and invisible to any naive eye.

He came to Halo's home more quickly than expected. His heart leapt out of his chest with glee, hurrying up to the window he heard her voice coming from.

He peeked inside, standing on the tips of his dirty toes to do so, brushing what remaining blond hair he had to the side. He heard two adults with angry voices.

At once, he began to survey the room. Scanning immediately to the left, he saw the horrible sight of a battered woman cowering in fear, clutching her face in the demeaning corner of the room.

His eyes widened in shock, and he almost lost his balance. He didn't know her or the tall, pot-bellied man looming over her.

The man shouted, practically spitting in her face, "Lirena, what kind of woman are you to let your own daughter have a friendship with that son of Agrona?"

He listened as he made haste with a rapid heart to lower out of view. This man's voice was slurred and lazy, and the air inside reeked of alcoholic stench of stale ulgg.

The woman began to plead but was interrupted when the drunkard turned and slapped her face so hard that the thundering sound stung Derjaun's ears. The woman was left crying on the floorboards.

Violent thoughts of fear racked him. He must stop it. His heart stormed with resentment he had never known before.

Once more, he heard a voice inside, but this one was very familiar to him.

"Stop this, you nasty pig!" Halo's voice rang out, eager to protect her mother.

Derjaun's heart froze, and he heard the sounds of wrathful heavy feet. He lifted his eyes to see the fat man point toward her.

"Get out of here, you little wench, or I will beat your blind hinds out of here! Ha, and you won't even see it coming! If you hate me so, perhaps you should return to your lame first father! What kind of a man throws his kin to the streets to sell bread? A baker man!" His belly bounced loudly with a horrible laugh.

Derjaun said under his breath in astonishment, "Baker man? She sells bread in the streets and is the baker man's *daughter?*" He lowered his eyes below the windowsill. It all finally became clear. His eyes widened anxiously and he whispered, "It *was* you!"

It all rushed into his head like a charging animal. He no longer cared if he was going to die that evening. Adrenaline infected every fiber of his being, and he gritted his teeth and found the strength to stand. All of the commotion his sickness had caused would end that night, either by being killed by a drunken lunatic or finally saving someone.

He grabbed a large stone from the ground, began to remove his shirt, and wrapped the stone inside. On his feet, he took his hands to the ledge of the window to will his sick body to fight in order to save his friend. He hurled it up and over, causing the drunk fat man to turn when he heard the interrupting thud.

He scrambled to his feet and saw the man had Halo by her hair. How *dare* anyone strike a girl, and even worse a *blind* one? He raised the cloth end of the rock weapon behind him, feeling the rage of an animal that was out for the kill and to defend its family. His father's bravery had to show through. It simply *had* to.

Derjaun called out to the brute, "Come here, fat pig! You think it's fun to fight the weak? Come fight a man!"

Lemson turned and cackled, "You diseased rat! You *are* weak and hardly a man. When I throw you out, my dogs will tear you to bones!" He lunged to try and grab the boy, but Derjaun ducked under the predator's first strike and hurried to Halo's side.

He stood upright at once and taunted back, cupping his mouth, "Ha! Not a man, you say. Well, what kind of a man gets drunk and slaps a woman or a blind girl? Looks like you have some insecurities, you smelly hog!"

"Boy!" Lirena shouted from the floor. "Get out of here! He'll kill you!"

He ignored the call and would not move. Again, Lemson went

after him, but the sweaty brown hair was suctioned to his swollen face, making it easy for Derjaun to bound around the room and avoid the drunk's clumsy attacks.

It was all he could do to keep Halo and her mother safe. A wince from his face caught his eyes before dodging another swing. He was losing his strength. But before he lost all of his energy he remembered the rock in his shirt. Bravely, he stood upright and spun it around fast enough. Right as the drunkard hurled after him, he released the grip, and it was a direct hit to Lemson's forehead. He fell to the floor holding his face in pain and whined furiously, "You bastard child!"

Halo cheered from the corner of the room, "Ha! Who's the man now?"

But Derjaun knew he could not distract the violent man much longer. Help was needed. The young boy fell to his knees and gathered all his breath to yell to his friend, "Halo! Go out and call a Guardian!"

Without a second thought, Halo rushed out of the house to the streets. Lirena hurried to the corner, cowering when she saw Lemson lazily stand again, and the chances of striking the sickened boy grew. Derjaun was desperate to escape the malicious stampede and tried everything that came to his mind, ducking, dodging, scurrying with all his heart until the feeling of slimy hands grabbed the back of his neck.

His feet no longer touched the floor.

Lemson was not thinking at all, nor did his abusive heart care. He flung that fragile body hard into the wall. "I'm going to break that filthy face of yours!" he bellowed.

Derjaun had trouble breathing, choking for dear life. He could not move. His air had been knocked out of him. But Lemson charged again. The boy scooted back into the corner to still face the adversary, baring his teeth. "I'll tear you apart with my teeth if I have to! I'm Radal's son. You can't kill me!"

That was when another sound broke into the room. Derjaun felt a burst of hope at the familiar noise of Guardian boots pounding after the attacker. Right behind the drunk, he saw Staghen appear with the hilt of his sword raised in his hands, his face scornful and snarled in anger at what he walked in to.

A tumultuous blow to Lemson's head sent him crumbling into a corner.

"Get away from him!" Staghen roared.

The small room rumbled with the deafening sound.

Lemson was stuck in embarrassment and, as most drunks do, began rambling to conjure his excuse for the behavior. "Your Grace," he hiccuped, "I was suitably punishing my wife for—"

"Not one more word from you!" Staghen interrupted. "You claim you were punishing your wife, yet I come in here seeing all of this!" Then the captain noticed Lirena's right eye was swollen and battered. He tightened his lips and with glaring eyes looked back to the drunk and lowly growled to him, "I have no idea whether or not to be more enraged at you for thinking you have a right to 'punish' your wife for anything or at the fact you said 'suitably punished.' There is no such thing. We men are protectors of our wives. We *never* punish them."

The drunk fought back, "But the boy interrupted and broke into our house!"

"Enough of this! Derjaun still has the bearing of a Guardian despite his ill health. You, Lemson, I know of your abuse to your family well, for I have heard it many times. It's over. You will be taken to the center of the village and shackled until I conjure up a suitable punishment." Staghen turned to his men and spoke over his shoulder, "Now *that* merits being 'suitably punished.' Take him to the pit, and I will need a few days to think of his due. But until then, little water and food."

Lemson was removed by two other Guardians, the captain walking out with them. The captain always enjoyed watching the lowlifes being forced to walk to their destination of judgment and shame. Lemson's hands were tied to the horse's side.

Lirena, humiliated, stayed inside to clean the house. It was embarrassing to have both the son of Radal and Staghen himself see the situation. But at least she could calm her nerves now.

Derjaun rolled over in an attempt to get up. He wanted to see Staghen before he left. He had hoped so deeply that he would have been applauded for doing something right; for protecting the weak. He stumbled out to Staghen's side and turned to see Halo already out there with him. She was ecstatic to see him up and moving.

"Oh, Derjaun!" Halo exclaimed. "You came!"

The captain turned his head and looked down at the two youths who were hugging furiously by his side. Derjaun placed his hands on his hips and hunched over as his breath was still compromised. "I had to come." He looked up to her eyes while she pulled his sweaty hair from his bruised face. "I had to try and protect you."

Staghen watched the Guardians set off into the night and spoke easily, "You did protect her. That was some feat, young man." He turned to the pair now. "Halo," he began sternly.

She turned to the sound of his voice in the darkness of the night. "Yes, Captain?"

The night fell lowly around him, and his figure became nothing but an ominous shadow to her. Softly and evenly, he broke the silence, "See to your mother's comfort."

Halo only groaned in agitation. In all honesty, her mother was never truly one who she felt close to after an event such as this. Lirena gave more care to cleaning up the house rather than seeing if she or Derjaun were alright and safe.

But she complied, "Yes, Captain."

Derjaun felt lightheaded, and his breathing quickened. One final gasp was given before he collapsed on the front stoop.

"Captain!" Halo cried helplessly. "He's hurt!"

Staghen, who was in the middle of descending the stairs, looked back in a hurry and without a moment to lose raced to Derjaun's side. The flow of his heavy cloak made Halo move back, and she watched with tears that could not be held back.

He came to save her this night. In all the times of her neighbor farmers ignoring and leaving when she needed them, it was this time around the weakest of them all came through to her safety. Staghen pulled the young boy to his chest. "Derjaun!" They held each other, Staghen full of worry.

Derjaun smiled. "I tried, Captain. I tried." His heart softened into his chest. Every possible broken bone, bruised muscle, and every single moment that happened was worth it all. This was what it meant to be a Guardian. To look into impending doom and then protect others, only to see these eyes. *These eyes.* The approving and loving eyes of his captain.

They were the only things that he could see. Despite the affliction his body was succumbing to, he could not resist the urge to smile. He was seen by his father's very successor. Weakness crept in his facial muscles at an attempt, but the joyous moment could not fully be endured due to his physical state. His eyes watered.

Staghen loved this boy's courage so strongly that he clutched him harder to his chest, "If only you could become healthy again, it would truly be an honor to have you..." The captain wept softly. "I have lost your father, and I see his endurance of life and love in your young heart." Staghen shook his head as his sadness made his heart jerk. "Must I lose you now?"

For the moment, the captain allowed his thoughts to honor his predecessor's death, locked in the longing he was barred with to have Derjaun live. But he was beginning to believe faith was running low.

The captain's strength made Derjaun's pain soothe until he fell asleep.

"I will take him, Halo," said Staghen as he lifted Derjaun into his arms. "Go see to your sheylee's side."

And the girl mourned in expressive longing. She had known that Derjaun came to her that night for a reason, but this reason was never told to her.

"Why did you come to me, my friend?" she wondered out loud.

When the captain mounted the ever-faithful Rikaana, he gently kicked the side of the steed with Derjaun held close, and with a turn the large animal was gone with a thunder of dust. Halo went inside while Staghen rushed toward his home within the Inner Circle.

5

When Agrona met with the captain to claim her child, she was beside herself with both terror and anger. With Staghen still in the room of her home and Derjaun lying in his room, the helpless mother pleaded for guidance, "Captain, what am I to do? It seems that he is now deliberately disobeying me in exchange for nothing."

The woman's eyes deepened in the need of fulfillment and deliverance from such confusion and frustration. Her face trembled as she firmly confessed, "I can no longer do this."

"Agrona, you have no choice. Keep him in bed from here on out." His heavy hand rubbed her shaking shoulder of soreness. "Allow him comfort until..."

Dead silence came to kiss the room away from any happiness or hope.

"Please, Captain, I do not wish to hear another sound," Agrona confessed with her head low. The only sound heard was that of the roaring fire's glow.

Ignoring her request, he pressed on, "Do not think for one moment of our lives, dear Agrona, that I am not tearing my emotions from my very bones with sadness. I longed for your son to be under my command. For he would have made a legend of himself. But we cannot mourn any longer. You may as well make peace until he sleeps. Perhaps bring Halo over to see him. I'm sure he would love this. Derjaun does not have much time left. You need to understand this. Allow him to stay in bed and for Halo to come and see him whenever he wishes. Allow him whatever his heart desires."

A moan came across her rugged lips. "Yes, Captain."

And with nothing left to say, he left her.

Alone.

Outside the small home, Staghen let the heaviness of his boots battle the heaviness of his body. The ground was wet and his boots sank with every step, as did his spirit with every breath. It was all he could do to keep his pride strong. As he moved to Rikaana, who was waiting ever so loyally, he began shifting the mane of his friend. "I must continue on. It is not my trouble any longer," he spoke softly. Yet he was swallowing lie after lie into his own stomach that was now poisoning his soul and conscience. The thunder rumbled and the rolling skies flickered with a heavenly flash.

He shook the thoughts from his mind. But no. It was one battle he could not win.

After losing Radal, it was now dawn, and he feared he would lose Derjaun as well. "Oh, Rikaana," he said with the weight of despair in his lungs. He brushed the mane once more as if to find comfort in it. His eyes narrowed, and his face tightened. "Have I failed?"

He allowed himself a peaceful moment before mounting his horse to leave the home behind.

Back at the house, Derjaun could feel death itself taking up his body.

Atop his bed and bundled in his favorite quilt, his eyes were empty, staring out the window. But it was not a window of beautiful, freeing light. No. There was nothing that could be seen outside. His mother had shut and curtained the window. She claimed that any cold air would make it more difficult for his body to heal. And with this, she had taken the last freedom he had.

With each passing moment, his breath became hollower. It was frightening. His pain was such that moving to find a more comfortable position was pointless.

He heard the familiar sound of his mother's footsteps approaching. Not wanting to speak with her, he shoved his aching face into the pillow. As Agrona pulled the cloth curtain of his doorway open, she told herself she must swallow her pride again, perhaps for the final time.

"Derjaun?" she asked into the dark. "Are you awake, my dear?"

There was a long pause.

A response came, though almost inaudibly, "Not for so long."

"Why did you disobey me?"

"Why do you not hold me?" he asked with his voice trailing off with innocent questioning. "I'm dying, Sheylee. And instead of holding me and comforting me, you choose to fight."

Her voice rose, "Fight? I'm not fighting with you. It is you, the one who continuously disobeys my rules and argues with me."

At once Derjaun sat up to scream, "Have you not been listening? Halo makes me feel better, and you deny me this only friendship I've ever known. I would come to you for love, but you hide from me. In your selfishness and ignorance, I'm losing stability, and you're not helping!"

Agrona lost her temper for the first time.

The woman rushed over, lifted her hand, and struck his face hard with the back of her hand. It sent the boy over onto his side.

"How dare you speak to me this way, you ungrateful child! I carried you to the doctor's when no one else would even lend me their ears. I begged Staghen to allow you to go to the Summoning Ceremony and make you a Guardian. You were a Guardian that day, Derjaun. Do you truly not recall? I have very little money, and I purchased those clothes to take you. Why, I tried to save you from that vicious cat, and you did not listen to me. Who is the one with the pride now? I should never have allowed you to join the Guardians, but I gave this to you. How could you be so ungrateful to me?" All she heard was his soft crying and cowering in the corner.

He was suddenly yearning for death with all of his heart.

But still, in her emotional outburst, she pressed on, "While you went to school because it was your heart's wish, I carried double weight in these fields. I have never taken another lover because I honor you and your paposa. Why are you so inhumane to me?" Her eyes watered, and she grabbed her chest, yearning for an explanation. "Have I not done enough for you?"

Her face scorched in fuming hostility and seemed to show no mercy when her young son's cries choked in fright. His mother had slapped him in the face, and it was the final sense he felt when he realized she no longer loved him. Perhaps his sheylee had been right. He was ungrateful. And now miserable. For the first time he understood that he was also a burden to his mother. His disease not only took his life but his mother's as well.

"Sheylee," he screamed in pain and confusion, "why did you do this to me? I have done nothing. I need her, please."

"Not one more word. My patience is gone for your disobedience. I am going to the village to gather fabric to mend your bed, and you will stay here. If you are kind to me, I will allow you to see her."

And she was on her way alone to gather materials to mend his bed. Even though she left with fighting tears, she wanted to allow him to pass comfortably. But even deeper and perhaps even more hurtful to confess, she no longer could bare to look at her son in such shape.

He cried out loud to the dusty air that filled his room, "No. Your patience is gone for my sickness."

It had become too much for his heart to bear.

Derjaun took the deepest breath he could manage and fumbled to roll to his side. He saw the closed window. Suddenly it graced his mind that he was fighting for something and murmured it aloud, "Yes, my life is what I'm fighting for, in more ways than I can say." His breath became harder as he sought out the last bit of strength he had. Slowly, he turned over to rise and held onto the wall to walk to the window. All he saw was the cracking wood, the soft webbing of a house spider, and imprisonment.

He grimaced tightly. He knew his destiny. His trembling fingers, soiled with dirt and disease, began to unlock the window, and moment by moment passed that the light illuminated his wild blue eyes, forever now youthful and unbridled. "I'm not dying here. I'm not dead yet."

Derjaun turned and began dressing as fast as the injuries and sickness would allow him to, knowing that today was going to be the final day anyone would see him.

But not from the fact that his body would become a shallow gray shadow of death's final embrace. No, he did not have to die yet.

It was because Derjaun, the young boy of Radal, was going to run away. And he would not simply run away. Something specific called to him. He was going to simply vanish. Disappear.

His direction was clearer to him than his absolute fate. He clambered around his room for certain belongings, a knapsack for clothes without the realization that taking clothes should have warned his own mind that he had hopes to still live on, some food to get him there, and an old blanket to provide something comforting to snuggle against in the darkness of the nights ahead.

However headstrong his decision was, he was completely left in uncertainty of whether or not he would see Halo before he left. He paused. For a moment, he could hear the soft fading of his heartbeat in his own ears.

"No, I won't. If I should let you see me like this, I will never be able to rest in peace. I wish for you to remember me when I was healthier. I will no longer burden you with my sickness, my friend. I'm going to do something even my paposa never did."

He moved to the window once more and saw the mountains in the distance. The light of the morning star was higher, and it would soon make it too difficult to leave unnoticed. It was time.

The mountains were calling him home. The soft breeze came to lift his lungs with fresh air, and he placed his two hands on the windowsill. He focused his strength and miraculously lifted himself out of the prison of his disease. He felt the grass underneath his feet, and the wind came stronger. He closed his eyes to enjoy the moment, much like he had done with Halo on the fence in his pasture not long ago.

The sun filled the stream down his cheeks with a radiance of warmth, and he sighed heavily. "I will see you, Halo...on the other side."

For a second his face winced from the pain, but he quickly stood upright and professed to the sky, "I am Derjaun Vin Gruinelle, son of Radal."

He began walking to the north. He fought every mound of uneven ground with his eyes focused forward. "I am the future captain of Nakhan, my father's beloved village. I am what one desires most. My heart is still beating!" He ran faster and faster. "I am not a diseased rat." His eyes began to tighten in remembrance of Mozkin's scorning. "I am not weak. I am not a burden." His pace began to quicken until he realized how in control he felt. His energy shot into the most unbelievable level as he ran through the kaku fields and easily leapt over the fences with the bursting energy of what was ahead.

"I will not die here. I will never die."

His body ignited into a full sprint of vitality toward the mysterious foothills of the roaring evergreens, the forbidden forest.

He saw the forest and stopped with his breath heaving in his chest anxiously, and he said aloud with bravery, "No, I am not a captain. I am a king. I am the king of my own life. For once and for all."

But wait.

Derjaun lowered his head and turned to see what he had left behind. His eyes watered. "I am sorry, Halo. I am too young to fall asleep. I will meet you...on the other side."

He hurried off from Nakhan forever and disappeared into the forest. What was left behind was the flowing grasses of the pabi fields, the scent of the flowers, and the little animals and insects and the birds overhead that were innocent to everything of his emotions. It was as if his voice had become the driving force of his own newfound power and strength. He was gone.

. . .

AND HE LEFT HER BEHIND. All of this, Halo was completely unaware of. The most unfortunate thing was that if she had known she would have gladly left all things behind in her own life to follow him. How she craved such freedom, and being with him was the best thing in her world. But she was at school when her friend left his life behind, completely naïve to what had happened.

At school, Halo carefully examined every desk in the first row, seeing one available seat left.

As she flopped down, it came to her mind how heavy the heart inside of her chest was, and the only thing that would lift it would be the sight of her dearly loved friend, the one who she sadly parted with too early the previous night.

The room was darkened from the sudden coming of a storm on the horizon, closing in around the village in preparation to consume it. At least this was the way Halo viewed such storms, because of their marveling strength and power.

The clatter of the children's gossip rang in a brutal sense of annoyance to her, but despite what should have been a distraction that brought her away from her emotions, Halo could not help but sulk. Derjaun had not yet arrived. She fixed the emerald ribbon in her hair and earnestly looked around, then a gruesome sound she loathed so severely interrupted her thoughts.

"Ah, Halo," came the heartless voice on the left. She glared at its source.

"Mozkin Ramath," she said with a sound of acknowledgment, and a snide one at that. "I was holding this seat for Derjaun."

He shot with a cruel response, "Your favorite breathing disease is not here."

"Yet!" she corrected angrily.

Mozkin folded his arms. "No, he will not be coming. His health has made him idle at home. I heard the captain speaking with his guards about making sure that Radal's son was not allowed outside."

Halo caught her breath. For the moment, she attempted to see if Mozkin was telling the truth. "He is home sick?" she asked with concern.

"Yes," Mozkin replied with a tone that lacked any sympathy at all for her worry or for Derjaun's well-being.

She shook her head in anger. "I still demand that you leave. I'll have Jastin sit by me."

Again, he laughed, "You mean your friend who loves me?"

The boys in the corner laughed in a united team of scoundrels.

"Leave!" she shouted into his face.

Thunder came with a sudden downpour of rain, and in through the side door came a plump figure whose hood and elaborate cloak were soaked.

"Halo!" squeaked the hidden face in a feminine tone.

Halo stood with a smile. "It's alright, Jastin! Come on over here. I saved this place for you."

The girl wandered quickly through the desks to her, nervously speaking, "Oh, I hate the lighting. I simply *abhor* it. And look at my boots! Just look at them!"

Mozkin and Halo looked down as she pointed toward her lavish foot attire.

Jastin griped, "They're muddy!"

"Haha, you're learning more words through your readings, I see," Halo responded. "I'm sure you'll live. Maybe you shouldn't wear your finest garments when it rains."

Before the well-dressed girl removed her hood, Mozkin edged closer and poked her belly. "And I see you haven't lost weight since the last time you came to school, Jastin."

She revealed her face to him and jerked back in fear. "Mozkin, if I had known you were going to speak to me today, I would have dressed better."

He laughed as he rolled his eyes. "Nothing you wear could ever hide that disgusting pudge you carry around your waist."

Halo slapped his face so hard that it made the skin of her palm burn as if she had slammed it down on glowing wood from the fire.

Everyone heard the slap and turned to see the boy rubbing his face and Halo's stance of victory. They all laughed.

"You rotted female!" Mozkin bellowed.

"She's not your doll! I refuse to let you carry on like this with her."

The horrible young man finally left them alone.

The girl from the Inner Circle sat down in the seat, and with her light-brown hair being freed from the hood of burgundy velvet she proclaimed happily, "Many thanks to you, Halo. I could never have done such a thing."

"Because your sheylee has taught you not to. Jastin, he's not your husband, nor does he have any right to order you the way he does. I don't know if it's because your family comes from a place so far away that this is customary for you, but I'm getting tired of constantly defending you around him."

Jastin noticed Halo's somber demeanor and extended a hand to hers. "My sweet friend, what troubles you?"

Halo looked down and answered softly, "Derjaun."

Her best friend's dark eyes glowed and grew larger in innocent softness.

"Do you know of him? Radal's one and only son?"

Jastin blurted a quick answer, "No. I did not even know Radal had a son."

"He does," Halo informed her. "You may not be aware of this, as Derjaun and his mother live in the Outer Circle near the fields. But since you have been absent, I have found a friend in him."

Jastin could not help but smirk. Her thoughts raced as one hopeless romantic's mind may race. "So, you and he have..."

"No, Jastin, he is a friend, nothing more. Although a deeply cherished one."

She frantically leaned in to whisper, "So if you have made a new friend, why do you wear a face of drama?"

"Oh, please," Halo shot as she sat back and folded her arms. "Your face is well rehearsed to display a drama one thousand-fold more than mine."

Jastin playfully rolled her eyes, and her feminine voice chirped, "You can see my face today? Even in this dark and cloudy weather?"

"For goodness sakes Jastin I'm not that blind."

Jastin paused. "Oh. Well anyway, answer my question, regardless of the term I used for your expressions."

Halo's breath stilled itself for a moment while she thought.

"He is sick. Deeply sick. So sick that his health may soon have him in his father's arms," Halo mumbled.

Jastin did not know what to say. She was never skilled at comforting those who wept. She could only offer one thing, and this was her heart. "Halo," she staggered, her hand on her chest, "I am sorry to hear this for you. Is there anything I can do?"

"I'm afraid not. But there is more to this story..."

Jastin leaned closer to listen.

"Derjaun came to me last night. I was not expecting his presence at all. I had no warning or call of any kind. But he came when Lemson was fighting with my sheylee, and he saved me. He took Lemson's attention away from me. And although he is our age and ill, I soon saw before my very eyes Lemson charging into him time and time again. If it were not for the stature of the boy, Lemson sure would have smushed him like a wood beetle. But he became too weak to fight, and when he told me to call a Guardian I left and summoned the only person I could find. Captain Staghen came to—"

Halo almost jolted out of her skin when her friend gasped hard. "Captain Staghen was at your house? He is so handsome. Oh, what I wouldn't give to be his wife!" Her head leaned back as she held her chest.

Apparently, Jastin began to ignore Halo's intense confession of everything that had recently happened to her and even more hurt-fully ignored her emotions to press on with her own desires. "He is so strong and brave and... and—"

Halo interrupted bitterly, "And eleven years over you."

Jastin continued, "But that has no meaning, my dear friend. I have only two more years to wait before I can marry. *Then* perhaps Staghen will see how well trained I am in both family and house-work, and he will ask me to marry him. My sheylee has been working with me without forgiveness because she knows how much I want his love in marriage. I refuse to have any other man." She flipped her hair with a giggle, placed her chin on her hand, and looked at her friend.

"Oh, I am so deeply sorry again," Jastin said in sorrow. "I have distracted you from your story."

"It's fine, Jastin. It brings me happiness to hear that for the past two years your love for Staghen grows stronger every day. It's nice to hear you are consistent with at least one thing in your life. I'll tell you about the rest during our social hour outside, that is if Lady Florn lets us go outside with this storm."

After hours of lectures and a few tests, the students were inside during their leisure time, which was nothing but a blackened curse to Halo's ears. Instead of being outside in the storm where the winds and lightning would drown out the screams and laughter, she was locked inside.

Halo and Jastin sat in a far back corner while Jastin painted on paper. "Do you care to hear the rest of what happened?" Halo asked.

Without looking at her colleague, Jastin continued painting and answered, "I finally have a perfect shade of green to paint your eyes. I got distracted. But Halo, he is sick. What more to the matter is there?"

Halo's heart was shocked with betrayal. "Jastin, he's going to die!"

"And there is obviously nothing that can save him or he would have surely been saved by now. I asked you if there was anything I could do, and you said there was none. Right? And you have known him for at least the month I have been gone, and he has only worsened." She paused with a breath while dark-blue paint dripped on her paper. Her sweet dark eyes looked to Halo. "If he is to pass, he will have had *one* good friend in his life, right?"

Halo hunched over Jastin's paper, forcing her friend to look at her. "When he came to me last night, his appearance showed his life will end in a mere few moons, and if this is how you feel about him, that there is no hope for anything, even for him to have a peaceful passing, then I must say I will not see you at school tomorrow nor after that. I will be by his side until his last breath draws. I don't care if my sheylee knows. If you would have ever met him, your heart would be weighed by grief as well."

School was dismissed, and the morning star had not won the raging war with the storm, making the girls rush home faster than ever before. Although the beloved rain had not fallen yet, it was coming close to.

Jastin had decided to accompany her friend until they reached Derjaun's home. After all, it was the least she felt she could do after the tense conversation they shared during school.

The two girls walked up to the front door, and Halo's intentions to knock were halted by a familiar whimper from behind.

"Halo?" Jastin began with her head low, brushing her hand against her olive-toned arm, "I can't bear to see someone ill. And if he is your friend, you should have some time alone. He may feel uneasy with someone new. I know your presence will bring him peace as it does me. I wish you well, but I am going home now. I will come here tomorrow and see how you are. I'm sorry I can't be of any more help to you."

The rich girl left without any further action of comfort or spoken word that would bring Halo some easiness to her spirit.

She watched her best friend disappear onto the pathways that lead to the luxurious inner parts of the village, and she felt the cool breeze from the storm clouding her chest. All over, her skin flushed with emotions that were nearly unbearable to withhold.

Shaking this aside yet again, she decided to race around the back to Derjaun's bedroom window. Knocking would interrupt Agrona if she were to be home, and her heart felt it best to endure a quiet time alone with her friend without any peering eyes from adults who may not understand her emotions.

She sought out the boy's back window by scurrying off the porch and darting around the vibrant flower bushes until the window came into view. The perimeters of the small house smelled as it always did. Rich, fragrant animal hide freshly hanging off from tree branches gathered insects that would eat the scraps of flesh so clean until it could be washed and prepared for clothing. Halo caught a scent of the warm meat. She was hoping to one day become a skilled huntress herself. Jastin would have made a wonderful wild gatherer, if she would have ever gone outside more often.

The flies and insects were desperate to swarm around the blood-stained furs and skins before the dimming sky fumed with violent showers. Thunder brought a hasty sound to the village once again, but for some reason the rain never came.

Climbing to the window was met with stumbling over chopped wood logs and other things that could have potentially been hazardous to a girl with cloth slippers. The wind of the storm blew the cloth tapestries about in a flapping banter that almost sounded percussive, and she began to fight with the annoyance of the curtains. Then standing on the tip of her toes she peered inside Derjaun's window.

He was not there.

Her troubled eyes focused harder in the dark room, but still, she could not see anything. She quietly tried to call for him, lest he be inside somewhere she couldn't see, "Derjaun?"

No response.

Halo's heartbeat sounded in her ears as she searched frantically for the sight of anyone. There was not one single trace of evidence to tell where he was.

Despairingly, she believed that Derjaun may have slipped into his ever-needed slumber—but if he did, where was his body? Her face tightened in anguish as she dropped from the window, jumping through the bushes and into the street. Nearly colliding with the other villagers, she called for the captain. A friend she had grown to love so shortly was lost, and by no apparent means of natural causes, at least in her mind. Derjaun could not have died. She believed he was simply taken. It was not in his nature to leave without telling her. They were best friends, and Halo trusted him to tell her everything. Something was amiss.

An expedition of great measures found her racing toward the Inner Circle against the capacity of her young heart, until she found Staghen with his high fleet of Guardians.

His voice carried on in the conversation of duties until the

approaching voice caused him to turn his head, and immediately he
steadied Rikaana and drew a cautious breath for a moment to quench
the worry of a dreaded occurrence. The voice, ever loud and explo-
sive, called for him.

"Halo, what have the stars done to worry you so?" he asked
sharply when she nearly fell to the hooves of his horse.

Gasping hard and in severe emotional distress, she was wild with
fury and fright. Halo could not even speak properly.

"Ease yourself." Staghen beamed down in command. "Your words
are quite adrift."

Her knees hit the dirt, and she yanked for his leather-clad leg.
"Captain, Derjaun is gone! He wasn't at school and isn't in his bed!"
Her hands that were dusted by the pathway's dirt snatched the
leather even harder. "Mozkin Ramath told me you ordered him to
stay idle! Where is he? Please, tell me!"

Staghen had to maintain a strong spine despite hearing the tragic
question. His eyes flared toward his men. "Radal's son has vanished.
Do not stop your search until he is found. Raid every house and over-
throw every stone if you must!"

He grabbed her arm and pulled her onto his horse, clutching her
against his breastplate. The stampede of men and horses drowned
her ears with the rhythm of something so far from graceful that it left
the people of the village scattering like fleeing rodents. The captain
kicked his horse to a faster gait toward the widow's home.

The only slight comfort Halo had was the embrace of the head-
strong captain, and it was not the rain that washed his armor. It was
her tears.

But how she wished the rain would come. Everything in that
moment was desperate to be cleansed and born anew.

When the two arrived, Staghen slipped off of his horse without
any struggle and trampled toward the door to bash his fist against it.
"Agrona vin Gruinelle, this is the captain. I order you to open this
door!"

Although the widow was the wife of his great inspiration, it meant nothing to him when her disobedience reigned in such ways. He knocked harder. "Agrona!"

Halo, while still mounted, wiped her eyes and told him, "Captain, she was not at home. I don't know where she would be."

He turned to her and listened to the pattering of rain on the roof of the house. The rain finally came. "The storm is above us, Halo. Please hurry home. I will wait here until she returns."

He sighed briefly and searched around the dilapidated stoop for a place to sit, and all Halo could do was allow the rain to dampen her clothes. She spoke softly, "But, Captain, I wish to be here when she returns. It's my friend we speak of."

"Halo, do as I ask of you. You'll get sick from the rain if you don't."

She lifted her eyes to the gray sky and pleaded again, "Please, Captain. I'm a farmer who works in the field through flood and frost. This weather is nothing to me. My friend is everything."

Staghen's lips parted in concentration while he heaved with breath. "I'm losing patience for her return. If it is your will to stay, then I suppose I can grant your request. I would go inside, but even I as the captain am not allowed to raid anyone's dwelling without their permission."

Rikaana stayed by the front stoop. Meanwhile, Halo flopped on the wooden floorboards of the porch. Only a few leaks managed to bless her head with droplets of cold rain, and Staghen occupied the only available porch seat behind her.

How frightening it would be to Agrona, Halo thought, to see them both upon her porch when she returned. If the captain waited at someone's home, dreadful matters were about.

He spoke while rubbing his face, "We have little time. She should have been home by—"

A little fleck appeared in Halo's troubled eyes, and she muttered, "Captain, she comes." Her pale and dirty finger pointed. "It's her, right?"

Staghen lifted from the chair and without hesitation but much irritation questioned the mother, "Agrona Vin Gruinelle, your boy has gone missing. I have sent every Guardian to search for him, but I demand to speak with you as to where he may be."

Halo raged, "Captain! She was supposed to be watching over him! She failed to—"

"Keep your tongue clasped! This is our matter now, not yours," he ordered.

Tension built between the three of them.

Agrona hurried toward them and hollered in confusion, "My Captain, I ordered him bedridden. He was there when I left!" She panicked and looked at the girl. "Halo, you have not seen him either? He mentioned a great deal about wanting to visit you. Has anyone checked the barn houses? The kaku coops? The hog pens? Anything?"

Her golden mane had collapsed from the walk home in the rain. Panting, she pleaded, "Staghen, I have nothing to say. If he is not inside this house..." Agrona paused in thought. Over and over within her mind she recalled the memory of what she had done to him that morning.

The widow suddenly shoved past Staghen and threw her front door open, calling for her son. "Derjaun! Derjaun?" she yelled. Her eyes widened as Staghen and Halo followed her inside. They witnessed Agrona desperately searching his room, throwing every item to the side. She saw the window. Her lips shook like falling leaves from the trees, and under her breath she muttered, "He left."

The mother's heart grew into a stricken panic.

Staghen came into the room with his arms folded and urged her, "Agrona, you must talk louder! What was it you said? He left? How do you know this?"

"This I can say," Agrona wept on her knees as she turned to grovel to the captain. "He demanded that I let Halo see him, but I ordered him home to stay alone for now. I wish he would have been more patient. I know seeing her brings him peace, but he could barely walk! I closed this window, and now it's open. He left deliberately. Are you certain he did not make attempts to see Halo at school and was taken by someone?"

He asked angrily, "You disobeyed my orders? I specifically told you to allow him to see Halo whenever he wanted to, not at a time convenient for you. To give him whatever he desired. You scolded him for disobeying you, yet you disobeyed me! He probably left to go find her, and if he dies alone days before his time because of it, may you claim fault for it." He clenched her collar and yelled, "You are his mother, for heart's sake!"

He lifted and brushed his cloak to turn away from the mother in the corner, who collapsed in terrifying cries. Sobs heavily rang through the wooden walls.

Staghen was burdened by his emotions. An impenetrable state of misery glazed in his eyes as he had lost his constitution of how to behave as a captain. Like an ill-tempered gale off the shoreline, he left. The mother glanced toward Halo, who was numbed by the incident.

Agrona's blonde hair clasped to her cheeks from the tears and sweat of what happened, and her golden face withered in sadness. "May I ask if I am worthy of your forgiveness?" she whimpered. "You are the only person to have loved my child the way his father and I have. What am I to do?"

But Halo wanted nothing of this woman any longer.

The girl rose to leave. "I only wish you peace. I will grant you this, and it is a promise. I won't stop looking for your son. He will be found."

She walked outside alone and faced a decision.

Not tomorrow nor the next day would Jastin see her, because she would not be at school, but that fact solely must have meant something. She told Agrona he would be found because she knew exactly where Derjaun was. She had spent enough days with him to believe that his fascination with the dangerous mountains finally pulled him in, pulled him away from his torment.

At least, she hoped that was where he went. What more beautiful of a way to sleep than to sleep where even his father never ventured to?

On she trudged around the village, allowing her sorrow to sink deeper, all the while questioning. Her lungs inhaled to feel the contracting sting of the damp, cold air. The rain still fell heavily. What was she to do now?

An answer suddenly came as a snapping pulse to her mind. Her decision set and sworn, Halo hurried toward Staghen's house so quickly that she could barely remember getting there. Nothing in her peripheral vision mattered. All she could do was run as hard as she could.

A few small knocks were given to his door, and almost right after he answered, opening the door in curiosity. "Halo, what brings you here? I can't waste much time. I will be leaving soon to the village circle to make an announcement regarding Derjaun," he said as he began fixing his scabbard to his side.

She looked up to him as his eyes saw her exhaustion. His sternness subsided. "Please, come inside. Let us find you warmth."

A few moments later, Halo was able to rest on a wooden chair that was endowed with handcrafted pillows. Staghen's house was massive compared to any other she had ever been inside of. Waiting for him to sit seemed to lag on for more than she could bear. He sat, crossed his heel over his kneecap, and began with a deep tone, "Why have you come? Make this brief."

"My Captain," Halo began with confidence, "I am here bearing humble dignity." Hesitation choked her courage. This very thought could turn into an argument, but she continued, "I am asking if I may join the Guardians."

Captain Staghen was curious, so unlike how other Guardians may have reacted. He responded curtly, "Not only are you a female, but you are young. I can't resist the feeling that you believe this will bring Derjaun home. And your eyes..."

She swallowed with a raucous sound.

"I have heard about your eyes. You can't see well in the dark and even struggle to see when the sun wakes."

She interjected respectfully, "All the more reason why I should have training, Captain."

He shook his head. "I will not recruit someone who needs specific training just to protect oneself and be an independent person."

"All villagers are dependent on the Guardians. With honor, my Captain, I don't enjoy a village of people who always need someone else's protection. Or are you, Captain, attempting to make us all sucklings, unable to fend for ourselves?"

The mind of the captain was blown by finding humor in the scathing response, yet the response was delivered by a young lady who was almost as persistent as he was. It was as if he was having dialogue with his youthful self all over again. At this moment, the captain had felt a slip of his emotional grip. He had no choice but to chuckle at the irony of it all. He paused, rubbing his lip. She was right. If only the villagers could have protected themselves better, the scourge of the beasts that night almost seven years ago could have had a better ending. He leaned over on his knees, and his blue eyes glared deeply at her.

His voice dropped in tone, "I will have to burn the written laws of the edict for you."

"Do we *have* to follow the word of every law, Captain? Derjaun's place in the Guardians is now vacant. When he is found, he'll need time for healing. I assure you that I will make a fine Guardian. I give my blood for it. It's also more than that, Captain Staghen. I wish to uphold Derjaun's blood destiny that he can't carry. I know he is still alive."

The burning in her soul increased. The very words she uttered with such confidence reminded him of when he was speaking with Radal for the first time about becoming a Guardian.

Staghen leaned his head to the side, his eyes still fixed on her. He was listening.

Halo continued with perseverance, "I have nothing to live for. I don't want a husband, and I feel I attend school without reason. I am twelve years old and have no meaning to my life as of yet. My destiny is bleak, but my spirit is strong." And with this, the soft green hues of her eyes gleamed. Her voice creaked with hope, "Please?"

They looked at one another. The man's eyes were vague in

contemplation, hers however were basking in the lights of desperation.

Halo exploded again, "PLEASE."

He spoke, "You state you attend your daily lectures without reason, and yet Lady Florn finds you to possess vast knowledge of your teachings and that you are such a stylish student. The idea that you believe you have no purpose for your studies is questionable to me. However, understand that there will be no special training for you. Yes, I will give the best I can to guide your training with the sight you have been given, but none other. You will run with my men and fight with my men. Do you also understand that you will be regarded as such?"

She asked with a curious demeanor, "If Lady Florn gives me such praise, then you should be happy I asked to join. But, you say, am I to be regarded as if I myself were a man?"

"Yes."

Halo answered bluntly, "Then so be it, Captain. I would expect nothing less. I don't want anything else."

When Halo ended her confession, the storm had almost seemed to end with it. Winds that rattled the trees and creaked the houses became dormant in a steady downshift while the thunder was long passed to rumble another settlement. She waited, and she waited longer. Halo began to fumble with her fingers.

Their eyes locked. His face of judgment was almost burdensome to her patience.

What she did not see was how much inside his heart was gleaming with memories of seeing her sneaking onto the fences to watch the Guardians train. Even before she knew Derjaun existed, she wanted to be a Guardian. She did not know he knew these things about her. It would be a kind secret he would keep to himself.

His heart was moved by the spirited girl. He realized that Derjaun was truly supposed to hold Radal's position. And since his sickness had rendered him unable to do so, why, here was a perfectly strong and determined girl who knew the Vin Gruinelle line almost as well, if not better, than Staghen himself. Even though he knew he was taking a risk, he saw the earnestness in her will to absolve Derjaun's plight. He had known her to be a true and sturdy worker. And with her energy of preserving and upholding the Vin Gruinelle legacy and to find Derjaun, he felt it almost cruel not to allow her to join. He had seen so much hardiness in her love. His heart softened with her bravery. Bravery, honor, friendship, and loyalty. These were all the things that a Guardian was. And she was already just that.

Miraculously, he spoke, "Then there is little time."

Halo's mind was utterly tangled and stumped at the same time. Quite rooted, actually. "I'm sorry, Captain. I don't know what you're trying to tell me. Where are we going?" She rose from her seat and attempted to see what he was doing. He was gathering his coat again and grabbing something off of a wall hook she could not see.

His deep voice answered, "To receive your paposa's blessings and catch a horse for you after I organize the search orders."

She stopped. Her breath almost left her body. "Captain," she gasped, looking to him.

He turned to look at her.

"Are you allowing me to join?"

"Absolutely."

The blind girl held her cheeks.

He continued, "I am moved by you. I know you will do fine. It will be difficult for many reasons. But all Guardians face difficulties in the beginning. And quite honestly, these difficulties never leave. We just acquire new ones. You'll learn this soon enough."

She smiled as she turned her head to the side. Not only were her most unfathomable dreams coming true, but she was given the responsibility of helping bring her dear friend home.

Her heart became woeful. "My sheylee and paposa will never approve. I didn't know I needed their permission."

Outside, Rikaana remained tied to the post under a shelter until the rain ended. Staghen untied him and while adjusting the saddle briefly said, "This is no great obstacle. You will live with me now. I can't have you living with Lemson. Come morning, your training begins once I make the announcement. After, we will proceed with your new work."

"My heart is full of gratitude, my captain," she responded.

"I'm sure it is. After all, finding Derjaun will be much easier if you're trained for it properly. I'm not sure how in such a short time you became the only person he trusted. You were only friends with him for a little over a month before he vanished."

Halo pleasantly responded, "He trusted you."

Staghen smiled at the thought. She spoke a truth he had forgotten. "Then I must continue to be worthy of that trust and train you well."

6

The search orders were given and afterwards they made their way to her mother's home. Following Halo's intuition, the request for custody brought havoc to her family. Inside her former home, she stood next to Captain Staghen Viktraana while her sheylee bickered back and forth with him. Lirena was angry at the thought of her only child leaving to join the Guardians. "But Staghen, she tells me she is blind! How can she possibly be a Guardian?"

Staghen laughed and looked about, stunned by the mother's words. "She *is* blind. For stars above woman you're her mother and you doubt her still. Haven't you taken her to Crenon to be evaluated at all?"

Lirena lowered her head. "We haven't the money."

It occurred to Staghen that the girl had been living under unimaginable circumstances that far surpassed how bad he thought it was.

In Nakhan, when a child's parents separated, the law was written to favor the mother's custody. But this gruesome display of parenting only left him with the thought that the law was in desperate need of revision.

Lirena and Lemson simply disgusted him.

There was nothing Lirena could do to prevent what was going to happen. She said her final farewell to her daughter and watched her leave. When they left the house, Halo realized how simple it felt to leave her old life behind, which was quite contradictory to the way she had expected to feel. She wanted this new life.

Afterward, across the many pastures they rode to the eastern side of the Outer Circle and came to the mud hut where her father, Aljen, lived. He was a hardworking farmer and baker and was proud to claim the role of being responsible for a majority of the crops and bread sold in the marketplace.

Outside, the captain found the noble man working in the side fields alone.

Rikaana came to an abrupt halt and caught the attention of Aljen, who wiped the long white hair from his face and squinted to see who it was. "Ahe-ye, who comes with hooves upon my soil?" he asked, placing his farmer's hat over his eyes to block the rays of the blinding sun.

"It is I, Captain Staghen," he answered. "I have come with your daughter to inquire of something."

Aljen, as playful as could be, chuckled loudly. "What is this? You wish to marry her?"

Halo's eyes popped.

"No. For heart's sake, old man, we come with important matters," the captain said. "Perhaps she should come near and ask you for herself."

Halo dismounted with ease. "Yes, Paposa. Derjaun is missing, and so Staghen is allowing me to join the Guardians. May I?"

Aljen dropped his shovel. His face looked frantic and reddened. "I'm confused, Halo. You are a girl, my little heart. I thought you were going to travel far and wide and study the stars," he said. "Tell great tales...become a philosopher. I read every tale from the *Travels of Bremlin* to you. You enjoyed the vast and dangerous feats of the gollets. My heart, I expected you to move on from this village. Why must you change your path here and now?"

Staghen was astonished she had altered her dreams so drastically.

"But I'm not," she consoled. "If anything, Paposa, I *am* living this dream now. Gollets are fighters, warriors. And they're hired by those who can afford their services to bring people home. Of course they steal and murder and pillage as well. But remember what Galden did? He brought someone of great importance home. He was the very first gollet. I want to bring someone of great importance home."

Aljen looked to the captain with confidence. "Well, if she has your blessings—"

Staghen spoke firmly, "She has my blessings. We come seeking yours."

Aljen clapped with joyous laughter. "Then a Guardian she shall be! You have it. Oh, my dear, please promise me one day I shall read the collection of *The Travels of Halo*."

Captain Staghen's impatience soon melted into respect as the old father hugged his precious girl. It was clear to him that Aljen would have a difficult time letting her go.

Yes, the laws needed much revising.

And so Halo left all of her life behind. She left her mother, her father, the beautiful fields she always tended to, and even her favorite wicker breadbasket would be traded in for a sword soon enough. To her gratitude, the captain made the parting brief in order to attend to the great task of finding Derjaun.

On their casual walk, with his horse at his side, he took notice of his men's diligent work in the pastures. They were searching for the boy. He looked to the girl and said, "Halo, we should obtain a suitable mare for your Guardian companionship."

She groaned.

"Now, now. I know you'd like a stallion, deeming them 'wild and fierce,' but the bond between rider and horse must be close and well tied in order for them to cooperate properly. I have learned in my trainings that male horses tend to be very feral for females, as if testing their riders. Yet when I myself mount a mare, she seems to place a heavy amount of distrust in me. They believe male riders to be too assertive, and sometimes we can be."

They had passed the opening gate that led to the vast region of the northern pabi fields. Feeling the squish of the soft, wet grass under her feet made Halo feel like she had been embraced by a loving mother.

The captain halted. As she looked up toward his sharpening eyes, she squeaked, "Captain, why do you stop?"

"There are the wild horses near this field, dear one." He surveyed the region. "And yet I see nothing."

The young girl attempted to look around, placing her hand above her eyes to shield the gleaming rays of the morning star away from them. "I hear nothing except birds, Captain."

He held his gaze firmly. He had to ask in astonishment, "You *hear* birds? But I do not see them, nor do I hear them."

She lifted her pale finger toward the Castonuje Mountains.

Still, he saw nothing. "Halo, my senses do not catch what you do."

"Captain, the birds are becoming rather restless in the forest."

Staghen gave up with a sigh and a smile. "Have you ever set foot near this forest?"

His partner stood in thought. "No, but I've wanted to my whole life. My parents said that it was too dangerous."

"Well, this day you are with me. And where there are forest birds getting restless, there must be some sort of herd moving in the steep valley. Inside the Castonuje Mountains there are long, deep paths that were formed by the river and strong winds. In them lie streams that are both gentle and strong. Wild horses move in herds alongside these locations since they supply an ample amount of both water and grass."

"But, Captain, going to the mountains is forbidden. Why are we going there now?"

He stopped again and happily answered, "We aren't. *They* will be coming to us."

Silence.

He leaned closer to her and extended his finger toward a part of the Gigannora River that was enshrouded in dense forestation and continued, "Look there. My intuition tells me that a herd of horses will be coming this way soon. Wait here. If any horses come your way, crouch and cover your head. You can't outrun them, so don't try. They'll ram you and trample you if you run with them. They'll jump over you if you crouch."

A gust of birds took to the sky from the forest canopy. She had been right. There were birds there.

Proudly, Halo answered, "Yes, I understand, Captain."

"Good, I will return soon." He mounted his horse and with a snap of the reins and a kick, Staghen raced toward the forest.

There was nothing more left for the girl to do but wait, so Halo dropped onto the pillowy grass and watched her captain ride toward the north, becoming ever more distant until his figure vanished among the grass. Even in late spring the exhilarating scent of the mountain berry pine trees blushed their perfumes all across the pastures and outer fields. Her mouth almost watered while thinking about those succulent berries.

She lay on her back and tried to think about how to find Derjaun. The time that passed was perfect for her heart to regain its stability, for a lot had happened that day. Among her rich grasses brushed her skin, and the wetness of the ground was cool to her back. But a sudden rumble of the ground was felt in her back. Due to her blindness, Halo had become incredibly sensitive to movement and sound.

The pulse in the ground underneath her body rumbled harder and carried on a faint echo in the trees. With every passing moment, it grew increasingly unstable. Halo jumped to her feet, and as she did the soil became dangerously unsteady. Her voice quivered, "Staghen? Where are you?"

It must have been the rare occasion where the ground moved vigorously from time to time, and from this she felt a sense of peace because her memory recalled it would only linger for a while and was nothing to be concerned over.

But she was wrong.

Halo toppled backward on her rear. "Ah! Oof, that hurt..." She rubbed her behind. It did not stop. The ground refused to halt its agitation, and the fury escalated into absolute terror for the girl who could still see no hint of Staghen's approach.

Once more, Halo fought with the distempered ground and stood. "There, this is not so—"

Monstrous shapes burst through the forest opening. Slowly approaching and trying to allow her eyes to focus, the girl curiously observed. They grew larger, larger, and when the ground's terror ignited with a deafening sound of thunder, it came so close that even her ill eyes could see what it was.

Her eyes grew with the reflection of fear. Horror anchored her legs and adrenaline burned in her stomach, and her lips slacked open while her mind told her to run as fast as her limber legs could. A stampede of enormous and hostile horses was closing in on her.

In her heart, she was hearing Staghen's voice telling her to stay calm and crouch the way she was supposed to. However promising his words, the large beasts that were less than a life's breath away did not seem to have interest in jumping or dodging, only destroying. Their whinnies and neighs were screaming a horrible sound.

Breathing hard, palms sweating, the terrified girl forgot everything Staghen told her to do, and she obeyed her body's howl to run.

The lead stallion rushed across her side with every glistening muscle tightening in his move. Around she saw them closing in with the head damaging outburst of atrocious movements, the animals heaved with loud hooves around her from all angles behind, and she began to panic. Harder breaths came from her trembling body while she kept attempting to outrun the stampede, but it was futile.

Turning her head to see how many more of them there were, she saw a surprising blessing. Staghen was racing desperately alongside the deadly herd. "Halo, I told you to stay still!" he screamed at her.

In her pants of breath, Halo cried hopelessly, "Staghen, please! I'm sorry!"

A younger stallion sounded his guttural horse scream when it came up alongside Halo's fleeing body, and she was certain in her that the animal was going to trample her into a bloody pile of bones.

She may pay for the mistake with her life.

"Halo! Get down!"

A horse rammed its head into her back, and within an instant her body smashed onto the ground. The frightened blind girl quickly lifted her battered face to see shadows manifesting into horse hooves in front of her very eyes.

"Staghen!" she cried in severe distress. Every which way her watery eyes searched. She couldn't see him and tried calling again, "Staghen, please help me! I can't see you!" Outward her hands reached in confusion. Either she was trying to find Staghen or hold her head. Never before had she been so hysterical.

Her vision was blocked by every color of animal legs and the gleaming of hooves. With every impact the hooves gave the ground, her jaw rattled. It felt like she was trapped in a fatal thunderstorm. Her screams rattled her skull, "STAGHEN, PLEASE!"

"Halo, lie still and keep your arms close to your body!" Staghen called amidst the chaos. Fortunately her ears were in tune enough to hear this life-saving call for help among the rage of horses.

She pulled her hands close, and with her back hurting from the impact she pressed her face into the ground.

All around, Halo felt locked in their lethal warpath until miraculously an opening of the horses to her right allowed for a sighting of Rikaana with Staghen mounted coming alongside. But the captain's face looked horrified, and he screamed with all of his heart, "Halo, look up!"

She fought her fear and turned on her back, seeing a white horse with its sparkling silver hooves rearing above her and snorting its nostrils as if fire would be exhaled. It was going to stomp.

Right as it was going to crush her, Halo covered her face with her hands until her ears heard a massive whinny to her left.

She looked to find the horse was on its side right next to her and fighting to get up.

"Got you!" Staghen called as he began pulling his rope harder. "Rikaana, back up! Come on, boy!"

The stampede seemed to fade to nothing except the lone white horse thrusting to turn over.

"Halo, get away from her!"

The girl struggled to stand up then hurried away from the horse, which also rose and began putting up an intense fight against the rope around her neck. Her eyes widened at the magnificent size of the animal. Its long, waving mane glimmered in hues of emerald. It reared and kicked around, but Staghen and his stallion pulled hard. The mare was insistent.

"Staghen, you're hurting her!"

Across the distance, Rikaana struggled to keep pulling back. "Nonsense. This horse can endure far more hostile treatment than this!" Although youthful still, the captain was used to the strain on the body when catching a wild horse. His arms continued to pull the ropes to steady the beast.

Several long minutes passed until Staghen could see the mare was tired. He dismounted Rikaana and pulled the rope hard enough to bring her to the ground. But it was not out of aggression to harm the animal. It was simply to force her to lie down and calm her lungs and heart.

Once the mare succumbed, he spoke, "Halo, go and steady her."

Halo covered her ears to the heart-wrenching sounds of the large horse struggling to call for its herd. The herd had not returned. There were no sounds of her herd at all. They were long gone.

"But," Halo began in confusion, "you told me to stay away from her."

The captain tied the rope around Rikaana's saddle. "She is calling for her herd. She is vulnerable now, and so it's the best time to show her that you are there for her when she was abandoned by her herd."

Both Staghen and Halo met standing above the wild mare that lay on her side in exhaustion, still breathing hard from the fight.

"Staghen," Halo said softly, "this horse is far too large to be a mare."

He knelt by the horse's muzzle to carefully loosen the noose from her muscular neck. "She is a mare. I studied her quietly with the rest of the herd. She is wild, strong, dominant, and very agile on the rocks. She would make a perfect companion for you. She's a mountaineer horse."

Uncertainty was the unkindest of gifts bestowed upon Halo.

"Captain, I can't tame her. A mountaineer horse? In Bremlin's tales they are written to be truly wild and always free." She affectionately attempted to soothe the throbbing of veins in the mare's neck. "Look at her. I feel her heart is saddened now that she knows she was caught. Her eyes are dilated, and her nostrils are racing. She's scared." She understood exactly how the animal felt. The young, blind peasant girl knelt by the animal's side and brushed her glorious white fur even more. "It's alright, pretty one. I know how you feel. But maybe..." Halo paused. "...you are like me. You were meant for something more." She wished the situation could have been different, as she never enjoyed succumbing another being against its own will for her gratification. But it simply had to be.

Staghen witnessed the tender moment of the girl bonding with her new mare. It gave him quite a different feeling than when he caught Rikaana. His mind wandered fondly back in time to when Rikaana was a young colt that challenged Staghen, leaving the young captain fleeing for his life and running up a tree. He had been left there for hours while Radal simply laughed at the situation.

The former captain had told him in jest, "Now you really made him mad, young man! Well, are you going to come down here and be brave or am I going to have to send a bird to deliver your dinner to you up there?"

At that time, Staghen was to catch his own horse, but he would never subject Halo to such a thing. For one, Rikaana was an onisian stallion, and they were far more docile than mountaineer horses that had skulls built to ram and tempers hungry for freedom. Also, with her eyes, lack of training, and strength, she would have had her body turned to dust. No. She was his treasure to protect and guide now.

Leaning over the mare to examine any possible injuries, Staghen replied affectionately, "She now knows that at one moment in her life her herd family abandoned her. Prove to her that you would never be like this, and she'll learn to trust you. This is not a matter of heart but more a matter of trust. You see, the Guardians are riders of their horses, not masters. Like how your friend would carry you if you were injured, you must think of the horse as your friend. I am not

asking you to tame her wild heart. I am asking you to build a friendship with her. This mare will be the best thing in your arsenal of
training to bring Derjaun home. You'll understand."

Sadly, Halo could only agree. "Yes, Captain. I understand."

She brushed the strong neck and felt through the fur that was
purer than the snow of the winter. "I shall call you..." Her fingers
traced in admiration through the brilliantly colored mane of rich and
sparkling greens. "...Zidori."

"Zidori?" asked the captain with a tilt of his head. "Why, that's the
Gruic word for emerald."

"Yes, in honor of Derjaun. And it suits her mane and tail," Halo
concluded in her growing love for the new beast. She noticed the
horse was relaxed. "She's so calm."

With a slight cough and rising to his feet, Staghen spoke, "She is
fatigued from the run. We will stay here until she is willing to stand."

Halo turned her head and watched the captain return to Rikaana
to comfort him through any trauma or agitated muscles. Apparently,
the stallion was fine.

Her loving stare moved back to Zidori, whose kind, light eyes
were closing from the calmness that her hand offered.

"Zidori, you will help me find Derjaun, yes? With your speed,
strength, and spirit, I *know* you and I will be together forever."
Leaning her head over the mare's strong cheek, she firmly kissed her
new friend. "Won't we?"

And yet, deep inside of her soul, the despondent girl quarreled
with the most awful emotions. They had recently become so steadfast
to her life that she began to worry if she would ever find happiness
again before Derjaun's return.

The captain came over to encourage them both to stand,
informing her how to fashion the rope as a makeshift bridle about
the mare's muzzle and head. But with a laugh, he said the most
important fact of all, "We're not going to do this right now. It would
surely send her into a maniacal frenzy again. She won't like it on her
face, so patiently lead her with it about her neck. She's a herd animal
and will follow you as if you were her shepherd."

Halo looked at the horse, and surprisingly the captain was right. She loosely placed the rope around the horse's neck, and Zidori followed her.

The size of Zidori's hooves and frame made Halo realize how carelessly crooked she walked on her two feet. Many times she bumped into her four-legged companion, and more often than desired her toes were nearly crushed under the hooves.

"Halo..." Staghen began from the front.

"I know," Halo grumbled. "I need to walk better."

Once the horses were safe inside the small barn that was behind the captain's house and the two walked inside Staghen's home, Halo felt a rush of encouragement while the kiss of dusk brushed away the morning star's light. She would find her lost friend.

Inside, Staghen's home had been built out of burkold wood to give it sturdy walls, and together these walls made five separate rooms: a kitchen, a living room, a washroom, his bedroom, and an obvious spare room that was meant to accommodate guests who happened to stay overnight.

As Staghen led her through the living corridor to her room with only a candle in his hand, he said, "You will have your own room next to mine. This is your home now, but it is my house. I trust that you will adhere to every rule I set for you."

In the back of the house, she was stunned to see actual wooden doors instead of cloth curtains that were used to separate the rooms. She was not used to a wooden door being used for any other purpose other than the front entrance of houses. They came into the cozy room with a bed big enough for a full-grown man, a resting chair, a small wooden table by the chair, one window, an elaborate rug under the bed, and a pretty burkold dresser flourished with candles.

She rubbed her chin when she noticed that this bed, unlike hers, was raised on a wooden frame and significantly plusher in thickness. She raced inside as excitement swelled her head, and he spoke once again behind her, "But understand this, Halo. I am not your father, but I *am* your nurturer. So if you are ever frightened, hungry, cold, or any other emotions that may keep you, I am here. I also expect you to trust me all you can. The bond between you and I, as a bond of a Guardian and a captain, has little time to grow if your beloved friend is to be found."

She could not withhold her love for him any longer. She dropped her bags to run and throw her arms around his waist. "My Captain, you brought me hope, a reason to live." She continued to rub her sobbing face into his armor. "Rescued me from a miserable life, gave me a chance to prove I am worth more than just being a wife and also to walk where Derjaun should. I already trust you."

Staghen's heart eased from the cool air of the night, yet he felt her longing for more things in life. So deep in her heart did she yearn for things that Staghen could not give. He could only hope that one day she would find peace.

He looked forward in surprise and whispered, "I don't know whether to be more moved by the words you speak or by the strength of your hold."

Her face darkened until her green eyes moved up to see his, claiming the sparkling ambers of the candles' warmth in the room. She saw him smile, warming her heart in all the most endearing ways.

He tenderly pushed her off. "You must prepare yourself for rest. I will wake you early. I have to lead the night search now."

Fortune found Halo that night as her slumber was granted many blessings. Never had she slept so...*hard*. Her rest was so deep that one moment she was wishing to the stars for Derjaun's safety, and the next moment her bedroom door flew open. The crashing sound of wood made Halo jump out of bed. It was already morning, but it seemed no time had passed at all. She jolted frantically and tried to salute.

"I am ready to get up and to...uh, Captain!"

Staghen nodded his head in a slight smile in the doorway. "Hurry and prepare a simple breakfast. We head to Xoegell's soon for your armor."

"Did anyone find him last night, Captain? Please tell me something good this morning," she asked as she looked for her morning clothes.

Staghen turned so that she may dress in modesty. "Unfortunately, no. But during our time yesterday, you told me that he always wanted to go to the mountains, so as dangerous as it may be for my men, we spent some time last night formulating a proper search."

"Last night?" Halo inquired. "That means you haven't really slept, have you?"

Staghen remained motionless.

Halo dressed and moved over to rub his shoulder. "Thank you for your sacrifices you always make for us."

After breakfast, they prepared the horses and rode through the village together. Halo noticed all of the people staring awkwardly at her and Staghen. It was strange for them to see him riding with the blind young lady. Halo rode on through the attempts to ignore the repetitive gawks from the villagers, but she lifted her head high.

"Feeling prideful, are we?" Staghen asked.

"Is it that obvious?" she responded, looking about.

"Only a lot. You remind me of someone in this very moment. I can't think of who exactly," he fondly fibbed, "but it's someone of great importance."

They arrived, and Staghen gave several patient knocks on the door with leather-gloved knuckles. He knew that at this time of the dawn that the old man would still be sleeping, so he stayed patient. The door creaked open, and Halo saw the slouched figure of a gray old man.

He bowed and croaked, "Ah, Captain Staghen! My loyal protector. What brings yeh here this day?" He lifted from his bow, but drawing himself upright was difficult to do. "Oof." He grimaced.

At once, Staghen assisted him kindly. "Ah, you old fool. Always trying to push yourself too much."

Halo saw that he was missing several teeth and only seemed to have one eye, or he kept the other one miraculously closed all the time. Xoegell appeared to have a plump soul and wore his long white hair in a braid, unlike the other elders who let their tresses go ratted.

He also wore overalls made out of a durable fabric that contained numerous loops to hold his tools.

Old man Xoegell's eye popped open a bit more. "What tells you to bring a young lady to me?" he asked in a crunchy tone of dry age.

"She's Derjaun's best friend."

Halo swallowed uncomfortably when that big, bulging cloudy eye opened more. Although she could relate, she still felt uneasy at the sight that the poor man's one remaining eye could bulge so large.

The old man croaked, "The boy who's lost? Radal's son?"

"Yes, she has joined my men in honor of the Gruinelle family."

"But she is so tiny compared to your first-year boys!" Xoegell exclaimed after an invasive examination of the girl. "Isn't this the blind baker girl? Er, farmer girl?"

Staghen boldly spoke, "None of that matters, and so boldly spoken by a creaky old man with one eye and is the best armorsmith we could ever have. Besides, you haven't seen her stature next to boys her age. Her bone structure and muscled figure is more than sufficient."

She followed the two men with great attention for everything around them. The workshop was a mess of scrap metal, wooden mechanisms, windows that were quilted in dust, and a large oven that constantly fumed a bitter smell of hot metals. Halo sneezed from the disgusting stench and felt her lungs regret walking inside.

Despite the thick blanket of dust, the windows were letting the dawn light in, and Halo saw Xoegell pick up a step stool and place it before her. She held Staghen's hand when he offered it, and her foot reached out to find the stool. Her heart grew sad immediately, and she could not see the stool in the slightest. Not enough light had come in.

"Take time, my girl," Staghen whispered sincerely. "I will never rush you." Even though Staghen wanted to hide her blindness from Xoegell, there was nothing he could do about it in that moment. Instead of trying to hide it, he embraced his patience and under-standing for her.

The statement, although a calming one, was something she

would have to learn to truly find sincerity in. Enough times in her life she had been emotionally abused and deemed a burden to her family for the lack of eyesight she was cursed with. She knew that she was going to have to learn to trust the captain.

The stool was accidentally kicked over. With feelings of hatred filling her own heart, she swallowed her tears and heard the captain pick it back up. He said to her, "Don't weep over this. It's petty. Remember, I'll teach you to use the eyes you have. None other have I seen with the lovely emeralds you've been given."

"Captain, eh, if I may..." Xoegell began with what seemed like critical curiosity.

Staghen helped her by grabbing her ankle to place her foot atop the stool. She heaved herself up. How giving he was to help her. It was almost to the point of flattery and endearing.

"No, you may not, Xoegell. I have knowledge of the feelings you are feeling, and I do not wish to hear them. May you praise her for her poor vision," Staghen continued with slight shame for the old man, "for there are many young men who do not even desire to be a Guardian. Her spirit and courage exceed where vision fails. But even with this, she is now one of your protectors, and you must respect her as such."

The old man began pulling out a measuring tape and stretched it across her chest and noticed how strong her posture really was. Xoegell finally broke an awkward silence with a slight giggle. "I think yeh made a fine choice, Captain. Her armor will be ready in a few mere nights."

The captain rubbed his leather-gloved hand across his jawline with a smirk. "Thanks, old man. I believe so as well."

After a few moments of happiness, the jubilant captain turned toward her. "Now then, we make way to the training fields."

And so, with the early dawn finally washing the entire village in its glorified presence, the hero and the new Guardian rode toward the outer fields to the north. And there stood before her the beloved training grounds.

7

H alo saw horses tied to the outer fences and men in the fields. Heavy men that all had barbaric height, muscles, and brute force. They jostled as their swords shone in the sunlight and crashed into one another. Her nerves felt quite uneasy. Many times before Halo had watched the training days from her little room's window or perched on some faraway fence, but to see the strength and massive size of the men up close was something she would have to get used to.

"Halo, dismount with me," Staghen ordered.

Quickly, she obeyed the command. She was ready. She heard the one Gruic phrase she always wanted to hear so closely. Staghen roared the command that was used to simply get the attention of the Guardians.

"Kok aras!"

At once, the men began to gather in an orderly horizontal line, drawing Halo's attention. She looked to the left and watched heavy black boots slam together with a loud slap of leather to leather. And to the right, backs curved forward and heads lifted high, eyes cut straight forward, and swords sheathed abruptly. The large men had become absolute statues. Staghen began moving toward them, noticing she had not followed.

"Halo!" he called. She quickly caught up. They peeked at her as to not make their stares unwanted, and a few let out a moan of dry distaste toward what they saw. Halo could not see the confusion in their eyes like the captain did, but she heard the groans. Regardless, she remained firm in her spirit.

"Guardians, I'd be wary of moaning in disgust toward the presence of this girl. She can hear you better than you realize. She has joined the Guardians on my permission. But you won't treat her like a lady here."

Silence fell upon the entire cast of the Guardians, and she felt a little feeble about the "lady" comment. She associated the term with being perfect, proper, soft-spoken, and obedient. She had never been proud of Nakhanian customs of women never being allowed to serve in the Guardians as well as the traditional views of what a woman's role should and shouldn't be.

As she surveyed the men, she noticed one who easily stood out among the others and immediately knew he was a Guarada. He had long, fiery orange hair and a scruffy beard that was groomed to reveal his jawline, cheeks, brown eyes, and rich skin. With a round nose and an aged face, his size and build was all fierceness. All it took was one simple cough from him, and she recognized his timber of voice. Theidran was his name.

Staghen stepped forward with his hands behind his back. "Now, men, we all have joined the ranks of Guardians for many different reasons. Some of you desire to protect your family and your village. Others merely have joined out of the feeling of obligation. Her reasoning for joining will be respected. Her name is Halo."

Her nerves were as tense as a cattle rope. She thought about her friend, and when doing so the line of skilled Guardians became a mere house task to her. Everything in her life *must* seem simple now if she were to make it through.

"Halo," Staghen said to her, "when I call an order, simply do as they do. If your memory fails you, you will learn much faster this way, and the physical reaction will be quicker as well."

"Yes, Captain Staghen!" She saluted and went to fall in line at the far end.

A few of the Guardians chuckled, and one of them even said aloud, "Look at her! She saluted like one of us!"

Another chimed to his colleague, "That must be Derjaun's friend. Poor thing, she must be sick with worry."

Staghen had trained these young men to love and respect one another, and it brought relief to him when he saw that they seemed to accept her, even if it was tenuous acceptance.

She took her end spot, next to a beauty of a boy who appeared to be at least seventeen years in age. Perhaps this was the reason for his face having a more supple appearance than the others and a smile that would have made the pabi flowers melt. He had kind lips, pronounced cheekbones, and soft eyes that were slightly hidden underneath blond hair that had been loosened from the tie during the warm-up sessions. He glanced with blue eyes down to her. "Welcome. My name is Oniden."

She glanced in return with a calm look of uncertainty, yet she felt comforted inside. "Thank you," Halo murmured.

"For your knowledge," he secretly whispered, "we run first and—"

But before Halo continued watching him speak, her heart jumped at the sight of Staghen nearing with a tremendous cottonfell seed sack slumped over his shoulder. She pulled her head to look straight again.

"Oniden!" Staghen barked. "Are you giving cheats to the new one?" He laughed almost playfully and dropped the enormous bag in front of Halo's feet. Her eyes studied it. From the knowledge she bore of seed grinding, that bag seemed to be a twenty-kigo bag and would weigh almost the same as a small field goat. The young man nervously looked around at the others, who remained calm and quiet.

"I...eh...erm..." Oniden stammered uncomfortably. He looked to Halo and then to the colleague on his other side and gave a meek, disheartened laugh.

While the captain's eyes looked brusquely at the younger male, his hands pressed on his hips in impatience.

"Well then," began the captain in a light way, "since you will not answer me properly, young Oniden, perhaps I should give you..." Staghen leaned down to unfasten the ties of the bag and grabbed a fistful of seeds, "a reason not to speak. Open your mouth." Seeds were stuffed almost brutally into the windbag's mouth so tightly that they almost seeped through the tightly clasped lips.

The captain stood upright. "You are to train this day with these tiny seeds in your mouth. If you have little or none left by the end, you yourself, alone, will sow all the seeds in this bag, and the punishment shall proceed until all seeds are nestled. Is this understood? After all, the entire fleet of Guardians has an important task at hand. And we can't waste precious time with idle chatter."

Oniden nodded, and Staghen turned to speak so all could hear, "Yes, I have been known to begin your training with vigorous running around the entire village, but I am also a man who enjoys keeping his Guardians on their toes."

Staghen returned to tie the knot once again on the bag, and a feeling tugged at Halo's gut instincts, for she was the only one without the extra weight of armor. When the captain stood, she thought to kneel and grab it, but it would have been an action without an order.

Firmly, Staghen commanded, "Lift this."

And these were the only words spoken to her. The men found it difficult to avoid watching the girl attempt to throw the bag over her back, and yet to their surprise there was no spectacle of struggling to watch. The bag of seeds was effortlessly flung over her shoulder and situated perfectly across her shoulders and behind her neck.

The captain thrust his black tresses behind his neck and spoke loudly, "Had it not been for our new friend, Halo, upon whom I do not wish to bestow our usual routine, we would push on with other drills. Gale-meh la!"

That means attention to the right! she thought instantly. The Guardians turned their stances to the right, giving one solid sound of moving armor. Calming her nerves as the fabric of the bag absorbed her sweat, she braced her racing heart. The cloth slippers she wore were far from the stable boots that the Guardians wore, and even though she had worn them out with her work and walking all over Nakhan, she had learned the captain was full of surprises and probably had some reason for her continuing to wear them.

When the bag began to slip, Halo made a quick shift to fix it. Her mind tried not to question the duration of the coming task, but the captain kept them lingering in an idle position so long that her arms began to quiver, and the unforgiving heat of the sky frayed the nerves in her stomach. She saw Staghen mount Rikaana and draw his sword. "Okaya meh-la!"

Staghen had fooled his entire troop, for they were not expecting to run, but the order given clearly meant so. At first Oniden confessed they would run as usual, Staghen denied it, only to truly go through with the command. The entire fleet moved with heavy sounds of feet and booming masculine chants. Her spirit rose as she followed.

Halo's heart nearly burst at the voice, and she immediately broke into a run. Her feet were rather large for a young girl and well-calloused with many a hard day's work, but even still compared to the booted feet of the men hers were tiring fast.

The fields, as she knew, possessed many patches of lumpy dirt, soft pockets, and also holes from the burrowing of pabi mice that would be agonizing if stepped in carelessly. Sweat began to sting her damaged eyes, making it more unbearable to try to sharpen her eyesight, and with the bag becoming heavier with every breath her spirit became burdened with weight, as did her body. In the beginning of the grueling task, she was an assault of energy waiting to explode, but now she looked up to squint and saw the distance was growing from the others.

With this, she also saw the entrance gate to Nakhan, which meant she may see the widow and childless Agrona in the fields. A happy dream flowed throughout her mind that if she trained hard enough, a reunion with Derjaun would come, but this was not easy to do.

Determination had to be her closest ally now. Halo's legs carried her onward, and she closed her mouth in agitation to avoid letting the pain show. Before too long however, the men had left her far behind and out of sight. Now, the knowledge of where to run was unknown to her.

In between huffs and pants, an approaching sound of hooves came from behind, and all she needed was a glance over her shoulder to see the sight of a miracle. Or curse.

Staghen came riding to assist on the navigation. "Guardian, listen to my orders! I'll command your path. Do NOT stop. Separate your muscles from your mind! This pain is only in your head. You feel nothing!"

Oh, I do, she thought. But her mouth spoke differently, "Yes, Captain Staghen!"

The girl pressed on. Larger lumps of dirt began beating into her feet from the impact. The Nakhan entrance passed without a sight of Agrona, and now Halo was coming to the stream that Nakhanians used for their source of water. It was a kind and free-flowing child that was born from the Gigannora, a tributary. Inside the village, the land-savvy girl knew of a bridge for crossing, but her eyes wandered desperately in hopes of seeing one in the fields. Although the stream may come to her knees, it was the jagged and sharp rocks below that made her worry.

Staghen's vicious tongue lashed while the horse came nearer, "Halo, keep light on your toes throughout this stream. I'll force you through it!"

With his guidance and reassurance, Halo proudly conquered the stream without much pain in her feet, and surprisingly Staghen's commands felt more loving to her than cruel and dictatorial. More than ever, the girl trained her spirit to become unbreakable as she lunged forward up the steep hills, pushing her soul harder than Staghen pushed her body.

On and on throughout the burning sun's light Halo finished an entire length around the village boundaries, and when she finished the daunting mission a celebration of supportive comrades was heard upon her arrival. Why, for them it was no such issue to complete such a modest feat, but in their strong hearts they knew it was special for her.

Staghen, who still was mounted on his horse, corralled the girl with the rest of his men, but to Halo's disappointment he wore no look on his face that showed the slightest bit of pride for her. He had to treat her like all the others.

Lowering her head to stand with the rest, she knew that making the captain pleased would not be easy in the slightest. Mounted, Staghen strode down the line once more to study the group in attempts to catch any sense of fatigue, sweat, or panting. If no such display was given, one more circle around the village would be issued, and even Halo would have to follow. However, Staghen was no devil. Such a kind man would allow her to walk lest she became injured. Fortunately enough for Halo's nerves, he did not do this for too long.

A moment of excitement came again when the bag was able to be dropped off of her aching shoulders, and taking a deep breath of warm air Halo let it slip off with a loud thump to the soil.

The black horse approached her with a disturbing sound of the captain's voice, "Halo!"

She stood up at once, as if lightning shot through her back.

She moaned upon seeing an angry captain. His arms were crossed as hard as his face was scornful.

"If that were an injured child or another Guardian, or even perhaps a dear elder, would you act so carelessly? Answer me!" he ordered.

He may seem vicious, but he is nothing compared to what I endured at home, she thought. "No, my Captain, I wouldn't."

"You are quite naive to our ways, but you shall learn to connect every single task you do with what and who you are now," he spoke with authority.

Far too often, Halo was left without reasonings why some actions of hers were misguided and wrong. The only reason she ever heard was "because I say so." And this never made much sense to her. Captain Staghen scorned with reason. And he scorned with love.

Halo had learned quickly that all the men who were present, with only a few minor exceptions, were miklana, the lowest rank and newest Guardians, like she was. The galakhan, or the next highest rank, made up the few that were helping the captain train the lower ranks on this day. Theidren the brute and another man of his size were also seen wandering around. They floated amongst the sweating and laboring miklana like bees drifting from flower to flower. Halo truly was honored to see these few members of the guarada brigade.

The captain immediately ordered for a set of pushups from the ground, and the determined girl dropped to her stomach and did as best she could. Overhead, she heard his loud voice, "Halo, your eyes must always look ahead of you regardless of your position. This will help you to separate your eyes from your body. You would never look at your sword before swinging it, would you? Don't let your head hang!" With a bit of effort, she corrected her form, and he patted her back in praise.

She was the last one to finish. Staghen appeared in her trembling eyes and cleared his throat, "Up straight, Guardian. You finished without falling, great work. Guardian Halian will be your partner and supervisor." He simply turned away.

In their own part of the field, Halian showed her how to hold a sword by letting her use his. He laughed merrily when she could not even hold it with two hands. "Your body is tired beyond exhaustion."

She cared not, but upon looking around she noticed the other newcomers were using wooden staffs. "Why are the others using wood staffs?" She leaned down to lift the heavy weapon again and nearly felt bile in her throat. Her lips tightened in grotesque manners.

"You naturally have less muscle to work with. Thus, you must work harder. It shocks me that you are disgusted by this. I felt you to be proud of such an honor to hold a sword instead of a staff. After all, don't you enjoy a challenge?"

His smile of adorable taunts filled Halo, as if his friendly demeanor gave her newfound strength. She *did* love a challenge.

Proceeding, the wise Guardian helped her learn the parts of the weapon. How to use the hilt to pummel enemies into the face, double grips, and proper foot techniques. Why, the sword was so heavy that even holding it in the proper fighting position led her weakened body to drop it again. And stars forbid the attempt at replacing it in the scabbard. Of course, naturally, luck and destiny would have it that the captain walked by to examine her progress at that very moment. Yet she did not scurry. Halo exhaled loudly, sat upright, and calmed her nerves.

"How is she doing? Tell me, Halian," Staghen inquired.

Halian informed him that although her determination was set at a standard far above the reach of the skies and heavens, her muscles were incredibly weak. This was no news to the captain.

After this day of bonding with her colleagues, he would work with her personally in the beginning. Halo's eyes met with his, and in this she felt that same warmth of comfort. Everything was all right.

Despite this numbing exhaustion, Halo forced herself to complete the very first day of being a Guardian.

Later on, the blessed quiet and cool breeze of the night came, letting the sun rest beneath the mountains. Staghen looked to Halo, as on their ride home through the field she rested lazily on Zidori. Rider and horse had undergone an impressive training regimen that day, and Staghen knew that Zidori would find comfort in willingly following the only horse she now knew well, Rikaana. This brought a smile to him, and therefore the captain let her sleep the rest of the way home, only if she did not slip off and fall to the packed dirt below.

Once home was reached, the captain led the horses to the stalls behind his home. Then, being very courteous not to wake Halo, he slid his arms underneath her and pulled her to his chest plate.

For a moment, he held her as she relaxed like a piece of cloth contouring every muscle in his arm. Seeing her soft eyelids closed and allowing for once his own heart to smile, a broad sense of happiness came to his face. The blue eyes of his soul lit up and warmed with the glow of love so strongly he could have broken her bones with the pressure of his hug. Staghen never would marry, and yet he found himself utterly attracted to the idea of now having a daughter of some sort. Yes, he could leave a legacy with someone he knew would live on.

Carrying her inside, he laid her with the same amount of grace onto the bed that would soothe her achy back and let his hands flip his hair before using them to brush Halo's dark-brown tresses from her cheek.

Quietly, he lit the little candle in the room, and the golden hues softened the room. His look was solemn and calm. A peaceful night could do many things to a soul, regardless of the soul's absolute energy.

Whether an evil and immoral person or a heartwarming child, the stillness of the night's calm could bring many emotions to anything alive or even deceased. Staghen felt that the realization crept back into his heart when he had lost his family.

His mother and father had died from the same illness that plagued and claimed the lives of so many others when he was a little boy, and being an only child he had no one left but the elder guarada named Ishlog Cantin who lovingly cared for him like a son after Radal's death.

Staghen interrupted his thoughts to remember that Halo's feet would be blistered and swollen, therefore they would need to be massaged and oiled if she were to walk when she woke. He had learned as a young malakae that it was quite necessary to do it. But he never did it for himself.

As he rose from her side, the captain's face became twisted in confusion. Never before had he been the one to oil anyone's feet or muscles, not even his own. Many maids and maidens offered to perform the coveted task, but Staghen always refused.

Yes, he had the oils and the materials to do so, at least he believed he did. But the biggest concern was how to actually do it without waking her. And with how Lemson behaved in their home, he feared that if he touched her as she rested, she may assume a dreadful thought.

A soft knock came to the front door. Hastily, he moved out of the room as so not to disturb her.

The only time someone had ever knocked during the evening was with the burden of bad news. Remaining calm despite the alarming timing of the visitor, the captain trodded across the wooden floor with every intention of being prepared for anything.

He opened the door and looked upon a familiar face of a wealthy young girl, younger in age and stature than Halo herself.

Why, it was Jastin. On her usually meek or excessively animated face, she wore a look of distress.

"Lady Jastin? How can I help you this evening? Isn't it a little on the untimely side for you to be wandering around the pathways right now?"

The night had settled, he saw. For in Nakhan, it was worrisome for someone of her age and gender to be so careless.

"Captain, Halo wasn't in class today."

He gave her a reassuring smile, but as her eyes glistened in the little lighting of the torches outside, she had more to say. A brief pause came, and she felt saddened. "She told me she would be at Derjaun's side until he passed, but word is echoing all over the village that he disappeared, and no one knows where he is, nor has he been found. She did not come to me and tell me this, and now..." She put her hand to her unsteady heart. "I cannot find her."

The floral scent of the evening came with a soft breeze of cool air. Staghen crossed his arms and shuffled his feet in the same fashion the Guardians would do. This girl, he thought, seemed quite immature. His black brows went up. "And it is obvious to me that you have not gone to her house to question her family. You came to me first, correct?"

Jastin gave her usual little whine, "Captain, I fear her household and did not wish to bring worry to Aljen. He has many worries as it is." She shook her head in dismay, which did not move the captain in the slightest. "I did not want to trouble his early sleeping. Besides, I'm not supposed to be out this late on my own. I wanted to come to you for help."

She did not speak firmly, therefore Staghen believed she did not speak honestly. While his brows went higher, he glared at the rich Inner Circle girl.

"Am I to truly believe your feeble mouth? If you were to have come to me for your lack of bravery, which is really the truth, I could easily scorn you for lying. Besides, there are plenty of other Guardians walking around to escort you."

In a severe retort and to his surprise, her voice rose, "It would be an honor to receive a lashing of the tongue from you, Captain, than to see yet again what my dearest friend can never part with!" She placed her hand to her forehead. "These horrible things that she is forced by birth to call a family!"

She was dramatic.

"You have no reason to feel this way, and level your voice with me, young girl. Although you speak poetically compared to others your age, it's still a poor choice to ask for my assistance then speak to me like this. And Lemson is no longer there."

His stubbornness was about as high as her desperation, and she continued, "It does not mend the scars that stay behind, Captain. Are you aware of the scars that this life gives her? Scars that are so prominent that they reflect and show no matter what clothing she cloaks herself in, and they are there, plain as Radal's resting stone, for all to see. And yet you apparently do not see them!"

All he could do was laugh at her behavior. Although she was right, she was still *very* dramatic. "Come inside before the insects infest your hair."

Inside Jastin followed him about his home. Without looking back, the captain heard the racing feet and rolled his eyes with a grin. The sounds were noisy and clumsy. "Jastin, your feet could wake the dead if they were buried under these floorboards."

She bumped into a table. "Forgive me, Captain. I am trying to be silent. But what should I be silent for? You are the only one in this household, and yet you are awake. Right?"

Through the quaint rooms of handmade furniture and decorations of armor and weaponry, Jastin clutched her chest to admire them all. He signaled her to a door.

"She's resting in here," he answered.

"Oh, I see. Thank you." She smiled. "Now I understand why I was to be quiet."

Jastin's blood pushed to the surface of her skin with excitement to see her dearly loved friend. Usually she would greet Halo with an excitable tackle, but upon entering and seeing her friend sleeping, she changed her mind. Jastin let her hand graze the other girl's hair and softly spoke. "Halo?"

Halo lifted her head to look at the blurry figure. "Halo, wake up, my dear friend," Jastin cooed with a smile of softness. The room was dark and calm. Another friendly coaxing followed, and the figure became clearer to the sleepy eyes.

"Jastin, is that really you?" Halo asked as she sat up. "What are you doing here?"

"What am I doing here? You told me you would be with Derjaun until he passed, but he has gone missing, and you were not at school. I have been looking everywhere."

Now was the time for the new Guardian to admit the life-altering decision she had made. She sighed. "Jastin, I'm sorry I didn't tell you. I have joined Captain Staghen and his men in place and in honor of Derjaun."

To Halo's surprise, her friend wasn't angered. Jastin instead laughed loudly and clapped her hands.

Halo immediately covered her tender ears. Her friend could be quite loud and abrupt at times.

"Oh my, Halo! My heart flies for you. What a brave thing you did." She cupped her lips, wondering if her voice could wake the dead as well. Being quieter, she asked, "Was today your first day of training?"

"Yes," Halo said with a twist of soreness.

The sound of the door opening made both hearts jump. Seeing Staghen, Jastin adjusted her embroidered and jeweled cloak and fixed her hair once more.

"I was just about to tend to the new Guardian's feet, as they are raw and hot," he said with a hand gesture to light another candle.

Jastin looked at his thick and dark mane and beheld in love his beautiful blues. She swallowed hard for how the lowly candles lit the definition of his cheekbones, the area of his eyes as darkened and mysterious as his openness to those around him. It was the same reason she consistently complimented the beauty of her friend; it was very similar.

Jastin turned to him and saw he had no soft cloth to rub heated water or anything onto the feet that were brutally injured. Not a single thing he brought to the occasion could give some true comfort and relaxation. She spoke with a cautious firmness, "And you have no cloth for a comforting touch? You really think, my honorable man, that your hands of fierce strength that hold similar roughness would nurse such abrasions?"

He looked over to her. "I have none."

"Then with permission, please give me a few moments with a lantern so that I may go to the village."

He stood. "No, it's too late. There is her water bowl on the table by the chair."

Jastin hurried to the bowl. "It is her drinking water you wish me to use? As you wish." Jastin put her foot onto the chair and pulled a dagger from her thigh strap underneath her petticoat.

Staghen was shocked at what she had. "Jastin! You are not a man, nor do you have the training to possess that weapon."

"Captain, please calm yourself. I merely use this to help strip fabrics that I purchase from the Inner Circle for sewing. As you can see, it is not a carving or hunting knife."

She proceeded to cut off a well-sized portion of that lavish cloak.

"Jastin, you just ruined your night cloak," he said in astonishment. "What in the stars are you doing?"

"I am tending to her feet. I have been trained well for such things." She dipped the cloth into the bowl of water. "Although this should be hot, it is actually quite cool, which will help soothe her inflammation."

After Halo's feet were cared for, she fell asleep. Jastin rose and rinsed the cloth as best she could. "Now, I will have to see to your water rations. She should keep water nearby should she thirst in the middle of the night. Being worked so hard, she should drink plenty of water."

Staghen watched as she proceeded with the other duties. "Thank you."

Her eyes met his as he stood in the corner of the room. "You are very welcome, my dear Captain."

As she left the room to find his water rations, he subtly called, "Jastin?"

She turned in the doorway. "Yes?"

He paused and rubbed his knee. "Would you mind, if it is no trouble to you, could you tend to mine afterward?"

Her eyes became lit like all the stars in the heavens above. "It would be an honor." The girl was captivated in a world of wishes with this order. And yet she needed to replace the drinking water by the bed. "I will return with fresh water."

Staghen watched her leave, leaning against the burkold walls. He glanced at Halo's sleeping face to see if it expressed contentment or pain, and to his relief he saw nothing but a soft face of sleeping rest. He smiled.

The candle's warm glow soothed his soul while its flickers had cast away his concentrated look.

Although Halo was now at rest, Jastin had been told her work was not over. This did not bother her in the slightest, for she was honored in a self-evident way to be there. Halo and Staghen both had done enough for her and the village respectively that she felt it was a way she could recognize their sacrifices. She returned into the room and slowly poured the cool, fresh water into a new pot and placed it on the table by Halo's head.

While she did so, her ever-racing mind could not repress thoughts of how her friend's new life may alter their days. With this, she whispered quietly, "Staghen, I fear Halo's new role will change our friendship. Is this so? Please tell me." Her eyes looked to him.

Staghen answered casually, "It will change how often you see her, but her faith and loyalty to you is unbreakable. How often does this need to be told to you? You seem to have insufficient confidence in your friendship with her."

Jastin only lowered her head. Her personality was known to be both flouncy and sullen, excitable and reclusive. "Forgive me, Captain. I feel that Halo's blessings are my punishment. She always dreamed of something more, and I always had her by my side. Perhaps even when I could walk alone, I felt I never could without her. And I am so joyous for her, but now I fear my punishment for my lack of self-strength is loneliness."

Staghen stepped toward her, arms folded. He spoke to her with color in his tone, but his sense of sympathy was bare. "It is honorable that you feel this to where tears are nearly given, young lady. But you then must learn this isn't so, and if you find yourself weak, it's a punishment you breed for yourself. But enough of this. I'm growing weary and tired and still need my care."

Jastin had no choice but to leave the matter alone and continue in her honorable duty.

Staghen led her out and through the living room to his bedroom. Before he opened the door, he turned to her and said, "Do not worry about the placement of the moon in the sky." He turned the knob and pushed the door open. "You may rest with Halo tonight."

Inside his room, she noticed his bed was decorated with hand-woven quilts that seemed to have been purchased from the Inner Circle, and clothes were tossed about carelessly all over the place. Books were placed in a disorganized fashion upon his nightstand, and dust accumulated in every possible corner and surface. His tapestries were in need of being washed and pressed.

She had to ignore this though and be prompt in her work, as her sheylee had trained her. While Staghen undressed himself behind the changing screen, she attempted to contain her excitement and simply prepare for the task. Afterward, the young man emerged in his night garments and flopped heavily on the bed. He was exhausted. His eyes trailed up toward the wooden ceiling of the room.

For the first time in his life since his parents died, he was allowed to just be in the care of someone else. He melted into the bed. The delicate hands, so soft and plush, tenderly massaged away all aches he knew, and all he didn't know he had.

Jastin knelt on the floor by his feet and wrapped a cool, damp cloth around them. "These are lovely quilts you own, Captain."

His voice seemed to roll off with an airy tone. "Yes, they are."

She studied the quilt. What a lovely and intricate design it was. The border was solid royal blue in color, and the square patches were all of different shades of blue and white. She recognized it as a simple shepherd's pattern, and it was soft and plush to the touch. Suddenly her eyes jumped as she noticed a worn hole that was starting to tear worse. "Captain," she stammered, "one of your quilts is wearing a hole."

"All of my quilts and blankets are wearing many holes. The fabric was from several blankets of my youth, all of which my mother made."

She urged the conversation on while knowing of a way to see her friend tomorrow, the day after, and for a very long time. Her excitement of the plan felt uncontrollable as she worked her fingertips into the arch of his foot. "I am a skilled seamstress. If you allow, I would love to mend all the holes in all of your blankets for what you have done for both this village and for Halo," she stated brightly.

"Is that so?"

"Well," she concluded, "I mend clothes for the men in my family. I have not yet mastered the art of knitting a quilt from the very beginning, but I do believe that fixing these holes will be a simple feat. After all, if it's a family heirloom I'd be honored to fix it for you."

"That is a very kind gesture, Jastin. But I feel I will have truly helped your friend when we find Derjaun," he said with brute honesty.

Yes, Derjaun had been missing nearly three days later. On the way to the captain's home, she had seen a search party out in the fields, and while looking for Halo she overheard many Guardians saying that Derjaun could not possibly be in the village. Nakhan was a very small village, and it would not take but one day's time to do a full search.

"I am truly grateful for the work you have done, Jastin. I should do it regularly yet haven't the energy to do so." He smiled in softness. "My soles feel very well rested."

She attempted to lift her head to peer above the blankets to see his face, but she could not. Kneeling on the floor left much out of her sight, so it was a great thing he spoke with tones representing such honest emotions. "However," he started once more, "I think it is time for you to rest with your friend."

With this, the girl stood and simply lowered her head in respect. When she raised her head again, their eyes met. Still his hand slumped across his forehead as his nude chest rose and fell in breath. She noticed his constant fixed look toward the ceiling.

"Please take pride in yourself," she said. "You are a great captain, and you should not go to bed with negative thoughts."

She moved to his side. Upward she pulled the blankets to his chest and easily guided his hand away from his forehead and under the cool blankets.

With such care she gave him, he smiled up to her.

"Goodnight, Captain Staghen," said Jastin. "It has been an honor."

She blew out his candle and left.

He was left alone in his thoughts. He could not recall the last time he had felt such a calming nature from someone. For a moment a smile dazzled his lips. And then, with so much weight and feeling in his body, he rolled to his side to fall asleep.

8

The sun woke and shuttered its beautiful eyes to greet the world, painting the roofs of the homes and buildings in a brilliant orange. The flowers all over the village had opened up to welcome in the warmth and light of the warmest day of the year. In this wonderful morning, the two girls had realized their lives were now different. Most different was Jastin being forced to wake before midday.

Halo was already up and dressed when the captain quietly knocked and entered. He noticed Halo's expression was distant and empty.

"Did you not sleep well?" Staghen asked with a tinge of concern.

Her eyes looked downward, and she stuttered, "I dreamt of Derjaun."

"Apparently it was a dream that lacked happiness?" he asked.

"Yes, my Captain," she responded.

And with a turn to light another one of their candles, he spoke, "You have my pity. I'm sure it must be a heavy thing to bear. However, I assure you this. He will be found if we all work with intelligence and swiftness. Let's leave to gather your armor." And he left the room.

Jastin stood to comfort her friend as much as she could, "It'll be alright, dear one. Keep your spirits high."

The blind Guardian felt the much-needed embrace. But her eyes searched without happiness. "I'm sorry, Jastin. I just wish I knew why he left without telling me."

"You know why," Jastin began. "You always tell me that you hate being a burden because of your eyes, and sometimes you'd rather be left alone. He probably left because he too felt the same. But the longer you stay here and think, the less time you have to find him. Now go." She kindly nudged her friend on. "Go find him."

Halo fixed herself, knowing Jastin was right. But she couldn't refrain from asking as she adjusted her blouse, "Since when have you become so matured and inspirational?"

Jastin twirled to collapse in her romantic state on the chair. "Oh, you know. I got to massage Staghen's feet last night. Being around him kind of makes me straighten up."

"Oh, good grief," Halo laughed, looking up and shaking her head. "Well, I'll leave you to your fantasies, and I'll be back later on in the day." She turned to leave but immediately turned back to her friend. "If you stay here, don't break anything."

Halo left the room, and she and Staghen joined together quickly to ride to the armorsmith's home. It seemed that the lush pabi fruit of the orchards had welcomed in the fresh sunshine so much as well, as now they were being offered in the cartloads in the Inner Circle. The giant orange orbs were Halo's favorite fruit, as they were extremely sour and sweet, dripping with juice and a fleshy pulp. She pondered if she could exchange what money she had for any of them. When they arrived, it was the usual chatter about the missing boy and other common pleasantries. Xoegell took Halo inside of a different small room to help her put on her breast plate. Little did she know, outside Staghen paced nervously about, wondering if she felt comfortable being touched behind a closed door with a strange man. He could not get out of his mind how Lemson had treated her.

She heard his pacing outside the room and happily called, "I'm okay, Staghen!"

Staghen stood in the dusty little room. He smiled. "Come on out. I am eager to see you."

She peeked around the wooden door. She had planned on being cautious until Xoegell threw the door open to her side and rushed from behind her.

His hand was thrown to the air with much hubris. "Look at 'is feat I 'ave done, young man! Why, this is truly the best work I 'ave done!"

The captain stood and approached. There she was.

Precious lineum metal conformed to her growing body, gleaming with the engraved symbol of Nakhan across her chest plate: the head of a pabi cat. And oh how the leather of the top gleamed like the endless night sky. She could not tell if it was black or deep blue, but she was certain once outside she would know. The lineum metal did not cover her entire chest, rather it crossed from one shoulder to the underside of her opposite breast so that her growing feminine body would not be so restricted. And the oiled leather supported her breasts with verticle stitching. However, her favorite part had to be the metal buckles near her lineum spaulders that could hold a fur cloak, or any cloak of any kind.

The captain could not resist the smile growing across his face. He had to speak, especially to calm the uneasy appearance of her face. "Why, Halo. Look at you," he exclaimed with his hands outreached.

"Yes, yes, yes. Go on about meh work," Xoegell said with another wild hand gesture and a playful bow. "I did the best I could for such an extraordinary occasion."

Staghen beamed, "Yes, you have!" He shook the old man's tender and frail hand. "I will give you twice the pences for such an act of kindness."

As Halo turned toward the mirror to see herself in her new armor, her eyes focused to absorb the beauty of the brilliant silver. Her fingers traced alongside every embellishment on the sternum. Toward her waist, dark-brown leather pleats fanned around her hips. "Is this supposed to be like a dress, Staghen? I don't understand. You don't wear this."

"Haha," Staghen chuckled at her frustration. "It's not a dress.

Because you have hips, it helps allow your armor to be more viable for your frame. Is it too heavy for you?"

"No," she lied. "It seems rather light compared to the bag of seeds. Is this intentional?"

Xoegell walked behind her and took an old rag to polish it once more. "Eh? I crafted it wit de heaviest metals you could handle, lady. Staghen told me you'd be clashing wit men of brute force. So you do not die on first blow, I made it quite heavy while trying to keep your frame in mind. I 'ave never crafted female armor before. You are de first lady of de Guardians. I am honored to be a part of this."

Halo looked in the mirror. Behind her, the captain stood. He towered over her small frame, and how his face of sternness had bloomed into joy. He happily spoke the truth, "You truly seem suited for this line of work."

She saw herself. She saw a Guardian. "Thank you, my Captain. But I still think this looks like a dress, yet I can move quite freely in it."

He felt his gloves in her messy hair and added, "We can modify it later if need be. But for a young lady, it may be best at first. Your hair is unkempt. Brushed but unkempt. Do you not know how to dress your hair in braids?"

She shook her head. "No." She looked up and smiled. "But Jastin does."

Afterward, the two Guardians went through the village to the field. Zidori trampled the center's cobblestones as if to draw more attention to herself and her rider. Halo gripped the leather reins and lifted her nose to smell the morning dew, glancing to the shops that came from all parts of the quiet and narrow paths.

But the captain was privy to her somber look and attempted to lighten her spirits, "Halo, have some fun! Let her spirit fly!"

When Halo felt the wind's impact increase upon her face, she squeezed those legs and snapped the reins.

The Guardian girl's adrenaline lifted her emotions to the heavens above. "Alright, girl! Take us to the fields!"

She felt Zidori's explosion of excitement.

She felt free.

She felt weightless.

Although the young rider's skills were weak, this did not matter. She was one with a powerful being, united now with the powerful force of men, and felt liberated when she heard cheers from the farm folk. It did not matter to them why or how she was wearing the armor of a Guardian. It just mattered that she was. The girl lifted her left hand to wave in return when Zidori whinnied loudly. The pace of the animal quickened.

Halo looked and realized, as the sweat dripped down the underside of her breast plate, that Zidori was planning to jump the border fence.

"Ah! Zidori!" She pulled on the reins with all of her might, squeezing her eyes and face together in fear. "Zidori! Halt! Stop!" she screamed.

As the horse was closing in faster, the young girl saw an image of a broken neck, a fractured skull, a shard of wood through her stomach, anything of that sort that would predict her fate. Her fear battled the winning fight with her bravery.

Once more, she attempted to call in a bellowing state of panic, "Zidori, listen to me! Halt now!" The traumatizing realization consumed her, and her body froze and turned numb.

"Zidori, you're going to kill me!"

Finally, Staghen's voice came from behind.

"Halo! Arch your lower back and dig your heels into the stirrups evenly. Do not take your eyes off of the fence!" Rikaana raced forward behind the mare's hefty move.

"Staghen, I can't!" she screamed back in terror. Her voice felt lost in the wind.

"Do it!" His voice carried as much as he could let it from behind her. If she did not follow his orders, it could easily lead to her death or to the severe injury of her mare.

"I will tell you what to do! When she jumps, lean your upper body only slightly forward, and let your rear gently lift!"

Halo could not listen. She did keep her eyes focused on the fence, but unfortunately the approaching situation left her paralyzed in fear. Not one of Staghen's words did she follow.

A light crack to the neck from the force of the horse's leap threw her head forward, and from there Halo was unable to do anything with her legs to protect herself from falling off. Her body went weightless and smacked the ground as the sound of the armor clanked in her ears.

The sound of her horse got fainter and fainter as the animal left her rider behind, mangled and hurt. She lay there for a moment with stings of pressure speckling her back and feeling their ugly way to her head. It never occurred to her that there would be a possible chance of falling off, that it would hurt so badly, and never would she have attempted to jump that bestial mare—ever. Forced to look only upward, Halo saw the beautiful blue sky that was painted with the wisps of the white clouds. Her hearing remained useless as the frightening incident left her in shock. Could she hear someone mumbling beside her? She did not know. The sky was too beautiful to care.

She tried to listen, but a large-snouted black horse came into her vision and looked over her, snorting his breath to blow away the hair that was strung across her face.

"Halo!" Staghen exclaimed as he dismounted and knelt to her side. "Do not move your head or your body. Just answer me with descriptions. Do you understand?"

She murmured with tears, "Yes."

The captain began checking her head, nose, and ears. "I'm making sure you are not bleeding anywhere. Can you smile for me a little?"

She attempted to show her teeth.

"Alright, no broken teeth. Remain calm." He waved his hand across her face. "Good, your eyes are responsive. Do you remember what happened?"

"I...I fell off my horse."

Staghen gently placed his hand onto her. "Very good. Can you move your fingers and toes?"

The caring demeanor of the captain carried on. Once Halo moved her fingers and toes and after a thorough examination, Staghen gently assisted her in sitting up.

"Well, you definitely had a hard fall, but nothing other than some severe muscle strain is what I see." He glanced up. "Let's be gentle now. Your horse is coming back for you."

Although her bones felt bruised terribly, she rolled over to her hands and knees and was ready to be angry with the mare. But she quickly calmed herself, knowing kindness would be better than hostility.

However, she did grab Zidori by the bridle when the horse's head bowed to her. She spoke to her wild friend, "How would you like it if I tossed you off a cliff?" She took a deep breath. "You need to be gentle with me. I'm learning like you, but I promise I'll be skilled enough to ride you the way you want to run. We need to work on our listening."

Without wanting to waste any more time, Halo fought the soreness in her body and allowed Staghen to help her onto the horse once more. "Halo, I have to tell you," he began as he helped her feet back into the stirrups.

"I know," the girl said with a low head, "I should have listened to you."

He looked up to her as he placed her feet back in the stirrups. His eyes were very purposeful. He calmly spoke, "Yes. I can't lose you. You are a Guardian, and you *must* listen to my commands. You could have been killed. And as sore as you may be, you will continue with training today. In battle one day you may fall off your horse, and should an enemy be near you must be able to push through the pain to do what is right. Understand?"

He was genuinely worried. Of course he had witnessed Halo's tragic fall with his eyes, but in his heart he had felt it. He wanted to express this, yet he could not tell the girl how much fear he had carried when he saw her hit the ground. He must remain confident and guiding.

She nodded. "I'm sorry, Captain. I will do better next time."

"There may not be a next time. Make it your first and only time."

With this acknowledgement between the two, Staghen pulled himself atop Rikaana. "Alright, let's go."

He gently tossed the reins, and Zidori followed Rikaana with an easy, steady walk until they reached the fields. Captain Staghen dismounted, called for his men, apologized for being late, and informed them all of Halo's incident. Not one seemed to mind. They all stood quiet and respectful while Halo carefully dismounted Zidori, who nickered at her as if to ask if her rider was alright. She walked to fall in line, attempting to hold her back upright. Even though Staghen said everything was fine, her back felt otherwise.

He announced the Guardians would be tested that day based on strength and divided them to follow an appointed guarada. Halo heard the guarada she was to follow was Ishlog and seeing him in person was just as righteous as it was to hear his name, for he was the one who cared for Staghen after Radal's death. He ought to be a kind man.

Out in the field, Ishlog spoke with a deep grumble from his lips, "Halo, Veneal, Nikolag, Lessi, Destin. All of you, follow me."

Halo began moving forward, but an unkind shove from another made her stumble. Immediately her eyes fought to see the man who would do such a crude thing. The blond man turned back to face her.

"Blasgardiget, Halo."

His laugh was simply the weakest and ugliest thing she had ever heard. Like a mockery of some shadow of disgust. She had never heard that language before and therefore could not properly retaliate. But she must think of something. Regardless, she snapped her attention directly to him.

"Your ugly face is unfamiliar," she sneered back to him. "Are you really intimidated by a girl so much you have to shove her and insult her in no common language?"

Halo had so many lessons with such a tormentor that this was hardly a thing for her now. She ignored the soreness of her body and hurried to lead him off. She refused to have just earned her place only to have to fight for it now. "I truly hope, young man, I fight you."

"For stars above, you blind grot, stop calling me 'young man.' It's Nikolag. Can you not hear it in my voice?"

She immediately turned to shove him back to where his gait was halted. "How am I supposed to learn the names of a hundred men in a day or two?"

He snarled and yanked her hand. "Place your dirty little fingers on me again, and I will break every knuckle you have. You should be baking bread, not wearing armor."

He was a man who must have been at least eighteen years of age, standing tall in his tanned skin with blue eyes. His face was well-formed and framed by a crown of blond tresses that he kept back in a hide band out of his face.

Their eyes burned toward each other with rivalry of the mountains feeling the crushing waves of the ocean.

She let her pursed lips open while her eyes narrowed. His nose was scrunched in disgust at her. She said, "Fine, I hope I fight you, *Nikolag*."

He pressed his forehead painfully into hers. Her head felt the soreness of the horse accident being amplified, yet she refused to show such things to him.

He asked lowly, "Why's that, girl?"

"Victory will taste much sweeter when it is over you," she shot back.

Flames burned inside him from the girlish taunt. His eyes widened, barely able to contain the desire to throttle her. The guarada, who was now hurrying back to them, called in a deep and dissonant voice, "Young Guardians, you shall learn that victory is only so sweet when it's over your own jealousy and pride!"

"Oh, I have none of them, Ishlog," Nikolag said in his ever-demeaning way. "Only the will to see if this little grot can really handle walking with men."

The sun burned from the high eastern direction, yet it was suddenly shadowed by that moronic male again. He simply laughed at her before turning to leave. "It'd be wise not to tighten your jaw now, Halo. You may need that strength to bite me."

"Oh, is that so?" she called out with her arms crossed. "I have more strength in my fists than you do in that stupid mouth of yours. And why do you refuse to tell me what language you use?"

She narrowed her eyes, following behind. His stride was stomping, hard and long. The boots he wore, Halo saw, were old and worn with many little objects fastened to them. Her eyes could not understand what they were, but they seemed fun to look at. It was the only thing on him she cared to look at. The rest of him was filthy, and he smelled like old sweat, dirty feet, and ulgg.

All of the trainees stopped in a line while Ishlog moved to the front and turned. "This is the field for fighting. The rules are very simple. You each will be paired with someone. Your enemy will show no mercy of their size in comparison to yours. Yet do not underestimate the courage, wit, or speed of someone smaller than you. This is fighting without the use of a weapon. So, everyone, remove your armor."

Every one of them were relieved with the ability to remove their armor, thus removing extra weight that retained excess heat. Once they all were free of the burden, Ishlog spoke once more, "Halo and Nikolag, please step forward."

Halo confidently walked forward and tossed her hair away from her face and Ishlog asked, "Why, you seem to hold no tension or fear. Tell me why."

"One should never hold fear with the attempts of putting a nuisance in their place, sir."

"Haha! Did you hear that, Nikolag? She threatens you," Ishlog responded.

Nikolag placed a hand upon his hip and approached for the fight. He smiled and shook his head. "I heard her. Loud and clear. Unlike her, I wasn't born a defect."

"Yes, you were. Being rude is the greatest defect. I have love and friends. You, Nikolag, will wander this world alone because of your ridiculous antics toward your fellow men," Halo said grimly.

Ishlog interrupted, "Alright, you two, I can see this is going to be quite the training session. Now both of you face each other while I pair up the others."

They waited. An eternity seemed to boil between the two.

Ishlog called, "The fight will be until one man cannot stand! Now, fight!"

In the blink of a weakened eye, the girl saw a powerful fist heave into her face, knocking her back. Halo stumbled with feet dancing backward, realizing she had been punched hard. The pain in her neck had doubled. She tasted blood on her lips, and when the numbing turned to pain, she opened her eyes to see Nikolag enraged with fury and readying to throw another near-deadly hit.

"You're stupid to be here!" he growled as he lunged at her.

Once more she was hit with a force more severe than the last, but Nikolag stopped when she looked like she may fall. When her body fell to the ground, the intensity of the noises around her grew heavier.

The other Guardians had suddenly frozen in their actions to shout the match onward.

All except Oniden, who moved other men out of his way and, to his horror, saw the girl with a bloody face stricken to the ground. "Ishlog!" he yelled. "You must stop this madness! She's a blind girl! What are you doing pairing her with him?"

Ishlog held his hand to silence the men.

There was a method, a reasoning behind this. It was Staghen's orders to have such an event. Halo saw those decorative boots before her in her vision. As the heels turned, she finally could make out the embellishments of those beautiful ornaments dangling inside of his boot ties. How beautiful they were. They were of things she had never seen before, yet oddly they felt familiar to her.

But the cold lashing of Nikolag's voice came, "Get up!" He circled her. "You blind grot. You're not getting up because you know it's useless for you to be here. Your stupid friend is dead, and you know it!" he spat.

He kicked so gruesomely that her body rolled to the other side in pain. And the proud man turned with his hands in the air to the others and the roar of praise feeding his ego, or so he believed.

Nikolag turned to Ishlog, and he angrily demanded, "Pair me with another. This grot isn't worth it. Oh, I mean *whore*."

Ishlog smiled, pointing a finger to indicate Nikolag should turn around.

In an instant, he looked over his shoulder.

Halo was standing.

"How do you know he's dead, Nikolag? Did you kill him? Found his body? Or like a coward, you're trying to make me mad. Well, I have something to tell you." She spat her blood out again. "As you threaten me, your fear of me is beyond my fear of you."

She pointed toward him and raised her voice, "Speak about him like this again, and I don't care about the punishment. I'll kill you myself. This fight is not over!"

Nikolag's lips curled so hard he nearly bit them. And he charged.

But this time, Halo kept away from his outrageous and out-of-control swings. Keeping a good distance between them, she could see he was very clumsy on his feet. She also was able to tell that her hits would not even faze him. Trying to stay away, her intellect kept on trying to feel how she could win.

Nikolag followed her everywhere. He was like an enormous, hungry animal that appeared to have a thousand arms. She was beginning to lose herself. Her body was tiring trying to avoid him. However, as the man breathed hoarsely and attempted to crash down on her, it dawned on her that he was becoming slower. She bound away with a chance in mind that she could win.

"Come at me, you grot! You call *me* the coward!" he hollered at her.

She let him charge once more, but this time she dove, rolled out of the way, and got up to run away again, leaving the attacker confused. Her tactic was working. The Guardians nearly fell about laughing, for it looked like Nikolag was chasing a kaku bird he couldn't catch. She looked at her surroundings. In the field, there were knolls. As many times as she watched the Guardians train from her window, she had learned that being aware of their surroundings and using them to her advantage was a must. The boots Nikolag wore were heavy, and surely climbing up a steep hill would be a challenge.

With the last attempt to wear him down, Halo scrambled up that hill. With all of her might, she crawled and moved upward as fast as she could.

"Oh, running away, I see," Nikolag tormented. With this, he pursued with a drive unmatched by any other assailant.

The top of the slightly challenging slope was nearly at hand while her heart was pounding into her jaw. And to her glee, the top of the hill arrived. She felt a cruel snatch of her ankle.

Nikolag had her. "You little witch. I got you!"

She rolled over onto her back, panting hard, feeling his nails digging into her calf.

And there was her perfect shot.

As hard as she could, Halo used her leg to swing it into his head with blunt force. At once, the blond man was knocked senseless, his head hit so hard by her boot that his jaw clacked, his vision blurred, and his grip completely loosened with his body softening in tension.

The other men cheered for her, even though they were supposed to be training themselves. Captain Staghen had allowed everyone to view the spectacle. He circled around the field, watching Ishlog's supervision as the fight carried on. He himself wanted to see how she behaved naturally when assaulted. Nikolag's grim and dirty approach to fighting brought out the best, or worst, in Halo.

Halo had fled up the slope and quickly turned to see that Nikolag was not moving the same. He held his head and attempted to stumble to his feet. And while he did, the other men roared for her to continue to attack him while he was weak. But Halo felt differently. If she fled down toward him, she could easily risk putting herself in harm's way again. Instead, she would let him stumble up to her, allowing him to waste more energy while she regained hers.

She spit blood again. She was ready.

She raced down to him, and out of Halo's lips came a deafening screech of anger. While Nikolag was trying to prepare, she leapt onto him, taking him down to the ground hard. Down the hill they rolled over and over each other until she landed on top. With every bit of her strength, she closed her fists and bludgeoned the man in the mouth, eyes, and nose as hard as she could. And yet it seemed through every hit his unkind eyes looked to her. He had been hit far harder than she could ever dream.

Suddenly to Halo's shock, she felt her body lift, and at once she was tossed onto her back with his hips crushing in between hers. But worse, his hands went around her throat. His hips thrusted again and broke her thighs further apart. She felt him. He snarled tightly at her. "Stop struggling and get used to a man on you!"

Staghen began to come closer, watching worriedly.

She had to act, because no one was stepping in to help. Allowing her airways to be closed harder, she removed her hands from his wrists, grabbed a lock of his hair, and completely ripped it out. The tearing sound was met with his yelp of pain, and Nikolag climbed off her, feeling his bleeding bald spot.

"You vile witch!" Away he crawled on hands and knees, but he was not left alone for long.

Gasping, she jumped onto his back and wrapped her legs around him. Her arms squeezed around his neck as her heels dug into vulnerable places in his midsection. At this moment, her face was clenched in the back of his sweaty hair, and she would have rather died than let go. He attempted to crawl, reaching his hands around, but she was like a tiny insect he could not reach. Choking, his face was turning blue. The men screamed for her. And it was then she heard Staghen yell, "Halo, release him!"

Her body rolled off as he fell to the ground gasping and holding his severely injured head. She did it. Her eyes looked up toward the beautiful blue sky. Her diaphragm bobbed up and down. She felt as though she may vomit.

As she was barely able to catch her breath, Nikolag's bloody face appeared above her. They looked at one another. She had expected some sort of dialogue to take place between them, yet none occurred.

Instead, he simply stood up and walked away. Utterly, shamefully, and despicably defeated.

She had won. She had defeated her very first opponent. Or had she really? Everything in her body felt in critical condition. With nothing else to give, she called for Staghen, her nurturer.

"Captain," she cried, "please, I can't get up. My body's giving out on me." Her weakened eyes searched the fields desperately for him. "Staghen, please. I can't see you. Where are you?"

Staghen heard her call and immediately hurried to kneel down, and her whole body became limp in his strong arms as he lifted her. "Congratulations, Halo. You won."

Her eyes watered. "No," she groaned heavily. Staghen expressed his confusion, and she finished saying with a hard breath, "If he continues to be so cruel, I haven't won. And there is no victory in death." He lowered his eyes to her and looked intensely, as if searching for her thoughts. Tears came to her with this as she breathed again, "Or am I to be trained to believe there is?"

"I will speak on this matter later, but for now, young Halo, you must willfully claim your victory over the fallen. As I can see, it was not an easy one."

Staghen turned to the others. "Guaradas, please continue the training without me as I take her to Dr. Crenon. I will rejoin you later."

And to the Inner Circle, their horses followed as the captain carried her the entire way. Her body was too damaged to ride any horse.

Needless to say, Halo had a very hard day.

9

She grumbled in soreness, feeling the sway of the movement. "I don't know if the fall or the fight hurt worse."

"Nonsense," the captain said. "I was testing you today. And I must say, you exceeded my expectations."

She chuckled weakly and flopped her head back again. "I bet you weren't expecting me to be tested by Zidori though."

As he continued to navigate the village, his kindness showed with a smile of his handsome, young face.

"True! But I deliberately placed such expectations on you, knowing you would break before the first part was over. And the reason is simple. I needed to break you to see if you would give up because of the pain. And if you did, how you would react. If you searched for sympathy despite giving up, I would not take pity on you, and my anger would easily rouse. However, if you felt disgusted with yourself and placed scorn upon your *own* heart, I would easily see that you were self-sufficient and truly desired to learn and work hard.

"I have little time for those who search for praise despite failing. I don't cast hate upon you for leaving training early. Your body is young and can only tolerate so much. However, you *did* win. And for this I give you much praise. Your character showed strong today. And I am vibrant with happiness to say that I feel Radal's blessing in knowing I made the right decision in allowing you to join."

Her whole mind melted as her head fell back into his bicep. Her heart was content. "Thank you for carrying me."

He lifted her closer to his eyes and his voice was deep as the stable soil below them. "Know this, Halo. I will always carry you. In one way or another, I am here for you. I will push you to and over the edge of pain and sanity. But it is home that I will always carry your broken soul and body. With me, you are safe."

There was a happy silence that fell between them. The silence carried on for quite some time as Halo's heart steadied. Her body felt peaceful.

The warmth of the morning star was still unforgiving on all it touched, and the villagers cleared the path for the captain.

Halo's voice broke the gentleness of the day, "Captain? Instead of taking me to Crenon, could you please take me to Jastin's home instead?"

His face nearly stumbled with the confusion of what face to show. "Why? You are injured and need medical care. You can visit Jastin afterward."

"You see," she answered, "Jastin comforts me. She used to rub my muscles and heal my wounds from my heavy days of farming and field work. And she's very good at it."

"Well," he laughed heartily, "I don't believe you truly sustained traumatic injury. If it's your wish, I'll do this instead. I will take you home and have a Guardian bring Jastin to you."

Halo nodded. She was thrilled to be able to see her friend again. It would comfort her to feel the soft, gentle and familiar hands of care instead of those of rough examination. She believed she was exhausted and sore, nothing else.

Staghen continued to walk, but his soul grew sad from a sudden thought. Winter was a difficult season to get through, and a cooling breeze that brought forth a much-needed break from the damaging heat came from the north, indicating the seasons were going to be changing. In the winter, the winds blew hard with icy bites from the Castonuje Mountains, food became scarce, and the temperatures dropped in severity that left even the healthiest in fear.

All of this meant that Derjaun needed to be found. Time was running low.

The women of the village were adding new goods to their quilt shops, and Staghen took great note that they were becoming thicker in fabric. The Guardians were assisting women in their duties and making small talk with the farmers, who were busy selling the final goods of the day. All seemed well.

As Staghen was nearing his home, a Guardian began approaching him with light steps so as not to wake the girl who was now sleeping in his arms. "A good evening to you, my Captain."

"And to you, Vathra. Please walk along my horse, as I must get this tired girl home."

The malakae Vathra, quick with obedience, followed next to Rikaana.

"I was to believe you were not claiming this girl as your own," Vathra lightly said. He shifted his blood-colored hair behind him more.

"Your belief has been falsely born, Vathra. She is mine to love, to guide, to teach, to protect. But I'm not her father. But this is not your reason to speak with me." Staghen turned to his malakae with a smile.

Vathra responded instantly, "No, Captain. I have come to tell you that Derjaun's learning material was found near his home. But not inside."

Staghen stopped the horses as his own pace halted. "Did you check the belongings with Ms. Florn?"

"Yes."

Staghen stopped at his stoop. "And the condition of the material?"

Vathra answered promptly with his head erected, "Dusty with the pathway's dirt all over it. I'm assuming this may mean he was taken."

Staghen shook his head and repositioned the sleeping girl in his arms. Even he was growing fatigued now. His instincts brewed a better and more educated assumption. "No, Vathra. I have spoken with Agrona, who forced him to school when I sent him home to stay in bed." He took a deep breath. "I firmly believe Derjaun ran away."

Vathra's voice grew in concern. "Then he is not in Nakhan, sir. Your men have searched every villager's home and have questioned everyone. We have even searched the furthest regions of the fields that we can within safety of your orders and boundaries. I am regretful to say that—"

"Then do not," Staghen interrupted. "I believe your words, Vathra. The boy is not in Nakhan and has fled the village himself. If I let my position lead me to believe I am always right, the boy will never be found."

Vathra gave a sigh. "What are your orders?" he asked with a tired face.

Staghen looked about the village square and for once he had to think longer than a moment. "Take your team to the fields. But first, I must humbly ask you to make your way to the house of Jastin Henson. Halo requests her presence in our home tonight. After this, you shall comb the fields from now until dawn. When the morning star breaks, you and your team will rest. Search in the forest if you must. And please be cautious. When your men return, I will take another team to search even further. Even if I have to take a formal search party and be gone for days, so it will be. He is sick and weak, so with any luck he will not have gone far. But please bring Jastin here and gather your men. The boy will be sleeping soon and will be stable. Make the quickest movements toward the mountains. I feel that is his desired destination."

Vathra bowed his head and hustled away to gather his men and perform the simple tasks given to him, leaving Staghen alone again with only his somber thoughts to keep him company. It was difficult for him to remain calm.

Inside, he laid Halo in her bed while the horses allowed themselves into their shelter. Something then crossed his mind's flow of thought.

Jastin was right.

The night before, she had spoken to him when she was rubbing his feet. Perhaps he should bring her to stay. As he moved to cover Halo's resting body, a stirring sound came from his horses outside. He looked out the window quickly, pulling the curtains aside. There she was, the eager Inner Circle girl. She was pouring water into the trough from a bucket and proceeded to give hay to the stallion and mare. He chuckled both in his voice and in his heart. Quietly, Staghen lifted the window and whispered abruptly, "Jastin?"

Her head turned in alarm. "Oh! Staghen, I'm so sorry. I felt horrible about approaching you so late last night, so I thought I could help by tending to the horses." She rose from the dirt to approach the window.

Her dark eyes looked up toward him while he folded his arms on the pane and looked down. "My young lady," he greeted her as he folded his arms on the window, "I believe we need your services tonight."

"Yes!" she whispered loudly. "As you wish, Captain."

Staghen smiled as he watched her disappear to the side of the house to come in through the front.

The moments passed, and the night was well into its darkest hours when Jastin found that she was needed in Staghen's home. From tending to the horses, soothing Halo's pain, and now gathering all of the soiled clothes from around the room so that she could take them to be washed tomorrow morning, all of this was a lot of work. But it was work she loved. No, she could not stare adversity in its cruel and ugly face, but she could wash clothes and cook for those who could.

Her heart felt joy as she sat in the chair in the corner of their bedroom. Her hands were raw and sore, and fatigue filled her muscles, but she was truly happy. It worried her mind what Halo's body may feel like that next morning, but it would be her duty to rise anyway. It was more peaceful in the low-lit room, and it made Jastin all the more tired.

A knock came on the door. "Come in, Captain," she answered with a soft hush of her voice.

He only allowed his head through the opening of the doorway. "Jastin, please come out here with me. I desire to speak with you."

Since she was too exhausted for fantasies, she fixed her dress and stood to walk out. "Yes, Captain."

She was calm, collected, and ready to listen to him.

He turned to talk to her and crossed his arms. "I feel I may need you to mend my blankets for winter. As you know, with our bitter climate, the summer vanishes almost as soon as it comes."

"I could have that done by midday tomorrow, Captain."

"Thank you, I appreciate that. And what of my siloks?"

She tilted her head. "Siloks, Captain?"

"The clothing we wear under our armor. It looks like you had gathered Halo's for her and put them in her wash basin. Could you extend the same kindness to me and have them washed and ready sometime tomorrow?"

Yet again she responded a little dryly, trying to hide the excitable lump in her throat so large that she could have choked on it, "The same, Captain. I could have them done the same as Halo's, if it is your will."

She would rather be a slave to him than a wife of some boring village wretch.

Staghen focused deeper into her eyes. "And what of meals? Is this something you could do for us as well?"

Obediently, Jastin gave immediate affirmation, "They would be freshly hot and ready for when you and she return after training, Captain."

At once Staghen grabbed her wrist with such assertion and force she thought she had surely angered him. There was nothing she could have done to receive such treatment. Regardless, she felt fear. His voice grew in temperament with her spineless behavior. "Jastin, listen to me. I don't want to force these things on you. I want you to —" He suddenly felt her pulse quickening in her wrist and noticed her eyes widening while she looked away. "Jastin, look to me."

"I can't. Please continue," she pleaded.

He saw her jaw clench, and she was beginning to withdraw

herself physically from him. "Why do you act like this?" His other hand placed itself on her small upper back to try to coerce her closer. "I would never hit you. But, Jastin, you are acting like a slave to me right now. I want you to *want* to be here. By love, not by force."

"Yes," she fumbled while her nerves settled. "I give my sorrow if I have angered you, Captain. I assure you it will be out of love." Her eyes felt brave enough to look into his. "I want to make you and her happy."

"My happiness is devoid of all gold if it comes at the expense of yours," he assured. "You can even bring your uana here and play it for us in the evening. It would bring both Halo and I solace. I don't want to own you. I want you to live here, happily so."

He finally saw her shift with a mood change so desperately needed. She grinned so hard her young cheeks grew sore. "Yes, of course. I would love this."

The next morning, Jastin surprisingly woke before Halo, and since the young girl had never cooked for Staghen, it took her a long time to find any type of cookware. She carefully maneuvered over the perfectly polished wood floors and the lovely burgundy rugs so as not to wake the captain or Halo. The hefty iron of the wood stove caught her attention, and knowing how to use one, she peeked behind to see if he had any wood to make its fire. He did. "Oh, this is good to see. But it won't do me any good to make a fire without pots to cook with."

He had no such necessities in his pantry or cupboard, so Jastin glanced to the left corner of the floor. There they were, piled in the enormous wooden wash bucket with old food stuck to them and smelling of stagnant water. They smelled like they had not felt the cleanliness of fresh water in many days. "Ugh, *vradva*," she exclaimed while pinching her nose. It was a simple word of disgust her family language used for things that smelled rancid. As she clamped her nose, she began looking around for an extra washtub that she could go fetch water in. Despite all of her attempts in another search, none was found.

A sound of heavy, slow footsteps came from behind her, causing her alarm. She turned. No one needed to see the captain to know that it was he who came. His pace was obvious to all. His nightshirt was hanging loosely around his collarbone, and his clothes were in desperate need of ironing. And from the grime on his shirt, Jastin could have believed he actually *slept* in his siloks. His hair was also tangled in its untied hanging around his chest. This was a far different look than what she was used to, for she usually saw his hair well-oiled with black jinfish oil, pulled back tightly and adorned with jewels.

He spoke, seemingly calm but confused at Jastin's rummaging. She was scooting yulan marble kettles around on a shelf. "What are you doing, Jastin?" he asked with a hefty yawn.

She was quick to answer, chipper in tone, "A wonderful dawn to you, Captain. I am in need of fresh water so I may wash your stoneware. I need clean things to work and cook, you see." She gestured to the days-old filth. "And when in the stars above was the last time you dusted all of these beautiful yulan kettles you own?"

He laughed and rubbed his nose in an attempt to wake up further. "I haven't the slightest recollection. But we'll go to the river together for water. Let Halo know."

Jastin gulped as her body clenched with love. "We will be riding together, I assume?"

Once more, his large arms folded. "Yes, Jastin." And since he took her statement as apparent fear, he consoled her. "Do not be afraid. I will be with you on the horse. But make fast paces. I need to see to my Guardians soon."

All Staghen could do was to think about his words with Vathra. He had hoped his wishes and hard work would bring Derjaun home, but his heart knew he would not know until later when he could actually speak with Vathra again. His sore hand rubbed his chapped lips, and he began pacing about. He had felt a wreck lately.

Inside their room, Jastin attempted to wake her friend. "Halo, my dearest, wake up," she called, leaning over her snoring friend and gently nudging her.

Halo's eyes opened with a disgruntled sound. She stared in confusion. "Jastin? Is this you? I can't see your face, but I hear you."

"Yes!" Jastin stated merrily. The young maiden lifted her friend to sit. "How do you feel?"

Halo glanced about the room blinking. "I feel...quite alright, I guess." She looked to Jastin. "How long have you been here? You should be at school, shouldn't you?"

Jastin's cheerful face looked up to the ceiling, and she answered, "I *should* be. But I'm not. I took care of you last night. I rubbed and stretched your muscles, cleaned and dressed your wounds. It was Staghen's order for me to do so. So I slept by your side last night. I have more great news! Staghen needs me to stay here to look after both of you. I will wash your clothes, cook your food, clean this home. And I will be here for your comfort. It's the least I can do to help you find Derjaun."

Jastin's hyper demeanor was almost too much for Halo to handle so early.

Halo's heart calmed. Her eyes closed softly with the good fortunes she'd been given lately. "Thanks, Jastin. I know that we will find him." She smiled at her friend. "Surely being close to Staghen makes you happy?"

Jastin chuckled, rolling her eyes. "You have no idea."

Later on, Jastin was holding on to the captain as they rode to the river. The large empty sacks of animal skin that were used for water were tied to Rikaana's side. She should have been tickled by this moment, but the captain was strangely quiet. Not wanting to anger him, she too stayed quiet. He showed her how to fill the bags and how to tie them to the sides of the saddle, how to find the freshest water, and even how to carry it more properly. She flopped a bag over her shoulder and stumbled while making grunts from her mouth.

Staghen watched her clumsy walk from the riverside back up the slight hill to the horse. His face winced with concern. "Is this too much for you, Jastin?"

She slipped a little. "Nonsense, my good man," she tried to respond with confidence. "It is my shoes. These slippers hurt my feet so terribly."

"Ha! It is because they are fanciful slippers and not boots. Come now, hurry." He clapped his hands to urge her on.

"If I didn't know any better, Captain, I'd say you were mocking me," she playfully said.

He looked about with a grin. "I am."

"If you're going to mock me, could you at least help me? These bags are heavy!" she protested as she finally made her way to Rikaana's side.

"I think this should be a lesson for you."

"What lesson is that, oh, wise one?"

"I asked you if this was too much for you." He turned back to look forward as she stared up at him. "You lied to me. Why would I want to help you now?"

"Oh, you!" She chuckled as she slapped his leg. The two shared their humorous moment, allowing each other to feel the silliness. Still, Jastin knew she needed to learn how to do things on her own. She was no longer a richly padded Inner Circle girl but a hard worker.

At home, the young lady was put to work in earnest. She cleaned with a smile though, for in the other room she heard Staghen showing Halo the simple parts of a bow, a quiver, and an arrow. She heard Halo faintly say, "Do you think I will ever be able to use this, Captain?"

Jastin listened. Everything she did was put to a halt. What would he say? How would Halo's blindness affect such a thing?

He spoke, "Yes. It's not what your eyes can and can't do. I have seen men with perfect vision miss targets thousands of times. Even targets right before their very eyes. I have seen men injure their own arms out of negligent stupidity. But I have also seen you defeat a gollet, Halo. And you defeated him without training. You should believe that anything you are equipped with heightens your chance of survival."

"A *gollet*?"

"Why, yes." Jastin heard Staghen stand at that statement. He continued on, perhaps readying himself to leave. "A gollet is what Nikolag is."

"I know what a gollet is, sir. Bremlin was a gollet. I loved his tales as a child and even now. But Nikolag? How could such an ill-tempered, disgusting human being be a gollet?"

"That's what they're like, Halo." Staghen concluded. He was moving again, likely to put his coat on, and Jastin continued to listen. *Who is Nikolag?* she thought to herself.

Inside the room, Staghen spoke once more, "Not all of them are as kind as Bremlin writes himself to be. Nikolag is—"

Halo stood up and interjected, "Where is his family? A gollet so far from the sea?" She looked about as her eyes filled with shock and confusion. "His family would have had to pass through the southern territory of Persu to come here. We are nowhere near the sea. Where is his family?"

Jastin simply heard silence.

Halo pressed on, "Staghen, where is his family?"

"His father was named Unregard Farog Tempest, and his mother was Joriga Midga Tempest. From what he has told me, they both died from a stomach illness while his family was at sea. His young sister, Filia Kaig, died from drowning, and he had lost his older brother, Burdock, during a squall that capsized their ship."

Halo's inquisitiveness turned into slight anger. "You mean to tell me you had me fight a man with a broken heart?"

"Halo," Staghen spoke sternly, "every man you'll fight wears a broken heart. I feel that it was essential for you both to fight. He is the most ruthless man I have. He would have taken no mercy on your gender or age. I needed to do this to see if you were truly able to handle the strongest I can give you."

"But could *he*? He lost his youthful sister, and you paired him to beat up on a young girl," Halo demanded.

Jastin still listened and held her chest while Halo carried on. "Can he really fight with a clear head with a broken heart?"

Staghen rubbed her cheek and gave her a reassuring smile. "I knew you would say that. Now that you know, I am hoping you can calm his maiming hatred. He is bred to handle the bloodiest cries of war and battle, but I can't get through to him. If he were to rush into battle with this dark spirit he has, he would not last a second. I have been trying to get through to him for years and have not had any sense of fortune with him. But you, who could heal Derjaun's terminal suffering, encourage Jastin to stand strong on her own, *and* stand against Mozkin Ramath? Why, if anyone can do it, it's you."

10

There were many things on the young captain's mind as he hurried down the stoop.

Everything rushed into his memory: the recollection of losing Radal, training a young and blind girl, trying to find the long-lost sick boy, and now attempting to remain strong in the eyes of all who saw him. All of the villagers had placed their trust and their fortune in him, and as he pulled Rikaana from his stall his mind attempted to frantically clear itself. His throat became swollen with guilt and frustration, his stomach laden with despair, and his muscles weakened with heartache.

Regardless, he pulled his horse from his stall and walked onto the path. However, he was immediately greeted by Vathra and his men. His strong chin lifted in the early light. He stood to turn to his malakae.

"Vathra, please tell me some good news."

Yet his blue eyes became aglow with worry. The blood-haired Vathra Saran sighed. Silence persisted, and the captain's body grew cold. Vathra steadied his horse and his voice rose above. "We came home this morning with empty hands, Captain."

Staghen succumbed to anger, for his last stress of calmness had snapped. He attempted to keep his tight hostility low so that the young ladies in his home would not hear. "Why must I remind you and my men so often that you were not to stop looking until he is found?"

"Captain," Vathra calmly interjected, "I journeyed to the mountains as you ordered." His eyes began to show the surge of tears that he fought to suppress.

Staghen's body felt hard and heavy, and he continued to listen with absolute attention. "Go on."

"We did not sleep, as you ordered, but it was dark." His breath quickened. "And at the foothills we were attacked by something we could not see."

"Attacked?" Staghen's eyes lifted and grew alarmed. Vathra breathed deeply as if he were nervous to speak. Staghen spoke again, "Vathra, speak to me!"

All was quiet.

"Ishlog is gone. We tried our hardest to signal the arrows, but we hadn't the time." Vathra widened his eyes with urgency. And with muted frustration, his voice broke again, "We did all we could do to keep ourselves safe. We rushed into hiding in the forest until daybreak. We tried, and we lost, Captain."

Staghen's legs went weak, and he leaned over the neck of his horse. His stomach churned inside and out, tossing about with the storm in his eyes and inside his heart.

He had lost again. From inside his heart, he felt the splitting crush of a thousand emotions he could no longer hold onto, and his mouth hung open in devastation. Silently in his voiceless screams of pain, one hurtful tear rolled down his tightened face. "Vathra…" The only thing that could calm his growing pain was the presence of his malakae.

Vathra moved his horse nearer to Rikaana and began to rub the back of the young captain's shoulder.

"Staghen, these beings were not like you and I. As you know, they were those…animals. The Annenji."

Staghen immediately sat up with a sharp intake of breath. He was livid. But still Vathra spoke again. "Their growls were loud near the foothill trees. Their wings cut the air like thunder. Ishlog's bravery was a sacrifice to us all. He stayed fighting while we tried to flee. We tried so desperately to get him to run, but his horse had been eaten beyond recognition, and with his size he told us he would have slowed us down to ride on another horse with another Guardian."

It was without any doubt of the mind that this news was hard for Vathra to deliver. And it was in this *very moment* that Vathra knew his pain could never compare to Staghen's, and so he had to try to mask his nerves for his captain.

Staghen's heart was broken.

He rubbed and held his face, trying to hide his hard tears. He coughed while his knuckles squeezed against his lips. "I am assuming you believe the boy had the same fate?"

"Yes, Captain," Vathra concluded.

Staghen lifted his head high and felt his shoulders attempting to relax from the rush of loss he was once again enduring. "Get all of my men to the Nakhan gates immediately."

"Captain, if I may, we may have invaded the beasts' territory. I would think twice to wage a war out of anger."

"No, Vathra," Staghen answered.

His eyes moved tiredly to see his malakae. He shifted his head with his brows raised. As he spoke, his voice cracked in tone, "You are forgetting the terrible night when Nakhan was attacked. The night Captain Radal was taken, it was the night before the celebration of my sixteenth year, when before I was ready I was forced to be a man. So it is clear to me that *they* have invaded our village." He looked at his malakae. "Our *home*." He pressed on after a brief cough, "War may not be necessary, as we do not exactly know what we are dealing with, and I do not want to place my people in danger. Gather my men." He mounted Rikaana. "We will discuss this in the fields."

As Vathra followed the captain, the pathways were filled with curious villagers who had wondered why the search for the boy had everyone in tension and why one guarada was missing. Vathra had already believed that the occurrence the previous night may have placed the people of Nakhan in danger. The home they left was still. Inside, Halo's eyes were still. She and her friend sat on the sofa in complete stillness. The silence was so loud, and it murmured in Halo's sensitive ears. She had heard *everything*.

"I knew it was about my friend, but he didn't come inside to tell me."

Even as her eyes twitched to look about, she continued, "Derjaun wasn't found, but the matter doesn't end here. I couldn't even ask of my own friend's whereabouts."

Halo felt a sensation like she could not make use of the air she was breathing, and her mind was at a loss for thoughts now. Jastin touched her friend's leg. "Halo, I have sorrow for so many things."

She could hardly begin her speaking before Halo cut in, "Jastin, spare me. I can't handle another emotion. Not only did Staghen lose Ishlog, Derjaun is gone, and I fear that where he has gone no Guardian could bring him home." Halo began to cry without sobs. Only tears were given. "I feel I can't even bear my own soul with this thought."

"Don't say this!" Jastin said with positivity as she leaned over to her. "Unless his body is found empty and gray, he may still be alive, and you know that! Besides, Staghen has to uphold his role as the captain. He must tend to his men first. I'm sure he'll come home and tell you everything."

Halo groaned in frustration, "You don't understand. Ishlog supervised me yesterday. And he was a good man. A man who raised *your* beloved captain after Radal was killed."

Once more, Jastin spoke boldly, "If you believe now he's dead, then there is no purpose for this status you have fought so hard for and earned. Look at what you've become. I wished so hard all night giving my heart to the moon for Derjaun, and if I must do it for you now so be it. Don't give up, not until physical proof is before you. After all, you are the one who says that the most. Am I right, my friend? An action without due memory is nothing but a lie."

Halo was deep in thought. Her mind plunged harder into the

words of her friend, for she found comfort there. Why, her dearly beloved friend who had been so notoriously selfish and immature at times was starting to show extreme, selfless care.

"You're right, Jastin. He's not dead. Perhaps he's still on the move. But I can't imagine what grief Staghen feels."

"Never mind," Jastin soothed. "Leave this burden to me, for it is one I long to carry. And if Ishlog is gone, then *you* must have the strength to avenge his death. Now I do believe Derjaun may still be on the move. But where?"

Halo laughed without an exact reason for doing so and very bluntly answered, "The mountains." She was trying very hard to surrender some of her woes for Jastin to handle.

But her laughter became manic, and it concerned her friend. Jastin thought the Guardian had gone mad. "Why are you laughing?"

Halo chuckled once more, but as she shook her head the tears came harder. This time, they could not be contained. They accompanied the faulty smile. "I don't know."

Halo jerked. Without wanting to, her spirit cracked, her face clenched, and all of the stress had come out of her friend's actions in hard cries, grasping clutches, and sobs. Jastin was in a rush to hold her friend, and she held her hard. The sounds of the cries broke her heart. Her friend was suffering.

"Jastin, I'm tired," the young Guardian confessed. "I have only just begun, and I'm so tired. I believe so much that he is still alive, but I miss him *so* much. He never teased my blindness, and although he told me of himself I kept so much of myself from him. From my own fears I didn't open up to him. Of all the horrors Lemson and my mother put me through, he liberated them all."

"You are tired, and as a baby cries from fatigue so does a new Guardian with a first few days of training and a lifetime of work ahead of her."

This soft statement nurtured Halo's sadness.

Her friend spoke once more with softening words, "If it eases your troubled heart, Staghen has asked me to live here as well because he will be taking on the search more directly. And he will not have time to cook or clean, as we mentioned before I left this morning."

Halo sniffled and relaxed.

Hours later, the two girls were sitting quietly on the living room sofa. The front door opened, and both girls turned to the door anxiously. In came the captain, who always looked proud and strong, but his current features made them panic. Jastin placed her hands atop Halo's shoulders to steady her friend's concern. He was filthy. Beautiful black hair coated with sweat, face dirty, and eyes tired. He could not even handle standing up straight. Jastin and Halo ran over instantly, hearts tearing to comfort him. Without any hesitation, Halo grabbed his wrists, and still he would not look to her. Instead his eyes stayed downturned, and his head shifted as if examining the floor. Jastin held her mouth and stayed a small distance away for respect.

Halo began quietly, "Captain...please, speak to me." Her eyes searched his, which seemed lost. Her eyes watered, and all the comfort her loving friend had given her drained away like a river going dry. But it was hard for him to admit what he had done. He had never had to make such a horrible decision before.

He finally looked to Jastin and then to the strong girl he had grown to love. "Halo..." He swallowed hard in an attempt to stay sincere. "I had no choice but to call off the search for Derjaun."

Jastin abruptly pulled her other hand to silence her gasp, and it took all of her strength to let her mixed emotions stay back. But Halo could not. Halo in a fury grabbed his wrists mightily and shook them hard. "You called off the search for my friend without telling me? You told me he would be found. You promised me!"

"Halo!" Jastin interjected for fear of Staghen's anger. She tried to calm the dangerous outburst of her friend, but Halo's resentment erupted. Staghen held Halo's fists and suddenly tightened them only to contain her but far from enough to hurt her. They both were tear-stained as Halo's words hurt his heart far more than he ever could hurt her in training.

"Listen to me—" he started.

But she roared, "Just tell me if he is dead! I need peace of mind!" Halo fell into his chest, like Agrona did to him many years ago.

"Jastin," he began as he held the crying girl, "go to your room now."

The girl, whose nerves were already coiled, went into Halo's room only to quickly turn and press her ear to the closed door.

He got onto his knees to look at Halo. Nothing in this world could have prepared him for what he had to do. Halo was distraught, inconsolable, and torn apart. It was rightfully so. And Staghen was searching for everything in his power to continue. In this moment, in this *very* moment, her sanity meant more to him than his own. After all, it was what real Guardians were to do.

"Halo, there is no exact conclusion if Derjaun is alive or dead. But we know of Ishlog for certain. And he is dead. Vathra informed me that Derjaun's books were found near his home, and from this we concluded he fled the village. You more than anyone else knew he was not happy here.

"I ordered Vathra to gather the strongest men to search in all directions away from here. Ishlog went with Vathra and some others to the mountains, and the Annenji beasts attacked them. They're still here. Ishlog stayed behind to fend them off so the rest could take shelter in the forest. We found his body in the field today. He and his horse suffered the same fate as...never mind. It's suicide for us to continue our searches any further. We believe we know the place where Derjaun went. To the mountains, as you have spoken of many times before. And we confirmed it with Agrona this afternoon. I'm not saying he is dead, but I can't risk any more of my men in this search. Please tell me you understand and forgive me."

Halo realized that she needed to ease her anger at him. What kind of Guardian would she truly be if she saw him lose a father figure and yet be outraged at him? "What of the southeast, toward Persu? Is there no possible chance he ran to Persu in hopes to find a cure?"

They gazed at one another. Several nights ago, Halo believed Derjaun would have fled to seek solace in the mountains. And at first, she believed herself to be happy for him. In this he would have truly found freedom, bravery, and a death suitable for a great soul. Who would not wish to meet their end by doing what they longed for? Now it was different. There was a possibility that this could have never been, that Derjaun's frail body did not even get a chance to get near the mountains. Halo was not naive. She understood what Staghen was saying. However, he never answered her question.

"Staghen?" she quietly questioned once more.

He rubbed her hands and sighed in dismay. "Halo, I wish I could say better things to you. But nothing was found. But if it is your wish, as an apology for not informing you sooner, I will arrange for men to search further in the southern fields toward Persu." He lowered his head again to make a movement to rise.

But she clenched his wrists to stop him. For she had believed she had hurt him deeply. "Staghen, I'm sorry. You have lost in a more difficult degree than I have. This search, I appreciate it, but..." Tears rolled down her pale face. "I wouldn't want you to lose another. I accept this. I have no other choice but to accept it."

It was a desperate need to hug him, to hold him. As of now Staghen had lost all the men he looked to for guidance. Now he had no one. The sensation grew stronger in her soul the more she saw his heavy expressions. It was not an easy thing for him to have done as the fears of regret came in large numbers. But they needed one another, and so Halo pulled him with sore arms, and he let her. Harder she gripped, and he held her with arms like the father he wanted to be. "I'm sorry, Halo," he wept. "I tried."

THE NEXT DAY, Staghen ordered Vathra to stay with Ishlog's wife, Mihora, for comfort and protection. The captain needed a few days time to think of how to address the village, knowing that they would be in a panic uproar. Two days had passed, and Nakhan's Inner Circle burned with low torches that night. The village's spirit was in tumult with rumors of the captain's orders. It brought worry that spread like an evil sickness, and no one was left with an easy heart. They saw

Mihora, hunched over and held in Agrona's arms. Both women had lost all of the family they had left.

Among the chaos of the concerned, the Guardians were gentle in pushing the people aside so that Captain Staghen could have a clear path to walk to the platform where he would give his announcement. Halo waited atop Zidori on the sideline, seeing how every person in her vision only appeared to be a faintly colored shadow. She knew the villagers were terrified. Those beasts still existed, and they existed closer than everyone thought.

At the foot of the platform, Staghen dismounted his horse and walked up, seemingly unaffected by the loud jeers of outrage from the crowd. Halo knew he could console them.

"My friends of Nakhan," he addressed warmly, "it is apparent to me that everyone is aware of the tragedy that has struck two women, and it has brought fear to you." He looked about with his eyes searching in an attempt to connect with every citizen. "I *demand* that none of you fear for your own life. Rather give comfort for Mihora Cantin and Agrona Vin Gruinelle. In times of grief, we come together. Although my men and I are unaware of Derjaun's fate, Ishlog's unfortunate fate has been met with much certainty. Let us all not believe it untimely, as it was his very death that saved many other husbands, brothers, and sons." He sighed and paused. " However, due to this incident we know that it's too dangerous to continue the search for the boy. Unfortunately, Derjaun will not be able to be found.

"I, along with my men, will be honest with all of you. We now have proof of the reason as to why we were never able to set foot near the foothills of the Castonuje Mountains again. And only for protection of all of you, in the utmost service and fearless love, will my men no longer search for the boy. This village must be protected. Please listen and adhere to these rules I will set, henceforth. This is not to punish any of you but to keep everyone safe."

Drawing a breath, he continued louder, "Absolutely no single woman, child, or anyone under any circumstance will be allowed outside of their homes when twilight falls. If you do, Guardians will take alarm that something must be amiss. When night falls, Dr. Crenon will be escorted to every home to check for illnesses or discomforts. Xoegell will also be placing bells at the front of every home so that if something goes wrong it will be able to be sounded, and a Guardian will be near every home to hurry to help. The bell is only to be used for emergencies. But that is all I have to say for now. I will answer any concerns you may have."

It seemed all at once that a wave of hands were held to the sky, each one desperate to ask a question. As Staghen looked about, he noticed Agrona more than all else. However, she bore a face of hatred. Even though he knew he would be her first target of accusations, he allowed her to speak first.

Still twisted with her heart, she bellowed, "How can I rest at night knowing my son is missing? How can you sleep well at night knowing Radal's *real* successor is dead? You must know my child is dead, otherwise you would not stop." Her face was shaken as she continued, "Radal would not stop. Who is to keep my proud blood flowing? You tell us not to fear and to love one another, but I have none left to love!"

Staghen calmly retorted, "You chose this, Agrona. You made the choice not to hold another lover or bear another child. And you yourself said once before that I am Radal's real successor. Why recant this notion now? Is it easier to cast blame upon me instead of yourself? As you cast scorn upon my name in the public's eye, I can easily do the same for you. I would watch my words, if I were you."

"No!" At once Agrona broke through the crowds until the Guardians up front caught a hold of her. "Derjaun is Radal's successor! And I don't care what you say of my name. Radal was not supposed to die. Go and find my son. He is supposed to one day stand where you are!"

Halo's heart raced against the scene of unhinged emotions. With each passing breath, it seemed impossible for her to calm her nerves. Her whole life was coming apart, and it pained her so to watch Staghen be made a spectacle out of. She believed Agrona was in the wrong after all Staghen had done for her. But suddenly she felt a hand against her shoulder. Immediately she jerked and turned. "Who's this large figure? Who touches me?"

"You really do have sickened eyes, don't you?" the shadowy figure responded in a husky voice. If she didn't know any better, she would have assumed this man had been drinking copious amounts of ulgg.

For a moment she listened. Her eyes tried to focus on something that could not be seen. This man was mounted on horseback as well. She sniffed. "Nikolag? Is this you?"

"Ha, your eyes are terrible, but your memory and ears are not," he responded.

"It's not my memory nor my ears but my nose." She held her hand over her face. "Heavens above, do you ever bathe?"

"When red ladies are available and I have means to pay them, yes," he laughed back. This time, his demeanor seemed different. The arguing between Agrona and Staghen was almost drowned into the back of Halo's mind.

"Is the river your only means of bathing? It's getting colder though."

He shrugged and scoffed. "Not entirely. I don't have many clothes. I'm almost positive it's my clothing you're smelling and not my body itself. I bathe in the river almost every few days. But I can tell you this," he said as he looked to Agrona's continued scene, "if I was Staghen, I'd cut her tongue out and sell it for a pretty pence."

"What a gollet you are," Halo responded. She did not really care to have any further words with him but could not refrain from asking, "Why did you put your hand on my shoulder?"

Although she could not see his face, she could see he looked forward to the crowd. "Because I suppose you looked like you needed it. No one else was doing it, so I did it."

Halo wished with great might that she could have seen his face then and there. She could hear there was a difference in his tone of voice. It almost seemed saddened or heavy with secrecy. A few breaths of silence passed between them. "Thank you," she suddenly said. "This means a great deal to me."

He looked once more back to her. "I know it does."

Halo's attention was taken back to the quarrel between the captain and the widow when she heard Agrona yell, "You cannot find half the man to take my son's place!"

Staghen smiled with confidence. "What about...a *woman*? Halo, please pull your mare beside me. I'm sure Agrona would like to speak with you."

For all of her life that she could recall, Halo never liked the idea of idolization or being put in the forefront of any occasion. However, this night was different. Inside her blood she felt the encroaching cries of revenge, and this was even directly at Agrona. It maddened the blind girl how Derjaun's mother spoke to the captain. Halo gave Zidori a gentle belly kick and steered her in front of the line of Guardians until she came to Staghen's side.

It was miraculous how Zidori seemed to know what to do despite her rider being poor of vision in such low lighting. She squinted her eyes to make sure it was by Staghen that the horse did in fact go to. She dismounted her horse and took her place by Staghen's side.

It was more than expected to have the people murmuring in question about seeing a girl. Perhaps they suddenly realized why they had seen her riding alongside Staghen in his early morning business. Halo steadied and attempted to focus her eyes on Agrona. The curiosity of what the mother's face must look like nipped at her. She decided to simply judge what her facial expressions may have been by the tone in which the mother would speak.

"Agrona, it is an honor to speak to you again," Halo began with a friendly tone. She did not want to rouse further separation.

As expected, it was quite a surprise to Agrona, and she spoke instantly, "Halo, it is you? You have become a Guardian?" There was a tinge of disbelief in her voice, and at this point the mother did not know how to feel.

"Yes."

Agrona marveled at the girl's newly acquired attitude. Now she saw a girl who had been mounted atop a strong horse that was bred with brute strength and vigilant behavior. And not just any horse, a mountaineer. With a sword strapped heartily by Halo's side and

Guardian armor tightly formed against her body, it was clear to all who witnessed that this girl's role was to be taken with great respect. A memory came to her. The day Derjaun went missing, she had asked Halo what she could do to keep the young girl's love and attain forgiveness. Now Agrona felt a surplus of pride that brought forth tears of hope. She would honor Halo's new position.

"Halo, I would not honor any other such as you to take Derjaun's place. I have no blessing to give, only honor." The widow lowered her weary head to accept what had been done.

After the event, Staghen guided Jastin and Halo back home. The walk was peaceful and soothing. Warm floral scents cascaded from every draft of the winds, and the clamor had resided into a serene scene, much like the wild waves of the ocean calmed after a mighty storm. They walked by the closed-up shops and across narrowing stone paths to their home. Jastin could only imagine how Staghen felt, so she tried to comfort him. "Radal assigned his role to you for a reason. He would have only given his title to a man he believed could carry Nakhan through anything. This is merely another task at hand, my good Captain."

He gave a sigh of what seemed to be relief as he looked up to the stars in the sky. The sweet sentiments may have even healed his heart had he not retained a calloused soul. All he could do was simply smile to her before leading the girls inside to go to sleep. But the two girls lay on their bed together for an eternity of silence. None of them could sleep.

Jastin broke the silence. "Care to share your thoughts with me?"

"It's not much. A gollet by the name of Nikolag was someone I fought just recently, but he consoled me at the village tonight. And I'm not sure why. His actions leave me, well, confused."

Jastin placed a hand upon Halo's back to brush it with affection. "I wouldn't think so much into this for the moment, if I were you. You, more than anyone else, know how gollets can be. Maybe if luck is in your hands, he feels sorry for what he did. I would rather you rest well tonight and think of these matters in the morning. Remember," she stated with her forefinger upright, "Derjaun is the front of your mind. Not some heedless gollet."

Silence befell the room in its unsettling blanket. Halo's thought burrowed deeply into her consciousness. She said with a concentrated voice, "You are right."

"Focus on resting and go to the fields tomorrow to become the Guardian you were meant to be, the one who will bring Derjaun home."

11

And it was so. The months passed, and the brisk spring air gave way to a more cooperating summer breeze. Although it was summer, the breeze was still chilly. Beautiful snowdrifts melted from the Castonuje and rushed in all of their lively offerings through the Gigannora, which was now plentiful with fish and deeper in its mysterious depths. Halo had spent many days and nights on that same fence glancing out to the mountains as their rocky slopes became more pronounced, and she loved the little white pops of field flowers on the foothills. Pabi flowers were lovely to her. In this time of seasonal change, the blind Guardian had attempted to take her friend's advice into her heart. But it wasn't easy.

It was early morning, and Halo decided to wake earlier than need be to allow her mind some peaceful recollection on that fence. It was a true time and place for her to be alone with her thoughts. She smiled, lifting her chin and to absorb the bounty of the summer air. The Guardian girl felt newfound strength. She jumped off the fence, gathered her horse and set for the training fields where she knew she was set to fight Oniden that day.

When they fought, Halo used every fiber of her demanding spirit to push him back harder, even though he was much larger in size.

Her sword knew no order now, and neither did her mind. Perhaps she was still secretly frustrated by Staghen's lost promise. Either it was this or the knowledge that she felt to be the only one who cared to bring Derjaun home. It stoked a fire that spread her wrath onto Oniden and all she knew and saw. Her eyes possessed no need to see, only to defeat.

With this, the exchange of swords clashing grew so intense that Halo decided to end it then and there. As she had defeated the lofty-headed gollet, she got a clear view of Oniden's vulnerability. With one powerful thrust of the sword to the face, she *thought* she hit him. Yet it was not to be so. For the life of her, she could not recall how she had missed and only felt her cheek being torn apart by his blade. Blood dripped down her chin. Her lungs expanded. Her heartbeat pulsed. Everything suddenly became very, *very* real, especially to the captain watching her. With every injury she acquired, his heart skipped a beat. He was not meant to be a captain until he was thirty-five years old, and with his still youthful heart he found struggles in trying to both teach her, love her, protect her, and watch her fight.

Yet time and time again he noticed Halo was fumbling more than what she should have, and he called the fight to stop. He approached quickly and grabbed her hands to deliver reality into her ears. "Please, I feel I am losing all reigns on my life. I can't lose them over you." He pointed to Oniden but kept looking at her. "Wake up, Halo. You're better than this! If you can hear birds in the canopy no one else can, you can hear when a man eight paces in front of you draws his sword."

Halo was absolutely bewildered at his action. She stared through the smears of black jinfish oil around her eyes. The captain was right. She heard *everything,* every blade of grass in the wind and every breath by the men. Her vision had left her incredibly audibly sensitive to even the presence of a wall nearby. Many times before she would navigate her home at night just by feeling the pressure change in the air.

She was more adept and stronger than she realized.

The world around her seemed to fade into nothingness. All of the actions of the Guardians, the sound of the wind, the captain talking to her, all of it blushed together in one seamless color of insignificance. Why was it she started losing her ability to separate all the details in her sense?

The shouting of the captain caught her ear, but she still dazed off in her thoughts. Her mind swam deeper into the ocean of her spirit, and she realized something so profound; if she was strong enough to fend Nikolag off on her own and strong enough to be placed among men, maybe she was strong enough to try to find Derjaun on her own.

After training, Halo made her way home with Staghen. She kept her thoughts chambered inside, for she had to make absolutely sure that if she wanted to go that she would be respectful and ask for Staghen's permission. She really did not want to though.

They arrived at home and business continued on as usual well into twilight. Halo examined Jastin about her duties and another debate entered her mind. Would she take Jastin with her? She may need healthy eyes, after all.

She thought.

She planned.

She deliberated and asked herself many questions.

After much time passed, perhaps too much as it was daybreak now, Halo decided to look for Staghen to ask him. She simply had to do the right thing. She hurried outside to find him but only found confusion about why he was not outside yet. However, she found a man just as helpful, the blood-haired malakae.

"Vathra, a good morning to you," Halo told him easily. Although she desired his rank so far beyond her ability to do so, she honored the man who found Derjaun's school materials outside and led many searches for him. She felt slightly melancholic as she walked down the stoop and passed him and his horse.

Vathra was a tall man, like most Guardians. Most Guardians were not at all as privileged in their looks, however. His eyes were by far his most curiously intriguing features. They were as dark red, rich in extreme rarity, and they always seemed to be watching. Maybe they were. The clothing of the chosen malakae was very easy to recognize as well. A well-handmade long coat of dark burgundy velvet trimmed with Gilda buck fur hunted in winter and laced with reflective gold shimmer. His boots were as folded and high as the captain's.

He bowed his young face, a face that was only twenty-four years old. "And a good morning to you, Halo. I came here because I wanted to speak to you. I couldn't help but realize that in taking Derjaun's place it essentially means one day you should be strong enough to hold the captain's position. I'd like to help expedite your training, if that's alright. Perhaps you and I shall fight tonight? While Staghen watches the other girl?"

She turned as the question he asked caused all blood to rush to her feet. He was glowing with a kind smile, and so she proudly accepted, "I would be honored, Malakae. But why do you ask this now?"

Vathra moved to her side while she brushed her horse down. He uttered, "This is my business to know, inquisitive one. As you wish for answers to all questions you have, sometimes the answers are best meant to be discovered and not heard."

For a settling moment, Zidori simply nickered as if waiting for the two to conclude their encounter. Halo continued to brush the horse. "Do you think me harsh, Vathra? Do you find me to be..." She paused as she simply found herself staring at the horse's fur. "...a defect?"

"No," he answered candidly. "Halo, let me guide you. You are weak, yes. But those who are weak are usually so from the great sufferings they've lived through. They're usually lost, confused, or desiring a greater purpose in life. Let's take Nikolag, for example, whose weakness is not physical like yours."

"Yes." Her eyes lit up. "Please tell me more of this man."

"Well," he said with a dry sigh, "he is highly disobedient, a male-factor if you will. But his past comes with great bounties of hurt. Radal found him wandering the western fields. He was barely ten years old and was alone. I do not know exactly what has happened to him, but I can only imagine coming from somewhere alone."

"He's been here that long? Why haven't I seen him before?"

"He spends a majority of his day in the forest alone. Either hunting, shaping his weapons, chopping wood, or even fishing in the creeks. If he is not training, he is always occupied with something else. But as you can see, he has a penchant for disobeying orders, and it has given Staghen more than a few headaches. But he is the strongest Guardian we have below the guaradas. And so Staghen welcomes him."

Halo remembered her plan to search for Derjaun on her own. Excitement consumed her. If Staghen was near the forest when he got Zidori, and Nikolag hunted in the woods, were they really *that* dangerous? "But I thought the forest was dangerous to venture into? And hasn't Staghen tried to comfort him?" Her mouth could not even keep up with her mounting questions.

"Nikolag goes to the forest without permission. Don't think he hasn't come back injured or nearly dead before either. And Staghen tried for many years. But Nikolag has built mighty walls around his heart. All I can simply ask is for you to differ from Nikolag. Do not build such strong walls around your heart."

She glanced to him in a pausing stare. So much was delivered to her in such a short time, and yet the malakae had made great sense to her. With this conversation finished, they said their goodbyes to one another. She had done her best to race Zidori to the fields, where she was hoping to have been welcomed with tasks more painful than the ones of yesterday. She approached, dismounted, and tied her mare. The rest of the young Guardians were warming up.

"What a surprise to see you finally joined us, Halo!" came a familiar voice.

It was Nikolag. Her spirit grew happy in hearing his voice was kind to her.

Others thought a battle would begin in an instant, for these two spirits were rivals beyond the point of a steaming river. Or so they had known. Time had a way of changing things between them. She finished tying Zidori and sarcastically laughed, "Vathra spoke to me about helping me train harder. He obviously knows my potential."

The large blond derided her with a snicker and turned away to

leave. Over his shoulder he taunted, "As a female always will be delusional. Poor thing."

Not out of anger but out of competition, Halo quickly leaned over
to pick a rock from the ground, and giving her eyes little time to
adjust, she threw the object hard and saw it hit him in the back of the
head. At once Nikolag turned sharply and rubbed where it success-
fully hit and attempted to tune out the thundering laughter of
the men.

It was almost like a memory relived between the two. Halo placed
her hands on her hips prominently and gave him a friendly smirk,
"How's that for delusion?"

But he gave a shake of his head. "What is your inextinguishable
obsession with hurting my head, you wench?"

"Sounds to me like you're whining. And besides, you have a big
head. It's an easy target. I heard a murmur in the Inner Circle a few
days ago that you were sick. I figured Captain Staghen would order
you on bedrest." Her frustration with the gollet was softening.

"Ha!" Nikolag approached her. His long golden hair was worn in
messy tresses about shoulders that were strong and rounded. Why, he
was simply *massive*. But it was such in a form that she was not use to.
He bore a smile and an easy pace. "Staghen said that with what
happened to Ishlog he needs all the Guardians he can get. And if you
think my sickness was enough to keep me down than you're more
stupid than I thought," he admitted quietly. "And also? You may hate
me now, but one day you'll lust for me."

The young girl exploded as he turned to leave. She moved to him
with a dagger drawn and forced him to turn around. She snarled at
him, "I'd never lust for a man who isn't strong enough to take me
down."

Nikolag looked toward the blade, and his blue eyes made swift
movements back to her. His hand bravely broke the clutch of the
blade to move in with a tactical reversal. Before she realized what
happened, Halo's throat was now being brushed with that same
blade. "You say this now, but there will come a day when you think
otherwise."

Halo felt him touch her lower hips with a feeling that left her feeling insecure.

"NIKOLAG!" a ground-shattering voice came.

At once Nikolag backed away, knowing Captain Staghen had arrived. The captain marched onto the field with his face scornful and tightened. "It was difficult enough to ask you to return, but if I ever see you touch her in a way like that again I swear to all spirits I'll kill you!" Staghen came out of nowhere like a disembodied phantom to grab Nikolag's throat and pull his body close with a violent speed. Staghen's mouth continued with his verbal attacks. The captain did tell the men to treat Halo as one of them, but only in training. Never did he ever want to see a man treat her with sexual degradation. "I should slice that uncontrollable organ of yours clean from your body!" Staghen snapped into his face. "I said clearly you are not to treat her differently than a man and never to disrespect another Guardian's body!" And Staghen shoved the younger man hard enough to make him fall.

"Captain, please," Halo interjected, coming toward Staghen, "this is how men can be. I have to learn to handle this properly."

Staghen looked to her in worry. "But not yet. I've seen you handle things like this before, but that doesn't give him allowance to do it. Not now." He gently nudged her on. "Go fall in line with everyone else. I have an announcement to make."

Halo quickly obeyed and all of the Guardians stood in their line, waiting for the captain to speak.

When all was in order and every Guardian was quiet, he spoke in grand demeanor, "I am the captain, therefore I hereby invest it into myself to create a new law. Someone in our league has proven a great deal of strength in a very short time."

All of the men and the one girl waited anxiously to hear what the captain had to say. It was a difficult thing for her to refrain from shifting back and forth on her feet with excitement, for it was almost as unbridled as Zidori.

Everyone waited. She and Staghen locked eyes. Oh, how she wished she could see them better. The sun was bright behind him, and so his figure was vague and had lost most detail. But all she saw and heard was him. Her heart lifted to the sky in happiness.

He continued, "Women will now be allowed to serve openly in the Guardians. May she be the first."

Halo Laankel felt her knees become weak with the burden of pride becoming so strong, and once again she fought to retain her composure. A single tightened tear came to her cheek, hearing the men all around her applaud her.

Staghen gave her this historical moment with silence, allowing her to feel her emotions out. He proceeded happily once more, "In our old ways, this was not allowed, but this waters down the fact that just because she may be physically weaker, it doesn't mean she is useless. Nor is she strictly born for bearing children and being a homekeeper. She has proven to me that girls, ladies, and women can be tempered with and bred into courageous Guardians."

He began lifting his head to look about. "I myself went against our own laws. I had disobeyed our edict by allowing her entrance. Let us all take heed of this. Perhaps some rules are meant to be broken for the purpose of our own self-discovery."

Her heart grew into a precious gem and melted with flaming love for what she was hearing. It was a great stage to be set for asking him such an important question later. Staghen waited, looked around, and continued in his noble ways, "Her will to overcome any obstacle will no longer go unrecognized."

Staghen began to pull a small hide sack from his side and after untying it pulled out two white beads carved from bones and two red beads that were bones stained with animal's blood. The girl knew better than to look at him as she did not want him to see her youthful face of excitement. She had to appear stern to him.

"Halo, look to me please," Staghen said with much tenderness.

She was speechless.

His eyes were dressed in pride. "Untie your belt for me."

For a moment that seemed to last as long as the winter's snow would fall, they looked into the eyes of one another. The men were waiting anxiously. Then finally, she spoke with humbleness, "Yes, Captain."

It was a moment of considerable magic. The farmer girl who was a blind nobody now was watching Captain Staghen lace four beads onto her belt, raising her rank. He spoke, "These beads represent a new woman who is no longer a miklana. She is now a galakhan."

Nikolag was ironically the first to cheer for her. He chanted as he shot his fist upward, throwing his whole body with it. The rest of the men followed suit, applauding for the young woman who was so warmly accepted and so righteously praised. "Let's eat in her honor!" boasted Nikolag.

"Oh, Nikolag!" Oniden proclaimed while clapping. "Must you find *every* reason possible to eat?"

Halo laughed in amazement and was charmed by the men dancing and clapping together all in her name. She accepted Staghen's grace. He looked down when he was finished tying the last bead on and saw her eyes close tightly with her face jerking in the belief of her life now, and the belief in his love. "I am proud of you, my girl, and most congratulations to you," he said.

"Staghen," she whimpered, looking up to him. But that was all she said. The girl could not resist the need to hold the captain so close.

They embraced one another, and his long fingers slipped through her hair.

It was a wonderfully welcomed rest from all of the turmoil their lives had gone through. Between the feisty gollet softening his ill-tempered heart to her and now rising in rank, Halo felt more assured of her decision to leave to the forest. She just did not know when. The summers never lasted long in that quiet northern village, and so even with fall would come frost and significantly shortened days. She needed to make a decision quickly to avoid the difficulties of fall and winter. But every time she attempted to talk to Staghen that entire day, he was distracted by a villager, a Guardian, Jastin's outburst of affection for everything in her life. It was always something. It left her unfortunately without her chance to ask, and later that night she was lying in bed next to Jastin, who was adorably snoring.

Now both of their lives were going somewhere happy. Somewhere worth being. Although Halo had not yet found Derjaun, the four beads that glazed her rope belt proved to all she was of worth to be able to even try. She kept this thought dear to her heart, and onward she slept through the night, dreaming of its promises of tomorrow as a gentle winter wind began singing its song outside her bedroom window. She was startled awake as the thought came back to her about looking for Derjaun alone in the forest, and she hadn't yet had the chance to ask Staghen for permission.

Does he know of my intentions? she thought to herself.

The next morning, Halo woke with more thoughts. Her eyes peered out the window and tried to rub the dust away, but it was not dust. She rubbed her eyes frantically and tried to look again. She gave attempt after attempt to wipe what was not there. Worried about her eyes, she checked to see if the room looked different to her. She noticed Jastin was obviously awake and tending to her morning duties, but that was all.

"Maybe it's dust outside the window," she thought aloud.

That day gave the wonderful gift of more time for her to think things over. With such a dangerous request, she kept fumbling over her decision on asking Staghen or not. Time slipped away from her that day and night came once more. She got into her bed and realized her body was becoming used to the work that surpassed the pressure of farming. While Halo was growing in her strength to complete her ultimate mission, Jastin's frame had almost shrunk with the passing days of her hard work. Another day of rigorous training had passed, and Jastin finished settling Halo in to sleep. But the house maid had one last task to finish, and that was to make sure Staghen was safe and happy. Her soft rapping was given to his door, and an exhausted voice groaned from the other side, allowing her entrance.

The young lady entered and saw the unfortunate sight of Staghen lying in nothing more than a pile of bones and muscles on his bed. It saddened her to know that he and Halo were undergoing so much. She simply wished she could help more.

His voice was barely audible for her, "I need you to help me to my bathing tub, Jastin. I can hardly stand on my own two feet."

Jastin's body almost ceased living. "Bathe, Captain?" her voice called curiously.

The hard-hearted man nodded. "Please? Don't fret, I can handle myself inside the basin. I just need help getting there," he finished firmly.

"Of course," Jastin almost interrupted. How her heart raced into the sky. She hoped he would need her.

The once clumsy girl was now bred into a respectable servant to the house, and she walked to him and gently placed her arm underneath his back and another under his legs. "As you sit up, I'll turn you."

"Your breath seems unstable."

She heaved him up with ease. "It's not that I can't. It's just that your muscles feel tauter than my uana strings are. The heat will do you some good. Your body is a miserable wreck. I feel it in every sense of your skin. You sitting here alone is making you shake."

Jastin allowed him to sit and rest while she prepared the bath for him. On and off he heard her frantic and yet more graceful scurrying about the backyard where his rain barrel was and to the bathing room, carrying pail after pail of water. When it was finished, she put his arm around her shoulder and lovingly helped him to the tub. Inside his bathing room, she turned and allowed him modesty. "Captain? Since you managed to get into the tub unassisted, I assume you can get out. I've left your robe on the door and your fresh night-clothes on your bed."

He called her and told her would be fine without her, and he offered sincere gratitude. Jastin quietly closed his bedroom door and uttered to herself, "Just rest, my handsome one."

Jastin stood idle. So much in everyone's lives had changed that she had forgotten about taking time to recollect on her own.

Although she was growing closer to Staghen, that was no longer important to her. She just simply wanted to see him well.

She went into her own room and lay next to Halo, completely worn out, but was left naïve however to Halo being awake. The Guardian's eyes were closed and perfectly acting like she was in slumber. Halo heard her friend snooze.

Halo lifted out of the bed with supreme stealth and left, making her way to the fence that she and Derjaun sat upon long ago. Guardians did not even try to stop her, as she was well within her right to move about freely. She was thankful she could still see the fence with the paleness of the moonlight casting a shadow upon it. She climbed and sat quietly, enjoying the smell of the trees and all their woodsy florals were sensed in. The night was quiet, and all before her was hers alone.

Halo glanced with her eyes lifting toward the Castonuje range. "My friend," she began as her eyes welled, "if this be your grave, it is the most beautiful of them all. And if I never see you again, I will assume it was near here you came to rest, and I will come here every night to speak to you in hopes the wind will carry my words to your soul." For a moment she went silent until her tiny voice broke in the sound of a heartbroken child, "I miss you so much."

Then she heard someone coming and readied her sword. As Halo looked at the flatly detailed grass, she called out, "Who's there?"

The figure coughed and she sighed with relief. It was Staghen. One would usually be fearful of being punished by their nurturer for being out so late without telling anyone, but she could hear in his graceful steps that he was not angry at all. He approached quietly and asked, "May I sit with you?"

She scooted to the left and allowed the young captain to sit. Together they watched the flickering moonlight wash the fields. Halo allowed the moment to be as it was, which was a rare moment where she and Staghen could just be in each other's company. It was good company. No orders, no routines, no quarrels to subside, nothing. Just each of them pausing life's never-ending stress. It would have been a great opportunity to ask him but studying his face in what light she could see, it was clear that he was finally serene. She'd rather not disturb it.

He spoke, "You can go. Go forth with your heart's will." His voice was a song of serenade. Low in timbre and mature in speech, he spoke fluidly with sureness in his words.

She lowered her head smiling. There were not enough words in their language to encompass the wonder she felt. He *did* know.

"I came here," he continued, "because I knew you were thinking it. It would only be in your nature to want this. I would want you to want this. So I came to tell you that I give you permission and my blessing to leave. Go find him."

Halo turned and yearning filled her heart to see his face better. Luckily, her ears were attuned to knowing by his vocal sounds. He was at peace. "How did you know?" she questioned.

He chuckled briefly, "I know more about you than you think. I've lived with you long enough now to know how you work. You and Jastin are easy to read." He returned her smile and playfully raised his brows. "I also know that Jastin is absolutely in love with me."

"Oh!" Halo exclaimed as they both laughed. "She'd be mortified if she found out you knew."

"Well," he groaned, grinning. "She doesn't have to know that I know. I find her character amusing and charming. When I first knew her, she was so fast to do way too many things. I've seen her calm down and pace herself more these days. I'm proud of her. I'm proud of both of you."

"I feel like I should tell you this in her honor. She just adores you. From the moment you became captain and fought for us all regardless of your youth, she was so wooed by you then."

"That long?" he asked, puzzled.

"Yes, that long. I know you're never going to marry, and that she's far too young for you, but I want you to know that she's happy being a part of your life. Even if it is a housemaid."

Staghen thought. "Yes, it's truly nice to melt into the care of someone else for once. She does it extremely well for someone her age. I know she was trained to be like this from her mother and father, but she's just so natural at it for being so young. Only a real man could be honored to be her husband one day." He enjoyed the momentary silence and spoke again, "But enough of this, I give you all blessings to go."

She shook her head. "I'm blind, Staghen. And I'm inept. How do you think I'll fair? I could die out there."

"Perhaps. Just as equally as you could, you may not. Nikolag disobeys my orders not to go, and he still goes and returns. I also tore the edict apart for you, so I'll do it again. I cannot train you then keep you shackled as well. You're a Guardian now, Halo. So go do what you're supposed to do. Who knows, maybe he's avoiding us but will come to you."

Halo's choked on her emotions. Her cheeks tightened and tears streamed down and became rain on the ground. "I miss him so much, Staghen. I can't let go of my past. I feel like a failure in everything, and I don't know why."

Staghen did not even think. It wounded his heart to watch her cry, and so he placed his strong hands about her waist and clutched her into his armor. She went immediately still and quiet. It had been far too many moons since he held her like this. His warm embrace hushed her fears and soothed her pain with only but a simple hold. Staghen leaned his head onto hers and began letting his fingers run through her scalp, and he hushed her once more, allowing the hold to settle her nerves. As he waited for her to relax a bit more, it came to the captain that he adored this moment. Actually, far beyond adoring it, he cherished it.

"Halo, listen to me. Let this go."

She pushed her face deeper into his armor as if trying to listen but being afraid to.

"Let this go, this whole past that you know. Because everything will be changing, and you will have no heart to spare or to be wasted on such memories. You have me now, and I will walk you through everything you need to know to grow and walk where you wish to walk."

He pulled her head for her eyes to try to look at him. Unfortunately what he saw were two light-green jewels that were stained with water, wandering aimlessly about. He had always found it odd that Halo was the only one in the entire village to possess eyes of such color. Dr. Crenon had summed it up to being from her eye condition.

Not once was she ever able to look him into the eyes, for she could not see them. It was a good thing perhaps, because the captain's strong blues became saddened with his heart tearing at the sight of such a young girl with such a horrible deficiency, and he did not want the girl to see he pitied her. His voice started with a weak tremble as the air grew colder on their skin, "Remember your future. Remember that to design your future you must build today. Derjaun is your future, not the problems of your family."

She sat up and wiped her eyes and after she was consoled, he dismounted the fence.

Then affectionally, she called to him, "Thank you, Paposa."

He ceased his stride.

"I love you," she finished.

Staghen's fists slightly tightened. He had not heard that since Radal died. With a shuffle of his cloak, he turned to her, "I love you too. I'm going to leave you with your thoughts as company. But please come home tonight so that you can rest. I'll make sure you're prepared to leave."

Once again, she was left alone on the fence. The pretty Guardian drew in a deep breath and let all of her tension flow out of her mouth in one relieving sigh. But then her heart grew heavy, and her eyes began to quiver. Her sturdy fingers wiped away her eyes. Never before had she felt so alone. "My dear friend, surely you must know how much I miss you. It seems not so long ago that you and I were resting on this fence, watching the storm overhead. We talked about everything yet said so much with nothing. And there was so much of you I had not learned. It seemed as if the moment we became friends, you were gone. Just gone. Now, even though I still see your face when I sleep, you seem to exist...only in my memory."

Her face clenched into its never-ending sadness. Her heart longed for him to come home. While her eyes cried effortlessly, she glanced to the mountains and whimpered, "You were meant to live for so much more."

12

The next morning was the most important moment of her life. The dawn's light was filtering in the dusty room, turning the brown colors of the area rug into its splendid deep burgundy, and reflecting pops of gold were seen against the glass of every oil lantern that sat upon the table and dresser. How in those passing weeks did she grow to love that humble room, so perfect in all of its finishings. She was very thankful that Staghen allowed her to reconstruct the setup of the room to better suit her vision.

She didn't have to worry about stubbing her toe on her bed leg in the middle of the night anymore or knocking over the water pitcher and sending its fragile porcelain crashing into pieces on the floor. Staghen was even gracious enough to let her remove the curtains at her will to let every possible light in.

In this room, in this exact moment, Jastin was sitting up in bed, dressed in her nightgown, and watching Halo sit on the chair and tie up her boots. Her nightgown was much looser on her, and she kept pulling the neckline up on her narrowing shoulders. She stared at the lady Guardian with her full lips parted, chapped from the chilly air.

"My Guardian?" Jastin peeped.

"Yes?"

"You are quite different this morning. Normally you're fast-paced, frantic, withdrawn, and quiet. But now you're calm and steady. Are you alright?"

Halo snatched the bootlace to pull it tighter and smiled, still leaning over. "Yes," she said. "I'm very happy. It's an incredibly important day."

"Oh! Wonderful!" Jastin clapped her hands merrily. As she stood, she opened her wardrobe to choose a dress. She placed her finger to her lips and began shuffling the dresses about. She said, "Which one should I wear? Is it someone's birthday? A wedding? Oh, Staghen has purchased so many for me! And then I made this one." She pulled it out and showed the garment to her friend. "How about this one? It's lovely and white, like the sky today! Like..." She clutched it to her chest and fluttered her lashes.

The Guardian approached and placed her hand on Jastin's shoulder. "I know, I know. Like Staghen's dreamy complexion." She laughed and instructed Jastin to put it up. "But nothing of what you said. I'm going to the forest to look for Derjaun."

"WHAT?"

"Yes!" Halo said in her happy tone, as for once she had found that youthful happiness all over again. "Staghen and I talked last night on the fence, and he knows I still want to find Derjaun. After all, Jastin, I shouldn't keep making these men sacrifice their lives for what I want. It's my duty to bring him home, so today I'm going to do it. The captain gave me permission to do it."

Jastin's lips parted in terrible fear. "As happy as I am for you, this is suicide for you and I both. Don't you understand?"

"Both?" Halo asked.

"Yes," she stammered. "I'll die without you. And then for you there's the Annenji. Thieves. Wolves. Pabi cats. Savri cats!"

Halo boldly spoke attempting to nurture her friend, "I understand your fears, but these fears aren't mine. I have to go."

"Halo," the soft-spoken girl pleaded, "I don't want you to go."

The lavish Inner Circle girl was still just that, a lavish Inner Circle girl. But she prepared food for Halo to take and drew fresh water. Staghen waited for Halo outside on his horse. He was stunned to see she came alone.

"You can't possibly be serious," he stated bluntly.

Halo responded casually, "She's not coming. And I wouldn't want her to if she didn't want it herself."

All the captain did was sigh in distaste and shake his head. "Very well. I'll take you to the fields."

Together they rode while Halo gripped the reins as hard as she could while her soul searched inward for guidance. This was her burden alone to bear. The dew was flickering against the grass and all above her were wisps of gray clouds. The air smelled as warm and humid as could be. They passed the training grounds and the gate right out near Derjaun's home and then changed direction to the northernmost part of those fields. They reached the coniferous trees and heard the birds had dwindled in song, recently taking flight to the south.

The horses jostled in their gait until they halted completely, and Staghen glanced to the young lady. He spoke in a neutral tone, "This is where we part."

Halo returned his gaze as Zidori's head reared, snorting a heavy breath. The Guardian looked onward. "Yes, I suppose it is. I can't thank you enough. I will come home." She leaned her head more toward him. "I promise you."

"Don't make promises that cannot be guaranteed, young lady."

Halo tried to study his face but couldn't. She rubbed her eyes once more to see if perhaps the allergies of the morning had made them hazy. But she didn't want Staghen to think something was wrong, and so she ceased her actions.

They suddenly heard another horse behind them coming up fast.

"Wait!"

Halo quickly turned, feeling her hope rise far and high that it could be Jastin.

And it was!

The galakhan's smile was so grand that it extended her belly in a deep breath of relief and glee. Jastin came with Nikolag on his horse.

"Please, wait!" she shouted once more.

Nikolag immediately shrugged his shoulder to his ear and scolded, "Ah, vile girl, stop yelling in my ear!"

Jastin leapt off the horse and quickly reached into her purse and offered the gollet a handful of gold. "Thank you for your troubles, strange pungent man."

The gollet stared at Halo and back down to the offering, immediately changing his character. "Ha, why of course! For an offering like that..." He snatched the gold from her hands to stuff it in his vest pocket. "...I'll take you anywhere you need to go!"

"Jastin," Halo called as she hurried Zidori over and laughed, "this is Nikolag, the gollet I told you about! I'm so happy to see you here!" She practically jumped off her horse to greet her friend.

"Oh?" she asked. She turned and looked at the mounted gollet and back to Halo. "It's a shame he reeks like hog sweat. He's just your type."

"Jastin!" Halo laughed, smacking her friend's back.

"What? It's true!" Jastin said.

"No, that's not what I meant. Hogs don't sweat. Stars above, you are an Inner Circle girl!" Halo chuckled again, leaning away for a moment as if to size her friend up.

That Inner Circle girl could be absolutely silly to her at times.

Halo looked at Nikolag furiously counting his gold. She said to him, "Thank you for bringing her here."

"Oh, of course. The moment I saw her attire I knew she'd pay me well. I just didn't think it'd be that well."

Jastin walked up to Halo and looked up to her. Her face was full of sweet expressions, and she asked, "May I still go?"

All Halo could do was reach down to pull her onto her horse's rear. "I wouldn't want it any other way."

Nikolag was respectfully quiet as he reached back in his pocket to count the gold, and Staghen turned his horse over to Halo's. "Now, you have to keep a promise, for both of you."

"The promise that I'll come home?" she asked.

"No, the promise that you'll do your very best. I could have taught you for weeks how to do a search, but you still wouldn't have been ready. You'll learn from this and grow quite substantially. Just come home if you must and know that if you come home empty-handed you didn't fail."

She felt Jastin's arms tighten around her, hugging her and holding her. Her friend rested her cheek against her armored back and let out a coo of breath as if she were content. Halo nodded strongly and snapped the reins to take off to the entrance of the menacing forest where so many men had died. That was all she could do. It was time.

The lady Guardian was locked in looking onward toward some sort of destiny. The color of the pine trees was deep and earthy, the patches of dirt beneath her were packed and wet, and the extravagant scent of the wood and soil made her think of childhood times. They were spicy, splendid. She said to Jastin, "I would love to gather this scent in a bottle!"

Jastin smiled gleefully, tucking her head behind her friend's back. "You'd be gathering quite a lot of things! How would you gather the smell of the air?"

Halo looked forward and grinned. Snapping the reins harder, she said, "I'd find a way."

They had left the entrance far behind, and together they felt peaceful. The Guardian feeling accomplished and ready, the younger wealthy girl feeling content. They had always longed for some sort of adventure together since they were little girls, but never could they have imagined it would be so soon and so...dire.

Zidori carried them, and they felt weightless under her more accomplished stride, whipping under low branches and leaping through shallow creeks. Every branch broke under her hooves. Every rock plunged deeper into the ground. They were joyful. They were all together.

Time had passed, and Halo looked to the sky and noticed the sun fighting with the clouds. "It seems that we've gone several miles now.

I think it'd be best if we stopped here and looked. This is close to where his reading materials were found."

She dismounted and began looking around in the beautiful forest. It was simply magical. When the sun could shine through, it dripped down those berry pine trees and gave spots of light to the lovely forest floor. The pine was so rich in hue it almost seemed blue. Or maybe it was blue. Halo couldn't tell. The trunks of the berry pine trees were jagged, rough, and the bark split in shards from age. The trunks were long, broad, and tall, allowing a human of average height to pass underneath the lowest branches. Young berries could be seen in all their brilliant cold hues, still kissed with sunshine and dew.

"Halo," Jastin whimpered from behind.

The Guardian turned and could not resist laughing. Jastin was struggling to dismount Zidori, lying across the horse's back and one leg swinging wildly about.

"I can't get down. She's too tall!" she said.

"Grab ahold of the saddle on the horn and back and guide your-self down. It's not that far of a drop."

"Maybe for you! You're taller than I am."

Halo approached and helped the timid girl slide off. They looked at one another, and the Guardian smirked. "Only by a thumb's length."

Jastin fixed her dress and her shawl. "What are your first orders, my brave galakhan?"

Halo said with certainty, "We need to check this area first. Jastin, stay close to me. And if you see anything that I can't see, and you know what I mean, let me know. But for stars above, do NOT scream. You understand?"

Jastin nodded then asked as she followed Halo's lead, "Do you find it odd that we haven't even witnessed an Annenji yet? Poor Ishlog was killed that night they came here. I mean, I felt that if this forest was truly that dangerous, we should have seen something by now."

Halo shielded her head to walk under a branch. "Not entirely. The Annenji seem to always attack at night."

The girls came under the low branches and Halo stood upright immediately. Something profound caught her mind. Her eyes looked sternly to the ground deepening the thought. "Jastin," she said.

"What is it?"

"I just realized the Annenji only attack at night. And not one villager has been killed in any of the previous attacks. They go after men who seem to be in some sort of leader role. And we didn't even know of their existence until the first attack almost twenty years ago. My biggest question is why they are here now. Where did they come from? Did we do something a long time ago that threatened them and I don't know?"

"It is ironic," Jastin said, "that ever since Staghen took the role they haven't attacked the village once. Even perhaps what Ishlog and his men did could have been seen as a threat to them and that's why they attacked. But it's been a while since then, and we haven't had any retaliation. Right?"

Halo sulked for what seemed like could have been an eternity. She couldn't put the pieces together. Something was awfully wrong with everything.

She fixed her silk scarf that was hanging about her neck. "Let's go. I'll remember these details, but for now I really want to get this search going. If they are after men of strength or in some sort of leader role, then Derjaun shouldn't have been attacked by one. Even if I find his remains, I don't care. I have to find something."

Jastin reached into her bag, still following Halo, and spoke, "I have my paper and quill here! I'll write these down for you."

She flopped down onto a rock and began scribbling away while Halo examined everywhere. It dawned on her suddenly that with it being nearly three months since Derjaun disappeared, he could be anywhere. He could have found a cave to hide away in and die, he could have attempted to scale the mountains and fallen into an icy river, or he could have found an unknown village and sought shelter and care there. Where in the heavens would she start?

"Jastin, look for footprints. I know it's a mere opportunity with soil erosion and rain but look for smaller footprints. But stay within my ears."

"Yes!" Jastin said as she stood up. She left and went on with her orders.

Left slightly alone, Halo knelt on one knee and felt the soil in her leather gloves, rolling each dirt lump through her fingers. "Where are you?" she whispered out loud.

But they had found nothing. No sign of any human life, no struggling, no lock of hair, no shred of clothing, nothing. And so the Guardian made the decision to mount and venture deeper into the woods thus closer to the mountains. While on their travel, Halo pondered about if Derjaun had made it this far, if he was as truly sick and near death as everyone thought him to be. Jastin was quiet the entire time, allowing her friend a moment to reflect, conjure up what to do, and think.

Until her sudden voice almost startled Halo, "Do you think it's possible that someone kidnapped Derjaun, stole his reading materials, and then dropped them after seeing nothing useful inside?"

Halo pulled her horse to an abrupt halt. "Not only is that a possibility, but I just realized I never saw what was inside those materials. He could have written about something. There could have been hints inside. A letter. Something." Once again, she dismounted and helped Jastin off. "Here. We're five miles deep now, and with the season at hand the sun will be our friend for a few more hours. Let's find a place to make camp, and we'll search in the morning."

When the Guardian turned to examine and touch the surroundings, seeing with her hands, Jastin felt her stomach rumble loudly. She gulped and held her belly.

"Was that thunder?" Halo asked.

"No. It's my stomach. I'm starving. We've been out here for hours with no food yet."

The Guardian stood up and turned, seeing her friend's facial expression of growing hunger pangs. "You can eat what's in the knapsack tied to Zidori's saddle. It's the food you prepared for me."

"Oh, alright!" Jastin said. "I'll leave enough for you. It should be enough to last us until we go home tomorrow."

Halo said, "Tomorrow? We're not going to go back tomorrow. We just got here. We're going to be out here for at least a week."

"A WEEK!" Jastin shouted. "I'm not staying out here for that long! We're going to starve to death!"

"Relax," Halo said as she approached her. "There are plentiful creeks nearby, and I have my bow. We can fish and hunt and gather berries and—"

"And starve to death! Halo, you don't know how to hunt! You can't see!"

She glared at her. "Listen, you asked to come with me. I didn't make you come! If you want to go home, go home! Staghen has taught me how to use a bow, and I may not be good at it, but I've got to learn sometime. And I know how to fish. I've fished my whole life. Just because you sat on cushions doesn't mean the rest of us don't know how to survive!"

Jastin went quiet and pressed her lips together.

"Life is not easy," Halo continued. "Our village is under constant worry that those beasts may come back. And what if they do? What are you going to do then? At some point in your life, you're going to have to endure hardships and discomfort. As Staghen once told me, 'only in the harshest of storms do trees root deeper,' and it's true."

Silence.

The birds sang a lovely song as if in attempts to ease the tension.

Jastin fumbled her lace-gloved hands and looked down.

Halo knew how to change her emotions immediately. She playfully teased, "After all, think about how much Captain Staghen would be proud of you."

She lifted her head.

"Come on." Halo patted the girl's shoulder. "He'd be most impressed if he found out you learned how to berry pick, prepare fresh-caught fish, maybe sew a wound or two. After all, isn't that what you like doing anyway?" She proudly lifted her hands about. "You're just doing it outside now!"

Jastin groaned, "Well, okay. I see what you're saying. I..." She looked down once more.

Then Halo hugged her. "It's okay. You don't have to be afraid. I'm not going to let anything happen to you. And we're not that far from the village. It would take us a few hours on Zidori to get back. You're alright." She pulled away but had one more thing to say, "Don't forget, I'm a Guardian now. I've been trained to fight and know when it's best to withdraw. I promise I won't be stupid with you in my care."

"Alright," Jastin said as she looked to her, "I trust you."

"Good, I'll teach you how to make a fast shelter with the animal hide I brought."

She taught her friend how to unroll the hide, find trees close enough to fasten the rope to, and drape the hide over it. She learned how to hammer the wooden pegs into the ground to keep them still, and after all was finished the two girls rolled out the animal furs inside and sat upon them. But Jastin's learning wasn't over. It was only a few moments of rest before Halo informed her it was time to gather wood.

Together they gathered wood from everywhere. Tiny broken branches, any type of dried vegetation, and all types of branches were gathered back to the little tent. They roamed until Jastin helped Halo find a tree small and dead enough to use an ax to cut down. The wood was chopped, Halo's back was sore, but they brought Zidori to carry the tied-up wood pile back to the camp. Jastin had no idea that her friend knew how to cut trees down, and she was proud to be able to finally learn new skills and offer any help beyond just her eyes.

The campfire grew, and as a chilly twilight came the two snuggled underneath the furs and dined over the exquisite food that had been brought. They peered up at the stars that were enshrouded in the canopy of the pines and finally enjoyed the silence in their lives. The stark wind blew softly about, as if not to disturb their newfound warmth or extinguish their fire. Some sort of owl hooted, and Jastin screeched and hid behind Halo.

"Jastin, it's an owl."

"A what?"

"An owl. It's a nocturnal bird. I hear them all the time out in the fields."

A stillness of quiet befell them once more.

"Come," Halo kindly offered. "Come around here and lay on my lap."

And so she did.

But as Jastin nestled down and felt Halo's hands on her hair, she looked up through the crackling snaps of the fire. How beautiful the embers popped then fluttered to the heavens. To the stars.

"Halo," Jastin said.

"Mmm?" she answered.

"Tell me about the stars."

Halo smirked and looked down to the resting girl. "Since when have you cared about the stars?"

"Since now."

"But every time I do you fall asleep in boredom," she laughed, petting the girl's hair in comfort.

Jastin said nothing, and in saying nothing she told Halo everything.

The Guardian lifted her eyes above the fire in attempts to see the stars she couldn't see there, at least not then. There were too many trees, and the firelight was obscuring them.

She sighed in a smile. "Ah, I see. Well..."

Her friend drew a deep breath and relaxed on her lap, and Halo proceeded, "Gollets use the stars to map their directions out at sea. In common conversation once, Nikolag told me that when he was younger he believed he saw a star that shot across the sky. Like a beam of light. But I didn't believe him. I can't imagine stars racing across the sky, but then again, I suppose anything is possible. But I don't really know much about them that I haven't told you already. I know that they shine brightly because of reflecting the moon's glow.

"But my favorite thing of all is something I learned recently from Nikolag. Gollets believe that there's a star shape in the sky called Veric, and Veric was once a rogue warrior prince who traveled far and wide and fought for the freedom of many people. Once he freed the last of the slaves, he was ambushed by those who didn't believe in his purpose, and they stoned him to death."

"Not a good bedtime story," Jastin interrupted.

"I know, but supposedly his work was so genuine that the stars formed a shape in the sky in his honor. There are more shapes though than him. There's Shain, the hunter. Wildecross, the king. And supposedly he says there's even the shape of a pabi cat up there somewhere. They use these star shapes on their guiding voyages across the sea."

Jastin continued to listen to the marvelous words of her friend as the words ventured from the stars into the Travels of Bremlin stories. And the Inner Circle girl was without strength to keep her eyes open any longer. The fire glowed brightly.

"And of this enormous white wolf that people talk about, the one who eats children and roams in these woods, have you no fear, my friend. He simply doesn't exist."

Halo leaned over and brushed Jastin's hair and saw her sound asleep, lulled by the magical tales. Her own heart was calmed from the beautiful evening, and she kissed her forehead. "He simply doesn't."

13

It was there she felt free. Free to roam as she willed and free to sleep and eat as she willed. The forest night was nothing harsh at all, quite the opposite. Halo was embraced in the unknown of the night, and to some it could have been a frightful thing to sleep in such uncharted territory, but to her it was serene. For once in her young life, she was in charge of her own existence in every single way imaginable. She could search wherever she desired, call out orders as she saw fit, and have her own way of doing things. The chorus of forest wolves sang to her, the darkness seemed to protect her, and the bitter cold refreshed her heavy woes into pristine gladness.

Until Jastin woke her up with jarring cries.

Halo fought to find her friend in the shadowy tent, but it was difficult to do so with the light of the fire now being so low and the night still so dark. She reached and felt her friend's leg. "Jastin, what's wrong?"

"I want to go home!" the girl cried back.

Halo immediately wrapped her arms around the girl to soothe her, but she cried on, "I want to go home. I'm terrified of being out here! I keep hearing things, so many things. Something moves in the darkness all the time! We're so far from help, I'm cold, and even if I wanted to go back, we can't see anything. Halo, we're absolutely vulnerable out here!" Then she fell into Halo's lap. "Oh, what was I thinking to come here with you? I can't calm down. I'm scared beyond my breath's grasp, and I feel I may faint!"

As dire as the situation seemed to Jastin, it was the norm for Halo now. The Guardian stretched her legs and guided the frightened girl to lie in between them and rest her head on her pelvis. She pressed her thumb and forefinger into a spot on Jastin's hand.

"Breathe deep through your nose, and exhale fiercely through your mouth. You're stricken with panic, my dear friend. But you're alright. This happens when we get scared, but you'll calm down and see everything is fine, believe me. Besides, Zidori is outside and is calm. She would alert us if something were wrong."

But it pained the Guardian to see her friend crying in terrifying misery, struggling to breathe in the instructed ways. It was definitely a new situation for the wealthy girl. And yet she knew her friend would be fine.

While the moments passed, Halo listened for any reason that Jastin was fearful of. Even with her sensitive ears, she heard nothing but sounds of the forest. In a motherly way, she brushed Jastin's sweaty forehead and said, "Do you hear that? It's the sounds of the forest."

She could not see her friend opening her eyes a bit more to listen, but she went on trying to console her. "Think of this beautiful moment. If Staghen were here, you'd be completely enamored by it. You would dream about feeling safe in his arms and celebrate the idea of being so alone with him. You see, Jastin? This night isn't a terrifying night. It's simply wonderful. Magical. Think of your heroic stories of adventures and romantic heroes. These are the nights they cherish most."

Halo felt her turn to look up at her. She touched Jastin's eyelashes, feeling them open. She spoke in a smiling tone, "There you go."

Jastin settled her nerves pondering the obvious truth in the words of her friend. One deep sigh was given and her stomach knotted, tossed, and turned in a frenzy of rattled nerves.

"Halo," she said suddenly, "I think I'm going to be sick! What am I going to do? I can't do this out here!"

Halo laughed and leaned over and used their poker stick to take the flames of their fire to the lantern. "Follow me."

Outside and away from the camp, Halo hung the lantern and comforted her friend. "Use our water with one of our many rags to clean your mouth and simply let it be left. It's just your nerves. You're scared. If you breathe deeply, you'll be okay."

She heard Jastin cry, whimpering in the fear of having to vomit. However, minutes passed with nothing happening. Eventually, Jastin sat up straight and sighed.

The two laughed, and the Guardian answered to the darkness, "You see? It's amazing what we can do when we let go of our fears. Let's go back, and we'll sleep closer together this time."

Jastin rejoined her and shuffled her skirt. "You know, you're right. Here," Jastin suddenly said as she took the lantern from Halo, "I'll be your eyes."

It was amazing to the Guardian girl. One moment her friend was crying in severe consternation, and yet already she was holding the lantern proudly and bravely to help escort her back to the tent. The ill-lit surroundings had suddenly meant nothing to her. She struggled to fix her eyes on the amber glow among Jastin's soft face, attempting to see what she was thinking.

But Jastin spoke aloud anyway, "I figured that if you're going to be so stalwart in your actions, I must be as well. It's only fair. While we're out here, there may be a time when you yourself are afraid because you can't see. I want you to feel safe with me as well and trust me too."

Inside her heart, Halo felt completely happy with this confession. Not only did it indicate that she had someone to look after her as well, but her lessons in consoling another who was in a traumatic emotional state had proven to be very useful and successful. Jastin kept her company while she fed the fire to burn brighter, and the two went back to sleep.

The following morning was brisk, the air light, and it seemed as if it had softly rained while they slept. Halo stood proudly outside of the tent and inhaled all of the magic that summer had to offer, with the wild herbs and forestation so fragrant it almost tingled her very senses to breathe it in so deep. There was no clamor of people. No carts. No foul smell of horse manure in the many stables either. She caught a sound in her ear and turned to the left seeing Zidori using the pine bark to shuffle her rump against, satisfying an itch. She had not tied her horse to any tree at all, wanting the mare to be able to flee if need be. But her horse still stayed.

Halo kissed her muzzle and spoke, "I love you so much."

"Aw, I love you too!" Jastin said in ignorance as she climbed out of the tent.

Halo shook her head in love and rolled her eyes, whispering to her mare, "She always needs the attention on her, doesn't she?" She looked over her shoulder to her human friend and spoke, "We're going to fish today. And then we're going to start our search again."

Jastin approached her side and nuzzled into Zidori's belly, stretching her fingers to weave them inside the white coat. Gently pulling the lovely green mane, she shuffled her face left and right and simply let her face press into the mare's side.

"Jastin, what are you doing?"

Jastin mumbled, "She's so soft and fluffy. Like a billowing cloud from the heavens sent here to be my comfort pillow."

Halo giggled and moved over to pat Jastin's back, "Well, get on the fluff cloud. We have to get to the creek with the little light we have today."

The two girls rode to the nearest creek, and the Guardian taught her younger friend how to fish, showing her all of trapping the live catches to snaring them by hand and even scaling them. She was impressed that Jastin learned all of this quite well, but Jastin choked up when she had to bludgeon the poor creatures with a rock. Halo informed her that it was either this method or to saw the heads off. Jastin chose the former.

Back at their humble tent, Jastin had brought fresh creek water to boil the heads, bones, and fins for a hearty and nourishing broth, in which both girls sat by the fire and sipped on gleefully, all while reminiscing about their days of childhood. Yet in the middle of their merriment, Halo noticed her vision dim ever so slightly and looked about. "Jastin, is there a cloud passing overhead?"

Jastin looked up. "No, my dear brave friend. Still the faint overcast we've had all morning."

"Then it's no longer merely morning. We should get moving for our search. The sun has apparently changed position a little, and we'll only have about four hours left of good light."

Jastin stood up at once with her joyful demeanor being doubled in energy. "I am so proud of you. Look at how well you're handling this. We survived our first night. We can surely find Derjaun now with you in charge!"

As Halo sat on the log with her leather-gloved hands rubbing together, she ruminated on what had been said to her. How her lovely friend spoke so much in such a short, hyper breath. "You really think so?"

Jastin pulled her to her feet and fixed her scarf for her. "I know so. Let's get going!" She hastily moved to Zidori and tried to heave herself up. She heaved once more, and once more again. Over and over again as Jastin tried, Halo came near and with one final attempt did she push Jastin's rump up and pulled herself up immediately after.

The friendship they had built when they were younger had simply grown stronger in those recent days.

"Alright, *zakuta* girl!" Halo snapped the reins, and Jastin tightened her arms. In one easy move, Zidori turned and left the campsite to look for the friend who could not be found by anyone else. As her horse gracefully maneuvered through that challenging terrain, Halo briefly thought in happiness, *That's because they didn't know you like I do, Derjaun. I know exactly where to find you.*

With nothing left to lose, Halo rode her horse into the mountains of uncharted territory. All around her the dripping branches had started to glimmer like jewels from the rain. The clarity of her mission was as bright as the wildflowers around them, and her lungs inhaled deeply as she snapped the reins harder. Jastin was becoming a much better back rider, and so they scaled every rolling hill, bounding through drifts and crushing through the creeks. Zidori was taking great care of them.

Freedom bound they were. Hoping to bring him home.

For hours they searched, covering miles far and wide, but nothing was found. And multiple times they attempted to cover a large radius of roughly ten miles, but the days came with little sunshine due to the frequent summer storms, and they were followed by wetter nights. Halo periodically checked her compass that Staghen had given her and was easily able to get them back to camp every single nightfall. Three simple days had passed, and Halo had decided to pack up their site and move elsewhere. But she knew she couldn't just search anywhere.

She had to be thorough and informed on why she would search where she decided.

It was the last night in that area, and she was lying snuggled against Jastin for extra comfort. Her younger friend had undergone quite a lot of strenuous changes in attempting to keep up with her, and so Halo had to ask out of courtesy, "Jastin, do you feel you have the strength and the will to search more of the mountainous regions? Today we saw that vast and open field, and I truly believe we need to look in the foothills."

The furs that covered them could now only do so much to keep them dry, even when partnered with the blazing fire at the front of the tent. The summer should have been pleasant with longer days, but the feisty coldness of spring was still clinging on. It was a tent that wasn't truly fashioned for such weather, and even Halo herself believed that her friend could be getting sick. She felt the younger girl push her face into her chest, saying, "I'm going to try. But these nights are starting to get to me."

The Guardian pulled her friend closer and thought deeply. The urgency of what was at hand was now leaving her mind in utter turmoil. Jastin was starting to suffer from exhaustion, but if Derjaun was still alive and out there he would be as well. But she had to think logically. She *must* think logically.

With grief in her heart, she knew they both could not go on like this. It was extremely difficult to think upon, but nonetheless she faintly spoke, "I understand. I can't sacrifice your life to save another. Please give us one more half day to search the foothills tomorrow. I'll call for him, and maybe he'll come to my voice."

"Call for him?" Jastin asked. "Are you sure calling for anyone is the right thing to do? What if those creatures come?"

Halo rolled over onto her back and folded her arms behind her head, staring up at the absolute nothingness. "It doesn't really matter now. They haven't attacked us once, and we've seen no sign of them anywhere. At this point, I don't really care."

And then she simply attempted to nod off to sleep, leaving Jastin curious as to what tomorrow could bring.

But the next morning, Jastin's health had made clear signs that she was sick. Halo brewed warm tea for her to drink, gathering the berries and the fresh herbs from around their camp. The girl who was so used to a pampered life was not bred for such things, and so with her pale face and nagging cough she attempted to bundle herself as best as she could for that final ride.

Out near the horse, Halo glanced at Jastin trudging through the wet ground, hanging her head low with each passing cough. She thought of Derjaun's ailing body and the trauma came flooding her emotions all over again. Her young friend approached, placing her forehead into Halo's chest armor. She coughed once more. Halo could no longer stand for it. She could not bear to watch Jastin cough or struggle for breath anymore. The pollen of the air had tinged their lungs, but Jastin could not handle it the same way.

She placed her arms around her friend and gritted her teeth. She drew in a deep breath. She was starting to get scared.

"Come," Halo said, "you're coming with me, and I'm taking you back to the forest entrance. I'll shoot the arrow there. But you can't stay out here another minute."

She saw Jastin withdraw immediately, backing away. "I promise I'll stop coughing. I don't want you out here alone," she said back. But doing so, she heaved over and coughed violently and began gasping for her air.

"Jastin, don't be ridiculous! And stop yelling. You're making yourself worse. Look, it's going to be alright. Get on Zidori, and I'll take you home."

She struggled to see Jastin's face in all of the shadowing clouds overhead and the dense canopy. She could see her cloak and her knitted hat and her frame, but her facial gestures were completely unknown. However, Halo had started to be able to *feel* what someone may look like, and this gift was abundant in that moment. She knew Jastin was looking incredibly upset. Her facial expressions became clear as she lifted her head to where the light was in Halo's favor. She *was* upset.

"Very well. I won't argue," she said in mumbling defeat.

Halo felt relief as she helped her friend on her horse, leaving all of her belongings behind. Even if she didn't return, there wasn't much value in that tent that could not be retrieved at a later time. She didn't want to waste a moment helping her ill friend find comfort and care.

Back into the forest they went, and the noble Guardian girl had her horse racing as skillfully as ever. Jastin coughed and settled into her back, holding on dearly for feeling misery creeping its ugly self up her body and into her muscles.

Zidori suddenly came to a grinding halt.

"Zakuta, girl," Halo tried as she urged her on. She attempted to nudge the horse's belly with her heel, but the mare's ears pulled back and her nostrils flared. Halo could feel her belly growing and collapsing with heavy breath between her legs.

"Halo, what's—"

"Shhh," Halo whispered alarmingly. "Zidori senses something."

Both girls became absolutely deathly silent. All around Halo turned her head attempting to hear anything, and suddenly she realized she heard *nothing*. She leaned to one side and noticed her horse's pupils were dilated, indicating stress.

She sat upright and turned her head and leaned back into Jastin. She whispered, "Do not make a sound. Slowly dismount her as quietly as you can and do not move."

Jastin obeyed her command, sliding quietly off.

Halo dismounted next and began removing Zidori's bridle and saddle.

"What are you doing?" Jastin quietly asked.

"Something is here. And if she needs to run, I don't want her to get snared on anything. Now be quiet and get behind me," Halo finished as she pulled Jastin behind her and backed up into a tree, discreetly drawing her sword. She spoke once more almost so quietly that only the pattering of her lips allowed her friend to understand her, "I need you to be silent so I can listen."

Jastin nodded.

Halo looked up and around the canopy of the pine trees.

She did not hear birds.

She did not hear the wind.

As she lifted her sword in a guard stance, her exposed wrist felt something that was curious to her. She looked at it and extended her arm. It felt stronger. Promptly, the Guardian removed her glove and tested the air. Her stomach tightened.

Her heart began to pound into her chest.

There among her pale and strong hand, she felt the cool air being interrupted by a warm draft. It rose in temperature for a brief moment before returning to its subtle warmth again.

Her feet went numb, and her eyes widened.

They were there.

Over her shoulder, she glanced to witness the innocence of Jastin's face, so naïve and vague to all around her. The wealthy young girl looked up and squinted, silent in her resounding sweetness.

Halo backed into Jastin more firmly, protecting her in audacious ways and spoke with calmness, "Listen to me. Under no circumstances are you to panic. But the Annenji, I believe, are nearby. And by nearby, I mean close. Closer than we want. Do not move. Do not fidget. And for stars above, don't even *breathe* loudly.

If it comes, do exactly as I say the moment I say it, and do NOT dawdle."

When she turned to look forward again, she was left unaware of Jastin's facial expressions, however her friend placed two fumbling hands upon her back. She focused up toward the sky more than anything. She peered and saw nothing in the trees, and Zidori was absolutely quiet and motionless like a statue frozen in time with both beauty and might.

A washing heat graced the tops of their heads, and they both looked harder through the trees. Something had disturbed the canopy to allow its leaves to shuffle like fluttering powder atop the girls' heads. And then Halo witnessed with her own ears the sound of leathery wings swaying rhythmically above. It flowed gracefully, peacefully, as if undisturbed or uninterested in anything below. The enormous black figure webbed in and out of view from the berry pines above, and eventually its winged sound seemed to grow fainter.

Jastin's clawing grasp on Halo's coat had lightened immediately, and she sighed, "Oh, thank goodness. It's gone."

But Halo knew better and prevented her dear friend from moving still. "No," she warned, "these beasts travel in flocks. If one flew over, others must not be far behind." Once more she tested the air and realized perhaps she had been wrong. There was no tinge of heat or warmth at all.

Jastin leaned into Halo's back and muffled her cough into the coat.

The Guardian girl stood upright and eased her stance. All the winds were tepid and gentle. Boldly, she spoke, looking up to the skies once more, "It was flying north. Thank the stars above. It's obviously not headed to the village."

"Oh, good," Jastin replied. "That's the last thing the village needs is—"

Halo turned and slapped her hand over Jastin's mouth. She heard something in the distance to the east. Jastin's eyes opened wider, simply petrified as her muffled cries were hushed.

Halo turned her ear to the east and heard another set of wings approaching fast. A sweltering sensation brushed their skin so horrendously in temperature that sweat began to drip down their necks. She saw Jastin's eyes watering in rising distress.

The moment the sound became too close for comfort, Halo knew exactly what was going to happen. She grabbed her friend instinctively and pulled her to the ground. She whispered hard, "Get down!"

Every inch of her body had a battling sensation of hot and cold when the canopy broke through with shattering wood and broken limbs. She covered Jastin's head and pulled her under her crouched body, looking to the right to see Zidori rearing and taking off.

She felt her helpless friend press her face so hard into her chest that it could have bruised. All around them the debris from above collapsed and smashed onto the ground, but she was left without a possibility of how to look up. The chaos had blocked her vision to see exactly what the Annenji were doing. Were they diving through the trees to attack them? Were they attempting to land on the trees and realizing their weight could not be held? Through and through, her eyes frantically tried to focus beyond the shrapnel with the blackened figures scrambling about, and suddenly an opening was torn asunder. The blinding sun singed her eyes with immeasurable pain. She jolted her head to the side and closed her eyes hard.

All she could do was hold onto her friend, but it wouldn't be able to last for long. The only choices she had were to attempt to flee but risk the falling debris crushing them or stay put and possibly be burned alive. Squeezing Jastin harder, she pulled the girl into her arms more and more, desperate for any possible second at an opportunity to act. Finally, she looked up after the wrecking seemed to subside. Beautiful skies were seen in a massive opening in the canopy. Somehow, they had lived. There were still no birds or wind, but the temperature around them was still uncomfortably warm. That great hole above their heads was still with the glorious blues of the day. Nothing else was seen.

Then, peering over the canopy hole and down to them, the enormous head of the great black beast appeared. Fragile limbs and branches cracked under the pressure high above.

"Halo?" Jastin asked, trembling in the fear as death loomed closer to them both.

Her lips quaked. Her jaw rattled. The pressure in her head consumed her so much she felt faint.

The Annenji leaned its head down, and the pungent smell flooded the entirety of the forest floor. How it made their stomachs turn. It was like a bath of blood and rotting corpses decaying in the summer sun, all mixed with ash and a smell of decomposing eggs and milk.

Halo pressed her fingers into Jastin's back, staring up at the beast. Their eyes seemed to lock as it started to stretch its neck further to look. She thought and thought. The pressure in her chest met with the pounding in her head, and she remembered. *These are the beasts that killed Radal, Ishlog, and possibly Derjaun.*

Derjaun. Her friend.

Leaning over into the tree with Jastin protected in her grasp, her breath quickened, and she looked up once more, seeing the hellish fiend opening its mouth wide. Enormous teeth and fangs glowed brightly with a searing heat from within its throat. As the flames built within its blazing mouth, she could see the fiery glows building within the blackened fur.

"RUN!" she shouted at once.

Halo yanked Jastin's hand and pulled her so hard to her feet that the young girl almost fell immediately. They ran as fast as they could over the fallen forest debris and through the wild weeds to wherever they could be safe. Her eyes were failing her, for the incessant colors of the forest were all blending in her vision. She could not determine a rock from a brush, or how close a low branch really was. All she could do was remember her training to run and ignore her fears of the unseen beyonds.

Roars of blistering heat swooped down from the canopy, and at once their safe spot had been consumed by fire, a terrorizing inferno cast behind them. Blackened smoke was thrown to the skies, and together they kept running as fast as they could.

Jastin ducked under the branches and felt one scratch and whip her in the face. She screamed loudly, "Halo, I can't run as fast as you! I'm losing my breath!"

She would not let go of her friend's hand. She called back in earnest, "You have to!"

The fires loomed behind them. It seemed like in a few moments the entirety of what they left behind was engulfed in flames. If they didn't make it out of the forest soon, there was a high chance they would be trapped. But the exit was roughly seven miles away, and Halo realized that they wouldn't be able to keep up this pace for that long.

Her boots almost skidded in the dirt, and she turned around to face the Annenji head on. She pulled Jastin behind her and clenched her fist around her hilt, drawing her sword.

"Stay behind me," she ordered her friend.

Jastin got behind her and looked around. Halo's shoulders rose in anger. Why, they rose and collapsed in absolute fury. Her lips tightened. Her teeth clenched and she sneered at the damned things that surrounded them. She would no longer run. Directly in front of the girls, one landed and let its wings rest, crouching and walking through the undamaged trees. A ferocious roar was heard on her left and another came with its teeth bared. A third sound of low growling, rumbling in a wicked throat was heard on her right. Three in total approached.

Behind her, her friend whimpered and began praying, "Please don't let us die out here."

Halo pulled her dagger from the strap on her thigh, "Like Derjaun says, 'We can't die.'"

She turned and gnarled her teeth. With one accurate throw, the dagger struck the Annenji on the left chest, but the dagger was hardly thrown with might enough to truly do any damage. All that happened was it taunted the beast to inhale for a flaming assault.

Quickly, she shoved Jastin to the right toward the other one, and the moment it went to leap and attack, the other's breath had launched across, and she pulled Jastin down immediately. The fire had been blown directly into the opposite fiend, blinding its eyes and scorching its face.

All around them, the massive black paws and talons stomped, burning the brush and crushing everything underneath it. "Go!" Halo urged.

Time was ticking quickly as Jastin and Halo scurried underneath the deadly paws, dropping to their bellies and elbows to crawl underneath and out the other side.

Halo pulled Jastin up and turned at once to see the two Annenji fighting each other, and the one who had been burned was losing quickly.

She pulled Jastin on and ordered, "Come, let's go! I don't want you to see this another second."

The two girls ran once more, but it was only a few minutes until Jastin began stumbling, trudging through the impossible terrain. She coughed again and again until she leaned over on her knees, gasping for air. The smoke from the initial location had taken to the sky, and now Halo could see birds fleeing from the situation. The beasts' breaths had been so hot that it was setting fire to nearly everything around them.

"Halo..." Jastin choked, "I can't go on. I can't breathe. I'm sorry. I..."

Halo approached her and leaned over. She grabbed her beloved friend's arm and heaved her up across her shoulders. But already her legs were buckling. Jastin had lost a considerable amount of weight, but it wasn't enough for a girl Halo's size to manage easily. She turned and took a few steps, feeling the adrenaline course through her body. Behind them were the howls of agony and a fatal fight coming to an end, and in front of her the third one suddenly broke through the trees and came down to the ground.

She gently and slowly laid Jastin against a tree and looked at her. The wheezing was loud in the girl's chest, and her lips were incredibly pale. "Stay here. You'll be alright."

Jastin could not even return any love for her friend before the blind Guardian stood and faced that terrible thing. She fiercely drew her sword and glared menacingly at it.

Lowly, she spoke, "This will be the last time."

She lurched toward the animal and opened her mouth and made a rattling scream that came from her stomach, "I'M GOING TO KILL YOU!"

The fight was on. Halo lunged after the animal and crashed her sword in its direction, but it easily shuffled to the right and attempted to bite the blade. Now being so close to one multiple times, she thought that if she was close enough to the beast, it could not scorch her flesh, nor could it bite her. With this, she hurried up against its belly and tried to stay along its side. It lifted a deadly paw to swipe at her and began spinning and backing up in. Halo pushed her back into the oily fur of its side and used all of her leg strength to groan and push it into a red thorn tree. It yelped in pain, hurrying away from her. She lost her balance and fell against the trunk. Lifting her head, the animal turned around and was ready to attack again. She looked up and saw a low-hanging branch, and she pulled it quickly, backing up and pulling it taught. The thorns pierced her leather gloves, and blood was felt on her hands. The beast opened its mouth, and with one final tug she let it go.

It struck its eyes and ripped a considerable amount of skin. The Annenji backed up and howled in despair, pawing at its eyes and crying loudly.

She drew her sword once more and hanging it with both hands to her side she drew in a deep breath and raced after the animal and thrusted the blade directly into its throat.

Black blood gushed out all over her deranged face, and she drove it in harder as she screamed in a horrendous symphony with the beast. She looked into its eyes and remembered all of what she fought for. She didn't want to simply kill the fiend. She wanted to murder it. Harder she twisted the blade and ruptured its jugular even more, and then she placed her foot onto its chest to remove her sword.

She backed up and slashed into its face and neck until it began to stumble away, leaving a trail of greasy and filthy blood. It looked and tried to call for something, but its throat could not mutter a sound.

With one final sigh, the beast fell to die.

Halo was left standing in absolute shock. Tingling was felt in her hands and feet and all in her stomach she felt she would vomit and faint. But she composed herself and lifted her head up high, steadying her breath and watching the excrement of the beast leave its body.

It was over.

She heard Jastin coughing, and she hurried back to her, kneeling down and wrapping her own scarf around her friend's mouth. "You're going to be okay. I'll shoot the arrow. We're not far from the opening. Staghen will be here soon."

Jastin tried to talk, but she hushed her, "Don't talk. Cup your hands over your mouth like this to breathe in moist air. You'll be okay. I promise you."

But Jastin had to talk. She simply had to. She looked at her friend's bloody face and used her own handkerchief to wipe Halo's face clean. "Your face is a mess," she said affectionately.

Halo's eyes glittered. She knew Jastin was going to be okay. "There's one more left still. We need to try to call for Zidori and get back to the village."

She suddenly heard a horse coming. No. She heard multiple horses coming. Halo stood and turned to see her magnificent mare charging through the trees and smoke, leading the captain and his men. She had returned to her rider after all.

Halo stood near Jastin, looked at the coming men, and simply tried to sheath her sword, but it missed her scabbard and fell to the ground. Her proud green eyes began to wither in her juvenile emotions when she saw Staghen arrive. She may have been a hero in that moment, but she was still a young and frightened girl. Seeing him made her feel that everything was finally going to be just fine.

Staghen pointed his men toward Jastin and ordered, "Go to her! She seems like she's ailing."

The men urged their horses around to tend to the coughing girl, and Halo looked back to Staghen, who dismounted Rikaana. He ran to her, clutching his black-gloved knuckles hard, and his lips were pursed tightly. She could not see his facial expressions well at all. But when he met her, his arms lovingly were thrown around her aching body, and he pulled her into his chest. His face snuggled immediately into her hair, and his grip was so tight that she was confused as to whether it hurt or felt comforting. All of her bones felt they would break.

She sobbed suddenly, "Staghen, I..."

"Hush," he whispered as he kissed her forehead. The captain squeezed his eyes harder, and his breath was that of excellent release. Halo felt his hand stroke her hair, and he whispered once more, "You're alright."

"Captain!" came the sound of the gollet's call. "Jastin's informed us that there's another one still alive. We need to get out of here."

Staghen removed his embrace from Halo and walked over, prominent in his disposition of the matter. "Then let's," he began. He looked at Jastin, who was now standing in her weakness. "Are you alright?"

"Yes, my darling," she responded feebly, fighting for breath.

All of the men looked at Staghen, stricken with what she called him. He simply stood upright and glanced at them, then spoke boldly with a brow raised, "Come now, men. Do you blame this girl? She had a near-death experience. Let her be with her emotions."

He turned and rounded all of them up with a wave of his hand. "Get moving. Halo, can you ride?"

"I can," she said calmly.

But they both looked at one another. Staghen paused and witnessed the exhaustion soaking among her body. He had tried to remain stoic about it all but had lost that war many times in the several moments he had arrived. All of what was beautiful to him was Halo's apparent victory.

Vathra stepped by his side and whispered into his ear, "If I may, she is like your daughter now. Carry her with you."

"Very well." He nodded sincerely. "Halo, you'll ride with me. Vathra will take Jastin, and Nikolag can lead Zidori home."

Staghen mounted his horse, and Nikolag was gentle in helping

Halo up. As she nestled in Staghen's arms, he removed his cloak and gave it to her.

"Nikolag, the rain is coming. Don't you need that?"

Nikolag returned with a kind smile and began reciting one of Halo's favorite gollet poems as he retied her bootlace, "In stories spoke a prince alone, who weeps of snow without a throne. This man with strength so pure in thought, his course was set, his ode begot."

He snapped her laces together tightly and backed away. The girl atop the horse remained completely calm in her returning smile. The men were still gathering Jastin up gently and readying for the return.

One of the Guardians walked past Nikolag and laughed. "As if you would ever be pure in thought."

But in that moment, the gollet had been.

The time had come to leave that world behind. The world in which she glanced over the captain's shoulder and watched the beautiful forest become nothing but a time in which she learned how to handle herself, to protect the life of another, and to stand firm in her boots. Staghen was immeasurably proud of what both girls had done, but still Derjaun was not found. It could have possibly been the very thing that led the blind Guardian to believe he may never be found. She softly laid her head upon his chest armor, weighing in with grief that perhaps she had failed.

Staghen noticed and tried to console her with his loving voice, "It is not the end of your world, Halo. It is only the end of your innocence. But take mind to this. When one sees what the world can be, it is nearly impossible to return to innocence."

And then the rain came.

14

Halo was a woman now. A full eight years had passed swiftly, like sand sinking into the ocean. And on this day, she was in her room resting. The crisp winter air felt good. In she breathed, allowing her stronger body to be filled of the wondrous effect. It was, at this time, the only thing that truly made her feel clean. For nothing else in the lands had ever come to bring her true peace.

When a bird perched on her windowsill, it barely caught her attention. The beauty of the morning sun's rays being captured in the sparkling blue feathers went unbeknownst to her. A gentle chirp had attempted to give her gentle company, in which she still held her head low. Long locks that had grown richer in color hung well in a braid to the side, flowing down her breasts, which were snug against her nightclothes.

She raised her head, not even needing to squint her eyes from the sun. "Sweet field bird, I would love to look at your radiance. I'm quite sure it will be the last time I could see it." Halo stood much taller now than before, and she allowed her nightclothes to brush the wooden floors as her feet moved toward the sill. Being peaceful not to disturb the little creature, she leaned her head forward and down, studying it. "You will be flying elsewhere for winter, and I am feeling my vision will fly away with you. Unfortunately, it will not return as you will."

Her own thoughts had made the coming knock of the door completely petty and therefore refrained from acknowledging it. After all, it could not have been any other soul than Staghen or the lady of the house. Her ears picked up the soft scrape of the opening door against the old wooden floor, but she still did not turn her head.

"My sweet girl..." the soft voice began. It was a voice so rich in depth. However the statement made was but a bittersweet one. In the light of the morning by the window, Staghen's grown appearance stood by her side. She stayed quiet. "My sweet girl, it is a merry day today. Is it not?"

Her vision to each side was nearly gone, portraying nothing but blurred images and distorted colors, and so by this unless she turned her head, she would not really be able to make out his gestures. She could only imagine them by the simplicity of his voice. She looked to him. In his hands, a well-adorned box was held. "It is the day you were born, my dear. You're a lovely woman of twenty years now."

She turned back to the window. The bird had flown away. In the voice inside of her own head, she heard her spirit call to the being, *Take me with you*. A deep breath was taken by her, and she lowered her head once more. "Captain, has it truly been eight years since I have lived here?"

Staghen set the gift down and beamed with happiness to her, attempting to lighten the lady's heavy soul. "It has. And it has been an exciting eight years. My, look at you. Every day you grow more and more. You grow stronger and braver by the day."

"No, it has not. And please..." Her eyes watered. "Do not use this term 'brave' with me. I am hardly worth the word."

"As much as I am aware of your lust for arguing with me, Halo, I must push forth with it nonetheless." He took her hand. "A hero is not measured by how many lives she saves but by how many times she has nearly lost hers for her work."

She did not believe him.

"Halo, without instructions to do so, you brought the old woman's purse back to her and brought Mozkin to justice. Before you were even thirteen years old, you rescued Agrona's entire herd from the forest wolves. You charged after them in the middle of the night with the eyes you possessed, flailing your sword and cutting into those beasts until they never returned. You protected Jastin and killed an Annenji alone before you became a woman!

"On the next day, you became a woman. It was an awful day for you," he spoke as his eyes searched for hers. For only a moment he paused and then gently pulled her to face him. "You ignored the pain and sickness your body underwent to jump into the rushing Gigannora to save the blacksmith's granddaughter. And at the innocent age of fifteen years, Vathra believed you to be so worthy of the title that he claimed you would become his malakae when the morning star sets on my time. As being a woman, you have to endure something every month that no man will understand. And yet you are still the only Guardian I have yet to hear any complaints of pain from during training." He quieted for a brief moment before he spoke again, "Does this not mean anything to you?" Staghen's eyes were soft and concerned.

Still the young woman's eyes were turned from him. For so long did she wear the burden of sadness that it was only in fighting did she have the ability to seem somewhat human. Her eyes glistened, reflecting the tragedy that the pain may never leave.

With his fatherly love did he look to her, and in his dominant care did he question lowly, "What more proof do you request, my child? What else in these lands could make you happy?"

It was some time before the Guardian woman spoke. When she did, her look reflected absolute loss. "Oh, dear Captain, you seem to adhere so much of your attention to me, and yet you still, year after year, ask me this same question, and I keep giving the same answer." She paused again with her eyes looking slightly away and sparkling. It was almost as if she forgot how to speak. So many words demanded the attention of the captain, but she was unsure which ones were important enough to come first. "I failed. Before I had even become a Guardian, I failed."

"How? Derjaun is dead, Halo." He came to her and held her shoulders. "Derjaun has been dead. He's no longer your concern. He is with his father now and with Ishlog. Your concern is your village, our people. Your family, and..." He leaned over to her kindly. "...your sanity. You led twelve searches for him in the forest and spent several months looking for him. He's gone, dear one."

They stared into one another, Halo questioning her spirit suddenly. What had time brought them?

"Oh, and it is a merry day, my dear friend!" Jastin gleamed happily, and she brought a freshly made cake into the room. "I was just thinking, we could—" She stopped. Looking at the scene, she immediately realized she had entered the room much too soon.

Halo pulled away from Staghen and fled past the young lady and left the house. For the moment, Jastin could do nothing more than hold the cake in one hand, while the other hand graced her chest. It was as if she was desperately holding her lungs inside, lest the air escape. The incident was so confusing to her she hardly knew what to do. Her eyes slowly moved toward Staghen, who was seen hunched on the bed with his hands to his face.

She looked down quickly to pick up her dress and moved nearer to him in an instant. "Captain," she pleaded, "please do tell me what led to this situation?" She sounded quite concerned. Kneeling down in front of him, the mature lady questioned his appearance. "I can't comfort your heart if you do not tell me why it hurts." She allowed the cake to rest on the burkold nightstand.

He lifted his eyes to her. And he saw them. He did not only see them, for once he felt them. Their soft brown hue had not even become slightly tainted or had grown any older since he first met her. They still sparkled and roared with their innocence that had been left uncharted by any aggravation that their family had known. He studied them. He watched her soft body barely breathe hard. It was clear to him that she had been being trained in not just the use of a house maid but perhaps that of a... mother.

With all of his strength falling apart, Staghen could no longer hold it inside. With grief stricken in his soul, he slipped onto the floor and fell into the young lady's arms for comfort. For the same amount of Halo's misery did he find his own soul weakening from life. In Jastin, he saw patience. The now slender and feminine physique of the lady was so matured in her peace and love. He looked to see her longer hair that was kept down in the colder months. The waves of lighter browns danced with the colors of blonde, and her face of kindness never really changed.

It only lost the plush skin around her cheeks that any young child possessed. The locks gently covered her revealed collarbone and gave way into a bosom that still had some growth to undergo. It was quite interesting to him how both women had developed so differently. At once he had spoken with Xorgoell about having to design multiple breastplates for Halo. But ultimately, she needed six in total.

It had brought unto their family quite a deal with the villagers. As any regular person of common intellect knew, a woman of that endowment must have taken a lover and borne a child. Naturally Staghen was always the target of the cause. The rumors were forced to rest when the years passed on and Halo never gave birth. However, her younger counterpart was not as fortunate to be the one rumored about. Her breasts were significantly smaller in appearance and would take some time to grow even if she was to be mothering a coming child.

The young lady was astonished. Her spirit had leapt into the opportunity to nourish his heart. Eight years of emotional training with Halo and many missed chances taught her well to control her fantasies. Staghen's hands clutched her slender biceps, smelling her fragrant floral oils. He nuzzled his sore eyes into her collarbone. She sighed with a calming breath and took forth the duty of comforting him. The captain seemed to shake softly when her hands slid through his long waves of hair. Her stronger fingers massaged his scalp. The young lady absorbed the honor of the moment, yet her heart could not quite believe the captain had shown his weakness for once in all of his days. His weakness was his daughter, Halo.

Jastin lowered her face to kiss his hair. "Captain, as you have once taught us and taught us well, the majestic Gigannora is never steady.

It carries with it the weight of the life of all the creatures. But do we blame the powerful river for when we thirst in the summer? No..." she spoke softly. "We don't. Halo also taught me that we all will go through hurt and suffering. It is what makes our souls show. But what judges the purity of our souls is whether or not we can accept help from others and give it in return."

Staghen listened. She kissed his forehead once more. "Allow her to weep, my brave one." She looked to him with a caring facade.

The captain looked up to her. "Lady, how am I to go on with this? For eight years I have been working my fingers raw trying to pull her out of sulk and despair. What more can I possibly do?"

Jastin shook her head. "You do nothing. You do nothing except love her the way you always have. Halo needs time to heal."

"But it has been eight years. How much more time does this demand?"

"Oh, my sturdy Captain, heartaches may never heal. And if they are lucky enough to be healed, they may take a lifetime."

Staghen stared blankly forward and realized that the girls weren't the only ones who had aged. "My little love..." he sighed heavily.

He continued on with a turn of his head to rest upon the maiden's shoulder, "My love, I will not have my youth forever. As you are aware now I have thirty years to my body, and I feel her misery has me with seventy."

Jastin held his jaw and stared deeply into his eyes. She searched their beauty and asked, "How is it that you carried the entire fear and weight of the village on your back when you were just a young man, but now that your precious girl is suffering you feel like all is lost because you can't help her?"

"That's just the thing..." he quickly replied. "For once, there is one person I can't save." The voice that came from his lips was dried and filled with burden. The lady felt he may begin to weep, for that lustrous voice was broken.

Jastin smoothed her hand along his jaw. "Then allow this to be her greatest self-accomplishment. You can't save her. I can't save her. And even if Derjaun were to come home this day, her heart would be full of joy, yes, but it would be temporary. You know of Halo's eyes and the trauma from her past. She was dealing with grief long before Derjaun left. Only in his absence did the truth of the burden wake. Everyone believes that regardless of her ailment there's nothing she can't do, and they're not wrong. Halo can do anything she wants. But doing it takes a mental load a thousandfold that we have to endure. Why, even if I set the pepper box on the wrong side of the counter, the poor dear is clueless as to where it is and must ask for help. It breaks her confidence and her spirit. She can no longer truly see my face or yours, dear Staghen. Imagine seeing all of your life slowly dying away. Where all of your memories of what you experienced can now only be that, memories."

The two were left in each other's arms, searching for an answer as to what could be done. They both believed Halo deserved unwavering happiness, but Jastin had been right. Sometimes immense suffering from the dealings of life couldn't be changed.

It was a great deal of frustrations that Halo had to deal with. Onward she walked through the Inner Circle, ignoring the constant cheers of the day being the one of her birth. The galakhan dressing was nearly a gimmick of the past, and instead she walked with her armor off, but still walked with her hand blade and the belt of her now sorakhan status was still hanging around her waistline. Halo's stride was a fierce and brute force of character, perhaps from the closer connection she brewed with her mare. Her long hair was glossed in a depth of rich soil tones and several ribbons of blue hung near her high cheekbones.

The skin of the sorakhan woman only became pale and sheer in color, while her eyes had lightened over time as well. Broader shoulders of rock strength and narrow lips that gave verbal bites were quite accompanied well with her profile of a noble nose she obtained during growth. It was a trait that at first she was embarrassed by, but her male colleagues told her that despite her extreme robust appearance it was quite an attractive contour. It wasn't so when she was younger.

Her destination was the village hostelry, which was built under

Staghen's orders for a fun place for adults to come and gather while the children were learning, but it had actually matured into a place where the adults, guardians, and village folk alike came to let their guards down and unite with friends to create strident and fantastic memories. It was quaint in size, and so the party inside sometimes took place outside as well, with some Guardians being seen stumbling home with a woman, or perhaps several women.

Yet in this gentle and quiet walk, she could not help but absorb something beautiful and meaningful to her. Every step she walked on, the dark-gray stones that had blended into the dirt paths had been painted with a chalky paste to give stark contrast. Around she witnessed the light-colored stone homes having deep burkold doors, and the buildings with dark wood were faced with a lovely white pine door. All of this contrast and small detail was something Staghen had done specifically for her over those many years together. Even the few extra hanging lanterns that had been placed had provided her extra help both morning and night.

The people moved around her in the busy Inner Circle as she stopped with this thought. The ladies would lift their dresses for her with a head nod to wish her a merry day, and the gentlemen would tip their hats, and even the children would stop to playfully salute her. With so much love surrounding her, pouring its richness into her heart, she should have reigned over this village with glee and no misery. But as she looked around, every bone in her body felt absolutely crestfallen. Miserable. Every day she gave Staghen and Jastin their due gratitude, but everything had become bleak in her life.

Her thoughts were interrupted by a little girl who called her name, standing right in front of her.

Halo turned and looked down and tried to decipher the little girl's face. She was wearing cloth slippers and offered but a single flower to the Guardian woman. The unknown girl stretched her hand out and sweetly spoke, "For your birthday, Guardian Halo."

Halo paused.

The endearing child went on with gentle persistence, "I don't know if you can see, but it's your favorite color!"

Halo knelt down onto one knee and studied the kind offering. She attempted to focus her eyes from the flower to the little girl's face, but everything seemed to blend, the colors bleeding into one another. And then she looked to the girl and smiled, taking the flower. She let out a heavy breath of gladness and spoke, "You know, this happens to be the most beautiful color in the world to me."

"What color is that?" the little girl asked.

"The color of kindness," Halo responded.

The little girl, who was only as tall as Halo was when she knelt, looked confused. "You can't see the color?"

"It doesn't matter if I can or if I can't. It's still the most magnificent flower in the whole village."

Then Halo's ears became attuned to a man calling for someone amidst all of the liveliness of the Inner Circle. Once more he called for the name, "Marla!"

Halo stood. "I think your paposa is calling for you over there. You should go to him."

The little girl simply gazed up to her—one wearing hide pants and a Guardian's coat and the other wearing a beautifully embroidered linen dress.

It suddenly seemed as if a giant emerged from behind the little girl, and Nikolag's gruff voice was heard urging her on, "Go on, get out of here, you little flower bundle." He gently nudged her away. "Your paposa's been calling for you."

She and Halo simply said their farewells, and she left.

Halo scoffed playfully and put her hands on her hips, "Ah, Nikolag, is my dear friend coming to ruin my day?"

He stood over her, towering above the height of Staghen and weighing enough to fit Jastin into his body twice. After all of those passing seasons and years, the zestful and adventurous gollet still stayed with them.

Somehow.

He could have left and ventured anywhere he wanted to go, but for some reason, he still stayed.

His blue eyes looked into hers with the same smile. "Ruin your day?" he laughed. Nikolag leaned his muscular and rounded shoulder nearer to her, attempting to lower his head enough to hear her or intimidate her.

"Yes, Nikolag..." Halo said.

Nikolag had sensed something was troubling Halo. With the years that had passed, he had a more logical mind and softened his spirit toward the blind girl. And so instead of playfully fighting, he offered to walk with her around the village instead of to the hostelry. It was truly a gift that she needed more than she knew. The cooling presence of the morning star found Nikolag and Halo patrolling the village together. He knew it was the day of her birth, but he bore deep curiosity of why she was not at home. She had seemed sad to him, but also he had to think of when she had not been sad. Nikolag gave the villagers no mind, except for a small excuse to introduce conversation. He looked forward after studying her for a while. "The village is peaceful again, is it not?"

She only nodded and smiled up to him.

Nikolag gave a slight groan while thinking of what he was going to say next. "Staghen has led himself to be a wonderful captain. And you..." He smiled back down toward her again. "...a more perfect sorakhan. I am so proud of how much you have accomplished. The fact that you never gave up? Quite a feat, if you ask me."

Although Nikolag tried desperately to give the woman a truth of comfort on her birthday, it was not found. "Halo," he stated firmly, looking forward, "Derjaun still has your mind?"

Halo choked, "Yes." Her voice had grown so warm in its femininity. "Derjaun still has my mind and my heart. And he will always have my mind and my heart."

The two friends made their way around to the village square. Halo took a brief glance up to the falling morning star. "I wonder what he looks like now."

He laughed, "Oh, Halo. Of the soil, I'm sure."

"No. Not at all," she answered. "I know everyone keeps telling me that he is dead, and they act as if I'm supposed to believe it. But I don't. And I never will."

"No?"

Finally, she smiled again. "I am sure he is a magnificently handsome man with muscles as strong as an oxgog bull and hair as radiant as the rays of the morning star. He told me once he thought of himself a king. That's how I imagine him to be. That's what I see."

Nikolag asked, playing along for the moment, "And his skin?"

"Like the virgin snow of winter. He would have the eyes of a pabi cat."

He moved in front of her and turned to walk backward. His laughter was alive with spirit, "With the blades of claws and the voracious thirst for blood like one as well?"

"Oh, come now, Nikolag," Halo playfully scolded as she looked down, yet deeper down her heart felt a sharp bolt of peace. It was the oddest sensation to come from nowhere. "Must you men always be thinking of violence?"

With a toss of lush blond hair, Nikolag's eyes twinkled. "Yes. There is nothing else in this life other than violence, mating, food, and ulgg. Oh, and the sea. I can't forget the vast ocean. The sky and the horizon. Gold is good as well."

She gazed forward once more. As the weather cooled quickly, Halo began to wonder with knotting curiosity of Nikolag's true thoughts. "Do you believe he is alive? Keep your honesty in those stale lips of yours, as I know that with any doubt I face, a desolate challenge I must embrace."

Nikolag's heart ceased to beat. For a moment he stood there, needing to think on the words spoken to him at that very time in his life. They seemed to be stabbing something at him, something that was worth taking heed to. "And tell me, Sorakhan, what am I to feel more suspicious by? Is it the word chosen to describe my lips that *I know* so easily tempt you, or is it the hint I gathered that..." His whole body turned to her. "...you may leave to go search for him?"

Halo breathed deeply and forced a hard look up to him, "Firstly, your lips have never tempted me. So answer my question, then I shall answer yours."

His mind said something so vivid it came straight from his lips, "I don't care if I make you cry with this, but Derjaun couldn't have lived this long. I can't abide by the idea that he is alive."

The agitation in the female Guardian rose with a heavy breath in frustration. The villagers were still packing up their opening up shops in the Inner Circle, and every so often her eyes caught the shadow of a Guardian extinguishing the torches of the pathways. "I cannot alter your beliefs with words. Nor can I alter the village's. I can only do so by actions."

The sorakhan left his sight before he could even catch her arm. He shook his head in despair, moving away from the town to return to his home. All along the walkways he feared that when he would arise, Halo would be gone, and it would be a saddening repetition of history.

Later that day, the streets were divinely calm, carrying with them the first frost of the season's night air. All around children were being tucked away in their beds of many different makings and colors, parents were washing up the dishes and floors from the hard work the days always brought, and Guardians were spotted by the hostelry and even the school. Her destination was her home, but the thoughts she felt in her heart told her that it was no longer really a home. The steps of the front stoop creaked gently under her weight, as she was not alone in her days of aging. The steps had aged as well.

The horses in the back pastures made soft sounds of existence. Not a single candle flickered its familiar warmth, nor did any shadow fake its movement inside. Both members of the young woman's adopted family must have been asleep. With this in mind, she made expert attempts in keeping her boots from sounding on the floors that held the same maturity of the steps out front. Still, she viewed that no one was awake, and so, having the entire outlay of the house memorized, Halo slipped with grace into her bedroom and sat on the bed.

She reached out to touch her lady friend, who was sleeping with her wonderful dreams. Although Halo could not make out a single face structure, she knew the young lady was in deep enough sleep not to wake. She turned forward, and a heavy slump found its way onto her posture. She saw the beautiful cake on the nightstand and thought. Looking out the window, she thought some more. They were thoughts that not even her high-spirited mare could catch up to, thoughts that when thought could bring even the captain himself to shambles. A slight feeling of a cold slither seeped a path into her veins in which now Halo believed there was no turning back.

To herself she kept her thoughts. *I can't stay here another moment.*

Hastily, Halo tossed the window tapestries away and heaved easily out the window. Outside the young woman met her faithful horse. The mare moved forward to greet her. Halo whispered into her ear that twirled forwards with alert, "*Zakuta-mahara, Zidori. Gesh dagan nut vit vela viciit hara.*"

Speaking her own family language made Halo's stomach sick. It had been so long since she even spoke the words that they seemed almost too foreign to her. Simply put, she informed the horse they would be leaving this night, and Zidori would not need to bear a saddle. Rikanna's presence was stale. The large black stallion was standing asleep near Captain Staghen's window, ready to be needed at any given time in the night. Halo heaved herself on top of Zidori with significant ease, and with one hard kick to the side Zidori turned sharply to leap the bordering fence of the pasture, making a steadfast run to the fields, or wherever it would be Halo would take her.

She was gone.

The following morning, Jastin rose and noticed that her beloved friend had not come home. She knew immediately something wasn't right. She looked in the kitchen, the bathing room, and nothing was found. Only when she opened the front door did she notice a note from Vathra that Halo had not attended her morning training.

"Staghen!" she cried desperately in her maiden shrills. All over the house she made her cries heard. She raced into Staghen's room, and immediately the shaken girl forced him to wake by grabbing his arms. "Staghen, you must wake!"

Staghen was already coming from her previous calls and his quilts fell from his chest when he rose, "Lady, please calm—"

"I cannot calm myself!" Her eyes were drowned in watery tears of distress. The young voice creaked in agony of a terrible happening that she knew took place in the middle of the night.

Staghen grabbed her hands. "Jastin, what in these lands has you in this storm of emotions?"

For a moment the lady could not bring herself to say it. Her chest collapsed with all her insides, and she whined, slightly coughing, "Halo is gone!"

Staghen smiled in attempts to comfort her. "My dear, you know that Halo leaves earlier than I on these days of her duties."

Jastin wailed with a reddened face, "No. Vathra came by, and..."

She lost it all. Staghen caught her in his arms before the torn maiden could fall to the floor. His strength pulled her to his chest. "Vathra what?"

She calmed her choking but only for an attempt to speak, "Vathra came by looking for her!" Her soft face fell forward into his body while a deep sniffle of breath was taken.

Jastin's sobs were so deep in their grayness that Staghen felt the presence of death itself in her tears. He did not even think. He acted at once on the impulse of his heart. He leapt up and climbed out of bed to dress himself. "Jastin, call for Vathra!" He walked quickly to his boots and pointed to her. "Tell him to take every single man we have and order an out search in the fields. If she left in the middle of the night, and it is midday now, let us pray she has not made it too far."

Once again it was a routine situation by now. Staghen grabbed his long cloak and threw it about himself. Panic struck like fire into the young lady's heart, and she stood. "Captain, where will your travels take you?"

He stopped. Breath of exerting strength passed between his trembling lips, and then his blue eyes looked over to her. The black hair fell carelessly about his jaw and temples. Should he speak honestly?

"To the fields and perhaps the mountains, my lady. It is the only place she would run to."

She began shaking her head slowly. "No." She hurried to him, "Staghen, please tell me that she will be alive when you find her.

Promise me! With all in the heavens above...ride swiftly. Have caution in those fields. I cannot bear to lose both of you."

He looked earnestly into her eyes, hoping the hardness would soften her heart and spoke bravely, "You will not lose me. And you have not lost her. But I guarantee you, my lady, if I do not go, you will. And I will not allow you out into those fields."

They looked at each other, the lady terrified of being alone in a darker way than she ever imagined and the captain fearing the worst of finding Halo's cold and dismembered body. Or worse, he may find her sword alone.

"Staghen, then you must go. Now." The eyes of the lady began quivering.

He glanced down for a moment, debating his emotions. He looked to her once more. His trance broke, and he moved toward her fast. She was pulled forward and did not need her eyes open to know what was coming. Her heart beat rapidly as her left arm went around his muscled back.

The captain kissed her.

Jastin felt his lips press lovingly onto her own, and a lifetime of waiting for that sacred kiss was felt at last. It was all he could have done at that moment to calm her heart. The young maiden felt a throbbing pull of weight in her stomach, and so she opened her lips to breathe quickly before looking up to him. Her left hand caressed his hair. She could finally cherish him, even if only for a brief moment.

Staghen looked calmly to her and said, "I will bring her back. You have my promise."

Her smile tumbled from her lips, which still had felt the warmth of his. She nodded quickly. "Your word is always kept even before it sees the form of words, my Captain. Now go, quickly!" With this, she gently turned his body to push him to leave, as difficult as it was to do so.

Then he was gone. Jastin was on the front porch waving her handkerchief to the Guardians' movement of thundering horses and loud armor. "May good fortune find you, my friends! Be in strides of safety and wits! Bring her home!"

A desolate heart was filled with fear in the captain. The entire assembly of Guardians was seen throughout the village as their horses crushed the soil with speed of desperation. Halo's antics of extreme gestures were felt by Staghen's soul many times in the past. This time death was involved, a horrible fate of destiny that no one could reverse.

Rikaana leapt freely over the borders of Nakhan, the other stallions following closely behind. Staghen's hair flew rapidly behind him as did the mane and tail of his horse. Vathra appeared to his left, and Staghen shouted over the rushing wind, "Vathra! Order Guaradas Nikoyehai and Velse to follow me! The rest of you, search outward!"

"Captain, do you desire us to search near the mountains?"

The captain was growing frustrated with every passing second. "If she be there and in danger, it is my daughter to protect! If she be there unharmed, it is my daughter to scold and speak with!"

"When will you understand?" Vathra's voice boiled at him. "She does not wish to live in Nakhan! Let her go! Let her find Derjaun!"

Staghen's eyes narrowed harshly. Vathra could not have possibly been serious. He had heard enough of the foolishness of all others. Without caring that the guaradas had not yet come to his side, he lashed his heels into Rikaana angrily, leaving the rest of them in nothing but remnants of cold dust. He must find her. His happiness and Jastin's depended on it. Oh, how he would feel if he returned to the lady without her best friend. He could never break a promise to her. Not another promise broken.

The shadows of the mountains threw their dark and haunting blankets over the forest and seeing them so close the malakae threw his sword forward to signal the men. "Follow the captain with every sense of strength! Keep your eyes upward and outward at all times! I will be your eyes in front! We shall kill these beasts here and today!" Vathra's heroic voice thundered over the reign of men, and in return they shouted with praising approval.

They moved after Staghen faster. He was nearly out of sight to the rest of the troop and the tiny speck that was his figure dissolved over the hills eventually. And yet nearly rushing closer to the captain was Nikolag. His blood-colored stallion raced toward the mountains, and all he could think of was finding her. With a tight swallow, he gripped the handle of his enormous battle ax on his side, ready to destroy anything he needed to.

Hooves thrust into the soil so hard that even they themselves were sweating. Rikaana's nostrils had never before been so swollen from the cold air, but it was not a time for slowing down. The strong stallion's instincts felt a clench of the rider's legs that he had never felt before. It was rather unsettling, bringing to his belly the sensation of unwanted soil critters crawling about his coat. His ebony head was reared up and thrown forward, dripping with heat and all at the same time cold to the eye sockets.

With a look of severe worry, Staghen stayed focused. "Come now, Rikaana! Run as fast as you can dream!"

The sturdy pair rode forward, and in the middle of this ride the skies rang loudly with the sound of horror. A ghastly screech that was from the breath of a blackened beast echoed up and through the sky, and Staghen feared the worst was yet to be seen.

As the two men reached the summit of a large hill, a black figure shot straight into the heavens and completely disappeared, a long tail hanging behind it. It had vanished so immediately without any trace of remnants as to what it was that Staghen halted his horse. His heart throbbed inside of his ears and inside of his skull. It was as if he had gone deaf from the fear of reality.

He jostled his head clear and looked down into the little valley. There was his daughter! She stormed a vicious circling path of anger, sword held high with swaths of the creature's black blood. He saw her limp, and her leg was completely torn from the hip down. It was clearly obtained from a grueling fight.

He was in shock. Frightened shock. For once in the length of his life, the captain could not move. She was significantly injured.

However, despite how bloody her body had become, Halo had lost all sense of common mindfulness.

Her leg being nearly ripped into bare flesh possessed no meaning to her. She wanted revenge. To her, it would not end until the last drop of black blood spilled onto Nakhanian soil.

"Come back!" Halo's blood-curdling scream called to the lands. The smokey mist of the mountains had engulfed that cold and northern terrain, leaving the creature's whereabouts unknown. Her face was blistered with madness. "You owe me your life! You have taken a father to many, a beloved captain, and my friend!" She threw down her sword and tore her coat and shirt completely open. "Come and kill me. You have taken my heart. Now come and free me of the physical realm! I dare you!"

With this, she pounded her bare sternum. The only thing covering her breasts was her hide maiden band.

Staghen had to sit and watch. He was charmed at the Guardian's display of such immense power. She was fearless, raging on for nothing but revenge, and miraculously it kept her alive. But now it was time for her to fall to the ground. Her fists were seen slamming onto the frost, grunting in frustration while her silent screams forced her to grab her own hair. She just wanted him back. She wanted to feel for once that her purpose in life was realized.

"Halo," Staghen whispered quietly with concern. He placed his hand over his heart to steady it as he questioned whether or not she would ever be sane again. "My daughter, even if peace found you, what could it offer? You have been wearing a thorn of agony in your heart since you were but a child. And now I see that you do not just long for peace from life but peace from death. But please take cautions..." The captain's face clenched as he sobbed looking down. He rubbed tears away. "Death will find you if you ask it to."

He could not intervene. Inside, his body begged for him to help her, but his soul could not. This was her fight alone. Again, high in the sky a dark figure appeared a swirling treacherous blaze of black.

"Captain Staghen!" came the sound of Nikolag's angered voice. "What is wrong with you? She needs you!"

"This is no longer our fight, Nikolag," Staghen answered. "I have trained her well enough. She has a hold on this. Allow her this victory."

Nikolag growled, and his blue eyes fumed with disdain. "You're inconceivable!"

He calmed the wild blond male. "Be quiet, Nikolag. We may distract her. You should be watching the beast's movement and studying it. I know as well as you there are more than one." It was all he could do at that moment.

As the shadow of mass proportions dove down toward the Guardian, the creature's large muscles pushed on. The body possessed four legs that resembled a pabi cat with paws that must have been larger than a man's head. However feline-like the body was, the shoulders were much too broad. The large animal stopped in mid-flight to rear vertically, and the wings sounded like distant thunder.

All Annenji had ears like a forest wolf, the paws of a cat, and yet the size of a horse, but this creature possessed large horns curved backward to form a lethal point. The beast halted quickly to scream at the Guardian before taking flight toward Halo again just as she picked her sword up from the ground.

Halo dove away from the lethal claws. The creature snapped vicious teeth and flew quickly around her in circles.

The sorakhan had no fear, for her training taught her well. The time in the forest was nothing as this moment was. It was the most glorious moment in her life. Face to face, she stood before the very animal that had been destroying Nakhan for years. Knowing that the creature was flying around her in circles, the wise-minded woman knew the beast would come around in front again. It was her chance. The beast's mouth came fast at her head, but Halo's sword was faster. Her powerful arms slashed open the corner of the putrid mouth.

A hard shock rocked up her arms, yet it was not enough to withhold her. Her sword dug wildly into the head. Growling and snarling, it struggled to get away. "I am not finished with you!"

She attempted to grab the long ear, but a hard curve on the creature's horn knocked into her hand.

From a distance, Staghen clasped his mouth, knowing that if the animal chose to use the horns as the oxgog would, Halo would be impaled within seconds. The wings fluttered harshly, and Halo growled in return using every fiber of her muscles to hold her grip. She would rip its ear off if she had to.

The ear was grabbed, and as she yanked it as hard as she could the animal cried harshly, trying to pull away. At once, Halo threw her sword to the side and removed her carving knife from her belt. Her breath heaved to switch the blade to a downward stabbing grip, and when the claws tried to grab her in another wail, Halo drove her blade deep into the throat. Black blood squirted into her face, but her eyes saw through it all. Another plunge followed, and she could hear the flesh inside tear and bleed.

"Go back to the fires from which you came, you wretched devil!" she removed her blade. The beast fell, and now it was her turn to circle. It struggled to get up, and she kicked its intestines hard enough that they came out from a previous underside wound. But it was not enough. All the Guardians, Nikolag included, stood next to Staghen and watched Halo observe the animal trying to get up.

It was not enough for her. Immediately she leapt onto the body and punctured every muscle, organ, and tissue that beast had. Moments of anger laced with sensations of sadness enveloped all who watched. The woman cried hard for things that could not be returned to her, and as the blood sprayed onto her with every stab Halo could only feel herself screaming inside. The beast had completely gone mute. The only thing left was the bare breathing it could give.

It rolled onto its bleeding back, scratching again in an attempt to stand. Winds came, and their coldness stung into her sores and wounds. Her chin lifted upward as her glare to the Annenji remained focused and thirsting for death. "I am aware..." the woman panted to the being, "that upon your death, Derjaun and the others would not return. But I don't care. You're not welcome here, you should know."

"Kill the beast," Staghen whispered under his clamped breath. "End it, Halo."

All of the Guardians, including Vathra and Nikolag stood sentinel and watched the occurrence right alongside the captain.

Her heart was the muscle that made her body move closer, and she grabbed one of two horns to lift the head high, allowing her sword to rise even higher. A tongue of length hung outside the mouth of slobbering blood, and all that was heard was the animal's approaching death. But something occurred to Halo as she saw the eyes of the animal.

She stopped.

They were watering.

She saw its pain, its suffering. Slowly, the black fur around the eyes closed to blink in its exhaustion. As the eyes squeezed one more time, the water trickled down the cheek of the beast.

She tilted her head in confusion. Out of all of the animals she tended to in her life, she never once could see them physically shed tears, only howl in pain. She turned and relaxed her stare. "How are you crying?"

Her lungs were tired. Her heart was fighting a battle that now could no longer be won. "You," she breathed heavily to the animal, "what if you were not the one who caused all of this? There were more of you, I know." Drops of sweat dripped trails of fatigue down her jawline. Halo turned away clenching her teeth. Her eyes tightened, and the animal's life was draining by the second. She shook her head. "I see you. If you are innocent," she choked through her emotions, "I only ask you find it in your soul to forgive me."

Staghen's body flinched when the blade slashed downward into the jugular. Eyes were squeezed hard; hands were clammy from the grip on his reins. A moment that was beautifully sacred to everyone in Nakhan, especially the woman who was now limping up the hill with the head of the demon in her hand. "Halo..." Staghen called softly.

Halo lifted her head and stopped along the hill. "Staghen, I should have known you would find me soon," she said coldly. Both loathing his pursuit yet honored that he must have seen her victory. She dropped the head at Rikaana's hooves. "For you, my Captain. And for Nakhan."

His lips were locked so immensely in smile that it stung his cheeks. The deep black brows of his head were forced together, and his iced eyes became the cool waters again. Yet for some reason Halo did not seem too joyous suddenly. "My Guardian..." Staghen lowered his head to sniff through his numbing nose. Halo was greeted by his pleasant face. "My love." Staghen dismounted and held her close.

She turned to the side to visit again the memory of moments ago. There was a great chance she would never speak of her feelings to anyone, although as her eyes saw Nikolag, perhaps he had already known them. It seemed as though an army followed Staghen there. The men coming in close were finally behind Rikaana, and Zidori had reappeared after the battle ended. Wherever it was she had been was out of her rider's order, not from disrespect or fear. Nikolag dismounted and rushed to her to hold her close. "Come, my friend. Lie down, and I'll sew your wounds and carry you myself if I have to."

And from here on out, Nakhan would always remember Halo's great story of bravery. Tales would be told for all eternity of the "woman who danced with fire," and young girls would now be able to train as Guardians to follow her less than mundane way of life. Halo was a hero, not only to her best friend and captain but to the entire village of people who had lived in fear for years too long.

15

"Oh, for all of the blood in my heart, Halo!" Nikolag shouted as his arms slammed around her. People were everywhere. Shouting, yelling, screaming, and rejoicing. The accused beast's head was staked high in the Inner Circle for all to see. Jastin was leading the troop of musicians and dancers throughout the pathways, prancing, and playing her uana, which hung around her neck. Other village maidens twirled their large dresses in circles, bells rang out for liberty. All the Guardians cheered with Staghen, who was feeling very light-headed with the ulgg quickly filling his stomach.

"It was all your doing, my honorable Captain!" Vathra wailed victoriously. He grabbed Staghen by his black locks to kiss his face with wondering love and praise. Staghen's laughter was loud and strong, and turning around to chant with the other men he bellowed, "How could it have been my doings? I only trained her."

Guarada Velse thought differently. He came from behind and squeezed Staghen's torso to lift him high in the air. With the captain's legs flailing about, all the men praised him more. Vathra held his mug toward Staghen, smiling wide. "It was you who brought out the beast within her. It was you who loved her and believed in her."

The handsome captain grinned but with caution. "Oh, come now.

We all att—" His voice croaked with a tightness as the guarada choked the captain's midsection in an affectionate hug. "—*ended* to her training in one way or another. My good man, would you kindly set me down before my ribcage breaks?"

Never before had Halo been so confused. She attempted to be happy because she was, but a dark secret bore deep into her heart, which one day would come spilling out as the black blood of the beast did. Jastin danced up to her, her whirling dress fanned with black and scarlet. She stopped and kissed the heroine on the cheek, and her brown eyes glittered with joy. "Halo, I knew it would be you. Out of all the Guardians, my heart told me it was you."

The charade of celebrations continued with night's blanket falling slowly. Halo could only question her. "What do you mean?"

Jastin's looked toward the diamonds in the sky, then with a jubilant touch of her chest she continued, "My dearly beloved, I knew it would be you to slay that last monster. I knew it all this time."

"Oh, is this so?" Halo spoke while she folded her arms.

"Why, of course it is so. Why would it not be?"

Halo laughed, "Because I believed you to be fantasizing of the captain being the hero. Besides of this thought, there are possibilities I may not have destroyed the creature that attacked the village or the one that could have taken Derjaun and killed Ishlog or Radal."

Jastin pressed her lips together with a childish grin and she slapped the sorakhan's chest. "Do not be so absurd. You have heard the stories of what these animals have done! *All* of them! It was not only one that killed Ishlog or plagued this village! It was time that we defended this home of ours!" She changed her demeanor a bit, speaking with a tone of mischief. "After all, Staghen was already my hero years ago."

Halo could only lower her head in thought. But this time it was not a thought of despair or longing. It was a thought of full self-assurance.

"Halo?" Jastin gently asked.

"Yes?"

Jastin was a little hesitant to ask the question. It would have been a question that would have either received a crashing answer of anger or a reply of happiness, and Jastin was willing to take the chance. Although her maturing age taught her to proceed with caution on sensitive topics, it was something she could not hold back. The young woman began with her full lips speaking. "How are your feelings toward Derjaun?" Although she longed to gossip about the unforgettable kiss that happened earlier, it was not the time to talk about it.

At once Halo spoke with a stern approach, "Jastin, you and I shall talk of this tonight."

The lady backed down, feeling rather intrigued. "Yes, brave Sorakhan."

The night brought with it a miraculous display of lovely blue, green and slight white streaks across the sky. All of Nakhan was bundled by the firepit of the Inner Circle, listening to Halo's wondrous story. And then it came time for Staghen to speak with her. It was at their home when he did so, never wanting to let her body out of his loving clutch. "My beauty of a Guardian, my heart binds itself to you at this very moment." The two pulled away, but Staghen continued to hold her hands out front on the stoop.

"Your heart is always bound to me, my loving protector. But how is it that you did not scold me? Not one word of anger or worry came from your lips."

She felt his thumbs rubbing over her knuckles. "I had to let you go. I had to let you fight that battle alone, as it was your battle alone to claim. Even like an angry paposa that I was, I had to."

"But that beast murdered Radal and Ishlog. Why was it that you did not intervene on this alone?"

Staghen always thought first before speaking, "I would have done so had I doubted your strength and abilities. I did not doubt anything in you. And although Radal and Ishlog were costly to my soul, you are my present concern. I can't bring them back, but I can make sure that you have your revenge, as seeing you at peace would soften my saddened heart from the loss of them both."

Halo thought, *No, he could never bring them back. Could he?* She nodded. "I understand."

"Halo, I must ask you something."

She looked up to him. The only way she was able to even barely catch a shadow of his face was from the lit torch on his stoop. Why, had it not been for the stark contrast of the gray sky blocking the blinding rays of the sun, Halo would not have been able to see the black beast approaching her so easily earlier that day. "Anything you wish. Ask of me anything."

Her hands were given a firmer grip. His breath released. "You did not seem the slightest bit proud when you brought the beast's head to me up the hill. Why is this?"

"Oh, um." She attempted to turn away. "I am exhausted from the fight, Captain. I need sleep."

Staghen pulled her back. "I assume it must have something to do with the guilt of killing a creature that..." He shifted his eyes and tone in a sense of hint that he knew her secret. "...you feel may have been innocent?"

She was quiet, and the moment he went to speak, she interjected, "I was taught to never believe there is victory in death. And, Captain, I saw the animal's eyes. I felt its heart." He stood upright and listened to her, almost with disbelief of what he was hearing. She continued on, "Despite the beast's hellish and demonic appearance, its eyes were expressive, sad, and kind. It cried tears like you and I. I've never seen an animal do this before. I felt warmth within when I looked into them. As if..."

"As if what?" Staghen firmly questioned.

She stalled. "I'm not sure. Perhaps it was wrong of me. There could be more. What if this was not the creature to kill? What if it does not hold vile intentions by nature?"

Staghen lifted his arms and dropped them to his sides. "Halo, this is a ridiculous notion. Even if this animal *was* in fact innocent, you must remember that although there is never to be victory in death we have a village to protect, and these beasts are nothing but a threat to us. You must remember that the villagers come first."

Although her heart disagreed, she spoke, "Very well, but there must have been another question in your mind other than that. What was it?"

He smiled and gripped her hands again. "The lady gave me much comfort while I wept over you on celebration day of your birth, last eve and this early morn when you had vanished. She has done well to heed to my sanity and my heart in times of when I felt I lost you."

"What are you wanting to ask?" she firmly questioned.

His mind changed paths. "Oh, let us forget it."

She was confused. His body just moved past hers to go inside where it was significantly warmer, but her eyes rolled, and she knew he was not confessing something. She followed him inside. "Captain, I can't forget an introduction to something that may be of a serious matter."

He laughed as he sat on the chesterfield inside. "It was simply nothing. Well, more or less it was of something very valuable to say." He leaned his elbows on his knees. "I wish I had words to express my pride for you at this moment. I am not sure you understand how well the village will be now from what you have done. I do hope that it has brought you something, perhaps some sense of strength. This should show you that even with the eyes you were born with, there is nothing you can't do."

As pleased as she was to hear this, Halo had to speak. "Captain, I am aware. But I don't wish to be fancied as some worshipped icon. You would have done the same, if given the chance."

A long pause was drawn. "And you did not see any others?" Staghen questioned.

"Other beasts?"

"Yes."

"No, just the one."

"This is perfect. As there were only a few who survived the battle between us and Nakhan. They took flight to the skies before any Guardian or villager could handle it," Staghen concluded.

"Well," Halo began easily, "this brings me great joy to hear. I wish you a beautiful sleep this evening, Staghen."

He laughed, "For once I won't need the lady's touch to help soothe me to sleep."

Halo grinned and teased, "I give this a few more moons."

While she giggled, Staghen shook his head in smiling, "Your antagonizing stops at nothing, does it?"

"Never."

Knocking came furiously at the captain's door early the next morn. It was ahead of when Halo was to rise, and the annoyance grew so fast that she was the one to rush to the door. Out of the bed she scurried away from Jastin's side, only stumbling into the room to see that Staghen allowed Nikolag in.

He spoke boisterously as he always did, "Where is Halo? We need to celebrate! Our time together last night was not spared a moment, and the words of praise barely left my lips before she was gone."

The captain bowed his head honorably. "She will be thrilled to see you again, Nikolag." Staghen carried a loud smile on his face, and his hands grabbed the young man's shoulders like that of a proud paposa. "I hope, Nikolag, you understand how much joy you have brought her since a truce was found between the two of you. You have changed so much over these last years, and your innocent quarreling with her has only made her stronger."

Nikolag waved the captain away in dismissal, "Yeah, whatever, Captain." He laughed with a bright-eyed nod of his head. He patted Staghen's back then walked inside, glancing for Halo. "Well, there are no red ladies in this here village, and I have been without a woman for a decade of time." Even though they had bonded quite deeply over the many passing seasons, Nikolag had kept most of his past to himself. The only thing he showed was his untamed demeanors and disobedient nature.

Staghen was not amused.

Nikolag professed with his hands outstretched. "Oh, come now. Don't be so dismal! At least I'm not trying to kill her now, right? And now that she's of age, I can do this."

Halo came into the room and interjected. "And tell me one thing, Nikolag, what if I deny you?"

He proudly spoke with a nod of his head, "Then I'll fight you for it."

At once Staghen parted the two from their soon-to-be grappling antic. "Not until I speak with Halo. There is something I need to discuss with her."

The gollet lifted his hands into the air, and while leaving the house his voice was heard outside simply saying, "Captains, they control and ruin everything!"

Halo was once again alone and confused by the captain's ever-changing behavior. "Are you going to be honest this time, Captain?"

Staghen's breath came and left, and he held her hand. "Halo, I have to ask you something. It is, yes, what I was going to ask you last night. But my mind needed time to make certainty of it."

Halo trembled nervously. She loathed it when people held things out longer than needed. "What is it?"

"I have given this a lot of thought. I have decided that because of you my heart is at peace with a mission." The statement made Halo's heart swell. "The village is entirely safe again. Radal, Derjaun, and Ishlog's deaths have been avenged. Although I sleep well at night, my bed has become a lonely place, now that my worries bring me no company."

She raised her brow. "Staghen?" she questioned with squeaky curiosity. A smirk lit up her lips as her eyes haloed her face. "Are you asking..." She stepped closer and looked up to him.

He sighed and smiled with his eyes closed. "Jastin brings me love in a way I thought was impossible to find in this village. She is loyal, faithful, and her strength of love for me has not broken in over eight years."

Although her heart was flying out of her body with glee, she had to correct him, "Fifteen."

"Fifteen?" Staghen's mouth was wide. "But you said on the fence years ago..."

"No, I said nothing. And I would say nothing to you for fear of causing you discomfort in her presence. She was almost four when she started to love you, when you became captain and soothed her fears. She fell in love with you that day. At that moment it could have simply been girlish infatuation. But every day she grew fond of you more and more. Jastin's heart is fickle, but with you it never was and never will be."

While he stared blankly, she continued, "A woman's heart is a deep valley of emotions, Staghen. When a woman knows what she wants when she sees it, she is forever faithful. Yes, Jastin had little loves throughout her life, but only a few, and they lasted but maybe one or two seasons."

Staghen sighed. "I didn't know. Her heart carries no interest in my status or my wealth. Or does it? I can trust you to tell me the truth."

"Well, she does find interest in your status. You are the captain. But she finds interest in this because it means you are strong, brave, wise, and comforting to her. Not because all other women in this village seek your companionship in your bed or because you have the final word overall. And yes, Jastin finds interest in your wealth, but it's because she needed to find a man of wealth to appease her parents. In your strength and ability to provide stability, Jastin finds peace. She finds you, to bring her stable peace.

"She isn't a woman who wishes to work her hands to the bone in a field as a farmer's wife to provide for her husband or family. She wants to wear her heart to threads and blood to keep them happy, protected, nurtured, and well-loved. She desires to cook, has studied medicine over these years, and you have no possible idea the joy it brings her when she can mend your clothes, make you new scarves, polish your boots, and more. She wishes to be a true-born housewife. Of course, she wishes for love in return. And now that you know what she is always after, you may make your decision."

Halo watched him sulk in his thoughts. And once more she spoke to him, "You are honored to hear the truth." She tossed her left hand out in a gesture. "Jastin may have been immature once, but one thing that always would stay mature was how strongly she loved anyone and everyone. For the sake of the stars above, she adored Mozkin for years! What does this show you of her love?"

But he grinned, "I have made my decision."

Halo could see a look of growing happiness and contentment on his face that she had never once seen before. His eyes looked down as he casually nodded. She questioned, "And?"

He grabbed her hands, and his excitement came fast from his lips, "I'm going to marry her!"

She clasped his mouth. "Captain, hush! She'll hear you. You have a commanding voice."

He pulled his mouth away. "I shall buy her the most beautiful necklace ever to touch human skin. It will be of Yulan marble, dense silver, and... something else!" He turned and grabbed his cloak. "It is cold this early morn, my love. Be careful when dressing, and I will return before midday."

Halo saluted. "Yes, Captain Staghen."

Yet in like a dark silhouette in the door, he stopped.

"Captain?"

His head slightly turned and he mumbled, "It's nothing. I realized that I've had a barricade on my own heart for my whole life. It's wonderful to finally open my heart to a woman. Especially her."

Halo's smirk released a soft snicker of happiness for him. "I'm truly happy for you."

Then he left.

Halo was furious of the fact that she must wait to hear Jastin's screaming and crying, whimpering, and wooing over the proposal. But even more so, she longed to see the faces on Jastin's brothers when the words would travel as rumors but land as the truth. Captain Staghen would marry, and since marriages in Nakhan were proposed and then held the next day, Halo had little time to get the word out. But never mind that. She would let Staghen handle that business.

She seemed to test herself with how fast she could get dressed and ready and found it difficult to look at the slumbering future High Lady of Nakhan. Afterward, Halo rushed outside to search for her friend, and she did not have to search extremely far. Nikolag was perched on the wooden railing of the porch, arms hung low in between his legs. Once again, his body was dressed in his old-worn hide pants and many furs from his previous hunts.

"I'm glad I didn't need to ride to find you, Nikolag."

While he laughed, he looked to the sky with his lips curling in a smile. "That old mare of yours has vigor still?"

Halo's hands pressed dominantly on her hips. "Yes, she is functioning well. Better than your belly-sagging stallion ever did, even in his youth."

Halo studied his dressings when he stood. Nikolag wore a very distinguishable long coat in the cold weather. It was of solid Gilda buck hide and its fur but was washed with oils to give it a dark luster. Unlike other Guardians, the self-centered man chose to wear his coat opened, allowing any females to take a wonderful—and according to his beliefs—lucky, glance at his well-contoured body. Most Guardians wore gilda-buck hide pants that were stained in black, only yet again Nikolag found a way to make his standout above and beyond all other Guardians.

The pants he wore had hand-stitched lacings that crossed all down the side leg, leaving only an inch's worth of tanned flesh to be shown, and the undershirt of his attire, although freezing outside, was left open more times than not. Another thing that covered his midsection was the back strap for his quiver. He was a man who bred himself to be immune to the cold by bathing in the Gigannora River during winter and feasting primarily on raw flesh of hand-hunted animals. He never cut his hair, only choosing to keep it trimmed and pulled back so that any tempted female could study his more than perfect smile.

"I wanted to celebrate your victory with you in a more private way. Every time we've been alone, they've been interrupted by either your mood or something else."

And so there they were. Nikolag and Halo walked all over the village only then to make way to the northern gate that would lead to the fields. She was enjoying his company, even though the company was small talk of current events. It never got much deeper than that.

"You know, Nikolag," Halo began cautiously, "I realized I know nothing of your family. And, I have asked you many times, and many times you don't answer. I want to know more about you. You're a gollet, after all. Surely you must be aware of the *Travels of Bremlin*. And yet you have said nothing of this book to me, even when I ask you of it. I have heard that gollets are all men, and they usually adopt this life from walking in the footsteps of their fathers. Their...paposas. Surely you had one?" She hesitated as she saw his figure walk across the bleak snow ahead of her. The softness of the cold air fell onto her lips. Her shoulders heaved in breath as she narrowed her eyes to stare at his back. He stopped. "Where is he?" she questioned with much concern.

For once in her whole life, Halo's voice fell like soft snow against his skin. Her temperament had ceased in the recent actions of the Annenji fight. She had realized how right Staghen was in his words. Derjaun was gone, but Jastin and Nikolag were right there in front of her. Although one day she would muster the courage and strength to find the lost boy still, she could no longer retain such a jaded heart. She allowed her voice to be calm with him. Nikolag said nothing. All his actions halted and he looked to the sky. "He is with Radal now." His voice was dry and heavy as he whispered the answer.

Halo held her arms around herself to shiver from the northern winds, and she suddenly felt sorrow for him. A memory came sweeping into her mind. It was the memory of when she had first fought him, and Staghen had told her a little about his family. Yet he had never openly admitted to anything of what Staghen said to be correct. But she could never let him know she did, in fact, know something. Instead, she wanted him to open up himself.

Acting as if she bore naivety, she asked, "Was it the Annenji?"

"No," he stated bluntly. Then he turned to approach her. "Some sort of stomach illness left him unable to hold food inside. He died from weakness of sorts. Or that is the way Dr. Crenon could explain it to a young child. After many other situations in my life, I left and came here alone."

Halo softened her harsh feelings toward anyone and everything in that moment. Why, it was a realization that many people in that village had suffered from some sort of loss. "What was his full name?"

He smiled with pride. "Unregard. Unregard Farog Tempest. My mother, well, she died from the same fate sometime before he did."

Halo heard how correct Staghen had been. But she continued asking, for seeing that he was softening made her heart feel warmer. "Do you have any surviving family?"

"No," he responded, looking away to the mountains. "I had a sister much younger than I."

Halo looked up to him with concern, "You say *had*? What happened to her?"

He walked away at once. "Come on," he said happily. "This is a moment of merriment for you, not a time to discuss my past."

Halo marched forth with disgust in her tone, "Nikolag Keljen Tempest, why won't you let me know these things? I see how strong and large you are. Your mass replicates your temper, and yet I feel somewhere it must replicate your kindness as well. You have been speaking to me of your family for so little time now, and all it has done is show me I truly know little of you. I wish to know more. As a matter of fact, your surname is quite interesting to me. Tempest? Isn't this a word that means *violent storm* of some sort?"

He folded his arms and grinned looking down to the ground. "Yes, that's right. Because we, as gollets, have to keep our identity as secretive as we can, our fathers usually adopt surnames they feel are appropriate to them. My father was one of the most skilled ship captains you could ever know. It so happened to be that as I grew older...," He chuckled in his reminiscing. "...Staghen told me that it also matches my personality. And I like it that way."

She politely interjected, "Where was your father from? He must have traveled through the forests and the mountains in *some* way for you to be so close to getting here as a child? If you did come by sea, as most gollets do, you would have had to travel through Persu to get here. Which means that these terrains are in fact accessible. We could learn so much together!" She pulled his coat so he would face her. His eyes only darkened with sadness. "It is in your blood to travel and to fight. This is what makes you a gollet, whether people like it or not. And I love it!"

He opened up to her on their joyous walk and shared with her stories of his childhood and made their way over the boundary fence, further into the fields. They continued to walk and Nikolag suddenly said, "I brought you here for a reason."

Halo turned to him. "What is it?"

"It is one rare day without training. I say you and I..." He walked up and stared her down. "...go to my home on these outer fields. I have never shown you where I live. And, you appreciate my culture more than anyone else in this village." He laughed. "I can't tell you how much your friendship has meant to me over the years. Staghen would always try to *fix* me. I never wanted to be *fixed*. I only wanted to *belong*."

"My dear Nikolag," she softly began as she watched his face turn back down toward the grounds, "you do belong. The world is your home. Not just in these barren and frozen fields upon which we lead such a life of seeming mediocrity. We never know what life may bring us tomorrow. Be it blindness, be it an illness, be it death from great bravery. I want to live first before I die. And I have yet to feel like I have lived. When I met you, I saw nothing but fiery life and pungent vitality. I despised you, yes, but I wanted to be like you."

The confession from the young maiden brought a sincere grin from his lips as he looked to her. "You *still* want to be like me."

Halo could not resist laughing at him once more. "Yes," she heartily replied, "I do."

Then the gollet stood erect with his broad shoulders and proud posture once more. Despite the pain he felt from his body's daily exertion, he still stood tall. "I'm glad to hear that. I think there is much that we can feel for one another, you know? I lost my entire family, and you lost your beloved friend. You are blind, and I'm unfit for any society. You want to travel, and I know how to do it. Perhaps being around someone other than a looming captain and an attached friend would be good for your mind. Would you come with me?"

Halo felt her heart move like shifting ground beneath her feet. She gently took the gollet's gloved hand. "I would like that very much."

Inside Nikolag's home, Halo found it to be very bare, but that was to be expected given his lifestyle. The chesterfield, bed, table, chair, and all other types of little household items were made by him and him alone. He knew how to prepare the meat that he had kept in the longhouse he built, and Halo also saw different cuts of wild boar being stored in frothy colored jars of whey. All around she walked inside the tiny home and, after not seeing many other ornaments about, she finally questioned him about his that were well-hung and laced into his boots.

"Nikolag," she began curiously as she looked about, "I'm still befuddled about those beautiful little things you have on your boots. They are not identical to each other in the least bit, and yet I see no resemblance to any of these items anywhere in your house." She glanced over her shoulder to see he was pouring ulgg for them at the table and preparing the bread on the plates. She continued, "I noticed them the moment you fought me the first time we met, when I fell to the ground. I have to say that they're beautiful to look at. What are they?"

He sliced the meat and served it, then patted the sturdy burkold table for her to sit. She did. Nikolag started very casually, "These are called *jovel*, which is the gollet word for ornament. When a gollet travels, he finds a certain representative piece of that place, and he constructs a way to fasten it to his boots, usually by laces, or if it's a fabric he'll sew it to the boot in some way. This way, other gollets can see how experienced you are in sailing or adventuring. They also make great starters for stories." He smiled to her as he set the knife down.

Halo's emotions jolted into her blood and she sat upright and spoke brightly with happiness, "Oh, that's the language you speak?" She leaned over the table. "I did not even know gollets had their own language! So, if I may ask, you used to call me *grot* all the time but stopped. What's that mean?" She sipped her ulgg.

Nikolag leaned back in his chair and crossed his large arms. "I am not proud to tell you what it means. I stopped calling you that because it is a highly offensive, if not the most offensive term to call any woman. It means 'vile and overused whore.' I don't want to call you that anymore."

"Why?" she asked.

He sighed and rubbed his leg while she held her cup at rest to her lips, waiting to hear what truly made Nikolag change. The wind was heard and the snow bit at the window with icy teeth. Whatever it was that he was about to say, was exceedingly difficult for him to do.

"I lost my little sister and my elder brother. It has torn me into an oblivion of hopelessness and anger with knowing this. And I did not initially know why you joined the Guardians. But one night, Staghen approached me and told me why." He slowly stared off to the left. He was so deep in his eyes that he was purely speaking his thoughts now. "He told me that you wanted to take Derjaun's place because that little sick boy was such a friend to you, and when he became sick and then ran away you joined the Guardians to not only help bring him back but to fill his place until he could return.

"That moved me," he stated. "That made me remember what it was like to be young with Burdock, and what I felt like when Filia... when Filia drowned. You have a sense of fortification that I don't see in many people, Halo. Whether or not I could admit it to myself, you were a lot like me. I also felt sorrow for your loss. At once it pained me what I had called you and what I had put you through. And the fact that you have vision loss did not make me feel any better."

Halo lowered her glass. "I want you to know I never held any grudges with you. I also felt sorrow for you. And because of how you look and the slightest difference in how you pronounce your words or how you dress, I gathered you must not have originally been from Nakhan. From this, all I could truly fabricate is that you were lost, perhaps in more ways than one."

If there had been any remaining tension between the two, it was now obsolete. Nikolag's eyes seemed to burrow deeper into the oceanic irises he possessed. He was so focused on her that he could hardly understand what his own thoughts were, if he had any at all. As the silence shifted between them, he finally drew in his chest to breathe. "Thanks. I'm not sure if I'm lost. At least not anymore. For the time being I have found a home, and I have found friends, and with these friends I have found a sense of purpose."

Nikolag stood to take her plate that had been completely wiped clean of all its contents. Halo had not realized how hungry she was. She had not eaten at all that morning. Upon taking the flatware, he turned and placed it into the wash basin. He lovingly said, "Know that whatever it is you search for, you can count on me to help you find it.

Unexpectedly, he felt her arms move around his waist from behind to hold him. He stopped. He listened, waited, and felt her head press affectionately against his back. Never in his whole life would he ever imagine her doing something like this. Why, in that very moment, she was allowing her vulnerability to show. It could have been the vulnerability of a woman falling deep into the vigor of a man, and if it were to be so, that was certainly not in Halo's nature. Holding the gollet so closely made her feel...innocent. She had often-times felt confused in finding the balance between being Staghen's daughter and a Guardian. Not with Nikolag.

"Halo?" he whispered. All he heard in response was a groan of near affection into his back muscles. She heard him but she was much too content in the moment to speak. He whispered again, "I'm aware that you're not a house maiden or a lady, but one of the reasons I do not wash myself as much as I should is that I am extremely tired by the end of the day. Although I have bathed this morning, I am finding pain in my shoulders and back that is becoming too much to bear. If it's not too much to ask of you, I was hoping you could help soothe the tension."

She pulled him around and gazed into his eyes. He had not changed his earnest face. "I may not be any of those, but I live with one. And she has cared for me very well. I know exactly what to do." She gleefully smiled and pulled him to sit on the floor in front of the chesterfield. She sat down behind him and began untying his heavy hair.

As his hair fell from the ribbons and ties, Halo's eyes began to show how enamored she was with his hair color. So many different hues of gold, blond, light brown and more cascaded down his broad back. Every strand gleamed with health. She wanted to play with it. Each of her fingers combed through the locks to brush them to the side, and at that moment her hands placed themselves upon his shoulders and squeezed deeply. Swiftly and with ease, he let out a loud sound of relief with water streaming down his face.

"Are you alright?" she asked as she leaned over.

All he could do was sniffle from the stinging sensations that were finally being tended to. "I'm sorry. I don't think you know what you're doing for me. I didn't even get you a gift."

Halo chuckled lovingly. "You have already given me a gift. Our walk and our talk were gifts. You listening, our friendship, they're all gifts."

He listened. And so, the gollet slumped back further against the chesterfield as her knuckles went deep between his shoulders. Every muscle fiber was being combed away of its pain. Several moments became several minutes, and when Halo moved to his neck, she felt how knotted and tight it was. He cherished every long stroke, every deep nudge, every affectionate sense of relief. As she began gliding her hands around the sides of his neck, his blood flushed to all parts of his body, and it flushed to one he couldn't control.

Nikolag was trying to control himself, as it would have been the worst timing in the history of their friendship to have such a thing happen. He shifted his hips, and Halo became aware of his uneasiness. She had assumed he was simply trying to reposition his frame, but she was sorely wrong. His breath became restless and hefty, and the more she massaged into the nape of his neck the harder it was to control his instincts. It had been far too many years since he had felt the warm touch of a woman, and Halo's body was fully matured now, and the skills of her hands were unparalleled to anything else he had ever felt before. His mental state snapped.

Quicker than rushing blood could handle, Nikolag turned around, and coming onto his knees he grabbed that beautiful blind woman by her cheeks as gently as he could so he would not come across as violent. Her face was like warm down feathers against his weather-beaten hands, and since even though Halo flinched from being surprised Nikolag pressed his lips so hard onto hers that he could not breathe. Immediately his desirable kiss took a hold of her entirely, and to his satisfaction she reciprocated.

She needed to. She wanted to.

Nikolag felt his chest collapse with relief when he felt her respond so favorably by raking her fingers into his long hair. Her mouth cried with the hormones that ravaged between them.

As he held her face, she could not resist the urge to succumb even more. Nikolag lifted himself, and in that heated moment he pushed his hands into her chest to force her back onto the sofa. He was on top of her, feeling her warm tongue so aggressively with his. The young woman's body lifted with arousal as she pulled that golden mane even harder, as it was simply luscious to feel. His lips were sweet with ulgg, and his breath was passing harder and harder with each movement.

Her hands slipped down from his scalp onto his neck, from his neck then to his broad chest, and she began shoving his heavy furs and coat away from him. He shuffled his body to remove it and grabbed her neck to kiss her even deeper. Halo sunk lower onto the couch and felt his entire mass on her, and when that passionate sensation was felt he only drove the moment into a bottomless rapture when he kissed into the warmth of her beautiful neck. Demanding to feel him closer, she lifted her legs to wrap them about his waistline. She touched his chest and began removing his shirt with loving hands. Halo glanced to his figure as best as she could, and it was saddening to her that her eyes could not fully understand what his body looked like when disrobed. She could not see it. All her eyes saw were shadows of his figure.

Halo's pelvis clenched without any mercy for the tightness that shook up her thighs and hips. The weight of him drove deep into hers, and his manhood was so large that her fervent adoration for him was heard in the heat of her breathing. Her eyes closed while he continued to kiss down her throat and onto her collarbone and chest. Immediately, Halo felt his muscled forearm scoop under her back to lift her off the cushions, and his mouth kissed between her breasts over the fabric of her shirt.

How much they enjoyed discovering each other's beautifully grown bodies. Nikolag was strong in his youth, and she had possessed an endearing female frame of suppleness with little muscular structure. But now Nikolag had become substantially taller, his muscles had grown to a point where Halo had felt minuscule in his presence. She loved it. Even now that she was taller with fuller endowments and a much stronger physique, no woman could deny the sense of protection and security when standing near a man such as he.

Now she was not just being in his presence. She was *feeling* his presence. In a few moments, the two lovers had removed every single piece of fabric that restrained them from enjoying the moment more faithfully. The partially blind girl held her lover's shoulders and simply enjoyed the beauty of his face. She knew what was going to come, and in her lower regions she had felt tender wetness while every fiber in her being tightened with tension.

With one more kiss, the gollet claimed her. Halo's body was filled with a sensation that was so deep that she could not resist calling out to the air of what it did to her. He pressed his face into her cheekbone to kiss her skin, and in this he absorbed every airy sound she panted. She was truly his to not only take but to treasure as well. The thrusting that came from his eager hips was both painful and joyful, massaging the taught inner muscles that had been bred by many cycles of frustration. More and more the lovers kissed while the air around them became a place for their pleasure-filled sounds to be heard. Nikolag enjoyed every passing thrust deeper into her, driving his hips harder and harder. And although Halo was an obvious virgin, the passion and love shared between the two was so intense that the discomfort that came was only coupled with desire that left her wanting more of him.

While she relaxed her body to accept him more, her hand reached atop his back. An interesting part of his skin was felt when she touched his back. Her eyes opened. Her fingers extended across...

why...it almost felt like a scar. Quickly her eyes closed with vigor when Nikolag began to rouse a sense from deep within her. No longer could she focus on feeling that long and deep scar across his back. Her hand felt every throbbing muscle curve on his back, and his powerful girth was driving her completely winded. His lips groaned from the pleasure she gave him as he placed his lips onto hers once more. He felt her nails dig into his thick skin with reckless hostility.

His eyes peered to hers, and he knew she could not see his face. He had known her long enough to understand that she was leaving herself completely defenseless to him in so many ways, but it made him love her even more. He had to communicate with her then. He simply knew he had to. In order for his dearly cherished friend to know he was really thinking of her and only her, he needed to let her know. Halo's body jolted when she felt his lips once more, and in the middle of the sweetest kiss his lips parted briefly to call out her name. With one more breath drawn from his heavy chest, he told her how good she felt to him. The coupling pushed forward into a profound movement of bodies that heated with one another, and Halo heard his voice gaining aggression.

With a fierce groan, he pushed himself harder into her. At that moment he lost his senses. The sweltering occurrence flooded her completely. Her hands tightly held onto his ribs, enjoying every bit of his release. He filled her, he pushed her body, and he left her feeling euphoric in the aftermath of heavy moans. His hand moved to grace her face with affection, and his thumb moved a tear from her eye. Halo was calmed when he pressed his forehead to hers.

Every bit of her despair, agony, depression, anxiety and self-loathing felt gone. Completely absolved. It was as if in that final sigh of release that Nikolag pulled every ounce of dread out of her, draining her body of all things horrible and filling it with pure delight and love.

She felt light, and within her feminine heart she sensed the urge to both cry and laugh.

"Halo, are you alright?" he muttered.

The young woman's response was simple and yet emotional, as it would be for a woman whose emotions and needs had been finally satiated. She had not been aware of what she was depriving her body of until that unpredictable moment. After attempting to gather herself, she finally spoke. "Nikolag, I..." She drew in a breath so deep that Nikolag felt her naked belly press into his, "I feel so...I don't know."

The words spoken from Halo's trembling lips were true. She held it in until her body and heart lost the battle. Nikolag watched her place her hand upon her face that began to contract. He stared in sadness and curiosity while he watched her rub her face in confusion and display of losing her grip. He heard her cry. Beneath his loving body, he felt her body jerk and shake from the emotional release.

"Come here. It's alright. I have you," he stated bravely. He pulled her up onto his lap and embraced her in every way. But Halo continued to clutch her hands into her face as if in shame. Nikolag worked many things out of her, including the desperate need to yell from pleasure instead of pain for once. She threw her arms around his neck and felt utterly secure and safe. His chest smelled fragrant with a masculine scent, and knowing he would still have soreness in his shoulders she frantically returned the loving favor by squeezing his left shoulder, massaging the pain away from the nape of his neck.

As she caught her air, she began speaking. "I don't know what's come over me. It's like I felt myself lose all sense of thought. I feel completely unsure about what we've done." She looked into his eyes. "But I want it more and more. Everything in my life has been confusing. And it was as if you knew something I needed, but I was ignorant to it."

He glanced down for a moment and let his hand move across her back. "Why?"

"I don't know." Her eyes glanced in the direction, and she found herself seeing his face. "I want it again. But I want it harder. I want you to make me forget everything I've ever known."

The gollet sweetly chuckled. "I'm *not* going to argue with that. After all, it'll be my belated birthday gift to you."

So once again it was. Nikolag threw her onto her back and gave her exactly what she asked for. After their second coupling, her friend sat up with persistence. A heavy weight of thoughts burrowed into his mind. "I must tell you something you should know." Even though who he was speaking to appeared unmoved by the firmness of his concerned approach, he continued, "One day the work you hold dearly to will fail to make you happy. And what should you do then? I've been a Guardian for almost years, and these days of repetition will bore you. As did schooling, as did your home life."

She began dressing herself, and she threw her coat around her slightly cold body. "Nikolag, those things were torturous to me. I was lost and withdrawn. Even though you were a nightmare to me, I wanted to conquer you and do something right for once."

"If this be so, then why is it you could not conquer your family and pupils? Why did you run away from them?"

"They didn't want me." She tied her coat around her waist. "The Guardians wanted me, Captain Staghen wanted me, and I wanted all of you. The Guardians mostly welcomed me. I felt more welcomed in that field than in my own home," she responded dryly. It was as if the conversation meant nothing to her, but it did.

He watched her hands yank the belt to clasp her coat closed, and she flipped her hair to fix its messiness. He said, "I hope my thoughts did not find ache to your heart."

Halo simply sat and looked to him. Her face turned downward as she rubbed her fingers together. "You are one of the very few friends I have left, Nikolag. I cherish your curiosity."

For once in all of his life, Nikolag was stunned by this woman. How wild and yet so soft she was to have the voice of thunder, but the soothing sounds of rain be her voice. She was perfect. Flawed in so many ways but dying in so many ways to correct her own imperfections that he saw her as nothing less than perfect. While they walked back to the village, Nikolag rubbed her upper back. "You are what legends are made of my fellow Guardian."

Halo placed her arm about his lower back in returning adoration. "I thank you, my friend. I have to return home. There's a gift that

Staghen gave me for my birthday. And I left before I could open it. I have yet to see what's inside."

They both stopped suddenly. The village was quiet, and Halo looked about. Nikolag licked his finger and lifted it to the air. He spoke curiously, "The winds are coming from the east today?"

"And?" Halo questioned.

"I am used to the handlings of a twelve-point wind rose, Halo." He squinted his eyes and looked about. "I've never really recalled the winds coming from the east here. And it feels a little warm and higher in pressure. Like a storm is coming."

Halo looked to him. "It's nothing more than the confused seasonal shifts, Nikolag. As the seasons change the weather is unstable. You know that. You are a seafarer. I hope it's a storm. How I love winter storms."

16

The soon to be High Lady of Nakhan was folding linens in the captain's chamber, and she was yearning for both another kiss and for Halo to return home. Oh, how she let her mind wander into the fantasy of such a thing! Her hands worked to press out creases in the captain's undergarments, and smiles were felt in her heart while thoughts danced over the idea of avenging Derjaun's untimely death. The village had drunk itself into a stupor of merriment that knew no end, and Jastin had seen a few young girls being a little bit more feisty than usual to the young boys. They were simply practicing their rights to be like Halo.

Nothing but glee was to be courted with as Jastin proudly began observing a little tear to Staghen's favorite night shirt, but a sudden disturbance in the home's floors made her turn with immediate caution. Her eyes were large as the sound of boots walked directly toward the door. Slowly, Jastin leaned down to lift her dress and braced her hand on the lady dagger she always dressed with, watching. She was unaware if it was an intruder. Without grace or fear of frightening the girl, Staghen opened the door and came inside, leaving Jastin's breath at an absolute rest of relief.

"My Captain," she began as she rose from gripping the blade, "I was ready to kill you."

The scene of Jastin acting as if she were so moodily tough and a true born killer that heaven forbid could have killed a man his size left Staghen extremely humored.

"My lady, you have not the strength or even half the muscles to handle me. And in the stance of which I saw you in just now, you would sooner fall on the floor than come after me properly."

Jastin's eyes glittered sweetly. "I could try."

He smiled and folded his arms. "And you would still fail, but you would fail from the floor."

Jastin tossed her dark-blonde length of hair behind her, and her tone of voice grew shy. "Captain, I would make myself use every muscle in my body to handle you," she said with almost a sense of innocent sarcasm.

He knew she was blushing uncontrollably with the situation, and so he wrapped his arms around her to kiss once more. She got what she wanted. As he pulled away, he noticed her soft face was looking down, and the lady was nearly squeezing the shirt in an uncomfortable death grip. "My lady, how are you this early morn?"

She nodded. "I don't think my heart has the room to contain any more happiness." Then she giggled sweetly, "I was hoping you'd kiss me again."

Jastin saw Staghen's hand approach her throat, examining a humble necklace she wore. "Where did you find this lovely creation that adorns your neck?"

The captain knew she was easily swooned. Jastin stuttered with her heartbeat. "My necklace?" She held her fingers to the creation of glass beads and small feathers, "You purchased the materials for me the night of the Feshtivig Vin Yulan, and I made it. Do you not recall?"

Staghen chuckled as he continued feeling the necklace. "My mind was in quite a web that evening."

"You intend no harm," she answered happily.

"But this should mean that this necklace is rather old, from your childhood to be precise. You need a new one to mark your womanhood."

Jastin's face grew defensive. "But this is the only one I possess, great Captain." Although his actions left her upset, Staghen removed the necklace anyway to set it on the small bed table.

Then she saw Staghen lower to one knee.

He took her hand to guide her to rest on the knee he was not braced with. As she came to rest on his thigh, her hands shook from what he was doing, both from anticipation and the grief of a dusty nerve being cleaned. Staghen marveled at the young woman's growing glow on her face, and her heart was beating so hard he could hear it from the close moment he gave. "Captain, what are you..." She looked into his captivating blue eyes. She could not breathe fast enough.

"It is time that you had another necklace to mark yet another chapter in your life, my love." He drew a breath, and with his eyes caring deeply for the gaze of hers, he began confessing his emotions. "I have not yet truly told you, but you have been a faithful friend to me and grew into a wondrously majestic woman who I could not picture my home without. Your company at night has eased my soul through night terrors and trauma from my past, and you have loyally remained at my side no matter how hard I treated you, and even though you loved me and wished me to be your husband—"

"WHAT?"

He realized he let Halo's secret slip. Regardless, he went on happily. "Oh come now, Jastin. Halo told me.

Yet even though you knew I wouldn't marry, every day you proved that your friendship was binding stronger and stronger to me. I don't believe you fully understand what happiness you give."

Jastin's heart moved heavily from the kind words, but she laid hopes down to rest. Her heart must remember that he would remain without courtship, even though he tortured her love for him by holding her in the ways of proposal, and even kissing her numerous times. The agony progressed when Staghen removed a luxurious necklace from his side coat pocket. One of a soft silver dust chain that was woven around rubies and held a larger, well-cut Yulan marble in the front, it too being encrusted in the soil's finest little diamonds. She gasped with a boisterous and elegant clasp to her mouth, "Oh, Staghen, this is simply stunning! Is this for me?" She held her chest with a faint feeling of overexcitement.

"Jastin," he began as he looked to her kind, brown eyes. She was still, seeing he had more to say, and held her heart. "Am I an honorable enough of a man on this day to ask for your heart in marriage?"

All of her past came flowing through her eyes. The young maiden's lips parted with a whimpering shock. Her eyes only watered, and her stare grew deeply blank at him. "Staghen...." she began in disbelief.

He interjected earnestly, "You are the only woman in these lands I want to share my love with."

A little sniffle was heard from the young lady whose day she believed could not have brought her any more happiness, "Staghen, I..."

And it was that Jastin fell into his body that almost knocked him off his knee. Her hug around his shoulders and neck was intensely moving, her soft cries in his neck accompanied the quivering of her body, "I cannot find a word stronger than the mundane 'yes' to suffice for my answer, my Captain. Yes! Over and over I'll scream it loud. I would love to marry you!"

While Jastin let her life's tension be released in that embrace, Staghen skillfully slipped the necklace around and fastened it. She sat back to feel it. While her entire face quivered, she had to reflect on all the rewards that life gave her. She finally was going to have the man of her never-ending love and heart. Before he had entered the room, she genuinely believed there were no further actions the day could bring to make her happier.

"I must say, my lady, the jewels sparkle all the more against your skin." Staghen grinned.

Jastin only wiped her eyes. "I can't even speak. My heart is confused with words to say."

She had no words to say. For years far too long did she write in her journal the love she felt and yet would never be able to show. It was nearly enough to bring her an untimely demise when Staghen brought himself in the proposal manners, but to have heard those immortal words.... *Jastin, am I honorable enough to ask your heart in marriage?* The young lady's heart began to feel complete, for the life-long dream of finally belonging to the most beautiful man her soul would ever know had come true. She lowered her head to cry softly in disbelief.

The captain snickered, charmed by her reaction. "You should visit the garment booths and find yourself a worthy seamstress to make you a dress. Tell all you see of the event, for I wish to marry you first thing when the morning star rises."

Hearing that made the soon-to-be High Lady come to, and she clapped with loud happiness and threw her arms to hug him once more. "Oh, I would marry you in this room if Vathra were here right now to wed us! And Halo of course, to witness the happiest day of my entire life!" Her voice nearly squeaked at the ending of her speech. She had clutched her hands to her chest when speaking, and her face expressed nothing but pure love.

"Well, he is not here at the moment, so make your time of use until he is." Staghen smiled to her.

"Oh, my Captain, as I said before, I promise I will be the most amazing wife you could have ever asked for. I will..."

She caused him laughter again, and he rubbed her rapid lips. "My love, you are the most amazing wife I could ever ask for," he chuck-led. "That is why I asked for your love. And you can cease calling me 'captain' so much now. I admire the ways you respect me, but..." He took his hand to tenderly touch her cheek. "You are nearly my true wife. I would love to hear you call me by my name more often."

Jastin's eyes were ablaze with honor. "Of course, Staghen! I give many thanks for this. But there is one request I must humbly ask of you. I know it is tradition for the man to wear his mane without a ribbon, but I am very fond of the way the rays of the morning star fall against the strength of your handsome features, and I have found that your ebony tresses, as wonderful as they are, hide these wonders.

Would you mind wearing your hair back in that beautiful style you wear when you announce newcomer Guardians?"

Staghen's face was calm to her, and his lips smiling all the same with a strong sense of contentment. "My little joy, if it is a wish of my coming wife, it is a wish I can grant. Halo makes fast work of the main braid. I would be honored to have her do it for me." He chuckled to change his voice with curiosity. "My instincts tell me that you have planned that look for me since you were a young girl."

She could only look at him. Still resting on his thigh, Jastin was not fully able to accept what her life now offered. There he was, the strong and noble man she had known for so long. The sense of innocence was alive in him. Now it was a time when seasons had changed, bringing with them the maturity of his body and a few lines near his eyes when he smiled. A smile that she favored with all her love. "And I am to call you...my...husband, now?"

"It is not official yet, but we need not the blessings of the malakae to know how our love lives."

It was obvious at that moment to Jastin that her love and body would be bound to this man the next day, and yet in her never-ending ways of her childhood, she tested her limits to get what she craved. "And is it wrong, my darling, that I desire to kiss you more than before? I know my heart cannot hold waiting for tomorrow to again know the ways of how deeply you could kiss me as your wife."

How sensually he answered. "It would be all the more sinful if your heart desired a simple kiss but your body desired more than what my lips can give. Is this what you want?" he whispered delicately to her. Both lovers knew the strain was building.

Jastin leapt into a dangerous dare. Strong nails ran through his hair and pulled him closer to her. The house was quiet and empty. The lady, with her hands braced in his hair, gazed strongly into his eyes, and he into hers.

"It is in our luck, Jastin, that my lips can offer more than a kiss. And not only can I give you more, but I also want to give you more," he professed.

It was more than a statement; it was a promise to the girl. Chilled by the confession, Jastin pulled her lover's lips to hers again, and Staghen returned the romantic affection the way he did before he left that early sunrise. With a rapturous approach of superiority, Staghen kissed her deep enough that her breath sunk under his lips, and his arm slid underneath her legs to lift her. However, an action she gave made him cease before he could do so. She began to weep.

Staghen was immediately taken back by the apparent display of grief. "What in our act of love have I done to make you weep, my dear?"

With her eyes flowing like the gentle stream of the northern forests, Jastin replied with her whimpers of uncontainable happiness. For the stream that ran so gently in the northern forests could not exist to be called gentle if something had made its heart break. "Staghen," she whispered lovingly as her closed eyes were pressed to his lips, "I cannot speak your name enough. I feel I should have my head knocked." Tears came a little harder and she shook her head in disbelief. "This cannot possibly be a fortune for me. I have never felt worthy enough to belong to you."

Words of the sweetest taste coated her lips. "You have been humbled in these years of our friendship, young Jastin. And as the role of my wife, you will learn that many women will attempt to sway you out of the truth that I love you," he warned.

Her face lit up to him. The woman felt his other arm embrace her back, and she was lifted. Blood rushed all throughout the young maiden's body, feeling the strongest desire locked in between her thighs, and without hesitation she engaged the fiery rage of lust with her lips to his. Such a remarkable warmth came to her at that moment. At once Staghen's display of strength was empowering over the female, delivering the strongest need for her in a moan of swelling desire, rendering her body a full scape of demands to be touched and nothing else. To hold back from a feeling of promising love was not in her nature. How could it be?

Her desperate hands flooded his breast plate in search of gratification by simply touching him. Staghen adorned her face with kisses, and his lips pressed warmly into her neck. The beauty of grace came across them as Jastin laid her head back. The pleasure quelled against her skin, and it was his body that was held against it. Their embrace led to the bed where he came on top of her, and his passion drove hard and bit against the sanctity of her luscious nape. Fingernails clawed deep into his coat, the armor of his chest heavily crushing against hers. The captain's physique stirred wildly against her smaller frame as the erotic fulfillment of his groin seared with rapid blood flow.

While Staghen's aggressive teeth held her still, Jastin's virgin body was attempting to understand the ways of mating. Was it normal for the man to hold the woman down by means of teeth to the throat? Or was he even going to attempt to court her? It was a rush of delirium to try and guess Staghen's intentions. All this excitement made the girl's heart soar and her fantasies fly. His nurturing hand stroked down the small of her waist, nerves flexed hard under her dress while the pressure of the touched skin grew deeper. His hand clenched around her hip, and Jastin felt herself being held down.

With a lash of worry, she held the captain's strong jaw. "Staghen," she panted, "if your plans do not hold the image of us making love, then please cease your passion."

His affection stopped.

"Forgive me. I am still so young that I know not the ways of this. But my body knows that it can no longer hold back what I long for. If it be against your dignity to have me now, then please spare my sanity and temptations."

Her lover's gentle lips spoke closely. "My heart is clenched with passion, Jastin. And as you I have pleasure to gain, I wish our love to come like rain."

A slow cadence began sounding in the rhythm of their bodies with every beat leading to a new exposed area of warm skin, neither one of them being more exposed than the other. He unbuckled his breastplate and lifted it to let it clunk carelessly on the floor. The most beautiful specimen was revealed as she removed his undershirt. Jastin's hands searched over his taught biceps and held them hard, feeling how supple his skin was despite the harsh climate of the winter, and in return her lover affectionately kissed her collarbone once more. It was erotic to his nerves, and even more tingling to feel her soft hands yearning to massage his muscles again.

Jastin had a healing touch to his body, a touch that took years to develop. But now he loved her as if it were his love that earned such a touch. His hips ached with a feeling that he was familiar with, unlike Jastin who had denied the same sensations she felt when she undressed him. Along with the aching, Staghen felt his body almost seemed to grow to a breaking point of blood vessels pushing against his skin, and every inch of him was thicker and longer. In this moment did he find the urge to bite Jastin's throat once more.

It was far more than her fantasy coming true that made Jastin's heart leap in and out of her body. To see such a feature of a man on top of her left her constantly in moans of joy. "Staghen," she quickly panted, "I wish we could enjoy this for all time. I can barely take breath for what you give to me." After forcing a deep breath, Jastin grabbed his neck to kiss his cheek hard.

He laughed happily with his eyes closed and began pulling her dress sleeves down more, and the young maiden shrugged her shoulders to lift her upper back so that he could slip the chastising garment down to her waist. She looked down and saw his kisses planted firmly against her sternum, and a little bit of hesitation was given when her breasts were nearly revealed in their healthy entirety. Staghen's manhood swelled when his lips felt the skin of her breast. He moved his lips until he felt the tiny erect nipple and his tongue licked fiercely against it. His body felt the rush of her excitement with the action.

She nearly jumped off the bed. It was so delicate but awakening, as if he had taken a dagger straight through her breast. Part of her body and heart would have been frightened further had she not realized who was doing it. He held her down to claim her, encouraging her to stay and handle him, and it let her mind rest as it proved he really did love her. Unexpectedly, there was that pinch of discomfort that rose again between her thighs. Except this time, it shook her nerves so hastily that she tried squeezing her legs together, but the placement of his body allowed her to only clamp them around him. How close his pelvis was to hers, so close that the vicious swelling of his endowment began making her eyes water.

When her body shifted to a different emotion, he looked up from suckling her breast and watched his love's eyes stay closed in adoration, waiting for him to penetrate the stiffness inside of her body. Staghen pulled her up to hold her, catching the young maiden in a daze of kisses and touching. She scratched her nails into his chest and returned the merciless favor of pinching his hard nipple.

He rolled her over on top of him, and Staghen, initiating to pull her dress down further, took her left nipple into his mouth. The actions became nearly unbearable to the girl who was straddling him, rocking her hips back and forth as she felt his muscled thighs pressing the leather pants between her feminine lips.

She dug her body deeper onto him and felt that the tension was being satisfied. Her chest grew in a hollow feeling, the blood flow coming to desperation, and Jastin pulled his hair hard enough to hold him down on his back. At that moment of amazing honor, his body was all hers. She tore his pants down, and his male instincts caused his hips to lift while Jastin pulled down harder.

When she saw his sexual entirety, it was far from enough. She loved seeing him naked. As she rubbed his hips, the flexing crease that led from his hip bone to his erection twitched. His mind clouded with a smile, and looking down he saw his legs being massaged deeply into pure eroticism. Then, as if by pure instinct, she licked Staghen's sweltering heat. The response was blistering as the hands of the man she loved coursed through her hair. He moaned loudly.

She listened adoringly to his audible moans that seeped through clenched teeth and took her licks up his length, stopping at the underside of the head and moved down again. The quicker she licked, the more violently his legs shook. When Jastin's sexual cravings took her to his end again, she kissed and placed her soft lips around. Immediately she sucked and stroked his length as hard as she could to fulfill a lifelong need. So much tension was felt in the captain's quivering lower body. So much that she wished her hands could ease it all immediately. This act of love took her some time to understand how it could satisfy him completely, so she went slower to fully feel every inch of skin and taste every pulse of sweat.

His hair fell to his left, looking down with breaths coming at their heaviest. Watching the sight of his own virginal sex being stimulated by her wandering lips felt just as perfect to him as she saw his figure, and he relaxed his head back with bright blue eyes closing softly. The pillow contoured easily to his head, and miraculously every fiber and blood vessel in his body sank into the bed. For once in his life, he relaxed. She took her love on him more aggressively, causing his breaths to quicken. With a few more moments passing, the raven-haired lover held her hair and a sudden hot liquid poured into Jastin's mouth. At first, she backed off, being unaware of what had happened, and at first being nervous that he had urinated.

It took her no time to taste that it was his semen, since it apparently had no resemblance in smell to urine, and Jastin wondered if it was unusual that she found the taste of it simply delicious. With a gentle kiss being placed on the tip of Staghen's manhood, she gazed up to him with her eyes full of wonderment and was pulled up to be rolled on her back. His hands came fast to hold her down and passionately, kisses covered her throat and breasts once more. What she had given him left the captain anxious for her love. His mind toyed with the teasing idea of giving her the same expulsion of pleasure she had blessed him with. Her dress was pulled down past her hips while every new bit of flesh being licked and kissed.

His nose suddenly drove into her soft lower belly, as her scent caused his skin to ripple in absolute contentment. For his entire life, he had been unaware of how much he needed this. The dress was removed, and Jastin's whole entirety waited. Easily, the captain slipped his hands under her thighs to spread them. The girl's mind flustered hard, questioning what Staghen intended to do. Although the sensation of his nose brushing against her pubic bone brought delight, she had never felt that a woman was able to receive the same satisfaction as he did. Yet the captain made this impossibility possible. His lips locked around her sensational spot, licking his tongue deeper into her womanhood.

She screamed out loud. It was a whirling rush of a miracle to her body! How much she craved for the feeling to last as it left the lady feeling superbly appreciated and truly treasured. The stars above could not grant her the ability to breathe fast enough, and the more excited she became, the more he pushed himself to pleasure her every nerve inside every hidden crevice. He was driving her mad, licking even further down until his tongue could slip inside. How wonderful she smelled and tasted, simply sweet and full of lust. He listened to her the way she had listened to him. At that moment, his hands gripped around her thighs to hold them, allowing the soft flesh to relax openly against his biceps. She felt his tongue tickling back up to that spot of overloading pleasure where it dug and moved firmly against it.

His hair was immediately pulled hard, her head was thrown back and louder Jastin called out his name. His muscles grew tight with the joy of finally having her.

She looked down and saw his eyes were closed, mouth buried into her female heat. She curled her fingers into his scalp and demanded to be licked harder. She wanted all of him, wanted everything on him to be inside of her. Her body began to palpitate in sweat and when the air in the room grew hotter, all she did was let go of his hair to pull her own legs back into her chest, which caused Staghen to get on top of her. It was such a wonderful offering as he accepted her request to be dominated. When she revealed herself to him in such a vulnerable way, it showed him how much she trusted him and mostly how much she was growing to need penetration.

Her thighs were clawed with nails as the captain came to his knees, leaned over, and kissed her wet womanhood so intensely that she was crying with his name. This time it was Staghen's hands that kept her legs back. Faster his tongue stroked up and down, and her body twisted with the contortions of a climax. Her teeth gritted, she panted, and he went deeper. Suckling, licking, kissing, and stroking until Jastin's body violently turned to the right. "Oh, I can't hold any more!"

But he inflicted it regardless. Her body held the strength of a mouse in comparison to his, and she was held down to bear more of his lickings. The captain had never tasted a woman before and was growing excessively fond of how one could sound, feel, smell, taste and appear when being orally pleasured, especially his love.

Weakly, she screamed.

But there was more to be felt. The captain ceased his torture to pull himself on top of her. At that moment, Jastin's heart nearly collapsed as she knew he was finally going to make love to her. When his body pressed onto hers, her eagerness overcame her patience, and she wrapped her arms adoringly around him.

"Staghen, make love to me," she gasped hotly.

He fiercely kissed her, and when his hips pushed hers apart her moans filled his heart and ears. Down her neck he kissed, and she held onto him as if letting him go would kill her. The two lovers felt each other's deep and wonderful bodies, finding heaven within.

Jastin could not keep herself quiet, not with the built-up tension for over ten years dreaming of him. The pain that came to take her virginity away was not enough to silence the urge to call his name again and again, and it was far from enough to keep her from enjoying it. They looked into the eyes of one another. With every thrust her body moved with this. As he saw her mouth parted, and her eyes focused on only him, he watched and heard her whisper, "I love you." It was almost so faint that he could simply just see it on her lips and hear it on her breath.

Although her insides felt like a thousand knives jousting up inside of her pelvis, the massaging penetration flowing with his passionate kisses felt nothing short of a miracle. The captain was held hard in the serenity of the moment, a moment that he had disregarded as a need his whole life. The embrace left him feeling that this beautiful young maiden's love would never founder, and it would never grow old. In this embrace Staghen also believed there truly was no other man she could have loved, as he felt it through her violent contractions that kept pulling him inside of her. He thrusted deeper into his lover, allowing the entire length to inject its warmth into her while the heavy thickness stretched her insides to a breaking point. He lifted his left hand to brush her hair away from her face. Now it was his turn to breathe. "I love you, my darling."

She heard the words. She felt the words. She *experienced* the words. She took him well for a virgin and allowed his thrusts of pleasure and pain to go as hard as he needed, for it was never too much for her to handle. Soft, feminine hands grabbed around the biceps that shuddered in climax. The lady panted violently with his name. "Staghen, you feel so good, so unbelievable!" Her back arched with her mouth gaped wide open when she took in an intense draw of air.

Frantically trying to ease her uncontrollable desires, she laid her arms around the captain's neck, pulling harder onto his hair and hooking her chin over his pumping shoulder. "Staghen," she breathed, "I feel you so...deeply."

In the mist of all turmoil in their lives, love was found in the sincerest of places. Staghen gave her his warmth while calling her name. She swept his hair from his slightly damp face and felt his eyes too had been watering. Together they had reached a point of pure erotic bliss that nothing could compare to.

After their loving affair, Jastin consistently either played with his hair or kissed his strong throat. His scent was washed all over her as he rubbed his face against her breasts. It was something Nakhanian men did. For Staghen's act, Jastin adored every motion he gave her. Nuzzling under her chin and rubbing his neck into hers so hard that her skin began to burn, but she loved it. A thought came to her. While the captain braced himself above her still, his arm muscles quivered as if to be tired, so in all her giving ways, Jastin massaged them. "Staghen," her breath flushed out of her mouth in one hot draw, "that was incredible! I feel I could cry forever!" He ignored her, only to keep his consistent affection going. She smiled, sighed in blissful relief. "But your arms are quivering. Should I ease your tension?"

He sighed with exhaustion. "It is not tension at all, my dear one.

Quite the opposite. I think I released every tension I've ever known into you."

She laughed merrily. "Perhaps we should lie together in a calming moment so that your non-tense body can rest. I can't get enough of you." Staghen looked to her with a grin, as she was taunting him with innocent humor. His heart flooded happily.

And still as the day was young, Halo was praised everywhere she walked. People chanted her name on high as this Guardian's name had officially become the most exalted name in all Nakhan. With her best male friend still at her side, she offered him a drink at the hostelry to give thanks for all that he had done for her in the years of their friendship. Without Nikolag, Halo would have been in ruins these days. It was a miracle to both see the village folk so happy and gleeful. The children ran freely in the pathways, the Guardians had time to flatter the unmarried maidens of the village, who in return had the ability to do their daily shopping without the need of an escort. Some Guardians were a little upset about the renewed independence of the maidens, as it left them without an excuse to follow a beautiful damsel around all day.

The topic brought much amusement to Nikolag and Halo inside the hostelry. When his belly was full of ulgg, he turned in a state of inebriation to his friend. He slurred his words with a lopsided grin, "Halo, if I asked for your hand in marriage, would you cut mine off?"

Laughter consumed her entirely. "I would cut off more than your hand!"

He snickered while he nudged his shoulder into her. "And why do you insist on being a manslaughterer?"

She looked. His face was nearly laying on her arm that was resting on the counter. "Nikolag, your blood is so intoxicated you do not know what you say." She spoke in humorous disbelief. "You never wished to marry a woman."

He rubbed her back and spoke lazily. "Yes, but uh. I forgot what I was going to say. Oh yeah! But I like what we did and don't want another man having it."

"Nikolag, you're the only one in Nakhan I'd ever do that with. Let's mate whenever we want, shall we, my gollet friend?"

The deal was set with mugs raised high.

Back at the house, in Staghen's arms, Jastin lay peacefully asleep. Before she slipped into slumbering, her mind was rushing with all the joyful thoughts of being Staghen's wife. Images of bearing children left her with nothing short of contentment since they were to be Staghen's children, and the anxiousness to tell her family wore hard into her mind. Even though she was certain they had made love during the least fertile part of her year, she had hope. Her protector was behind her, molding his body directly into hers, and every now and again his soft breathing stirred her lust once more. It was not until the cold winds came again that she woke up feeling very frustrated.

She easily rose away from her loved one who remained asleep despite the movement. The window was left open when they were attempting to cool their bodies after lovemaking, but it was time for it to be closed again. She moved to look outside. She sighed, smiling. "This winter shall bring much more warmth to us this year."

The shutters were stubborn. Jastin tried to loosen them from the locks that kept them open, but her attempts fell short. The wood creaked and cracked a little bit, and her patience began to fluster. "Come now, you stubborn old thing!" she whispered harshly.

And then the oddest thing happened. The wind miraculously stopped. Nothing else to accompany the feat, such as the clouds parting or anything else, the air currents just ceased. "Well then," the young maiden breathed as if relief was given from it. "That will suffice. And may you accept my gratitude, dear gale."

She slipped back into the bed, being more than thankful she had not woken Staghen. But he did stir, and he did wake. Jastin groaned. "Forgive me for waking you and disturbing your sweet rest," she said to him.

As he rubbed the weakness from his eyes, he moaned back to her. "It was not your warmth that woke me, my love. It was the sudden change of the winds. It is still light in here, and the windows have remained open."

"The locks are much too difficult for me to manipulate," she confessed.

"Ah, you do not need to hold worry," he said as he kissed her. "I shall close them. Perhaps the strength of a man is what the disobedient locks need."

She blushed when the captain showed his muscles in a playful visual aid of his statement, but even he himself could not close them. "Jastin, will you please make a letter for the woodsmith? I cannot fathom how—" He paused to look out the window.

For a moment, the lady waited in bed, but she questioned him to finish. "You pause, my heart?"

Staghen still did not move. Something outside the window had rendered him frozen.

"Staghen?" Jastin pleaded.

As he looked, his eyes were attempting to focus on something far away. An unusual flock of birds were swooping down from the mountains and heading in the direction of the village. "Jastin, can you recall a bird that flew in flocks as large as this?"

When she came to the window, the solid dark objects were a little larger and were gaining size quickly. "Well, of course, but...I cannot recall a bird that would be as large as these."

At once, a terrifying sensation possessed the captain, and his heart quickened.

His eyes trembled while his stare was stuck. "Jastin?"

"Yes?"

An unshakable fear was building. What were those beings that he could not identify? He looked to his love and held her shoulders. "Listen to me. Stay inside. Whatever you do, stay inside and hide."

The order made Jastin's soul cry with agony, and at once her soft eyes watered, already knowing he would leave again. "Where will you go?" she whimpered.

"I have to go gather my men and see what this—"

From out of the sky, the shrill call of several hundred beasts blasted their voices toward the humble and unsuspecting village, calling immediate intentions to destroy all in their path. They came upon everything at the speed of death. Staghen pulled Jastin to the floor and held his arms around her. She screamed loudly while covering her head. With the sound breaking the moment of the lovers embrace, Staghen pulled from his lady to see the sky was enshrouded in absolute fright.

The birds that swept into the pathways only possessed the wings of such a creature, but the rest of the body was recognized as the horrible animal that Halo had slain. Staghen's eyes enlarged.

The Annenji had returned.

His heart hardened at the onset of battle as he pulled his lover away from the window on the floor. "Jastin!" He began wrestling her to move, attempting to ignore her crying. "Get under the bed! Hide under here and don't come out!"

She kicked with all her worrying strength. For her it was also a situation of fight and protection. She knew, with a twist of pain, that Staghen was going to fight. He had to. "Staghen, please let me go with you!" She made her motions to crawl back to him, but he pushed her further underneath the bed. Her screams were horridly distressed, perhaps even more so than the wail of the beasts outside. All of her body quaked with the attempt to go with him, but the bells around the village chimed the song of threat and all the Guardians were rushing to get the villagers inside. He was losing time.

He managed to force her under the bed and looked to her breathing hard. "My love, you will be safe here."

But she shook her head, for all the misery as the risk of losing him played through her strongest desire to keep him. "No," she groaned in despair.

He spoke sternly to her, trying to stay as calm as possible. "Jastin, please, this is not the time! Promise me you will stay here! My village and my men need me!"

Heartache led her to clench his hand and kiss his lips. "I promise, but you promise me you will come home."

His mind fell into darkness. The bells continued to sound the warning toll louder as he heard his men assembling and calling for his name. He had to quickly kiss her, yet he disappeared without holding her request for a promise to be kept.

Jastin screamed in fright. She attempted to climb out after him." Staghen! Staghen! Promise me—" She could not finish her cry. The young maid laid her face to the wooden floor, alone, without knowing if she herself was going to live to see the morrow star. The sound of her home falling to a brutal slaughter was not the sound she wanted to be drowned by, but as it passed outside, Jastin stayed in. But the thought of Halo and her family as well crossed her mind. The eruption of shattering glass sounded across the path, and Jastin immediately yelped and hid back under the bed.

At the village hostelry, Halo and Nikolag almost choked on their ulgg when they heard the attack followed by the haunting bell. And they did not even need to look at each other to know it was an urgent time. They both raced outside, and Halo whistled for her horse, already on a thundering path toward her rider. This was not something Halo was afraid of, even though she and Nikolag ran outside and saw the unfortunate fate of what could have been an apocalypse. As Zidori raced toward her, Halo wailed, "Zakuta my lady! Let's shed some black blood once more! Nikolag, I'm sorry I doubted your instincts!" Her hand caught the passing emerald mane, and she pulled herself up, Nikolag coming on his horse close behind.

He held his ax high. "This is not the time to talk. To the masses we show no fear. I am a humble man, but on this day I am not to be one! It will be an honor to fight by your side, Halo!"

She laughed. "Just make it happen that you slay more than I!"

"It is set!" he cheered after her.

The positive confidence stayed with the two Guardians regardless of the havoc the village was enduring. They felt that together they could be victorious. The monsters were everywhere, tearing into homes and crashing the village circle into absolute chaos. As Halo fought bravely with Nikolag as her ally, her mind was not naive, nor ignorant. A few were quickly destroyed from her skillful blade while Nikolag's well-aimed arrows tore down the ones in flight, and in all directions the Guardians were proving they had no time for assembling plans. The orders were clear, to track and kill. As the beasts flapped their wings aggressively at the defenseless villagers, Halo's weak eyes caught the slightest glimpse of a monster busting through a demolished set of rubble, with the vocalized distress signal of a trapped Guardian inside.

The sorakhan yanked her horse to pursue the antagonist that was snarling his snout closer to the man and took one leap of faith to the back of the beast. She was thrown all over with the wild motions of an animal that was obviously angered by the presence, but Halo held hard onto the thick coat of fur at the back of the neck and felt by its size that the one she killed was merely a baby. The small knife in her belt loop was drawn and punctured several times in the creature's neck. It screeched, tossing its body in an attempt to claw her off. Halo saw the young man still bleeding in wilt and completely afraid to move. She pulled the petrified man away and shoved him off. "Hurry, move! Get underground if you can! Find a cellar!"

Claws latched deep into her coat, yet the leather barely allowed the grasp to grace her skin. Halo was thrown hard to the ground, bashing her head violently, and she lost her breath. With her weakened eyes she saw the horrific vision of the heavy taloned feet coming closer with a prowling roar of superiority. Blood ran as freely as the spring's storms, bodies in Halo's peripheral vision lied dormant in all of their darkened sighting, and still the cries from villagers and Guardians alike made Halo attempt to stand. Her vision saw the black paws coming closer with the claws flexed for the kill.

"Halo! Get up!" Nikolag's voice shot after her. He would have come for her, but he had creatures so frequently on him that it was enough that he could stand on his own.

Everything went numb. The Annenji had not even begun to breathe their flames onto the meek houses. The taloned paws stepped closer, and yet a sound more disturbing than the one that greeted her was heard as she looked to the left, and her eyes could do nothing but weep in disbelief. A creature had lifted young Oniden overhead, and Halo's mind immediately pushed her body to move at once. All over her muscles were withered and jostled, the fear of losing the sweet young man had brought her love to scream out his name. An attempt to stand fell in vain, leaving her soul weakened, for the last thing she would have known that kind and generous young man by was his audible pain in desperation to escape the merciless attack.

What have I done? she thought to herself.

"Halo!" he cried loudly. "Halo, help me!" Harder he thrashed to fight off the attacking beast, but her strength was not enough, and neither was his. The beast lashed onto the throat of the victim and feasted hungrily. Against all horrors, the wretched sound of him still attempting to flee echoed. Then, as if she had gone deaf, Oniden's life passed when the crying silenced. The creature's body covered his while he was pushed to the ground. The sorakhan's scream was loud in desperation to still rise to his salvation. In shaking trauma, those weak eyes bled tears of regret. She failed to save her friend.

Another life was lost. Another innocent life was destroyed, and the spirit of the sorakhan had sensed her soul's fire was coming to a dimming weakness. She was old enough to recall the first attack on the village. But the Guardians had led the cruel beasts away in time enough to spare everyone's life. This was not the same. They came in droves that far outnumbered the first encounter. In the wake of tragedy, when all hope seemed lost, Zidori rushed from nowhere and lowered her head for a fatal charge right into the belly of the beast that stood in front of Halo. The animal growled and turned to lunge at her, but without a pause Zidori turned and kicked her deadly hooves into its skull. The animal soiled itself, collapsed, and its entire body began twitching. Halo felt someone pulling her to stand and saw Nikolag's face. "Halo, come to your senses!"

She nodded quickly. Fear caught her eyes, "Oni—"

"Halo, he is gone!" he shouted fiercely at her.

"Oniden..." Her body shook uncontrollably.

"This isn't the time!" he hollered. The woman nodded again, but with a face iced white with panic while he continued, "We must save as many villagers as we can. I will be with you."

Halo lost all of her senses. "No, Nikolag listen to me! Radal and Ishlog were both taken! Staghen is next. We must find the captain and keep him on this ground. Look!"

Nikolag's eyes followed her thrusted finger, seeing the Guardians fighting bravely as all the villagers tried to hide. "They are after men of power, not the villagers!"

She reacted quickly to pull him away from a diving attacker. He looked up around and back to her. "I'm with you always! Let's go!"

The strong pair raced back into battle, and Halo left her horse behind. If they were truly after Guardians, she did not want to put her mare's life in jeopardy. All over the two searched for the captain, who was not yet found. Both were wearing thin of their energy and came to a standing rest underneath a collapsed awning, breathing completely out of panic and yet trying to stay calm.

"Your home, we should make haste to his house. Perhaps he is keeping Jastin from harm?"

She shook her head causing sweat to drip on her bloody lip. "No. Staghen is for the protection of all things, not just one. He must be somewhere. We have to find him!"

A horrible clouding thought came to her, and she looked at Nikolag fast. She wheezed. "The captain had intentions to propose to Jastin this early morning. I give my blood on the proof he has!"

Nikolag looked and quickly pulled Halo to duck under a large wooden plank that had fallen from above. "What are your orders? Tell me what to do, and I will do it!"

"Jastin is to be his wife! Go to my home and find her! She does not know what to do and will risk going after him!"

For a moment, the two friends looked at each other. With their chests growing sore with exhaustion, Nikolag's eyes watered. "Nikolag, go!" Halo screamed as she shoved him hard. His love for her had brought him to kiss her hard promptly. "I will find her, but don't you die on me!"

Bravery imbued Nikolag's daring acceptance. He ran out into the gruesome sight of a war zone gone deathly wrong. He dodged the falling remnants of buildings making his way swiftly to the captain's house. Halo squeezed her eyes and held her heart. "Radal, please. I know you can hear me. I'm so afraid." She squeezed her eyes and gasped. "Radal, calm my heart and give my body strength." This was it. A long time ago, Staghen had warned her there would be one day she would be alone in a hard situation and would have to think for herself. It was her chance. She earned those beads for a reason. That day was going to be the day she proved she earned them. It was to end, there and then.

No more moments could be spared. Halo rose to her feet and lashed out into battle, cutting into everything that was in her path. All she could think of was her family, of Staghen and Jastin, her home, her horse, and her strength. As if Zidori heard her rider's thoughts, she came thundering up against her. "Zidori, my trusted friend!" She climbed onto the wild mare's back once more, moving faster toward victory. Zidori's health had been properly sustained through all the years of their friendship. As the strongest horse, she faithfully led Halo directly to where she saw the demons flying over the village with a clear shot away from the buildings and chaos. "Zidori, hold your ground. Do not move!" Halo pulled her quiver from her back and prepared for the first shot. She squinted her poor vision in the corrupted skyline. "Radal, give my eyes the accuracy to kill."

She let go, and with a miracle one of the beast's growls had launched into the air and a rain of blood cast its ugliness onto the village soil, and it too had fallen from the sky to its death below. Halo laughed and screamed joyously as one after another went down. Surely this was a positive turn on the fate of the village and her people, and her home. But then she remembered her true mission. What was she to do? Five of the countless beasts had fallen from her arrows, but the captain was still not in sight.

All seemed still and silent to her. The fires taking to the sky and the cries of people fleeing for their life.

She heard a familiar whinny coming from a direction and looked. Right there over the burning rubble and slain victims, she saw Rikaana leap over the blazing destruction, coming toward her. Her eyes widened in happiness when she noticed Staghen mounted atop. Why, he had not even had the time to properly dress himself for battle. "Captain!" she yelled for him.

Staghen called back desperately. "Halo, prepare the arrows. They come for me! I'm leading them away from the village!" He looked over his shoulder to the Annenji and snapped the reins harder.

And he was right, as she had been right before. The three remaining swept down through the village paths and were gaining fast on Rikaana's heels with the captain herding the attackers to lead them away from the village. She felt for her quiver to only feel...two arrows left.

"Halo, get your arrows!" he bellowed out to her.

She thought in panic. He came closer to her left, and as she witnessed their intense speed she knew that it was too risky to take all three down. The horse was getting tired, and Rikaana would never be able to outrun them. There was only one chance she had, and she saw it coming fast. Halo shot the two final arrows, which struck miraculously two demons that fell to their deaths. Immediately she threw her quiver to the ground just as the last Annenji dug its claws into Staghen's coat and took him off his horse. At once his body contorted with the attempt to remove his coat. All over he twisted to free himself until the sharp claws dug straight into his skin. When Halo saw his head lean back and let out a shrill cry of pain, she knew help was needed immediately. He felt the talons through the most precious part of his body, near his heart.

"Staghen!" Halo could only do one final thing in dire attempts to save her loving protector. A hard kick sent Zidori to follow. The mare's breath raged as her storming hooves got close enough. Halo judged her distance and jumped from Zidori and grabbed hold of the tail of the black beast. Higher into the air she was taken, and with nothing but desperation she climbed, thanking the heavens the beast had long fur to use in her advantage to hold on. "Staghen, do not thrash about wildly! I'll get you down!"

She pulled herself finally on the back of the creature, but her stomach lifted nearly out of her throat as it plunged down toward the ground in an attempt to throw her off. Halo struggled toward the neck, and once she grabbed it, she drew her knife and injected it straight into the demon's neck, as she had done so many times before. "Staghen, he may drop you! Try to hold onto its paws!" she called.

The captain attempted to reach his hands up, but the talons had a horrible clench that blocked his shoulders from moving. "My arms can't move!" he whimpered in agony, trying to reach again and again.

She would not give up, but neither would the Annenji. Halo felt the neck muscles throbbing while the wind itself was nearly enough to knock her off, but Zidori's wild temper had trained her enough to hold on in such fast-paced situations. The beast was making a fast flight toward the mountains and over the forest canopy it flew. The muscles underneath Halo were throwing themselves back and forth and once more the beast dove down. "Staghen! He heads for the trees, and they may hit your legs! Try to hold them up so your skin does not pull harder!"

His stomach muscles were worn to their very last strength, with blood being lost at a rapid pace, the captain could not even flex his muscles, let alone lift the heaviest ones he had. Halo heard the lashing of leaves and Staghen crying hard, she leaned her head over and saw his legs being torn into. "Staghen, lift them!"

A loud scream came from the creature, echoing over the deep cliff he flew across. The rushing beginning of the Gigannora River's infamous path flowed vastly underneath them. Halo yanked the creature's ears hard, and once more her stomach flew out of her when the beast dove down toward the river. Apparently, she had not punctured a vital part near its neck. At that moment, Halo knew what it planned to do. "Oh no you don't!" she ordered it. "Staghen, hold your breath!"

With one hand holding against the ear, she drew her sword and with one immense blow cut the left wing completely off. The beast reared in its painful fate and could no longer fly straight. Easily Halo could have used that sword long ago to pierce from the back straight through to the heart, but being halfway between the clouds and the ground would have surely led the beast to fall with them to a crushing death. Halo lifted her head and saw the animal was faltering in flight toward the wall of the jagged cliff, and her entire body froze in fear.

Finally, the beast released Staghen, casting him a short fall to the rocky banks below, and Halo jumped off as well right before the creature's head smashed into bloody bits. The sorakhan's body rolled wildly, and she immediately pulled itself to stand in defense, but the beast was dead from a broken skull and a spine that had been crushed. Air from her lungs became still with thought. Although the horrible animal was no longer able to attack, Halo still had one fear that was far greater than if the beast was still breathing.

The sorakhan rushed toward Staghen, who showed that his skin color failed to hold any blood. She wept loudly to him. "Captain!"

His lips were cold to the touch. She did not want to lift his head in case he had sustained critical injury. But she petted his cheek gently. "STAGHEN! WAKE UP!" Then she lost all care of her training. She lifted his head with sincere caution. All through his leather pants she felt the cooling of his body. "Staghen," she said with fear to his pale closed eyes, "please wake up."

And then when she believed she had lost him a miracle of love allowed his eyes to open but a dry cough heaved in his breath. "Ha—"

"Quiet," she whimpered, "you're going to be alright."

This was a twisted truth that would be the first Halo could have attempted to believe in. Staghen was as alright as Halo's eyes had great vision. But that irreversible truth could hold no meaning now. Staghen was going to die. Not warm in his bed as an old man with his wife to nurture his body to sleep, not as a heroic legend of Nakhan should have passed, but here in the bitter cold of the banks on the rocks from which he honorably fell. Suddenly, the pure beauty of the snow around her was all but washed with hatred, malice, and blood. Her hands trembled without control to hold one of his many wounds of deep injections closed.

"Halo..." He turned to her with a smile.

"Stop talking!" With that she lifted her head to scream for help. "Is anyone out there? I need help!" Her voice shook as the thunderous rolls of the lands and her tightened face muscles were worn with trauma.

A hand touched hers. "Halo..." the captain's voice cracked with dryness, "my chest has been ruptured. It melted my armor." A single tear rolled down his whitened face.

She leaned her head to kiss the cold skin on his face. "Do not speak like this." She pleaded with the voice of a child and placed the kiss of love onto his mouth. She felt his lips getting colder. Her eyes opened, and she stroked his cheek.

The eight years that had passed appeared to leave no marking to his lips or face, as they still appeared younger than ever before with the exception of his beautiful lines near his eyes when he smiled. If a human could have the chance to touch the lips of death itself, this was her time to truly understand everything of life, and to answer every question about the life that he would fall asleep into. And the flow of blood was tasted on her lips as her eyes tightened painfully with tears.

Horror dug its merciless fangs into her heart, and she opened her eyes. "Paposa?" She spoke softly with her face against his, "I love you."

In all his glory, in all his bravery, she watched those beautiful eyes of fading blues become flooded as the river itself. "Halo..." he cried weakly. It was in this moment that he had known true love and family once again. To hear her call him such a noble title after all they had been through brought joy to his dying heart. He coughed, "I've always loved you." Staghen's voice broke with violent shakes.

She held him as if she were struggling to keep his life inside. She turned her head to press her cheek against his. "Hold on. Please, you must hold on. I can't lose you. I love you so much." The inevitable would never become a solid state to the stubborn Guardian. She was determined to keep him alive, as it was a fight worth struggling for. She had to force herself to believe in victory *over* death, never victory in it.

But the captain's pain showed through, and he wept. He knew his fate was coming closer. "I will miss you, my daughter." Halo's heart fell apart from the inside as she cried with tears that fell to his strong jaw. He was dying, and there was nothing that could have saved him now. The loss of blood from the claws that tore his insides could not be stopped. "Please, tell Jastin I will wait for her, wherever it is I will go. And you need to know..." He attempted to smile. "...that I'm so proud of you, and it has been an honor to love you. Please believe this. And do not lose sight of your purpose as a Guardian. I had lost faith in Derjaun, but I never once lost faith in you. Don't stop looking for whatever it is your heart and soul need. I'm sorry I could not bring him home," he whimpered with his eyes closing.

Halo nodded. All she could do now was listen to his final words. But inside she was at her final edge of restraint. She watched his eyes as his breath went shallow. The pretty Guardian began to cry. The tears came to her eyes like petals from a dying flower. "Paposa, all of this is in the past. I will do as you ask of me, I promise," the young girl cried. "I will never let go, my paposa. Thank you for giving me a life worth living. I love you so much. I'm sorry for all the times I made you mad." She kissed his lips once more.

And without fear of the inevitable, the glorious young captain's muscles became limp as his eyes lost their life.

They would never wake again.

The captain had died there in his loving daughter's arms, the bravest Guardian to ever risk her life so many times to honor and protect him, but never had she felt so alone. With despair, she clutched the lifeless and bloodied body to her chest, pulling his tattered black mane with her hands. Because of him, the three remaining Annenji were led away from the village. "We thank you sincerely for your sacrifice, my father. I will protect your wife and your people..." She kissed death's skin that had covered his throat and whispered. "I swear my blood on it."

Harder, she clutched him. Her body rocked back and forth with him tightly in her arms. Inside, her stomach swelled into her heart, as that vital organ began pounding uncontrollably. She felt his body unmoving and so limber in her arms. She rocked harder. And with each swaggering motion her teeth clenched tighter. Here it came. It was coming. She squeezed her fingers into his muscles, and her breath began to hyperventilate.

Lips quivering.

Body sweating.

Until her soul could not contain it any longer. She'd had enough of life's unfair games.

Her eyes squeezed with tears, and as her face contorted with reddened emotions, she screamed. It was a scream that echoed throughout the gorge like a banshee dying. She felt inside that she had died. Again and again she allowed her agonizing trauma to be heard among every damned thing of nature, her voice rattling in suffocation of a life gone fatally wrong. Halo threw her head back and allowed her stomach to push the cries louder, and then she burrowed her face into his neck. "Please, wake up!" She sat up and shook him harder and harder. "I can't have you die! I don't want to live without you! Please!"

Once more she collapsed on his body. She thought and immediately got up to hold his nose and placed her mouth to his. She attempted to resuscitate him. As much as she tried to pulse into his heart, there was not enough blood left in his body to help it beat again. She tried once more, and once more and for an astonishing loss of time she attempted to revive him. But after almost an hour of trying, his skin was powdery, and his eyelids never blinked. His pupils had dilated regardless of the blinding light of the sky and snow around them. He was gone. And she was alone.

The snow gently fell around them like a thousand soft kisses of ice. In Nakhan, Halo had learned that when a Guardian died in battle, they died with honor in their memories. Staghen had nothing less than honor in that moment when she looked down and gently closed his eyes.

"Paposa, I feel your soul is still with me. I was told today that I am what legends are made of, and by your death I will prove to you that I will not stop fighting. I will not stop hunting, and I will not stop training. You said I became a legend when I was the first woman Guardian, but I'm nothing compared to you."

She rose to her feet and began stepping into the bath of blood upon the snow, and leaning over, grabbed the arm of Staghen and kindly lifted his head. Halo attempted to heave his lifeless body over her shoulders. Her heart was broken, crying for the release of all evil she had known in this world, and now it was time to find strength in her muscles and spirit to make it up the cliff. A few steps were given, and the sensation of ache bit viciously into her thighs. Muscles quivered while her breath heaved from sadness, and another step followed. She fumbled with her steps to find the strength to move on.

The struggle with the demon and her emotions had rendered her without any vigor to carry forth. Still, she moved on with Staghen's body around her shoulders. But without much distance gained, the young woman collapsed onto her knees only to fall hard onto the ground with the sound of distress coming from her lips. Her eyes tightened together in brutal pain, and alone she wept with the body of her fallen father on her back, the side of her cheek stinging from the cold of the crimson snow. To be alone and far away from the only home she had ever known and the most unmanageable emotions clawing into her chest left Halo with nothing but the wish of death upon her own spirit. However, she had promised Staghen she would protect Jastin. She remembered.

Knowing she had her dreams still ahead of her, Halo pulled all forces of hope into her blood and stood again. No step ever became any easier. Never in her life did she ever want to carry her captain in such a manner, but in a sense Halo could not find more honor in the matter that it was she who began the treacherous ascension up the cliff. A sound of a whinnying horse was heard on the cliff from the other side, and lifting her head to look Halo saw Zidori rearing. The strong companion had followed her rider all the way through the forest and to the edge of the cliff. The sorakhan's eyes glistened. "My friend, you are here in time to help me carry the captain home."

She shielded her eyes from the blinding sky.

Zidori's whinny and presence was like a guiding spirit sent from the stars.

It was not an easy feat to carry the captain's body up the rocky slopes, but Halo felt so invincible and indestructible that her will to place him at rest amongst his wife and people strengthened her every move. Before the slope got too steep, Halo turned her eyes upward to the seemingly impossible task. She had never been truly trained to scale such a cliff. One misstep could send her to her own broken death. She surveyed the area and walked back and forth. High above, Zidori was racing back and forth along the ledge. Then Halo noticed the mare move to a specific area that would have been much easier to climb, so she began ascending and pulling up each rock and ledge, feeling as if she would faint. Another step and she heaved all of her breath and dwindling strength and caught her balance before she slid on an icy surface. However, instead of Halo being left to rise above such a difficult situation, Zidori used her swift-hooved skills to descend to her rider. She was a mountaineer horse, and being such a breed allowed her sturdiness to traverse rocky terrain.

The horse came to her rider, and Zidori's eyes showed she understood what had happened, and respectfully she lowered to the ground so that Halo could easily hoist Staghen on her back, and she stood. Her rider came to her face and stroked her muzzle, "Thank you, my friend. Please take gentle steps. The captain's deepest slumber is here."

They walked through the forest together. It would have been dangerous had it not been for their victorious battle. They made their pace toward Nakhan where she feared the sight of Jastin's face when the captain would not have returned alive. Mostly, she feared when the realization of her protector's death would strike her heart once again. She had wept innocently by his side, but it was sinking into her like treacherous sand. All the while she and Zidori walked, she thought. The journey through the forest was an odd one. Halo had more than enough time to reconcile with everything in her life. Her eyes of sorrow kept glancing to the right, seeing the captain's slumped body and hair hanging past his downward head. Mostly her mind tried to determine how she was going to manage without him, how the village was going to manage without him, and was Vathra ready to stand where Staghen had fallen?

She knew that when she returned to the village there would not be much of it left, and there would not be very many Guardians left, and there would not be very many villagers left. It was going to feel as if she had walked into a part of Nakhan's early settlement before she or her parents were even born. And Jastin, the wonderful wife of Staghen, would be depleted of all abilities to carry on, as she was certain that Jastin had not yet fully learned the lesson of emotional strength. Perhaps when Halo returned, her greatest battle would be to contain the village turmoil. She had time to think of this, and her past, and to reflect on all the miraculous things that Staghen had lovingly allotted her. With these wonders in mind, she affectionately rubbed her fingers into his scalp...and cried. She was a little girl again, one completely without a father now.

She walked around to the other side of her horse and noticed one of his boots was untied, and so she pursed her lips and tied it for him.

The village came into sight, and it was a terrible sight of destruction of families and homes. The flames had practically engulfed every structure. Nakhan was completely torn to the ground. As she came closer, a small group came to greet her. She saw Nikolag, who was walking hand in hand with Jastin, and it was a sight full of tension as Halo's heart squeezed into itself, preparing for the news. Everything seemed to drag to her, hearing Jastin's loud happiness soar over to her, calling happily as she saw her Guardian friend was alive. What she did not see yet was the dead body on the horse. Jastin called for her as she lifted her dress to run through the fields.

"Halo!" she laughed merrily. When Halo failed to move with the same stamina, Jastin stopped. Without the knowledge as to why her friend was without glee, she approached cautiously with hesitation and confusion. Yet the men knew what had happened.

Nikolag whistled. "Come about, men! It is the captain she brings!"

The small group of remaining Guardians, with Vathra in front, came to see the truth. Finally, Jastin managed to move forward. Halo simply stepped to the side as Vathra came with a sun-kissed, aged face looking to her. What words could she find to describe his face? She saw Nikolag come to her speaking in sorrow.

"Halo..." he breathed. All she could do was hold her finger to her lips, hinting at him to be silent. Vathra did not even need to see the face; the clothing, sword, and hair ribbons told the story of who was on the horse's back. His spirit was traumatized by the event and falling back on his rear was the only way he could express the severe panic. "Halo..." he murmured, "the captain is dead!"

"Vathra, silence yourself! Jastin comes. Let us pull him from the back of this horse," Halo answered. Inside her body, all of her world was becoming unraveled.

She ordered Nikolag to help first, but as he did the approaching lady made him feel uneasy as all things in Nakhan were about to change again. The malakae was weak in his state, seeing now it was his time to lead these villagers. *But lead them to where? Lead them how?* How was he going to be able to pull the sadness from those who remained, when he himself could not stand from it?

Jastin looked from one man to the next, and as her lips tightened it was the time when she came close. All of the surviving men, Halo included, held the captain off the ground on his back so that his face of peace would look toward the heavens, as well as allow his wife-to-be a closer look. Jastin leaned over and saw the face. Anxiety flourished in her eyes of absolute grief, as her eyes saw the gaping holes of blood in his chest straight through his armor. The talons of the beast were searing hot as well, and had melted the armor they had punctured.

They all watched her. The young lady's body stiffened with loneliness, her face drowning in longing, and her eyes then clenched together as they could no longer hold back her tears. Her warm fingers moved with great delicacy to the lips that were stone and cold with death's breath the only sound to be heard, and Halo could not recall a time in her life where her heart was locked in suspense, waiting for an action. It felt as if only a breath of moment before this were those lips so warm and passionate. And as sudden as the north winds came did the heart-stricken woman emit her suffering with loud shrills of sadness.

"Staghen!" Her scream broke the silence. Jastin threw her arms around his neck to beg with all of her strength and faith that he would come back to her. With his ebony locks still being soft and luxurious, his lover held them hard by the roots, "Oh, how could this have happened?" She wept into his neck. "Please come back to me!"

Harder she cried into his body, and even more viciously did she scream in despair into the cold, damp skin of his throat. Once more, her loud voice cried for an answer, and it was an answer that Halo could not give. The sorakhan continued to hold up the captain's lifeless body with the rest of his men despite her growing exhaustion. Jastin had given her entire life to him, her past, her future, and had done so willingly. All over his chest, the widow's hands coated themselves in his blood to feel the last remnants of his warmth.

She was horrified, gasping at the stains. As Jastin moaned softly with despair so thick she felt nauseous, her memory took her back throughout all the times in her life she had seen him. These were moments in her life when happiness came to her the most, and never once did she take these moments with him for granted. Not once. Her love for him resonated deep inside of the ground upon which they stood. It stained the virgin white of the snow.

Halo allowed her eyes to flow with sorrow. Utter turmoil cluttered her mind as to whether or not she would allow herself to be weak, or if she would be strong for her friend.

She swallowed hard. "Jastin, I am here at your will."

Her friend's words came in a staggered breath of a sore tone. "Please, I ask humbly to leave us alone. I wish to spend the last moments together in silence."

Halo felt impaled with confusion. For she too had lost. She looked at the men. "Allow her to mourn in peace."

And they laid him to the snow easily, while Vathra removed his cape, folded it so, and placed it underneath the captain's resting head. Jastin was alone with him. A bleeding pain of weight bolted her heart heavily as she leaned over him to kiss his lips and stroked his beautiful jaw affectionately. "Staghen..." she began in whispers, "I know not if you can hear me, or if you are even here..."

Death seemed so odd to her. The captain's body seemed alive to her still, as if she was waiting for him to stir with a breath or hear his heart beating again. "I will wait for you..." Her eyes squeezed again in pain, leaning to lay her head on his chest and holding him in attempts as if to keep him warm. "I promise, Staghen, I do not need to marry you to keep these vows." She nuzzled into his neck. "My vows were already made when I first saw you."

He did not move or respond. She sniffled when nothing happened. A pause of hesitation was given as if Jastin believed with all her might that he may still answer. Silence. "Then I will not be selfish. I would be a fool to lose respect for all the lessons I have learned." She held his hand without care of its coldness and spoke again, "You have served us all with selflessness and valorously, and I understand that you saved us all from absolute death..." She looked to him. "It has been an honor, my captain, my husband, my friend..." And her hand moved from his waist to his cheek, and she wept in realization. "My hero."

She pressed her forehead to his. The north wind graced the field once more. "I will miss you so much."

LATER IN THE DAY, Halo and her colleagues were standing inside the border of Nakhan that was destroyed with all remains being recklessly tossed around the ground, and with her fellow Guardians they were all left to ponder the destiny of those who survived. She turned to Vathra and questioned firmly, "Have you counted those who live?"

He stammered, being at once embarrassed as he had not yet held the time to do so. "No, I have no answer yet, but you have lost a great man this day. You should be consoled."

"What are your orders.... Captain?" a man of weakened Guardian stature asked.

Vathra looked around with worry in his mind. Even if it were only to be a seldom few who survived, he had not the slightest idea what to do, where to take them, or how to even make the long and dangerous journey across the icy tundra to the nearest town. The sorakhan had had enough of waiting for his response, and so she walked up to him heavily and demanded. "Captain, tell us your orders. We all lost a great man this day. We have little time for stalling." Her green eyes searched for his uncertainty of the expression he possessed.

Once again, he fumbled while blinking. "I... I have no answer yet." Perhaps he could have had an answer if he had not lost one of his dearest friends that day. Vathra suddenly knew what Staghen had felt many years ago on that horrid day that Radal was killed. He did not know one bit of what to do.

The response of ignorance burned the patience to ashes of the woman's spirit. "Captain, we have little time! How do we know if there are not more of those beasts?" With her statement, she threw her hand to the air. "Staghen told me there were only a few who escaped when Radal was taken, and that is why he believed I had slain the last! But now look at us! Look at where our arrogance has brought us! Our village is destroyed, over half of the Guardians are dead, and we have the right to claim one Guardian for every twenty villagers! This is not enough! The captain is dead, Vathra, and you are to rise in his place alive! Now make your move!" And once more Halo marched up to him and hissed angrily, "Or I shall run to my own decision without you."

It was far enough that yet again she had lost someone she loved that she had to wait for another leader to even fumble an answer. What hurt Halo as much in the back of her mind was that she still did not even know if her blood family was alive. Perhaps she did not even care.

"Well," Vathra muttered, "we all know that Staghen and I wished for you to claim the malakae status after I claimed his sword, and the malakae is to adhere to the council of the captain. What do you believe is the right thing to do?" His tone grew quite mature with a glint of rudeness. "You tell me, how we are to live now? You tell me where we are to go."

Halo snapped. "I will answer once that layer of sarcasm is removed, Vathra."

The men stood around and felt the ground move uneasily with

the tension of a fight. Nikolag was standing guard and watched all of Halo's emotions boiling to the surface. He began to worry. But Vathra answered quickly, attempting to console her, "I'm not trying to be sarcastic. I'm allowing you your place you've earned. But I believe since Persu is the nearest settlement, we should make haste there."

"I disagree."

At once the entire fleet of men were astonished at her remark, finding themselves lost in bickering at her decision. Halo cared not, pushing on with her reasoning. "Persu holds nothing but corruption. The king there is about as pure-hearted as a cow's feces is white." She looked about to the others. "We all know this. You take us there, and you sentence us to enslavement with pickets higher than the stars of our heavens."

A man spoke up, "Then tell us, Malakae, what are we to do?"

Halo had the answer. Nikolag grinned with arms folded. He knew she would have an answer. She always had an answer for everything, and they always rolled quickly off her tongue. She spoke with strength in her words. After what she had been through, she refused to do a disservice to her late captain. Instead, she rose above. "This village was founded by men and women like you and I. It was built by hands fatigued from slavery and unjust law." The malakae walked around to talk with each and every one of them, making absolute sure they heard her. "It was built from the paths of stone and dirt upward. And then came love, and then the laws of virtue that we as Nakha-nians all agreed upon. Our edict was written. Therefore, I say that we move far from the mountains, as this is where the creatures tend to thrive. We *need* to move as far away from the mountains as possible."

Halo paused and looked about. She saw Nikolag leaning against a broken remnant of a fence. "Nikolag, you are a gollet built of vast travels. You know this land more than anyone here now. Tell me, is there refuge for us further south?"

"I have more than this to answer," he calmly spoke. "I will give you your answer the moment these men thank you for being the only one to even attempt to save Staghen's life. I watched where that creature flew off to. I watched you chase it down like a rabid boar before you were too far to see. Given how long you've been gone, and given what Staghen's body looked like, I can only assume you ended up in the small gorge, somehow."

She sighed. "I did. But what does this have to do with this conversation?" she questioned lightly.

He moved forward. "I'm embarrassed for these men who have not yet thanked you. I don't even know how you, a young girl, managed to get Staghen up that cliff and back here."

The sorakhan answered easily, "I would not have been able to do it if it weren't for my horse."

Then the gollet walked toward her, and his eyes stared kindly into hers. "It matters not if Zidori helped. She is an old mare these days. You are young and not of the strength of a man. You both have braved a treacherous feat this afternoon. I cannot thank you enough for trying your hardest. And I thank you for bringing him home, Malakae," he said with raised brows.

Halo felt the eyes of the men upon her. Nervously, she looked about. It was a confusing thing for her to be given the opportunity to speak while having eyes turning to her. Stillness. Within her, she felt once more the numbing loss she had suffered through. But in his eyes, she found peace. For what seemed like an eternity, she found herself within him. As he stood tall over her, everything inside seemed to come to the surface once more. For a moment, he calmed her. But now she was faced with the terrible situation of refraining from falling into his arms and crying. If she could have had it her way, she would have taken Nikolag and Jastin and left the remains of the village.

Out of the quiet of the cold winds, Vathra spoke, "Yes, the gollet is right." He glanced to her. "We owe you our sincerest gratitude, Halo. Forgive my harsh tongue. I am—"

"Distraught?" she interrupted. Her gentle voice spoke again, "I know. We all are. But we no longer can stay here. I appreciate the apologies...Captain. And Nikolag, these men do not need to thank me. I simply did what I was trained and born to do. All I ask for in return is their respect."

The men fixed themselves to stand upright, although they all longed to mourn, weep, cry, and scream. Nikolag simply nodded in understanding. "Very well then. As you asked a question, I will give you an answer." He narrowed his eyes, looked to the south in the opposite direction, and pointed. "Beyond the southern fields lies the Southern Fault Plains—the place that millions of years ago gave birth to the gorge upon where Staghen found his eternal rest. A rushing fresh stream that comes from the Gigannora passes through there."

"How is the wildlife?" Halo asked.

"Plentiful. And there's a wood not far within the Southern Fault Plains."

Halo turned to the men. "It would be an excellent place to build a new home. We could make more weapons than ever imaginable, use the wood to build up a defense wall for our village, and seek refuge in the forest if another air attack should ever happen. Men, this is not an intelligent time to travel the long distance to Persu." She turned toward Vathra. "With all due respect, Captain, Persu would take us almost five or six days to reach with the coming snow, and given the condition of the fields with the snow and ice we already have. With women, infants who still nurse, children who grow sick from long frost exposure, and the elders, how can we be so sure we would even make it to Persu alive?"

Vathra curiously interjected, "And yet you expect these villagers to manage in the desolate ice and snow for nearly longer than that without shelter until a village is built?" He turned to ask a nearby Guardian, "Imek, have the villagers been cared for?"

"Yes, Captain..." the man responded easily. "A search party is well established, along with Doctor Crenon's care. Thankfully, not many villagers have been killed. Those who have been slain to have died from the destruction but more so as if they were collateral damage. It's mostly our Guardians. I actually do not know exact numbers, sir."

"Wonderful, thank you. Apparently, I was incorrect in my

assumption about the villagers," Vathra concluded. "So there you have it, Halo."

The Guardian's eyes narrowed in disdain for Vathra's leadership.

"You are out to transport several hundred people and lay them to rest in this frigid bed."

"There is the forest," she murmured.

"A forest that waits with what imaginable terrors? How are we to know these same beasts do not reside there either?"

The question of the captain made the entire fleet speak with assurance, and they all agreed.

Once more, Vathra pressed on. "Halo, I admire your council. But I am firm that Persu is where we shall go."

The malakae had heard enough, and so she pushed past the captain. "It is easier to rest on the ground than it is to walk over it. You have sentenced the weak to death. You will see once we reach Persu that you have made a grave mistake. And if Persu were to be so desirable, Staghen would have led us there years ago."

Nikolag immediately followed Halo in a rush to catch up with her. His well-loved friend was living through the most tragic day of her life, and he was amazed she had not lost her mind. Well, perhaps it was because it had not yet happened.

"Halo..." The blond friend sighed gently as he walked alongside her.

The malakae only grumbled, "What is it?"

"I say we all leave together. You, Jastin, and I. Let us leave this place!" He spoke with harsh whispers to allow them privacy. His large hand threw about. "Let us leave this place. You yourself said that the captain was the only thing you wanted to risk your life for, and now he is dead. Derjaun is gone. What else do you have to stay here for?"

While the loyal friend spoke, she thought about every word and syllable, pondering the meaning of every pause of breath. Halo knew that he was right, yet there was one thing wrong. "I understand you, my friend, but I made a promise to Staghen that I would watch over his people and his wife. I cannot leave now. I have sworn my blood to him."

Nikolag grabbed the malakae hard and fiercely pulled her to face him. His voice grew intense. "Listen to me for once, Halo. You believed Derjaun was not dead. Why in the stars above would the beasts go after such a sick child if they lust after men like Ishlog, Radal, and Staghen? For what purpose could Derjaun give them?" He jolted her shoulders to keep her attention. "Staghen knew well that you loathed your home life. He allowed you on the Guardians because he believed you had something special, that you would one day lead Nakhan proudly and stand up for its safety against tyranny if it should ever come after his death."

It was all too much for her to hear. Halo whimpered and in anger shook her head. "Please, stop."

"I don't care! This is what you are to do! You feel it, Halo." He passionately touched her heart while the heartsick green eyes of the malakae looked elsewhere. "You have an instinct that is what brought you here. Don't ignore it!"

"I won't break my vow to Staghen, Nikolag! I am sick of being told what is right to do! In the end, it never is!" Halo burst into tears with agony no longer being withheld. "I will not break a vow to him as he died in my arms! I cannot go against the captain who Staghen chose to give me my commands! He believed Vathra to be appropriate, so it's Vathra I obey!"

Nikolag's eyes filled with emotion for her. Once more she wept, shaking her head, and her voice was swimming in fatigue and strain. "Now please allow me time to find my family."

That time, letting Halo win was the most challenging battle of his life with her, for he had to let her go.

But then he called loudly as she walked away, "You need time to mourn, not to find a family that never cared for you!"

17

It was the first time in too long that Halo was with her family. A surprising feat, as they all were together, huddled in front of their ruins that once was a home. Yet the most important figure of Halo's childhood life, her father Aljen, was nowhere in sight. She had understood from a passing Guardian that he was safe outside his home with minor scratches and bruises being cared for. Lirena looked down with her dress in nothing but rags after the attack, and watched her daughter wrap her ankle tightly.

She had fallen, and her skin around the bone had turned purple. Her eyes studied that of her daughter's, which were focused without hesitation on her work. She knew the captain was dead, and all along these years Lirena had suffered through her hardest times without her daughter. At once she had hated Halo for leaving her all alone, but to see the young malakae so stressed, she could only attempt to care, even if it came off as feigned.

"Halo." She smiled tenderly.

"Mother, I do not wish to speak with you," she retorted without even looking up.

Lirena sighed. "Then I shall speak to you solely." She shook her head in dismay. "I know that Staghen meant the world to you. He loved you and protected you when I was acting like a child instead of a loving mother."

Halo seemed to ignore. Lirena pulled the blanket around herself more and continued on, "I don't wish for you to stay here with me."

That was the final thing that made her eyes lift to her mother's. Lirena's dark irises were softened by concern. "There is nothing left for you here. If this is the one thing as a mother I should say, it is this. A true hero follows their heart and never falls in line with the rest of the herd. Do not become a sheep, my daughter, for you have the heart of a wolf. This village means nothing to you, and I have grown in some years to accept this." The mother looked down with gentle streams of love coming to her cheeks. "I only wish you happiness, and I know Persu would never make you happy. Even if you never found Derjaun and grew old with death, at least you could say you tried."

Halo immediately yanked the bandage to give it the tightness it needed and tied it. "Come now, Sheylee. You talk with delusional spirits. This town needs me now more than ever before," she boasted angrily in spite of Vathra's commands. "I made a promise to Staghen on his last breath, and I will adhere to it until the day I die."

Lirena smiled, for she was preparing to remind her daughter of a valuable lesson Staghen had taught her, especially her. "And what happened to living for yourself?" Her voice grew in maturity and spirit, "You did not join the Guardians to help our village. You joined the Guardians in a selfless act to find Derjaun. Staghen knew this of you, and he allowed you on regardless, knowing that with the newfound knowledge and strength, you would find what you were looking for. If it is to protect this village, he left the duty of the captain to Vathra, not you, my dear. So..." Lirena smiled as an old wise woman would when she had something witty to say. "I think this means that Staghen knew you would run when his death came. He would not want to burden you, would he?"

She could only simply stare. Was her mother finally caring after all this time? Was it Halo's absence of home that finally made her mother mature? "Mother, please stop this at once. I'm older now, and my beliefs have changed."

The response made her mother's heart sore.

"Come now," the malakae said as she pulled her mother to stand. "You, my brother, and Lemson," she groaned, "follow me. The Guardians are gathering every villager so that we may leave as soon as possible. Take livestock and necessities from your home and bring them to the village gates."

Lirena nodded. Halo began helping her mother as the older woman asked, "What of the captain's body?"

Halo marched aggressively onward. "We burn it when the morning star begins to sleep."

The hours had passed, and Halo had left her old home behind once more. She joined Jastin at Staghen's home and sat by his side as his body lied on his bed—the same bed in which he and Jastin had made love not half a day's time ago. The bed in which she, as a little girl, had crawled practically underneath him when she was frightened of the dark. So many memories hung in the dismal atmosphere of the room where Staghen was sleeping. His blankets, which Jastin had spent an hour mending before he was placed on the bed, were tucked neatly up to his chest, allowing his arms to fold so that his hands held the hilt of his sword over his stomach. The blade was parallel down his body and wrapped with beautiful white flowers of the season. The house was in shambles.

Both ladies were unsettled and quiet, watching their fallen loved one sleep. It was a precious time to be there, as the morning star had begun its descent behind the horizon, and the friends were allowed to have their own time to say their farewells. Jastin had broken the stillness of their bodies by turning and looking at her friend, who wore nothing but hatred in her eyes. It was hatred that was vengeful and cruel, cold and empty, and this brought her fear that her friend would never heal from the tragedy.

Perhaps it was a time when she needed to step forth as a mother and nurture Halo's emotions again, as she had done so many times in their past while she trained. Yet the bereaved could not bring herself the courage to disrupt Halo's thoughts. The room was dazzled in low-glowing candles, and the malakae was losing sight from the falling night.

Miraculously, it was Halo who broke the silence. "What are your feelings about Persu?" The words of her mother had racked her mind so much that she was wondering if Jastin agreed with anything. After all, she had promised Staghen that she would protect Jastin and the village, but Lirena had been right. The village was already under Vathra's watch.

The maid replied with cracks of sadness, shaking her head, "I go where you go. I always will." And her dark eyes looked to her friend. "I told you this as a child, and I still stand by my word. I'm afraid of Persu, but I hold no fear as long as you are with me." And the maid stood.

"Where do you go?" Halo questioned.

"I have had my time alone to mourn," she sniffled. "I believe for a while, while light still blesses your vision, I wish you to be alone with your nurturer. I apologize for my selfishness in the fields. I never truly got to thank you for nearly losing your life to try and save him. Nikolag told me you were quite brave." Jastin left quickly. She was unable to endure the sight any longer.

Halo stared from her chair to the dead man's closed eyes, and she pondered what his eyes were seeing. However curious she was about death, her curiosity could not suppress her sadness that lingered within her very soul. Loneliness invaded her heart once more, but this time so strongly that she climbed under the quilt and wrapping her arm around him, laid her head upon his chest. All of his armor was buckled and strapped underneath his finest captain garments, which suitably so, were the garments he died in. All underneath the quilt her fingers traced alongside the hardened fabric that had stiffened from the blood, and the only sense of peace was that despite his fate Dr. Crenon had sewn the wounds closed. The blood had been washed from his skin, and she wondered if Jastin had cleaned him.

Her eyes shut tight in fear. Losing him was never going to be avenged. Nothing in that wretched world could have replaced him, as he replaced her obsolete family life, as he replaced Jastin's broken heart for true love. And then she cried. Pulling onto the shirt as hard as her strong grasp could, Halo shoved her face into his neck. It was different being alone with him now. Perhaps her mind had still held on to the idea that he may still come back to the living world when she was trying to keep him warm in the forest, but now too much time had passed, and it was the time she realized he was not coming back.

She had lost her love for everyone save for Nikolag, Jastin, and the doctor. No one had attempted to save him, and no one attempted to rescue or help the very man who risked his life consistently for others. Where was everyone else when their savior needed help? Suddenly, Nikolag and Lirena seemed so right in their words, and so perhaps Lirena's status with Halo had been saved from her growing hatred.

This time of mourning her loss was understood and felt because she was so warm—and he was truly cold—and she was lying in his bed with him and being able to focus on sorrow instead of regret. The woman's cries grew loud with the pain in her heart that was of tremendous hurt. While her eyes flowed uncontrollably, she wept looking at him, and screamed, "Staghen, why did no one help you?"

The commotion caused alarm of Jastin outside. Sounds of rage and discontent forced her concern to rush inside. "My darling friend, what is the matter?"

She saw the horrid display of the blind Guardian lying on Staghen with her limbs wrapped around his body, face pressed hard into his neck with wails of frightening threats to everything in her life. She screamed incessantly to the point where Jastin was confused whether to cover her ears or reach out to her friend and pull her away. A split decision was made, and so the widow rushed immediately to her friend's side. "Halo, please compose yourself! Your throat will surely bleed if you keep screaming this way!"

Before Jastin could even touch her, Halo shoved her away. "You've had your chance in peace. Now leave me alone!"

Footsteps were heard coming into the bed chamber, and Vathra shouted, "What is the meaning of this? Halo, how dare you—"

She quickly scrambled off of Staghen and stood to threaten the new captain face to face. "How dare I? You have nothing to say here. You cared more for the villagers who insulted you than Staghen himself! This man who is dead gave his life for us every day, and not one of you ran to his aid. I have little vision, his beloved wife is cowardly, and yet we both nearly lost our own lives trying to save him. You are not worthy of his sword, Vathra!"

Jastin began crying and tried to cover Staghen's ears. "Please!" she whimpered desperately. "Not in here while he sleeps!"

The other men who came in saw Halo and Vathra in unison draw their swords toward one another. Captain Vathra paused. Halo growled in pure revulsion of the new captain. "You who consistently questioned him, you who secretly bore anger toward his decisions, you who lusted after maidens while on duty! When all was safe and the village watch had ended, I easily recall all the Guardians except Oniden making sinful remarks about how they no longer had excuses to mingle with women! Instead of being thankful that children no longer had to be escorted and could continue their education and play times! Shame on your soul!"

Vathra shouted deeply while Jastin begged them to stop for Staghen's peace, "Then come outside, and we can talk this out. As you can see, your little friend is in tears with the fighting, and your beloved hero is trying to sleep, so—"

Halo immediately interrupted, "He will never sleep peacefully knowing what you have done and what you will do. He always listened to your opinion and valued your intelligence, and you shun mine eagerly. I will not fight you, but mark my words..."

All was quiet as Vathra listened, his heart pounding nervously, and Halo continued, "I will keep my vow to both you and Staghen to protect the villagers and yet obey you. But Persu is not my village, and I refuse to obey any law there. Once these villagers are safe to Persu, I will no longer be under your command and will leave."

Vathra's eyes glowed in loss of what to say, and Halo ended her warning. "I despise this unfair world," she said hatefully. "Now all of you, except Jastin if she wishes, leave this room until the morning star."

Vathra stood still and looked to Halo. "Believe me, Halo, I do not intend to get harsh with you. And you should have known all the times I had spoken to Staghen in hopes of trying to raise your rank. Why, you almost stand where you are now because of me, and it pains my heart to hear you talk like this to me. Do you honestly believe that I wish to take our people to Persu? Do you really believe I am happy with this decision? I am not. Yet I have no other choice. Our village is gone. These creatures have attacked us three times now, and each time we lose people near and dear to us. We cannot carry this on any longer. The Persuvian army and their mighty walls can give us peace.

"But I understand you are tired. Our tempers keep calming and flaring with one another, and that is not something I desire. We haven't the ability or the strength in men to start all over again. And maybe Persu will hold answers to the reason of these attacks, and they may hold answers for your eyes. There could be great things ahead. And imagine such a thing, if you could train under Volucard himself. It has been over thirty years since anyone has been to Persu. Times there could be quite different now. I wish for you to remain peaceful with me. If we are to work together in the honor of all those lost, we have to work together."

And all but the two girls had left. The two old friends were left alone once more. Jastin, who had decided to stay, had made her decision to do so solely based upon the principle of friendship. She watched Halo sob into Staghen's neck, clutching onto his glorious mane of raven fire, a fire that still seemed to both of them so alive. There was not much she could do to soothe her friend's emotions, but there was a growing concern in her heart about what Halo had believed in, so she questioned her, "Halo, why will you not fight for Staghen's blade?"

Halo shook her head, still buried deep in the stoned flesh and muffled, "It is not my blade to fight for."

Jastin calmly defied her, "But it is."

"No, it's not. It belongs to Vathra now."

When Jastin rose, she moved gently to lie next to her lover as well, in an embrace she recalled easily. For once, there was a slight bit of peace there that was felt. All three of them resting on his bed as they had done during his tales of Radal's bravery when they were little girls. The sensation warmed Jastin's body, as if perhaps his heart started to beat once more, and it was a lovely feeling. It was the feeling of family.

"Halo, my heart, do you feel this warmth that I feel? Against all the frost and ice in this season, and against death itself, do you feel this warmth in us?"

"If hatred bears the sensation of warmth, then yes."

Jastin sighed, lifting her head over Staghen's chest a bit more to see her friend's face. "I believe Staghen is in this room still." They were lying on each side of him.

And then Halo grumbled, recalling their belief of the spirit world. "He will be until his body is burned."

The idea of seeing her husband's body going to the flames made Jastin cry softly, "I do not wish to see him burn." And she kissed his cheek easily.

The candles had grown dim, and Halo whispered, "You must have been so enthralled when he proposed to you, my friend."

Jastin tossed her dirty blonde hair of great lengths and waves behind her shoulder. "I'm not sure how you knew he did, but I was and still am. As I told Staghen after he died, I do not need marriage to keep my vows to him."

Jastin delicately pulled her necklace so her friend could touch it and see it.

Halo felt a horrible pull in her chest as she touched the necklace. "It's simply perfect. He told me he had plans for doing it, and I couldn't wait to hear your story on it. My sorrow for you is as deep as the wild oceans. I know how hard you tried for him and how faithful you were, even when you first laid eyes upon his."

Jastin wiped her face. "Yes," she whimpered, "but there is some peace in my heart. That he did grow to love me, even if I only knew it for a small lot of moments before he was taken from us. There is also peace in my heart for you." Halo's eyes surged in waters of hurt as Jastin continued, "His love and devotion, his courage and his strength, his patience and his virtues seeded your blood to grow to become the most miraculous woman Nakhan will ever have seen. You now know your destiny, and now you can claim it. I know Staghen's life was obliterated before we all were ready, but perhaps...maybe we were ready. Maybe Staghen's purpose in his life has been completed.

"We can only wish him peace, since he had given this gift to us all so much, let us give it to him in return. I can only say one thing, that you, my love, are the greatest hero. My happiness and my gratitude for your attempts to save his life run higher than the Gigannora during the falls of the rain. And I am thankful that you loved him and comforted him until he passed. My husband, our dear loving friend, did not die frightened and alone. I am forever in your debt." Jastin laid her head down to rest.

Watching Jastin speak... She seemed to have grown many years in the cloak of the night air. Halo was more than proud to see another chapter close in a tale that was seeming to never end, for it was true. Staghen had died, but a miracle had come to them both that night of sleeping next to him. In Jastin's words, Halo had felt that warmth she spoke of, and this warmth led to something so muscular in its warnings...

The burning of the fallen captain's body was postponed to allow the young ladies their mourning time. And that night, for the first time in many years, Halo dreamt of Derjaun.

18

The rays of the morning star were unable to fight through the bitter cold, so there was no possibility for the snow to melt. This morning, Halo decided to keep the dream to herself.

Thinking of Zidori made her think of Rikaana, who was now without a rider. The question of who would claim the animal ran viciously throughout her mind, and it never seemed to have a happy ending.

She feared the worst, that Vathra would be seen outside mounted on top of the most valuable steed of the land. Radal had rode his own horse by the name of Volga, a magnificent beast significantly larger with five times the strength of Rikanna and five times the temperament of Zidori. Sadness struck the family when Volga was found dead next to the stone of his rider. Everyone knew it was from heartache. The valiant horse had died barely a week after his rider did. Halo could not even fondle with the idea of riding such a thing, but the door to Staghen's room was knocked upon, and it disturbed her from somewhat happy thoughts.

She was already dressed, as was the widow who was moving to open the door. Jastin had done herself well to resemble what she would have looked like on their wedding day, with her long tresses flowing against her back the way Staghen loved it, with only flower pins to hold her side locks away so that he could have seen her pretty face more easily when he kissed her. All the jewels that he had specially made for her were worn proudly, her garments of crimson velvet flowed alongside the most intricate gold embroidery. She truly, even on a gruesome day, looked lovely. Halo was sitting in the corner chair leaning over and tying her boots up. She wanted to present herself to Staghen in the way he knew her best, a Guardian and nothing else.

Lady Jastin forced a smile as she opened the door. Vathra stood there with five strong men and the gunni, which was a large wooden board with handles used to carry the dead to their pyre. Except this time, the gunni was adorned with laces around the edges.

"A good dawn to you all, and you, Captain," Jastin said as she bowed.

Vathra spoke gently, "And to you, fair lady. Have you and your friend said your last words of love?"

Jastin turned to Halo and paused to make sure her friend was ready. The only thing she saw was that Halo stood and began fixing the fallen captain's hair. How desperately she wanted to yank it and scream, "Wake up." Jastin's emotions were not ready to meet Vathra's face again, but her bravery showed and she spoke, "Yes, but allow me to place his favorite pillow underneath his head on the gunni."

And so the men came in and began to place the board next to Staghen's bed, preparing to pull him onto it, "Alright, men," Vathra said, "let us be gentle with him." After his body was gently laid, Jastin placed the pillow she made for him under his head.

Both women looked to one another, and what her little maid friend said shocked her. When all of them were gone, they stood behind in the room. Jastin closed the doors and spoke, "We will take control of this situation. I cannot bear to see Staghen's sword in any other's hand than yours. I will not stand for it." She shook her head in silent anger. "I will not."

Halo suddenly recalled something she learned in the edict long ago, and she wondered if Jastin even knew of it. Jastin, upon Staghen's death, was to be cared for and respected. The betrothed woman of the captain, in his death, will have power just as he would have. The wife of the captain would be given the same amount of respect and be allowed to make decisions as the captain would. They were completely equal by marriage.

"If it is your wish, Lady, I will see to that it is so."

They made their way hastily to the pyre, somehow no longer being sad. If Staghen did not die in vain, there could be no sadness, for in some sort of way Jastin's orders could possibly overturn Vathra's. There was some hope left after all. But this game of dominance was never played by Agrona when Staghen took the order of the captain.

As the morning star warmed the snow, the wind had calmed itself almost as if to honor the day of Staghen's eternal rest being finalized. No more did death wreak its havoc upon the land, and neither would there be any more sorrow, and neither would there be any more suffering. The entire village, with citizens still alive and unharmed, had been preparing the previous night to leave, to depart from their beloved home of many years far too large in number to count. Tradition bore strong yet again that day, as they all huddled in mourning clusters of warmth around the blaze. They all were waiting for the Guardians, with Vathra leading, to bring out the deceased hero.

The widow Jastin was in her old chamber, having her sheylee, a noble lady, Devarah, lace one final garment around her waist, one that would provide the last hope of warmth for the long journey. How tall Jastin must stand today.

Devarah had seemed not to have one wrinkle added to her age, as she herself was still young, at least in Jastin's eyes. She was a tall, lean woman who was the one solely responsible for Jastin's finely cut and well-mannered upbringing. Throughout hearing the quiet of the room, Jastin heard some aggression of anguish from her mother. She did not even need to turn and look, taking a deep breath and speaking calmly, "Mother, I truly wish you would not shed another tear. This cannot possibly go on but a moment more."

Devarah shook her head. "I always dreamt of seeing the large and royal Persu, but never out of harsh circumstances. Ahh, if only I had the chance to see your marriage come to be."

Then, when the mother began to weep heavily, her tears invoked a powerful cut into the widow and made her turn at last. "Mother," she politely counseled, "I share your tears, I have shared your grief, and also I share your sympathy. But I have much to think about." She lifted her dark eyes to look out the window of her home for the last time. "Staghen would not want me to cower."

All was ready. Jastin lifted the uana that was still leaning in the corner of the room and took it outside. She was going to lead the musicians in her late husband's final ceremony. It was her absolute honor to do so. She stood alongside Halo next to the pyre's firing inferno. It was mandatory that all Guardians formed a line on either side of a well-plowed path to the fire, and there Halo was closest to the fire, with her eyes shut and silent. First, the new captain would come down on his new horse, which could have been Rikaana. Jastin loved that horse, nearly worshipping it. It was the only living thing that could bring her the comfort of the strength and nobility that Staghen displayed honorably.

In front of the firepit was a small stump where the new captain would make his induction speech and would inform everyone as to any new laws he wished to implement on the land, or any first decisions as captain, where he would also make promises, and swear an oath to keep them. The oath was always done by laying the captain's sword to the ground and holding the book of edicts to his chest, showing he would never act violently against Nakhan.

The musicians of the small village began their drumming, and all stood to watch the new captain come with the body behind him, and the chosen high guaradas carrying the body with the rest of the lower rankings to lay flowers behind the path. Jastin carefully placed her feet on to those petals as she walked with her uana and played her lost love's favorite song, all while watching him be carried in front. This was to signify a new, fresh, and fragrant beginning to the land due to a death. Nakhanians always attempted to believe in new beginnings after the darkest of end-times. As the drumming sounded, all the villagers looked to the new captain.

He came riding on Rikaana in an attempt to show the villagers he would be strong. In all of his long, blazing crimson hair and handsome face did his eyes show extreme certainty. His chest seemed like an iron boulder cast with aggressive formation of muscles and was wearing black coal water and jinfish oil around his eyes that was something Halo had never seen before, and all the jewels and golden strands were well strapped to his ears and mane of waving blood. The gauntlets he wore had been faceted by a golden-plated pabi cat, which was another thing Halo had never seen before.

But this could never be certain. Although Vathra's confidence and wide smile could offset many fears of uncertain truths, those who lie hold a smile so wide. Halo could see inside of the new captain. She may have been blind, but she was not stupid. Vathra was frightened of the future. He smiled, but his eyes watered and the smile fractured for a second before returning to its full potential again.

Halo bit her lip and resumed looking forward as the perspiration of suspense dripped under her armor. Suddenly anxiety plunged into her stomach. She tried to breathe deep to nurture it. She missed Staghen terribly. It was going to take all of the mountains in the world to keep her upright and focused. The drumming immediately ceased as Vathra dismounted the stallion and began to step onto the stump. Everyone went quiet to listen.

"All of my wonderful, fellow brothers, sisters, mothers, fathers, children and so forth," his voice boomed loudly and with mighty strength of the Castonuje. "It is with a humble heart that I assume the role of your new leader, nurturer, and captain. Not two days ago was our hero, Staghen, taken from us. And despite Halo's desperate attempt to save his life, her attempts fell short. But we shall all honor her bravery on this day, for none of us had the strength in our spirits to do such a miraculous, selfless task.

"As a Guardian, one ranked highly, Halo knew the laws were to protect the people of the village, and not the captain himself. Staghen was a selfless man who risked his life for a sacrifice to this village, for you, and I, and all of us. And Halo challenged that by ignoring the laws set for her specifically by Staghen. It seems as though greatness has a notable history of repeating itself. Staghen ignored our laws to allow Halo as a Guardian, and in return Halo ignored his law in a steep risk of faith in the ocean of hope to save him. I can only be sorry, Halo, that your risk was not rewarded. Please step forward."

Captain Vathra turned to see Jastin, who was holding dearly onto Halo in worry. Halo truly recalled the times when Vathra stood against Staghen in hopes that he would allow Halo to train with him in the times that he was the malakae. On many accounts he had stood strong for her.

Halo moved forward and stood before him. Their eyes were finally settled with one another. He said, "As Jastin is the wife of Staghen, I am sure you know that she has as much right to hold the law as I do. And you would be a fool to think I did not hear her talk to you last eve. She wishes for you to hold the Vin Gruinelle sword, and I am honored to give it to you. After all, it needs to be returned to its true, rightful owner. And only you can do that, my dear one."

Halo's body became absolutely golden. Vathra removed the hilt from his side and stretched his hands to her, offering it both with love and admiration. "It is yours now."

She slowly looked to him and placed her hands about the most noble item in all of Nakhan, and no one would ever be able to see how much Nikolag and Jastin were glowing with happiness for her. There she held it. The sword was finally hers at last. She truly was standing where Derjaun would have been. Her grip tightened around that beautiful blade, and she looked up to see Vathra's face. In that serene moment, she realized her heart had become calloused in ways it shouldn't have been. He did care for her.

She bowed, holding the precious blade, and responded with honor, "I am humbled, grateful, and honored by this, Captain Vathra."

And so it came to be that Staghen's body was adorned with offerings of the people. With their farewells said, they stood to watch Jastin walk in front of him while he was carried to the pyre. All stood to sing while her fingers plucked the strings. Halo watched the widow's eyes tremble with both pride and sadness. Never once did Jastin believe she would lead the final song of her husband. The survivors of the village joined in a chorus of the song as Jastin slowly walked forward. As she came to the pyre, the men softly laid Staghen on the safest side, and each villager proceeded to set dry flowers upon him.

The melodious sound rang to the skies while one Guardian set fire to the fallen hero. While his body burned, the malakae made her first words known. Halo looked to all as her armor gleamed in the snow that somehow, some way, seemed purer than ever.

She spoke with a voice as precious as a sheylee to all of the people who witnessed her, "And he had said to me once before that I would find what I was looking for. So I, as I stand here now, am the reflection in the waters of possibility, that alongside our grievances, alongside our flaws or disabilities, and no matter our differences, we must know the truth of our existence. Reality is fantasy, and fantasy is reality. Reality is not truly real, because sometimes we don't desire it or accept it. But fantasy, what our hearts truly desire, is what should be realized. First a simple dream is dreamt, and then it allows a clear path for reality. Remember this, my friends, we are the reflection in the ocean of possibility."

Halo learned to flourish freely and love without restrictions of conformity lest her soul plummet into the never-ending lake of sorrow. This was a primary lesson that carried on in Nakhan's memory.

Hours after the ceremony, Jastin found herself at a familiar northern field, mounted on the handsome Rikaana that, after all, had been given to her. She stopped to gaze back at the sky-high blaze with its most memorable captain along with it, and tears of bitter honey and romance coated her cheeks.

"I don't think I can ever love again, Staghen. You were a man amongst all men who raged as savage beasts do. And for all forgiveness and good deeds in this world..." She paused for a moment, one that crept into her skin through the wintry air. "...how could one love a beast?"

"Jastin!"

The widow turned to see Nikolag and Halo coming on galloping horses. It was Halo who had called for her. All three of them came together and looked to the great Castonuje of the north.

"What are you thinking?" Halo asked.

Nikolag cocked his head. "She's probably thinking of how in love she still is and always will be. Not that I blame her."

Jastin paused and looked to the most amazing friend she had ever known. Her lips gently smiled, and quietly she chuckled. "I was thinking about how I will never love another man again. What are you thinking about?"

The magnificent blind Guardian looked forward to the mountains that still beckoned her, calling for her. "I was simply thinking about what lies beyond the other side."

All in those lands as the sun set on misty lakes and frozen grounds, the three friends stayed mounted on their horses side by side, looking off in the same wonderment.

FINISHED at 5:37 PM 11/27/2023

Afterword

This entire three book series was cultivated when I kept having recurring dreams of two men in castle ruins. I was much younger at age 21 then and became so obsessed with them I decided to give them a story.

As I grew older, my narrative and thoughts evolved as well as the changing of my writing style and over fifty-five times I've added to or changed the plot, the character behaviors, and so much more.

It's hard to find your voice as an author. But from scribbling in a journal by hand on the metro busses of Los Angeles to typing until sunrise in Finland, this book is for you. I have so much more in store, and I truly hope you enjoy reading this as much as I enjoyed writing it.

ALSO BY JAK ANGELESCU

A Promise Remembered - coming in 2025

Sassy To The Rescue! - A fan made third installment of the Homeward Bound series coming in 2025

What Happened to Mr. Tucker? - A short story of suspense and horror

Born a Hero - A fanfic of the Resident Evil franchise featuring a silent character

About the Author

J ak Angelescu, born Lindsay Hoffman in Port Huron, Michigan, is a musician and author. Her early life was marked by adventure, moving from Florida to Alaska, where her imagination flourished.

After her family settled in Missouri, Jak faced challenges, including the loss of her sister in a car accident. She found solace in music and poetry, eventually becoming a guitarist and forming several bands. Jak's passion for music led her to Los Angeles, where she worked at a rehearsal studio, rubbed elbows with famous musicians, and joined a Judas Priest tribute band.

Her experiences inspired her to write her debut novel, "A Promise Kept," which was influenced by her love of vampires, classical music, and her best friend, who became her muse. Jak is currently a guitarist for the heavy metal band Unknown, performs country songs locally, and resides in Kansas City, Missouri. She is a devout Methodist Christian, supports animal rescues, veteran and law enforcement benefits, and enjoys Italian culture.

www.jakangelescu.com

www.facebook.com/missjakangelescu

www.instagram.com/missjakangelescu